MARTHA!

LET THE SH

RESPONSIBI

TO THE BEA

CONCERN

The Cottage: Recondite

IT IS EASY TO STATE
THAT ONE SHOULD CLEAVE TO
THAT WHICH IS IMPORTANT... AND
SHED THAT WHICH IS NOT.
THE DIFFICULT TASK IS TO DETERMINE
WHAT ACTUALLY IS
IMPORTANT!

David Cocklin

FIND THE TIME...
MAKE THE JOURNEY!

FriesenPress

Suite 300 - 990 Fort St
Victoria, BC, V8V 3K2
Canada

www.friesenpress.com

First Edition — 2016

ISBN
978-1-4602-8327-1 (Hardcover)
978-1-4602-8328-8 (Paperback)
978-1-4602-8329-5 (eBook)

1. *Fiction, Literary*

Distributed to the trade by The Ingram Book Company

To my children, Meagan and Brendan; may you always find the strength to love one another, despite the failings of life's journey.

To my sister Debra for inspiration, reflection and guidance.

Table of Contents

The Cottage Recondite

He leaned forward ever so slightly, feeling the balance of weight shift outward and onward towards the edge of the cottage porch. His legs were together, and his arms spread upwards slowly as if dragging wings behind them. All he had to do was continue his tilt a few more inches, and he would teeter over the edge. His worldly musings and endless barrage of explanations or contemplations left behind for those who pursued his wisdom. How they would ponder the senselessness of his decision. How they would judge him and share opinions on what drove his final actions.

"He was always a little confused."

"Those blasphemous words were bound to bring trouble."

"Don't you know? He was very much in love, but she left happily in the arms of another."

"No, no, I heard he was embarrassed by some action or rejection and couldn't bear it."

"No, that's not so. It runs in his family. I think his uncle also killed himself."

Fools, he thought. *You and your limitations* ***are*** *my catalyst. How can I share the vision you are unable to see? How can I chase your wonderment into open space from the lonely corrals it settles into nightly? Sheep and chickens, wandering the earth under the weight of manmade chains, happy in captivity only because even the existence of freedom has never been conceived, let alone seen or embraced.*

His head bent back and looked upwards to the universe, brandishing a growing smile that opened to inhale the ocean breeze that never ceased to gust up along the cliff wall. The rocky beach lay half a mile below, the tug of eternity but a breath ahead of him. He continued his lean until it was far enough, gravity taking over and pulling his body effortlessly down towards Mother Earth.

As he felt the exhilaration of descent, his spirit leapt forward, sliding from its cocoon like a butterfly in its summer ritual, driving out into the light with an unexpected acceleration. His hands were in front of him now, leading the way to another dimension, steering him through the inexplicable wash of light and energy, twisting and spinning his evaporating thought and emotion into dust behind him as he embraced an entirely new existence.

What joy! No regrets, no blame, and no loss. And how immediate was there, indeed, no recollection of earthly life. He was free from his physical confines and thrust into a new chaos of unknown excitement and tangled mystery. An entirely new eternity, caught in the blink of his eye, a snap of his fingers, in the last wisp of breath that fueled his launch into the misunderstood realm of the unknown.

His body, now a vessel empty of spirit and soul and a burden to Earth's gravity, hit the beach with enough power to loosen dirt and small stones from the surrounding cliff wall, which tumbled down after it. The crooked twist of what had, moments earlier, been the confines of his enlightenment lay crumpled and distorted on the twinkling sands of dusk. Within a few seconds, everything returned to exactly how it was before the sudden impact. What a feast was served for the crabs and scavengers and birds of prey.

—

Far north of where those famous white sandy beaches bounced the captured waves off a breathing sea, out on the edge of a giant cliff that held back the relentless crash of that ocean, where night collided with day and history met tomorrow, a small cottage clung desperately to the jagged rocks and spider leg roots that ran away from the towering fern trees, sentinels guarding the limits of the fog. Their trunks as thick as dreams and older than tears, they waited resolute for the next generation to grow worthy. The cottage was nearly as ancient. It had been there from such a distant time that real memories of when it was not, no longer existed. There remained just old recollections, timeworn into legends of how it came into this world. The stone porch melted its secrets and sympathies onto the rocky precipice of the cliff, and the vines and shrubs that tangled the forest around her embraced the walls hungrily.

The front of the cottage was whimsical and dainty. It was a face of contentment with a wide, grinning mouth of a door flanked by two small windows that were reminiscent of the unmistakable wonder seen in the eyes of a child who had just encountered another of the many amazing things that growing up offers for discovery. The once bright white walls were suitably weathered enough for the cottage to be considered a mature structure. Although it wore its age well, it would never be mistaken for a recent build.

From the porch, the great expanse of the earth spread out as if a carpet unto paradise itself, with the pounding waves and tossing currents smoothed by distance into a shimmering tapestry of flickering sunlight and vessels of mist. One could easily become lost in the panorama, perhaps reclined on one of the benches that flanked the front door with a cool summer drink and a long, smoldering cigarillo for company. The sun would bring the day slowly across the horizon, pulling it effortlessly towards its eternal destiny of dusk. The hours wouldn't matter. Their counting would only blur the honesty of the day and close the imagination that shared its beauty. This place could inspire a defining moment in someone's life. It was a place to make decisions, to heal old wounds, to chase rainbows, to pray for salvation, to wish for love and happiness and, very likely, a place to die.

Closer to the edge, off the porch and peeking with a guarded, sliding step to look over the threshold, the entire planet bowed to the vision. Up there, it was as if you were a bird soaring on the winds that always climbed the steep steps. Or perhaps more than that. Perhaps it was even more significant than mere flight and lingered before you as if you were a star dangling from the black on blue above, watching time turn endless circles on itself, feeling like a child who was guilty of seeing more than you should have. Stealing the perspective from greater forces, perhaps even gods of some ancient culture, you could peek left and right, expecting the call of, "Hey you, what are you doing in this place? Who gave you permission to be here? What have you done to deserve this moment?"

Feeling the powers of creation and existence collide in a symphony of illusion and interpretation made visitors feel compelled to share it with everyone they loved, everyone they knew, but how could they explain it? How could they describe a colour to those who were blind? Language was too burdensome. No, too personal. Any recounting of it would not do it justice, and sharing it through insufficient words would only reduce its value in your memory. It was a view into mortality and immortality; both unsure of their place, both willing to risk tumbling out of control. A breathless moment that continued to grow more beautiful and powerful, but never older, each time it was seen. An experience that sat there endlessly, always ready, waiting to be shared. A vision that could awaken tired souls and broken hearts, it remained ready to expose itself always, even when no one was there to see it. Perhaps this particular point was not unique in this wondering world, but it was, nevertheless, one of the places that could fulfill a quest, a place where long journeys ended and new ones began.

The front of the cottage was cut off from the mountain and by the mountain on all sides. It could be accessed only by moving though the cottage from the back door. Thick brush and the dark, steep precipice prevented circumvention of the structure and blocked any ideas of shortcuts or alternative paths. It was unknown whether this was a planned aspect of the building. If it was, the architect was surely cleverer than credited, unless, of course, the architect was merely cleverer than those giving credit. In any case, it was more likely that this important aspect of the cottage's personality was created accidentally or necessarily due to the limited space available for the builder to capture the open view of the world below. At all other points along the cliff, the forest grew so tightly to the brink, even dangling over it at times, that one would not even see the edge until actually falling over it and glancing back towards it as the plunge to blackness gained speed. Whether built with great foresight or by accidental perfection, by studied architects, weary travelers, or ancient deities, the cottage stood firmly as a gateway from the dark and tortured forest behind it into the inspiration and clarity of light that shone upon its face.

From the back of the cottage, an entirely different escape awaited. There stood the forest that fought for a view of the sky with young stallions of wood punching through the rustling canopy to shake hands with the sun's warm embrace. Below them, saplings struggled to spread their budding roots into a solid footing before they, too, arched skyward. They knew the truth about life and love. They knew that the early growth of the unseen foundation and the strength of its every part would support their existence.

The forest floor was littered with the rotting wood of impatient young ferns either building their base on shallow ground, where their roots could not develop deep and wide, or else searching too soon for the sun's warming rays. But they were not mourned. Their passing provided fertile ground for less ambitious plants and shrubs or lodging for the busy inhabitants of the woods.

The forest delivered constant shade to the cottage and, ever thirsty, kept the rain from pouring in by drinking its fill of drops on their way down. It also gave respite from the winds that climb the cliffs and carried the vision of the world upward. In passing, it might be thought that the forest had a purpose in protecting the cottage with its sheltering blanket from the weather and undergrowth embrace, but it posed surreptitiously to the casual encounter.

For all its benefits, as unintentional as they may be, the forest was extremely jealous of the cottage. It had been placed in its path and was the only blemish on the domination the forest enjoyed over the terrain. The cottage was a passage from the depths of the forest to the wonderment of the world beyond the edge. It opened out to a place where the plants and personality of the forest could never go, for they were destined to grow on top of one another eternally, springing anew only on the backs of the fallen.

The cottage had been built and nurtured with purpose and a general symmetry, though the walls are roughly hewn and partially worn to dust. Just the opposite of the forest, which raged out of control but always within the boundaries to which it was a slave. Forever renewing and dying back upon itself, its only pleasure was a successful attempt to draw other life to death. Making each death a new part of the bigger whole, dissolving and evolving upon itself, incorporating the living into the dying, and stirring the swirl into the struggle for the next consumption. It grew thicker and denser but never larger or broader. That was its destiny and its affliction.

Moving away from the cottage into the deeper world of the forest was a journey that affected all who made it and could even find them lost hopelessly in its darkness and obscurity. The lure would come through visions of hidden wealth, stories of buried treasure, or a simple misdirection during an ascent of the mountain. Ironically, the very sun the forest blocked out was also the life-stream that nurtured its growth. The forest gathered its strength, power, and lust from the sun, yet it blocked and hid the warm light with zeal, possessive and petulant, neither susceptible to influence nor familiar with forgiveness. Its greatest pride was hiding those treasures the cottage revealed from its front porch and remaining thick enough to obscure and hinder the path towards it. It was pleased that there were so few travelers so high up and away from the mainstream of life and learning.

It was impossible to live a lifetime there. The emotion was too intense, the anticipation too gripping, and the time too long to arrive and too slow in passing. It could only be lived in moments and only enjoyed when passionate. It reached far past the mere experience of being there. The dislocated legends and untidy history surrounding the cottage lent themselves only to the truth. The truth being always whatever is believed.

The Young Lover

Some believe the cottage was built by a simple mason and cabinetmaker named Joseph who had lost his way traveling east from the great sunrise to the glaciers of time. It was no more than a point of reference, a juncture of convenience on a journey towards something more than he was. Just a man who was skilled with his hands and who could work wood or stone into objects of admiration but was sorely inadequate in matters of the heart and who suffered endlessly at the hands of lost love.

He had spent most of his youth learning his trade in concordance with his father's wishes and had missed out on much of the rumblings and ramblings of adolescence. It wasn't that he didn't notice the opposite sex, but he never found himself in situations where he could develop any kind of relationship or understanding of their nature. Most of his encounters were short and stubby, lost moments of incomplete sentences and unbelievable regret at the wrong impression he had surely left on some unsuspecting young lady.

His love and passions were chained and channeled into the confines of family responsibilities and limitations. Parents of classical stature. Father slightly aloof and reserved, obedient to his craft and determined to build a worthy heir to his small estate, recognizing that it was not much but honestly gained and wholly owned. It was a principle of pride that all true craftsmen had, even those who were unable to bring such independence and self-employment to fruition.

He was not a father to dwell on emotional or domestic issues. He worked hard and long, was proud of his quality, and was respected in his community of customers and contemporaries. That was his reward. Home was the domain of his wife, and the caring and upbringing of their son was left to her whims. His only demands were for domestic care of his needs, those being clothes, nourishment, and occasional relief with some recollection of distant passion. His satisfaction and purpose were gained from his work until he was a master at it, and then it was gained from the development of the craft within his heir, his son.

His greatest accomplishment, his most important work, indeed, his only legacy, was the skill, competence, and ability he could teach his son. His own work would always be his, of course, but in the world of such skilled labour, beyond the simple tasks of measuring and building, the tutelage of a son to carry on the art was the true quality of a master, the most respected and cherished contribution to their trade. A son as skilled as the father was a worthy legacy. A son who carried the trade further than his father, who developed new techniques and built a broader spectrum of knowledge, was the greatest reward life could deliver, and it brought contentment to the dying soul of the patriarch and pride to the family.

Unfortunately, Joseph would only realize this once his father passed away. The lack of emotional interaction between them was the very thing that prevented them from enjoying the pride and respect they felt for each other. As the young man sat with his father on his deathbed, both lamented the lack of closeness between them and smiled knowingly as they discussed the "should have" and "could have" situations they missed. Although Joseph had learned much about working with wood, both architecturally to shape furniture or buildings and conceptually to select type and grain to visualize the finished product, and though his skill was well beyond that of a gifted layman, he was far behind the kind of expert work that his father was capable of. Still, it never occurred to any of them that Joseph would ever be anything other than a tradesman equal to, or better than, his father.

Joseph would never sit with his dying father when his mother was there. Their visits were always separate, his father giving him fatherly advice and maintaining the role of patriarch until his last breath. Joseph wondered what his father and mother spoke about during those last days. He asked her, but his queries were always stalled by her distant comments of "not important" or "just things between us."

Joseph's mother was a delicate and demure woman on the outside, but he knew this was only to camouflage the strengths and energy that really defined her. She was content in knowing that he knew this. She considered her own responsibility in life to be that of guardian and care-giver, finding reward in her ability to sacrifice her desires for the contentment of others, comfortable in her purpose as a supporter of her "men."

When Joseph was young, he quizzed her often on her ambitions and interests, but she always turned his curiosity from adventure to responsibility. In her later years, she regretted that she had not laughed more with her son, had not rolled in the grass more, and had not challenged him with questions of importance. She was not disappointed with her life; she had performed as expected and delivered the heir in top form—obedient, curious to learn, armed with a sense of responsibility, and respectful of his elders, even the ones who were fools. She was only disappointed in the lack of spontaneity that Joseph enjoyed. She felt it was an important part of living, though not necessarily an important part of life. His destiny was born, with his body, from her womb. They were neither separable nor individual.

She cleaned and cooked, fed the hungry house, and managed the finances. She ensured the mortgage was covered, the bills paid on time, a fair allowance provided for father and son, and some savings put away. Her husband was a good man, bringing home sufficient funds to support a decent life and seldom indulging in poor judgment or misdemeanour. They shared moments of tenderness and even lovemaking from time to time. Not the passionate lovemaking of youth, but the kind of physical assurance that reiterated their commitment to each other and stroked their memories of love. It was important for them, and she was happy he was as indulgent of her initiations as he was demanding of his own. She also enjoyed a community of friendship with her neighbours and even more complete closeness with a couple of her friends. It was life happening with each sunrise.

As a young boy growing up, Joseph was reminded constantly of his responsibility to carry on his father's trade. That did not oppress him. He loved watching his father work with wood and stone and was especially proud when he allowed Joseph to chip away at some cast off piece of granite or saw a broken plank before drilling some straightened nails into it. His father never gave him new nails but straightened old ones so Joseph could attack them. He explained that using new nails for folly would be poor judgment, but nails that were destined for the dump would prove to be valuable tools in his education.

These justifications didn't matter to Joseph. He was much happier knowing that his father had straightened nails for him with his strong, skilled hands rather than just giving him new, unattended ones that were bought in some store. He valued them much more and took great care to ensure he applied them to the wood in a proper and purposeful manner. He would beam with pride as he held up his mosaic of nails and wood for his father's inspection.

A great day in Joseph's life was the first time his father brought him to work. It was early one Saturday morning, the dew still cool on the blades of grass that dampened his pant legs as he brushed past them, and the brisk breeze still blowing chilly before the sun was up to her daily task of warming its breath. He was only eight years old, rather young to go to the workplace. His mother had expressed her concerns, but he knew his father's decision would be final. It was a special rush job that had to be completed, and several tradesmen were working together to get it done. The Saturday was really just a clean-up day so the client would be happy on Monday morning.

Joseph was put to work collecting various bits of rubble and putting them in a large collection box that would be hauled away. As he collected the bits of broken brick and shattered planks, he saw numerous nails sticking out through the wood. He borrowed a hammer from one of the older boys, who were also there helping their fathers, and started knocking the nails out of the boards, collecting them in a pile to be straightened out later. He never knew that his father stood a short distance away, proud beyond words as his friends and co-workers commented on his son's natural ability.

As Joseph grew older, he became a skillful nail-straightener himself, and his nail mosaics became more complicated and precise, gradually gaining even more descriptive comments from his father.

While Joseph grew into the role of son and apprentice, he also developed some other interests—interests that he kept hidden or at least disguised from his father. He was proud to be the object of his father's pride and recognized his role in the family culture. He genuinely enjoyed the work of his destiny, especially the creative part of design or, later in life, the intricate latticework for which his father had become well known. He figured out at a young age that building and creating, whether for functionality or for art, was a process that involved much labour, patience, training, and passion. Labour was the easiest qualification to realize and passion the most elusive. He was fortunate to possess all the traits. He was a tireless worker, never shying from physical responsibilities, whether that meant helping his mother carry the laundry out and the groceries home or dragging the huge boxes of tools to help his father before each day's sunrise departure. They both expected him to help, and he expected them to expect it. It was never a question.

His patience when receiving an explanation on some worthy matter was another strong trait. He realized somehow, that questions were best asked after explanations were complete, that answers were best examined and calculated before being sought frivolously, that finding the answer required a complete understanding of the question first. He had faith in, if not awe for, his father's abilities, and his father knew he would impart all of his knowledge to his son at the pace he could absorb it. These were traits that helped him develop quickly and correctly.

Passion was the least recognized but most important trait of all. It was seldom implanted in anyone. It was a gift that everybody had for something; it was only a question of what. Joseph definitely had a passion for carpentry and masonry. Creating something from nothing excited and exhilarated him. When he walked past a structure his father had helped build, he held his head just a little higher and his eyes looked just a little wider. Something about the immortality of creating captured him. He would wonder about the great old stone cabins that littered his community, now crowded in by ever rising new houses, and magnificent buildings he had seen during trips to the city. He wondered about the men who had built them and the story of their lives. They were lost in the history and magnificence of these structures but were forever part of them. He envied and coveted that legacy.

His mother was aware of his other interests though, and she tried to encourage them passively. More than once she had found him reading poetry and prose from books secured from the library. She knew her husband would find such endeavours to be frivolous, so she defended it by not mentioning it. It was only the Bible that Joseph was not discouraged from reading, although his father was not so inclined. Joseph read at every opportunity and in any circumstance, ensuring that his responsibilities and commitments were not affected but veraciously engaged otherwise. He also knew his father would not warm to such activity. He could not really read and had commented often on the demerits of school. He agreed that basic reading and math were important, especially if his son hoped to be able to read blueprints and cut angles, squares, and perpendiculars, but he didn't feel that an entire adolescent lifetime should be dedicated to such enterprises that would be called upon so seldom in adult life.

"There's no point learning how to grow corn if you're never going to be a farmer," he would state.

But Joseph could no more quell his passion for text and verse than he could for chisel and stone. Reading occupied his moments alone and even cut into his study time. His school marks were in good shape though, and his teachers enjoyed his attention and attitude.

As he grew more mature and accomplished, reading became even more important to him. By age sixteen, he had defined his paths in life clearly. While those around him fumbled with relationships and indecision about what the future held, he stood with both feet planted on solid rock. His first passion and his source of livelihood would be as a builder. He had the foundation, mentorship, and aptitude to do it and to do it well. He knew he would always be able to earn a good living from his trade and to support a comfortable lifestyle for himself and his family. His other passion was reading, and he knew that would be followed by writing. He felt most content. Labour to serve the body, literature to serve the mind, and both artistic workmanship and writing to serve the spirit. Of course, he had not yet encountered or contemplated the heart, neither love nor the sorrow it could bring.

His father first took sick when Joseph was sixteen. He spent several months in and out of hospital, recouping at home otherwise and sinking gradually into a depression of the spirit brought on by the feeling of mortality his sickness installed and the sense of inadequacy his lack of work delivered.

Over those few months, the disease drained the family of their passion and joy. It was a sad time in Joseph's world, and it put everything else on hold. His learning, his energy, his reading, his dreams, and his happiness all fell into some kind of limbo. It was his first—but certainly not his last—taste of real pain and sorrow of the heart.

The sudden announcement of his father's complete recovery was unexpected and euphoric. The remission of the disease and the rebirth of his father's character and physique unfolded in less than a fortnight. The celebrations of spirit and family that followed over those next couple of weeks were genuine and lifelong highlights.

But the episode of illness had brought on a great change in his father. Lost was his patience and understanding, his calculating and measured design of surrender of the secrets of the trade he was imparting to Joseph. They were replaced with a hurried and humourless pounding of the skill details, as if he feared he might pass on before he could accomplish the completed construction of his son. His outlook on life and its purpose was twisted and confused by the rush to live it in massive amounts without any joy or taste, just consumption. It was a time when Joseph needed his father most. Not the skillful carpenter or master bricklayer but rather the experienced and understanding man who was living now in some internal struggle of panic, a man who would never emerge again.

That spring brought an end to the school year. Joseph had not even talked to a girl outside the confines of what could be termed a school-related reason. He prayed he would be paired with a girl for reading assignments or science work but then stumbled and fumbled wishing he hadn't been when it actually happened. His father used to say, "Be careful what you wish for, it might come true." Joseph had never appreciated the significance of the comment until then.

He had classified the girls in school, assigning them various categories that allowed him to track them and evaluate their potential as someone who would not refuse to talk to him, or worse, who would laugh at him for approaching them. He had no real indication that this would happen; he just protected his feelings with such assumptions. Any girl who was dropped off and picked up from school by a parent or nanny was off-limits. They would be too wealthy to associate with a tradesman. Any girl who had, or ever did have, a boyfriend was off-limits, because she knew too much about boys and would see right through him. Any girl attractive enough to be mentioned in every conversation between boys regardless of the topic was automatically off-limits, because she would never associate with a normal looking boy like Joseph. All of this analysis limited his potential conversation mates drastically. As a matter of fact, he had classified every single girl in his grade as off-limits to himself. This was mildly distressing, but it was also safe. If all the girls in his grade were off-limits, he had no pressure or obligation to actually talk to any of them. Perfect.

As fate would have it, however, he did meet a young lady named Mary who was included in one of his study groups. Although he didn't know it, she enjoyed his company.

As the school year was ending, they were together frequently in a group studying for exams. With the year-end party being planned and boys and girls coupling their intentions to go together, Joseph had already resigned himself to missing the event. No one would miss him, and he would not have to answer any embarrassing questions about why he had come alone. He just told everyone he had to work, because his father had been ill. His friends all understood, and there were sufficient expressions of sympathy and empathy. His young study mate didn't know his situation, however, and as she didn't think he would ever ask her to the party, she asked him instead.

Mary's question hit Joseph like one of his father's freshly laid bricks, and his heart pounded as his mind calculated the certainty that he now owned a flushed and blushing face. Joseph, after running the gambit of emotions associated with the prospect of actually sharing a complete event specifically linked to a single girl, could say nothing but "Yes," and then regretted it immediately. Why hadn't he just said "No"? But it was too late.

As the party date drew closer, he was forced to engage in conversation with Mary more regularly. He enjoyed it though, and his entire outlook on how the evening might turn out shifted from disaster to adventure. He even began initiating conversations with her and saying a casual hello to her friends as they passed in the hallways. Things were definitely rolling on round wheels.

Their affection for each other grew gently and in a juvenile way, much as it should at that age, and both Mary and Joseph came to anticipate their first morning encounters with some delight. Neither had told their parents about the budding affair, Mary fearing her mother would claim she was too young and not yet ready for such nonsense, and Joseph fearing his father would claim he was too young and not yet ready for such nonsense!

While this was going on, Joseph's father was working on a special and delicate stone gateway for an important and wealthy man who lived many miles away. As fate would have it, his father felt it would be the only opportunity for him to show his son some of the important methods of forming the finish and texture required to create uniqueness to the work that might also attract other potential clients' attention. He told Joseph they would travel that Friday to see the job and, because it was so far away, they would remain overnight and return on Saturday. This was the same Friday as the year-end party. Joseph had not mentioned the party to his parents. His mother commented on how happy his father was that he was able to show Joseph this particular style and type of masonry technique, as it was rare and seldom called for. Joseph had no choice. He could not let his father down knowing how much he wanted to show the work to him and knowing he had been so ill and was so anxious to accelerate the learning process. So he cancelled his plans for the party.

Mary understood outwardly, but that was superficial cover for the hurt she felt at facing the party alone. Joseph, embarrassed and unskilled in the ways of emotions, reacted to her chilled demeanour by claiming his work was more important than her anyway, and it was only a silly party of no consequence. It was not the best reaction available! She backed away from him, and he knew there would be no other opportunity with her. She felt he was disinterested and could not understand why he didn't just do his work and make it up to her on another occasion. He suffered greatly with his dilemma but did so in his own world, not letting his friends or his parents know the pain this situation had brought him.

His father's "complete" remission turned out to be not quite that. Within eight months he fell gravely ill once again, and this time his dying bed was not to be uncovered.

Once he realized that death was inevitable, a great calmness swept over his character, and he was immeasurably content with the most casual topics of conversation and the most trivial of anecdotes. Joseph's shy and tenuous attempts to engage his father in conversation about the opposite sex were futile though. Although such thoughts were ever present in his young mind, not to mention elsewhere, he was never able to find a way to begin such discussions with the dying man. They did discuss many techniques for straightening nails though.

After his father's death, Joseph heard the doctor tell his mother that the disease that took him was to be expected; it was hereditary, and she should be cautious to have Joseph checked carefully when he was past thirty.

Toast, Jam, and Tea

It was warm, as always, and the window lay open to allow the breeze a chance to shift the heat from side to side. The opening was too small however, and despite the fact that ample breeze was riding the late night airways, the opening restricted an efficient flow.

They slept in nightshirts with their day clothes folded carefully and piled beneath their beds. The ritual of changing was as precise as the meals, teachings, meditation, and prayer, all orchestrated by the stern, stoic Patriarch of the orphanage and by the guardians of life and purpose who doled out the pat-on-the-head rewards and the strap-to-the-bottom punishments.

It was difficult to sleep when the air was so heavy. Even the touch of a sheet brought on a sweat, almost as if the young residents were dressed in winter parkas. But they would never pull the sheets down. It was forbidden. Even if, during the restlessness of sleep, the sheets were kicked off to allow some respite from the warmth, one of the floor monitors would note the broken rule. There would be a punishment the next day, usually a simple scolding with some humiliation added in and, if the culprit was a repeat offender, perhaps a quick strap across the open hand. One could wake from sleep wide-eyed with optimism and hope for the coming day only to learn that while he slept, he had committed an offense, and punishment lay waiting for him at the breakfast table along with toast, jam, and tea.

Almost every boy received some form of punishment almost every day, sometimes just because they hadn't been punished for a while and their dorm brothers had suffered more. The daily routine and the routine punishments were woven into the fabric of their lives and seldom received more reflection than they deserved. The meals were regular, and the camaraderie among the boys was something more than they had experienced in their former lives, those being a wide range of unfortunate scribblings on the face of humanity—orphaned at birth, born into brothels, abandoned on railroad platforms, branded thieves, and sometimes just unwanted waifs.

From this pile of mongrel lives left to shore up the feelings of importance and charity within the spirit of the brothers who ran the orphanage, there emerged from time to time a promising and potent little life. A young man who would overcome the burdens life had delivered, who would unshackle himself from the self-doubt abandonment always lashed to the soul, who could absorb the teachings and challenges of schooling, and who could learn fast enough to turn the tables on the brothers by having them serve him, building his social skills and foundation on upright terms despite their need to have a dependent and submissive flock. With so many boys running in all directions in their lives, it was virtually impossible for the brothers to spot the one who might become a valuable adult until it was too late to prevent it. Then, after realizing this young man was heading out into the world with a winning way, that he possessed such internal fortitude he had not only survived the test of childhood but actually conquered it, the brothers and their school would parade the successful young man and profess the value of their order, using him as a poster child to solicit donations and build words of reputation.

The order had the expected cast of characters among its brothers. An elderly, caring Patriarch led the way calmly as he guided his disciples in the ways of spiritual development with a stern and unwavering set of values and principles. With him the time could be a hundred years earlier or a hundred years later. The demeanour and principles would remain constant.

He employed a council of four right hands. He chose them carefully to be efficient at whatever particular area of importance was needed on occasion. One was a skilled administrator who ensured schedules, books, donations, and dispensations were regular and accounted for.

Second to him was the spiritual mentor of the orphanage. He was a man of great strength and little patience, one who was adept at explaining to the boys what their beliefs were and how they would appreciate and honour them. He led the services, prayers, and all special occasion functions.

Yet another lieutenant was tasked with the husbandry of the orphanage. Meals, garbage, cleaning, purchasing, laundry, and general maintenance were all part of his responsibilities. He had the greatest presence in the outside community, as he went often to the local town to gather wares and provisions. He was held in rather high esteem, since the orphanage was considered to be a valuable asset to the world and a place of close service to God and his plan. Inside and outside the orphanage's walls were different worlds. From outside, the perception was one of sanctuary for poor lost boys who would otherwise suffer at life's hands. Inside, it was perceived as a prison, walls to house their crime of being unwanted or the product of misfortune.

The last pillar of the orphanage was that of discipline. This task was shouldered by a callous and crusty ogre of a man who felt bitter towards these youths who put such a burden on the world, and unfulfilled in his life's work, hindered and held back, he felt, by this torrent of undisciplined children. He was not only willing to set discipline standards and enforcement protocol, he did so with zeal and without conscience. He was the Ogre, but he was not the true tyrant of this orphanage. As the young boys grew into young men they feared his eyes and his lash, but they welcomed his presence. He was the most honest of the brothers. He dealt his punishments with integrity and commitment. He hurt the boys' pride and their skin, but he did not bruise their souls. That was the task of others. When he punished them, there was a reason, albeit often a ridiculous one, but nevertheless a reason that was laid out and presented clearly. Even if it was a reason unfairly levied or unjustly accused, the punished knew from where it came.

Other brothers were less noble in their confrontations with the children. Some had hands that wandered beneath the night-shirts on those hot summer evenings and brought confusion into the souls of these young boys. Some had private punishment sessions that scarred the skin only lightly but gouged the spirit, creating lasting scars that would direct life's path from the bitter trail of hardship onto the brutal trail of frenzy and mania. These brothers were far more menacing than the Ogre and more feared than any lash.

The Ogre vehemently opposed such activity among the brothers and considered those who plundered the boys to be charlatans in both their frocks and their faith. The brothers were well aware of his position, as he had confronted them at any opportunity and made clear the wrath he might bring to bear on those he could prove were such villains.

The Patriarch of the order was not such a villain, but he knew there were culprits among the brethren. He did his best to calm the Ogre and maintain peace among the ruling class, but his motives were not as noble as they should have been, and his tolerance was far wider than it should have been. He realized the life of celibacy was a difficult one, and he did not want to lose any of his followers. So, he turned a blind eye to a few indiscretions and harboured his guilt inside the stone walls of his ignorance, his head buried firmly and deeply in the sands of self-preservation. His true fear was that these despicable activities might become known to the outside world, bringing shame and accountability knocking at his door.

Indeed, there were a few occasions when the Ogre encountered such heinous acts as they were unfolding, and he confronted the offending brother, usually leaving him bloodied and broken before completing his circle of anger and guilt for not being able to prevent such activities by beating the young victim, ostensibly for making himself available! Some of the offending brethren were even forced to leave the order, notably if some permanent physical damage had been inflicted on the poor victim or some especially horrific action involved. Such expulsions, no doubt, turned evil men out into the world with bitterness, revenge, and hatred driving them toward their next encounter with the purity of youth. The Ogre's reputation for intolerance of these activities was well known among the boys, and this was why they welcomed his presence even though he was the disciplinarian.

One such dastardly and abusive Brother was known as Winter. Although it was his inherited surname, the boys felt it was appropriate for his cold heart and stormy inclinations. When the Ogre caught Winter forcing a young boy—freshly arrived from a tragic fire that drove his entire poor family and future hopes into the scorched black earth—to perform in a way that was beyond humane description, he unleashed his wrath and pummeled the man to a near death condition. The infirmary remained Winter's home for some time while the young boy locked himself tightly into his own inner world, unable to comprehend how so much tragedy had befallen him in a mere wisp of time.

As Winter recovered, he threatened every kind of revenge and hatred towards the Ogre, but the Patriarch made it clear he would be wise to leave the order and seek a new life elsewhere before the Ogre was given permission to finish his task. Eventually, Winter saw the reasoning behind this and departed without too much fanfare but with unlimited hatred for the orphanage, the Ogre, the Patriarch, the entire staff, and, of course, the victim.

The victim himself, but a wee boy, managed to bury the episode so deeply that, for a while, he lost recollection of it happening at all. He lost the memory of the entire night's events, moving from the day before to the day after, paving the assault over with black asphalt cooked somewhere in the belly of his soul until he was older and able to confront the episode. The only piece he did not bury or pave over at any time was Winter's face. That portrait would remain if front of him forever. He used it to help him overcome situations and as inspiration to achieve what he was told regularly he could not. Winter's face became his strength and motor of conviction, driving him to meet life head-on and part the burdens heading his way despite the fact he was commencing his journey from the bottom of the road.

As mentioned, from this orphanage, seemingly a madhouse but more likely a fair representation of reality for such institutions, there would, on occasion, rise up an individual who was able to insulate himself from these brutalities and waddle out from the oppression of the institution and into the world of sunlight, rain, and swirling winds. It was a truly great accomplishment, more amazing that any achievement of success or fame and more exhilarating to the spirit of mankind than any epiphany. The foundation of such an individual was built on rocky shores indeed, but the strength of character, built and held to enable a flowering from the ragged bed of weeds into which the seed was cast, would serve more than the man who embodied it. It would bring positive character out into the world as well for many to lean on and learn from.

As difficult as it was to believe that Winter's young victim would walk such a difficult path, it was all the more wonderful to understand that he did. From the horror of that early experience and the strength built from the boy's internal confrontation and self-absolution came the solid groundwork of a fruitful life. Despite numerous punishments at the hands of the Ogre during the boy's ten years of confinement at the orphanage, some of them much undeserved, the young victim always felt that some great power was looking over him and had delivered the Ogre to save him from Winter and the coldness he brought.

As the boy matured and his indoctrination continued, he learned from the brother designated as "spiritual mentor" that the great power was God, and although the events with Winter following his arrival at the orphanage were never mentioned again, the boy began to recall them in his mind every day. Winter's face juxtaposed forever with a perception of God's face, drawn from the numerous depictions scattered among the pitted walls and rooms of worship the orphanage held. As the event became less significant than the life-jarring memory it should have been, it became the most important aspect of the victim's relationship to this God, of whom he was reminded so regularly. He promised himself, against the charred bodies of his family, that if he ever found a path out of the orphanage, he would seek out God and extend his most humble and sincere appreciation for sending the Ogre into his life—and then he would seek out Winter.

Because of his notoriety following the incident, even though discussion of it was forbidden, the victim gained a slight admiration from the other boys. The whispered tales of the incident grew in scope and storyline with each retelling. The victim's legend also grew, and he became known as a fighter, then a favourite, then a blessed one, and then a protected one. Though none of these were actually true, and he was only a scared young man seeking purpose and closure on the events of his life, the perception usurped the truth and became the reality.

One day, a young ragamuffin, probably no more than four or five years old, was sitting silently on the curve of the staircase contemplating some daydream world, when he heard a few of the brothers talking on the landing below. They were discussing Winter's departure and how the young victim must have been under the protection of the Man above. He listened in awe as the brothers mentioned, almost sarcastically, though this fact was lost on the young scruff, that the boy in question was lucky the Ogre happened to be nearby and that it must have been God himself who intervened on his behalf. Under God's protection indeed. They winked at each other as the folly of this thought rose to their eyes, and then they rumbled off to meet their next appointed tasks.

The youngster who overheard their comments about divine protection raced upstairs to his small dorm room and repeated his eavesdropping to some of the older boys, assuring them of the importance the brothers had attached to the discussion, especially because they had used the name of God as well. He tried to explain how they had measured the serendipity of the Ogre's presence and that the victim was under God's safeguard. But he could not pronounce his words very well, and instead of mouthing the word "protection," he could say only "'tection." The boys were confused at first and asked what that meant. Not even the senior boys understood right away. They asked the young eavesdropper if he was sure about the word, and he repeated it clearly: "'tection, 'tection." Eventually, they got the message. The brothers thought this young victim was under God's protection. How obvious!

As they contemplated this possibility, they began to see the same light. After all, he had suffered so much and yet was becoming a rising star among the population, seemingly oblivious to his hardship and impervious to influence. His reputation grew quickly and relentlessly like the very flames that had stolen his life, replacing it with a new reality. Soon, the young victim became known as "Tection", his unsolicited nickname reverberating through the halls with murmurs of veneration and reflections of glory attached. Even the brethren, when they heard the name, thinking it was a nickname generated by the boys, began calling him Tection. And it stuck.

Tection was not overly impressed. He did not really understand why he was getting so much attention or why he had been singled out as someone worthier than the next poor orphan.

Many boys, even older ones, began speaking with him about their personal matters, feeling he could provide valuable advice and comforting opinions on their particular dilemmas. He responded with the best logic he could muster and, being from the same environment as the inquisitors, usually doled out a point of view or assumption that was harmonious with their own.

Occasionally, with some experience from the local town visits under his belt, he surprised someone with his "worldly" knowledge and enhanced his growing notoriety further. His reputation built rather quickly, and before long he was a focal point of the population, a de facto leader without any official status or special appointment.

One day, a new arrival was standing in the dorm when the boys returned from dinner. He was not too young, but he looked scared, shaking noticeably with his head bowed. The boys went through the usual teasing process. Even though it was a cruel procession, it had to be survived. The new arrival covered up, and some of the boys started to push him a bit. It became a little more violent, and then he was pushed to the floor. A round medallion fell from his hand and landed at Tection's feet.

Tection was not participating in this initiation, but he picked up the medallion and looked at it. It was a crescent moon raised on a smooth metal disc with a five-pointed star beside it. The boy looked up at Tection with anxious eyes, and Tection called out to the group of rambunctious orphans.

They ceased their bullying and looked at him. It wasn't often that he spoke with a raised voice, and with his growing reputation as a favoured child of the Almighty, his words were heeded. He put an end to the initiation and led the boy over to one of the spare beds. The other boys swung by eventually and patted the newcomer on the back, bidding him welcome. He would be okay.

Tection handed the boy the medallion, but he refused it, telling Tection it was his to keep. Anyway, the brothers had forbidden him to wear it, because it represented a different faith. Tection was curious about that and decided he would have to look into it later. He kept the medallion in his bedside locker, hidden under old shoes and a magazine about boats and knots. He pondered how a crescent moon and five-pointed star could represent a different faith.

All this fuss about Tection was not lost on the Patriarch. He could use a boy with such command of the orphan body to help hold the grip of order and reason more efficiently. He began to entice Tection with flexible reviews of his schoolwork, frequent opportunities to go into town, and duties of only minor hardship, mollifying him and sliding him effortlessly under the wing of sanctimonious servitude.

The other orphans recognized the special way Tection was being treated, but rather than build animosity and jealousy among them, they considered it part of his special relationship with God and actually came hither to his presence.

Tection flourished under this newfound importance. He relished the days of little hardship and afforded admiration. He had time to read and discover, to ask questions and receive answers, and to spend some time in the outside world, often strolling through the town and bidding casual hellos and goodbyes as he went. He rode into town with the brother in charge of purchasing and assisted in gathering provisions and loading them. This was a most enviable job, as it provided momentary escape from the orphanage.

Tection used his position of relative strength to help the brothers keep the orphanage harmonious, but he also used it to generate some alleviation of punishable offenses and enhancement of living conditions for his fellow creatures. His balanced approach to his responsibility allowed it longevity, and he remained a key figure in the orphanage throughout his time there.

Over the next several years, Tection became the leader and preeminent resident among the orphanage population. Newcomers were brought to him for initial introductory remarks, and his words of wisdom were heeded without question. During this period, with both an abundance of time and a cooperative staff, he completed his studies, being one of very few to graduate from secondary school; and he did so with attestation and recommendation from the orphanage and its status as a religious institution.

As time went by, changes in the outside world forced changes to the orphanage husbandry as well. Rules were augmented, reports were required, and the church in general became more watchful of the goings on there. Inappropriate behaviour or counterproductive actions were always at risk of becoming noticed by the outside authorities, who were under public scrutiny themselves and cognizant of the need to build an appearance of just and noble performance. The brothers knew this and pined for simpler days when decisions were internal and no eyes saw in or out from the large wooden doors that sealed the institution. The boys inside were not so aware. Newcomers were young and had no understanding of such matters, while older boys had been enclosed so long that they could not be aware of the subtle changes. So, as these social and institutional changes morphed the routines of the orphanage, much for the better, and swung the attitudes and demeanour of the brothers towards a harsh kindness, Tection was often credited with being the purveyor of such good fortune, receiving credit for an improved diet and reduced volume of punishment, even though he had no more to do with it than the wiry feral cats that sunbathed along the top of the exercise yard walls.

One summer day, with a warm sunlight hiding small wisps of wind that nipped at Tection's ankles. the Patriarch informed him that his days in the orphanage were over. The Patriarch did not want to allow for a long drawn-out goodbye period, and he was, quite frankly, concerned with the potential reaction from the general population. The Patriarch gave Tection a shoulder travel bag with a change of clothes and some general provisions, enough for at least a week. He also gave him a small stipend as a reward for his years of service to the orphanage, but not too much, he explained, to attract the interest of thieves or scam artists. Most importantly, he gave Tection an official document crediting his completion of secondary education and a recommendation that he be admitted to seminary. The Patriarch assured Tection that he had enough supplies and currency to get him to the seminary and then handed him a folded map explaining the route there, as if it was a piece of gold. There was no discussion about the possibility of not going to the seminary, and Tection had little idea about the outside world, save for the few experiences he'd had when visiting the town.

The Patriarch had planned it carefully, and his anticipation was flawless. The other boys had barely enough time to say their goodbyes and hold a small farewell breakfast before Tection was up and gone.

Surely he will stretch the reputation of our orphanage once in seminary and bring our great name forward to the learned brothers who teach there, the Patriarch thought. *If Tection performed well,* the Patriarch hoped, *his name might even reach forward to the bishop of the diocese.*

Surely Tection would find great success and a beautiful wife on the outside, the orphans believed, *and create blond babies destined for a wonderful family life with Tection and their mother.*

Surely I will find Winter and the face of God somewhere out there, Tection thought.

The Adventurers

The boys raced around the corner of the town wall, running and skipping, waving their arms, holding their few belongings in makeshift travel bags. They had been friends for many years. Julian was the most joyful, alternating between running, skipping, turning, and running backward and then forwards again, urging John P on towards the only road that led away from their small town.

The dust whirled behind them, and the pedestrians turned their heads at the commotion. Most of them, carrying their heavy loads or tugging along growing families, cracked a knowing smile. They remembered the exuberance of youth, the lure of the unknown road, and the desire to travel it. They had not traveled it, preferring to remain close to the place of their youth or perhaps acceding to the demands of life and responsibility. Families so close or friends so dear or children too young or callings too strong. Whatever the reason, they had remained in this town. But it was not the same for Julian and John P. They had no such attachments they weren't willing to liberate. As a matter of fact, they had too many reasons to leave.

John P was not sure he would have had the courage to pursue the invitation to adventure that the road delivered on his own, but Julian had never doubted it. Julian had enough desire to move away from where he was for both of them. John P was older and less anxious for adventure, but he loved the spirit Julian brought to their friendship despite the hardships life had delivered him. John P was a veracious reader, and for his young age of eighteen was a very knowledgeable individual. He preferred reading books with a religious tone, especially Christian, but would devour any material he could get his hands on.

Julian was sixteen on this day, finally old enough to leave the miserable hardship in which he had grown up. Forever cringing and cowering before the tyranny of his parents, forever longing to be free of their demands and diversions. The beatings were not too bad, but the humiliation and servitude were unbearable. He had fled their cruel grip twice previously, only to be returned by the authorities that managed to show up somehow whenever he began to feel safe elsewhere.

Like John P, Julian was fascinated by new things and the discovery of new ideas, but he had been ripped from the joys of school when he turned twelve to work in the family store. His mother and father made sausages and processed various meats for consumption by the local townsfolk, and their reputation for quality and tasty goods was well earned. They saw Julian as free labour and relief from the long, tedious task of grinding and blending the animal by-products they used in preparing their wares.

Julian's father believed he needed no more schooling. After all, he himself had never been to school, and look at the thriving business he had built. He was able to pay his bills on time, purchase the goods he needed to keep his production smooth, and still have enough for him and his wife to enjoy their liberal drinking habits. It was only Julian's mother, who could at least read and write, who convinced her husband it was important for the business that someone besides her be able to read the invoices, keep the accounts, and send out the letters for permit renewals, even though her motivation was to be free of those tasks, not because she wanted Julian to improve himself. She had never really liked Julian, viewing him as an intrusion on the happy and carefree lifestyle she and her husband had enjoyed before Julian arrived, blaming him more and more for the slow spiral into unhappiness and bitterness that was actually the by-product of long hours of work, a lack of any genuine family affection, and heavy alcohol consumption. His father agreed to some schooling for those reasons but swore Julian would have to begin work in the shop as soon as he had the basics in his little mind and had grown big enough to pump the meat grinder.

Julian's sadness was due not to having to work twelve hours a day, waiting on customers, cutting slices of cold meats, bringing small cafés to the few mushroom tables sitting comfortably outside the small curtained store window, or even by the understanding that his parents resented his existence, often alluding to the fact they could have done better by using all the money they spent on him to hire a labourer to do the heavy work instead. His sorrow was fueled by the thought he would no longer be part of the world that those other twelve-year-olds shared, learning about new places and new ideas; kicking an old leather ball into the form of a bright white one, with visions of adoring fans cheering him on down the bright green pitch; lifting a tree branch to the open sky to set course across the dusty field behind the old schoolhouse; or just sitting in the bowels of a sleeping sand dune with some friends, laughing out loud at ridiculous things. None of these things, taken for granted by many, were to be part of his childhood anymore.

But John P was his salvation. He understood the dilemma Julian faced from the first time they spoke. Julian never had to present long-winded explanations or mask his embarrassment about his life, and he never had to feel ignorant when asking a question or obligated when he got a response. It was a mutual time of enjoyment that they spent together.

John P was a natural teacher and sharer of information. He had an unusual ability to read, decipher, comprehend, interpret, and translate and a corresponding talent for dispensing the concepts and principles he gained from the text. He took great pleasure in sharing his understandings with others, not because he felt superior or even important, but because he knew that whoever had written those words, whoever had lent their perception and wit to him, had done so with personal anonymity and without expectation of reward. It was like books were a global movement to share whatever one believed to be the truth and an opportunity for the reader to constantly change what the truth was. Sharing what he knew and learned with others also allowed John P to garnish his own understanding of it. Words and wondering thoughts that he might have passed over too easily when reading them were spotlighted by someone else's curious question, especially by the unique ability Julian had to question those things that John P also found significant. Their friendship grew rapidly and solidly over those four years before breakout day, Julian's sixteenth birthday, today!

John P had lived a much kinder childhood than Julian. Although his mother told him his father had been some traveler who passed through the town about nine months before he was born, she had always told him to respect and honour him. She said that even though they had only known each other for a few hours, his father was a very intelligent, loving, and understanding man. When John P questioned how she knew that, she said because his son was also all of those things. She never let John P feel that he was just an accident spawned by a night of passion. On the contrary, she always reinforced that she had selected his father carefully and used him to bring herself the only thing she ever really coveted, a child.

She encouraged John P to read and remain curious, even when it got him into trouble. She introduced him to the church and brought him there faithfully every Sunday. The church was full of fascinating books and kindly old people. They loved young children, especially when they were cute and curious. Besides the many religious books and periodicals that he grew up perusing, his friendships with elderly patrons of the church allowed John P to secure other books, both fact and fiction. He would merely express his joy of reading to them, and they would respond by expounding the wonders of their most recent readings, even if they had read the book five years earlier. "You just have to read this book," they would say, and he would.

His mother also encouraged him to confide in Joseph, their local priest. It was clear that she had a rather special relationship with him, bending with his support, something a single mother needed desperately, and fostering a kinship between him and John P that provided her son with a worthy male role model and possibly even a suitable father image, even though priests were not to be fathers! John P felt Joseph was especially fond of him, and he grew to love and respect him greatly, although he never lost the longing to know and understand his real father.

John P's mother provided quite adequately for him through her job as a town clerk. She worked for the mayor's office and handled much of the bureaucracy involved with licensing, permits, and taxation. She knew a lot about almost everyone and enjoyed the town's respect, because she never divulged any information that was not public knowledge. The townspeople knew she was trustworthy, and her presence and reputation was part of the reason the mayor was elected for his fourth term. Honesty and politics was such an unusual yet powerful platform. Her close relationship with the priest also enhanced her standing, as she was accepted and liked by all the social components of religion, politics, and family. She had John P involved in numerous activities, from music to sport to community service. All in all, an outstanding woman and mother!

It was through his mother that John P first met Julian. When Julian showed up at the town office to collect the annual license renewal for processing meats that his parents needed for their shop, his face was clearly battered, and his head hung low, eyes to the floor. John P's mother was too official to question the circumstances that brought him to such a state, but she spoke with John P about it later that night.

John P was casually familiar with Julian's situation and explained what he knew. His mother was disappointed. She knew that Julian's parents made a good living at their business, because she saw the taxes they paid on their profits. Why would they pull their son from school? More importantly, why would he be so obviously beaten? Even if he had misbehaved or otherwise drawn their wrath, parents should not treat their child so harshly. She confided in the only person she knew she could trust: Joseph.

John P was impressed by that fact. His mother was the person he respected most in the world, including the worlds he visited in his books. The fact she was so trusting of Joseph left a lasting impression on him, one of respect and admiration for the man and his position.

Joseph suggested she try to get Julian to the church on Sunday, but his parents were far away from any connection with their spiritual selves. They told Julian to use his only day off to go and play with his friends like other boys, not hide indoors at some church where they would fill him with ideas of obligation and restitution. Besides, they would also ask him for money if he went there. So, John P's mother asked him to speak with Julian.

John P found him one Sunday sitting along the river digging mud out of the recently showered earth.

"Good morning," John P said.

Julian didn't reply. He didn't even look up.

"You think this river goes anywhere important?"

"Anywhere is important," Julian whispered.

John P took a step closer. "Have you ever been anywhere besides here? Like past the hills over there? I never have."

"Nope."

He only said half the word, but John P understood. "I'm gonna though."

Julian looked up. "Gonna what?"

"I'm gonna go somewhere besides here. Anywhere besides here."

"Where you gonna go?"

"I dunno. I know all about a lot of places, but I've never been there."

"So how d'ya know about 'em?"

"Books. I've read a lot of books."

The boys talked for a while. About places they had never been, which was anywhere and everywhere. About destinations, transportation, and motivation, and even a little about ambition, which neither of them had developed into anything formalized. Julian's main ambition was to get away from his life, away from where he was, and to leave behind all he had known so far. John P, on the other hand, wanted to exercise the imagination his readings had inspired, even though it would be at the expense of leaving behind all he had known so far. From this first meeting together they both sensed a camaraderie that steered them towards a common path, even if the motivations were dug from different foundations.

A few days later, John P heard that Julian had taken off the previous night, and now the entire countryside was looking for him. He wasn't gone long though. He was back the next day, and it was evident he had received a pretty severe punishment for getting everyone so upset.

Over the next few weeks, they saw each other a few more times, and although they never spoke of Julian's lost night, it was obvious they shared an interest in travel and far off places, even if it was for different reasons, one escaping from his life and one escaping to it.

Eventually, John P got Julian to come with him to church on Sunday morning. After the formalities and sermon, they went into the basement, where all the non-religious books were kept. They scoured the atlas and maps, making the kind of plans only dreamers can. Julian found great refuge in the church basement with John P, and John P found great fellowship with Julian. Even Julian's second escape attempt wasn't too significant in their relationship. It was just something Julian had to do to remind himself he had a destiny beyond his current life. The physical punishment for such escapes was compensated for by the exhilarations that such demonstrations of independence delivered him. John P understood that and never questioned Julian or admonished him for it.

John P never cried as a youth; he had no reason to. That changed when his mother died. She expired due to a long-running disease that she knew was going to bring her life to an end and deliver her from this world. Joseph and her doctor were the only others who knew, but the doctor was far away, and Joseph, honouring his promise and commitment to her, never said a word. Her desire to continue with her normal life until the end was something he respected, and even though he counseled her to seek broader sources for potential help, he never betrayed her request for silence on the issue.

John P resented Joseph for a while because of that, feeling he had the right to know. There were many things he would have liked to say and to discuss with his mother before she died. He wondered about his father. He longed to have more information about him, even though his mother claimed to have shared all she knew. John P had a constant feeling she would reveal more about him as he gained age and maturity. He wished to know more about her as well. His understanding of life had sprung new buds, and he was only beginning to communicate with her at a more substantive level, embracing opportunities to banter of those things more serious than playgrounds, meals, and why the moon found a home during the day sometimes as well as at night. She was his sounding board and echo chamber, and even though his books were the wind that blew his sails towards imagination, she was the rudder that let them find direction. Her passing rewrote the lines of his destiny in both immediate terms and, though he did not understand it yet, in the very path he would pursue through life.

Those feelings of resentment towards Joseph passed, however, and Julian realized the priest had an obligation both professionally and morally to respect his mother's wishes, but the bond they shared was damaged or twisted somehow and would never return to the blind trust they had shared before. The truth was always what was believed and never what was real. Reality was an interpretation of perceived truths. This understanding of the way the truth was delivered and accepted was part of John P's evolution to adulthood, perhaps before it should have been.

When Father Joseph delivered the sermon at her funeral, John P thought it was the most beautifully written work he had ever heard. The eulogy expressed the sadness of her situation and revealed a deep understanding of who his mother was and what she valued, and expressed so vividly the feeling of shared love she had with her son. It expounded on her beauty, commitment, fortitude, elegance, ethics, spirituality, and other attributes that he felt she embraced.

Following the funeral service, Joseph handed the pages that held the eulogy to John P, claiming he could never read it again. John P was genuinely moved by the gift and clutched it close for many years. During the nights that followed, John P's crying was so sustained that his tears dried long before his whimpers did.

Although he was only sixteen when his mother passed, John P was legally allowed to be on his own. His mother had left him a healthy bank account, and he was a bright and well-liked young man. Joseph was quite taken with John P and felt a sense of fatherhood, though everyone knew he could never really enjoy that in his chosen profession. So, it was a natural progression that John P moved into the spare room at the church and continued his schooling under Joseph's watchful eye. The priest spent much more time with him and opened up a whole new understanding of the Christian philosophies and the study of the Bible. John P found great solace and strength in the teachings and spent much of his time pursuing an understanding of them. Joseph also taught him the basics of carpentry, an entirely new experience for John P. He gained much reward from creating physically as well as intellectually and let the hammer and saw carry away much of his sorrow. He never imagined that Joseph had such skills; repairing broken altar stairs as well as healing damaged souls.

The friendship between Julian and John P also flourished as they grew up together over the next couple of years, each comforting the other for different sorrows and each firing the other's passions in life. John P was two years older and very much the steadying force behind Julian's gradual maturity. As their time together became more important to them, they realized the bond between them had grown strong; Julian replacing the loving family that John P no longer had, and John P filling the void that Julian's loveless family could not.

They made a decision to strike out together into that unknown world as soon as Julian reached the legal age of sixteen, when his parents could no longer lay legal claim to their child slave. As the days, weeks, and months grew closer to birthday sixteen, their discussions centered more and more on their plans. John P was the pragmatist, insisting they should only go a short distance, perhaps one or two towns over to begin with, and work to earn enough to finance their further travels. Julian, on the other hand, was already dreaming of crossing the oceans and deserts of the world. He devoured everything he could find that dealt with adventure in faraway places and curiosities about other cultures.

Aside from the great sorrow John P felt when bidding farewell to Joseph, nothing about the town held him tight. At first, Joseph admonished him for such plans and tried to usher the traveling thought from John P's mind. When that didn't work, he tried to at least get a commitment on communication, calendar, and destination, but the excitement the boys mustered was not going to be diminished by such barriers. When they left, it was for wherever, whenever, and whatever.

The midmorning air was still a little crisp from the night's chill, but soon the power of the sun, sitting unmolested in the eastern sky, would have the whole town looking for shade. Julian and John P settled into a steady pace of youthful strides along the roadside and spoke little after the first jubilant minutes had passed. They were finally on the road, actually doing what they had planned, and steadfast in their determination to become explorers, if not of the entire world, then at least of the next village. Each was gathering his thoughts and realizations of what was happening. There was no need for words. Each had his reasons for leaving, and they knew what each other's reasons were.

It's funny, John P thought, *even though Julian has led a remorseful life, and he has more reason to want to leave the familiarity of our lives behind, he also has more confidence and trust in the certainty of our decision than I do.*

Perhaps John P held a little trepidation, because he knew more about the realities of the world and living in it. His time and place with Joseph was safe and secure. But much more than that, he truly enjoyed the narrative of the Bible and embraced the teachings, principles, and convictions he found there. He admired the priest greatly, although he didn't idolize him. He thought his life was a valuable one, because he brought love and understanding to people who tended to misplace it. He dedicated himself to a singularity of purpose, and despite the curious doubts that John P often caught wrestling in the eyes of the aging man; he carried a confidence and sureness that lent strength to his flock. John P longed for such acceptance and self-worth. Little did he know that such was the very thing he walked towards as he left the town. What more could a man want than to be admired and respected in his community and content and committed in his mind and soul?

John P felt that being a priest was an honourable profession, but Joseph was growing older and poor, leaving him no further adventure in life other than that of a local priest. John P could not have realized the impact his departure would have on Joseph, whose entire life was centered on John P and whose spirit was to gain insurmountable loss. The passing of John P's mother followed by John P's departure from Joseph's life left the aging priest beyond sorrow. John P was young and inexperienced in the ways of family other than his mother, and her departure had left a void in him that he had filled gradually with Julian's friendship. Joseph had hoped desperately that it would be he who filled that lost space.

John P had his books and Bible to feed his mind and really was giving up more than Julian, or maybe not. Julian, for all the hardship he endured while being raised by loveless parents, never lost the hope, or perhaps dream, that his parents would change one day and learn to love him. As a child, his private games and daydreams usually included some attachment to a loving parent or imaginary sibling. The fondest memories of his youth, before meeting John P, were those of time spent companionless in his own fantasy world, where mothers and fathers loved sons and daughters; where huge extended families gathered once or twice a year on special occasions to renew their gossip and admire how big their nieces, nephews, and cousins had grown; and where good deeds and kindness were a customary part of life. His night-time dreams were quite different though, usually including some form of falling, separation, searching, or longing.

Julian had great difficulty appreciating the wonderment that John P had with the Bible and its teachings. He had spent too much of his life on the flip side of happiness. He enjoyed the swaggering characters and larger than life situations that were ever present in the book, and despite the many tragedies that were endured, the endings were usually happy, especially the way John P recounted them. It was an orderly story with distinct timelines, clear and consistent rules of law, and occasional flowery diversions from all the guts and glory. Littered with parables, allegory, and analogies, it could always be counted on to provoke thought and conversation. Even death was validated and made meaningful in its pages. Sacrifice and commitment were held in high esteem, and the personage demonstrated good character regularly. Much different than the world he knew and in which he lived. All in all, he enjoyed the time spent listening to the stories, but he never really felt the application of incorruptibility and honour would find their way into his heart or soul. How would this book, or this belief structure, help him gain a huge loving family? How could he ever expect to realize those fantasies he had built? He couldn't know then just how directly the seekers of faith actually would bring his dreams to him!

They walked endlessly along the road, occasionally finding the energy and focus required to have a light conversation and accepting short lifts from sympathetic fellow travelers who longed for their own younger days, and admired the spirit of these two adventurers. They stopped only in late evening, their tired bodies sinking to the selected clearing at the same time as the exhausted sun. They drank from their water bottles and ate various items they had packed or purchased whenever they slipped through a little village. Their small tent served as shelter, and fortune smiled on them, as they had not seen a single drop of rain during the six days they had been traveling.

On the seventh day, they came to an intersection which housed a large produce market, and turned onto a secondary road leading away from the main road they had been following so far. Traffic was light, and they walked continuously towards a horizon that never seemed any closer. Gradually, the terrain became more undulating, and the short relief from walking downhill was defeated by the struggle to climb the next incline. It was clear that the up was longer and steeper than the down, and those large hills, almost mountains, they had seen so far back in the distance were quickly, though imperceptibly, gliding towards them like the hands of a clock, never seen moving but always in a different place whenever you looked at them again. They knew the sea lay beyond those hills, and the sea was the gateway to the real adventure of which they dreamed. Their conversation always moved towards discussions of the passage boats, costs, destinations, and intention. At least it was the adventure Julian dreamed of more vigorously.

John P had learned that across the sea were lands of different cultures, full of people with beliefs that came from other books and other teachings. He was not nearly as sure about the prospect of sailing that far. He was nicely comfortable in a world where he understood the citizens and could follow his ambitions to read, discuss, acquire understanding, and sermonize, homologous with the ordained and confirmed. He had no plans to return to his small hometown, yet he had no destiny other than to do so.

Palpable Melancholy

After his father's death, Joseph found a significant void in his life. Not the void of being without his father, for that was true sadness, though not as wrenching as it may be to others who were more attached and enjoyed a loving personal relationship with their father. Joseph's void was that of purpose and commitment. He enjoyed his carpentry and masonry skills, but without a father to be impressed with them, they became more of a hobby. They had been the bond between the two men, and that had provided them enough value as a connection to be pursued. Now it was different, and Joseph's interest in framing a career around such labour faded quickly.

During his period of mourning, Joseph wandered frequently and somewhat aimlessly, caged by his thoughts of remorse and regret and incognizant of his surroundings as they trickled by at his humdrum pace. On one particular morning, after an especially edgy night, Joseph gathered enough food and drink to sustain him for several days and then set out on a more extensive outing. Without a clear direction or destination, and after a journey that consumed most of his supplies, he found himself labouring uphill along the edge of an ever-tightening forest. As the density of the forest grew, his curiosity towards it did as well.

He stopped and gazed uphill towards the growing mass and viewed the distant darkness of cover, void of the light that was shining down on him now and sheltered from the life that formed an upper canopy. Joseph was drawn deeper into the forest by a sense of emotional symmetry with the representations the wooded landscape provided, both dark and contained, indeed, secluded and perhaps abandoned, with a certain sense of natural anger. Unconsciously, Joseph tied the physical image emanating from the forest to his own grief and was drawn deeper and deeper onward, up the side of the mountain in a trancelike condition, until he pushed through a particularly dense thicket and found himself in a small but distinctly carved clearing. Someone had been there before, but it was certainly some time earlier. The sharp edges that would have formed the original clearing were well rounded by new growth of vines and leaves. The fallen plant debris in the clearing was deep enough to have a spongy feel, and the buzz of gnats and bees hard at work filled the air.

As he surveyed the full length of the clearing, Joseph noticed the shadow of a structure at the far end. It was partially hidden by forest growth, but there was no doubt it was a constructed object. He pushed through the tall grass, keeping his eyes trained on the structure as if it would disappear if he looked away. As he swept aside the final few remnants of growth, he found himself face to face with a roughly hewn cement wall, still raw and without finish, seemingly applied but abandoned hurriedly for some unknown reason. The long dried remnants of loose material could be brushed away easily from the coarse surface.

Joseph felt his way along the wall, yanking away the tangled vines that clung to it and shuffling along through the thick forest base that had grown up to and upon the wall itself. After several feet, he found the first edge of a doorsill and used it to pull himself through the final entanglements before grasping the lever handle and pushing the door open. It squeaked and then whined as it opened for the first time in what seemed like forever, the hinges woken suddenly from hibernation and reminded of their responsibilities.

As he crossed the threshold and entered the contained and cobwebbed room, Joseph felt an eerie sense of recognition, a shiver that swept through his neck and back, making him very conscious of his surroundings. He played the feeling off through some internal logic about entering a dark room with anticipation and without reference, but he knew it was something else. Something foreboding yet enticing lurked in the air, and he would not fully understand what it was until much later in life.

Joseph's first inclination was to seek some light, so he stumbled through the clutter of furniture and debris towards the sliver of sunshine slicing the edges of the heavy wooden shutters that framed a window at the front of the cottage. He swung the first shutter open, hearing it whine in solidarity with the door hinges, and was blinded at first by the influx of bright light. Shading his eyes, he reached around the window and pulled back the second shutter, filling the room with sunshine, highlighting every edge and angle, illuminating every particle of dust, and beating off the darkness that had rested there so comfortably moments before.

As his eyes became accustomed to their surroundings, he took note of the simply furnished room—an old stone kitchen hearth with top burners of heavy iron and an iron spring handle to shuffle them on and off the heat; a small pile of firewood beside the stove, thick with cobwebs and dry, peeling bark; a roughly hewn counter with a sink sitting solitaire and unconnected to plumbing, emptying into a pail hidden below it by a hand-drawn curtain; a rudimentary but sturdy table with two equally hearty chairs; and a platform that served as both sofa and bed, the thick straw mat covering it in complete disarray and uninviting to even the most weary visitor. There was no proper toilet, and Joseph assumed either some unseen pail or the woods themselves served for such functions. Upon reflection, the entire structure served but to provide warm coffee and shelter from the rain on any particular night, though even the integrity of the roof was suspect until proven otherwise.

Turning around, Joseph pried open the front door. He swept cobwebs from the opening and glanced out through the portal with eyes now adjusted to the brilliance of the late afternoon sun. He was impacted immediately by the visual form, the sun setting against the vast blue grey sky, the cosmos open in front of him like the heavens themselves. The view was unhindered, stretching beyond the horizon of sea and sky as they melted together in the glare of sunshine.

He stepped out onto the rickety porch, a little leery of the proximity of the precipice, and leaned forward to glance down. The cliff to which the cottage clung lipped out over the mountainside, and no matter how far he leaned out, the inside edge of the rocky descent was not visible, only the front side of the rocky beach.

Far below lay the soft wiggle of waves, too far away for their height to be determined and too far at sea for their shore to be seen. They simply rolled back towards the curve of the earth before dwindling and blending into a harmonious horizon with the rounded sky. It was a wondrous sight, breathtaking in every sense of the word, not merely in the common use of the word, usually used to describe anything more than normal. If there was a visual dictionary, this view would be tied indelibly to the word and provide instant understanding of what it meant.

New words would need to be found to replace the common use of "breathtaking."

Joseph smiled at his train of thought, as if he had just discovered the true meaning of a previously misunderstood concept. He stepped sideways from the door and lowered himself onto a small, lonely bench, knowing he wanted to spend more time enjoying the sight but still a little tired from the long trek up the mountainside.

As he sat, the bench creaked under his weight, and he sprang back to his feet, certain it would have collapsed with its unexpected burden. He would just have to stand, lean back against the front wall, and bear the weight on his own feet so his mind could ride the beauty lying before him.

After this first visit to the cottage, Joseph was determined to affect some repairs and service to the old structure and its contents. He wasn't looking to change it or take ownership in any way, but his frequent visits begged him to regenerate at least some creature comforts and allow him to rest there overnight so he didn't have to make these long journeys up and down the mountainside without a day of rest.

Over the next few months, he made numerous visits to the cottage, bringing various pre-cut wooden pieces, nails and other means of attachment, carpentry tools to complete his work and even dry plaster in buckets to repair and heal the walls and grout scarred by age. The stove fire pit, tested once the tin chimney was cleaned, worked with such efficiency that Joseph wondered why this particular type of stove had ever been replaced with anything more modern. The table and chair, constructed of such thick and hard wood that they could be sanded to a fine finish and glazed with a varnish, became the centerpiece of the building, standing strong and proud though void of anyone to whom they could boast, except the very carpenter who had reworked them.

Joseph replaced the mattress with a long foam sheet covered with cloth in a brightly coloured pattern, bringing some humanity to the lodging. The old mat served well as kindling for some time. He also reworked the exterior benches' one-piece handle and leg supports to strengthen and weatherproof them before new benches were installed. They were the most important pieces of furniture, as they allowed the visitor to spend countless hours lounging while attached to the natural screen of infinity and seeming immortality that the front porch delivered. Joseph hatched a series of plans on how he would refurbish these benches. He reworked the plans repeatedly, and it was some time before he actually carried them out.

One bright Sunday morning, Joseph leaned back on one of the benches and reflected on his growing discontentment with his current life. He lamented that he was not pursuing anything of real interest, and for a young man to be this bewildered, without job ambitions, without a girlfriend or even a single female friend, without prospects of fortune, fame, or folly, he was completely unfulfilled and uninspired. He wasn't depressed, at least not yet, but he would have to have to find purpose and social affiliation somewhere soon. He languished on these thoughts for far too long.

The Philosopher and the Broken Step

Some believe the cottage was built by the Philosopher, so enraptured by this particular spot in the universe and so inspired whenever he managed to make the ascent that he decided to build a simple dwelling for himself so that he could be there always and always be inspired. He gave up all other passions in life—his lover, his books, his music, and even his dreams.

For many years, he dedicated himself to constructing the cottage. He carried every stone, every nail, and every plank by hand. He left behind his philosophizing for those many years and dedicated himself only to construction. His friends thought he had lost some of his faculties, but he didn't care. They had not seen the view or experienced the transcendence, and he did not desire to share it with them. And if he didn't build it, he surely claimed it as his own for those times he was there.

He had grown up surrounded by this area. The town could be hot, dry and dusty, or cool, wet, and muddy. He possessed a curious mind and nature. It had often brought him trouble during his youth as he put himself in places he shouldn't be while trying to find out things he shouldn't know.

When he was very young, after saying his prayers and being tucked in, he would feign sleep and then slip out of bed to listen to his mother and father discuss the topic of the evening. They loved each other deeply, though not as passionately as earlier in their lives, and they shared a lot of time reminiscing, planning their dreams, and sharing their feelings of kinship with their young son. The Philosopher enjoyed nothing more than listening to them late at night sharing their lives together. Usually, he slipped back into his bed once he tired of the conversation or nodded off with contentment that everything was all right with his small, comfortable world. On those rare occasions when his parents discovered him, they feigned disappointment and scolded him appropriately before shuttling him back to his bed with smiles, tickles, and go-to-sleep kisses.

As time went by, the Philosopher gained great interest in the world by participating in his parents' verbal adventures. He also began studying the people of the town, wondering about their lives, their dreams, and their hopes. He read vociferously about foreign lands and foreign people, about beliefs and approaches to life that were dissimilar or even incompatible with his own. He made detailed exercises with pen and paper to apply other ideas and lifestyles to his.

He had a strange calling towards these differences in the great mass called the human race, but he did not really understand what it was. He thought it might be a desire to travel and see what the world was doing, but that wasn't really it. He wondered if he should examine more closely the political structures that governed the world and influenced the growth of people's ideas, but that was not what he sought either. Perhaps world religions were what really attracted him with their undeniable strength and power over "yes" and "no."

But he was a believer in his own interpretation of religion, and as he studied, he formed what he thought were some rather unique concepts about the way religion should be embraced. Unfortunately, he could not find any recognized religion that actually allowed him to bring a unique perspective along with him when he undertook such appropriate and specific recognition of the faith in question. He was full of vigour to pursue these matters, but he also had to profess acquiescence to the sturdy and essential religion by which his parents abided, as practicing any other would be a great burden for them, especially if he strayed too far. After all, he still prayed to God nightly wishing for those things he did not have and asking for the good, and sometimes not so good, favours he might deserve.

He pondered for a long period about his life's course. He knew and felt there was a purpose to his existence. He was a solitary individual, though not isolated or reclusive, and he did not want to be forced into the mould of an existence someone else had lived over and over again. What a waste of the great gift of being. Why was he here? What was his purpose? These were the questions everyone asked and the questions that eluded him.

As he began asking them more frequently and more profoundly, he realized these questions were his reason for being. Wasn't that a fundamental question that each and every person must ask? Why am I here? What is my *raison d'être*? He found clarity of purpose in a journey to answer these simple questions. He lost interest in travel to other lands. He did not need to analyze other people's politics or religion except in the context of their effect on the perception each person developed to explain, and perhaps even justify, their existence. It didn't occur to him at that point that most people didn't take much time to analyze their existence. Life happened, and it brought with it many joys and sorrows. We affected but a few, and if we were lucky, we fell on the heavenly side of the road. Fate and destiny enjoyed almost blind obeisance. Were people so wrapped up in their daily lives that they found no time to seek answers to these basic queries?

The Philosopher made a long and soulful inquisition of his thoughts. He had faith, he knew that, but he was not sure in what exactly. He did not develop any inspiration from the institutions that politics and religion represented. He did not understand why a multitude of people in some far off city, through their entrenched political process, would determine who was best suited to decide on issues of civil health and welfare as they pertained to his small town, when they were so far away and had never even visited the area. How did the needs of the townspeople take on such insignificance in the eyes of the political institution? And how was it that he could not engage this omnipresent God except through the faculty of a person and church building that he neither knew nor visited?

As he pondered these questions, he became angry and even more determined to expose the inherent peccancy of these basic institutions. He came to some realizations about them—money and faith, the evolution of survival and belief. Banks provided money for people to spend, although they had not yet earned it. This not only gave them hope that the future held a positive path, it kept them content and busy working to repay the debt. There would be no time for civil unrest or political opposition. The hunter and provider were guaranteed a kill, and the great institutional leader, the bank, provided his family with shelter and security. Man's other great need, belief, was packaged, controlled, and distributed by the Church or its equivalent in other faiths. No variance and no variation. The governance of faith was as essential to the harmony of society as the control of currency.

For many years, the Philosopher pondered the problems and issues. He came to the conclusion that every person should make an internal journey to discover his or her potential and purpose. He became particularly disappointed in the struggle each person took to remain faithful to an institutional belief structure they neither helped build nor had any influence upon. This was a great turning point for him. It allowed him to understand the structure of his society, recognize the need for enlightenment, and left him confident that his philosophizing was not in vain.

During these earlier years, while he sought the foundations of his concepts and understandings, he barely noticed that the warmth and love between his parents he so admired, had begun to show signs of wear. It had been losing passion and patience slowly for some time, but he had not really noticed.

His first realization came one evening when he overheard them discussing life and its ongoing evolution. Gone was the soft cuddling and sympathetic ear he had witnessed so often; replaced with a strange sense of discontent and almost regret. Each parent was lamenting their situation and complaining to deafened ears, as the other parent was disinterested and only waiting his or her turn to do the same. Although his future encounters with their private lamentations were too often about money and the lack of it or about vacations or new things for the house or just about any topic that could be complained about, this first experience, his first recollection of such an encounter with the breakdown of his parents' tender and loving relationship, was his mother carrying on about the broken step on the back porch. How she always tripped on it when she took the wash out, how it was a distortion that prevented her from bringing her friends to the backyard, and, how much it would cost to have someone come in and fix it. This first experience had occurred sometime before, during his early childhood, but he recognized it as a significant point of reference for his inward journey. Why didn't his father fix that step?

In return, his father complained about his manager at work. He pined about the fact he was more experienced and could do the job better than his manager but had not been born into the right circumstance to be considered management material. He complained about the pay he received while others became rich from his efforts and about how successful he could be if he started his own business. The Philosopher wondered why his father never did start his own business. He wanted to tell his father that he would help him and they could do it together, but he never did. He also wondered why his father didn't fix the back step. He found it curious that they spent so much time complaining about their lot in life and almost no time trying to rid themselves of the things they complained about. The Philosopher began to pray every night that God would fix the back stair. It became a symbol of the melancholy that had invaded his parents' previously serene relationship.

At his young and inexperienced age, he did not realize there were many other underlying reasons for their discontentment. He focused completely on the step. The step became a significant symbol for him. It was a mirror of the affection between his parents and a standard by which he would know their true feelings for each other. He wanted to fix the step himself, but he knew that would be a disservice to their relationship—not to mention his tender age and complete lack of carpentry skills. Surely between his prayers and his mother's lamentations his father would fix the step! But it did not happen. Little did he realize his mother had also begun to see the step as a symbol of the rift that had developed in their marriage. She also prayed that her husband would fix it.

The Philosopher's nightly prayers to God centered on the step. However, after some time, as the importance of the step repair grew to be the center of their disintegrating household, his faith in God became battered. He began to blame God for this dilemma. It was only a step, after all. Why wouldn't his father fix it, and why couldn't God just go and do it? It was almost like God was a barrier surrounding any thought of fixing the step.

Eventually, the Philosopher stopped praying altogether and turned his thoughts to anger and resentment that God would allow this tiniest of issues to rage uncontrolled through the emotions of his life. He decided right then that this so-called God did not exist. *Let's see if I stop believing altogether, what happens to the step. Let's see if that might be what's needed.* And so he stopped believing in his parents' God. He stopped praying to him for relief from his problems and maintenance of the step. This would be his test of determination towards the value of valuing God.

A few days later, after half a night of fitful sleep, he awoke to the sounds of his parents giggling and whispering passionately together. He had heard their lovemaking before through the thin walls of their home, but not for a long time. He laid back and smiled, feeling safe as he had as a child, and let the buzz of the ongoing passion blanket him. He did not hear the words or the individual sounds, just the hum of love.

Suddenly, he bolted upright. What about the step? He slipped out of his bed and tiptoed across the kitchen towards the back door, cringing with every squeak and creak that his weight elicited from the old floor. His parents were far too occupied to hear anyway, but it made him feel sensitive about the moment by trying to be as quiet as possible.

He pinched open the back door just a crack and peeked down at the step. It was completely repaired! It sat like a throne between two old steps that were worn and weathered, hampered by a longer existence. The new step was of some different wood, hacked and hewn from some far off forest no doubt, dark and mysterious in its natural colour and littered with a soft continuous grain running across its width. The appearance reminded him of a tiger's stripes running dark against its amber skin. Of course, why else would his parents be back in a lustful and loving mood? Finally, his father had done something about the situation. It also hit him hard when he realized that this event had taken place immediately after he had denounced his faith in God. He would have to think about that. It was obvious to him that, one way or another, God had nothing to do with it.

The next morning at breakfast, it was as if the sun had grown larger and spilled its warmth onto his life. His mother fussed over his father throughout the meal and left those tender lingering touches on his neck and shoulder as she passed him during the scurry to serve everything hot and fresh at the same moment.

She looked at her son. "Did you notice the back step is fixed? Your father has made me very happy at last."

He realized she also thought of the step as symbolic of their commitment together, and by repairing it, his father had restated his desire to return their marriage to the original joyfulness it once boasted. The Philosopher looked with admiration at his father, thinking perhaps that he had struggled greatly in his decision to fix the step. Why else would it have taken him so long? His father looked back rather blankly, but the Philosopher just assumed that was his dismay at the sudden attention and accolades he was enjoying.

In reality, he was completely dumbfounded as to how it had become repaired. He knew his son had not done so as he was still but a child, prone to dirt castles and muddy backyard rivers, void of skills sufficient to complete a work of carpentry. He knew his wife had not influenced its repair by the way she was hovering and fussing over him. God must have intervened; that was his only plausible explanation. Truly an act of God! He inwardly praised Him and felt comfortably assured that his faith was properly directed and his commitment sufficiently constructed. He would definitely give a supplementary donation with the next passing of the church basket.

As the weeks and months went by, the Philosopher thought extensively about the timing of the step repair and marveled at the fact it was so significantly intimate with his decision to doubt his mother and father's God. This critical analysis was the first real step he took in formulating the thoughts and contemplations that would direct the course of his life until its end. He evaluated his reflections and postulations carefully, becoming increasingly convinced that God existed, but it was the responsibility of each individual to seek him out and build the roads and bridges necessary to engage him. While he had unconsciously planted the saplings destined to grow into his future discourse on the challenges involved with encountering his perceptions of the God image, it was when he had committed consciously to a questioning of the God residing in his parents' church that his will had somehow affected, no matter how limited the extent, the step repair, helping to bring a healing process into his parents' relationship.

The Broken Lover and the Broken Step

Joseph cut three benches originally in anticipation of creating a third seat for the cottage porch but then reconsidered his plan, feeling more than content with the two already in place. His efforts were capped with a thin coat of whitewash paint to the interior and exterior walls, not wanting to change the fundamental appearance of the building but happy to renew it. The final result was a home-away-from-home that Joseph could venture to as the spirit moved him. A place to contemplate, speculate and reflect on the direction of life's path, the development of spirituality, and the mapping of some unknown future. It became a warm sanctuary for him; an escape from all that he felt encompassed by and a private point on his compass.

Joseph was careful to remove the waste and debris from his work, leaving behind only that which would be needed in some future endeavour to maintain upkeep. His most arduous task was returning the third bench to his workshop, which was quite far away.

He departed very early one day, carrying the heavy bench and various other trimmings. As the morning sun grew higher in the sky, he stopped for a small breakfast beneath a mature tree next to a quaint little house, neither in the village nor outside it, just parked at a point where either description would not be challenged. It was an odd place for it to be. If the village grew, it would soon be incorporated, but if it shrank it would be left lonely forever.

He listened as a mother hustled her young child into the house for his breakfast and wondered for some time how wonderful it would be to have his own child to raise. Someone to teach the things he knew, to share in their growth and discovery, to comfort them in their pain and praise them in their accomplishment. What a highlight it would be. His complete lack of any female relationship brought this fantasy into question though, and his thoughts turned sour as the idea of meeting a young woman with whom to share some time found its way to the forefront of his mind.

He was lost in those musings for a while until he heard the mother open the back door once again and descend the steps into the yard. She stumbled on one of the stairs and cursed more than he expected before she overcame the situation and gathered in her overnight laundry from the clothesline. She was oblivious to him as he sat motionless beneath the tree just outside her yard. He was not hiding though, and he thought about calling out a "good morning" to her, but he remained silent, lost in the shadow of the large trunk.

He watched as she carefully ascended the few stairs leading up to the back door, taking a double step to avoid the third one, which appeared to be broken. Joseph wondered why the step had not been fixed, as it was obviously a dangerous spot, especially with a young child running up and down them countless times per day.

After shaking his head at the carelessness of the father for allowing this situation to persist, he realized that maybe there was no father. Maybe, as had happened to him, the father had died and left the young mother and child to fare on their own. Maybe they were both struggling to survive the emotional and financial burden that death always brought. Maybe she had to risk her safety and that of her child, because she could not afford to fix the stair.

As he built the scenario more dramatically and more clearly in his head, Joseph heard the young lady leave by the front of the house. He couldn't see her at first, but then she came into sight, strolling purposely down the road with her son in tow, walking as one does when late for an appointment but either unable or unwilling to move from a brisk walk into a run.

As she toddled out of sight, Joseph rose to continue his trek back to his workshop. He had spent much more time under the tree than expected, and he was definitely behind schedule. He hoisted the heavy bench and stepped down off the small bluff, walking right past the backyard fence of the little house. He could see the broken step clearly now and realized that it would be terribly easy for him to fix, being so skilled in carpentry and useful with his hands. As he held the heavy bench, it occurred to him that he should do just that—fashion the now obsolete bench into a new step and replace the broken one. Of course, he had no other choice. A poor mother grieving over a recently deceased husband, struggling to support her devastated and confused son, impoverished by the hardship of life! How could he not perform this act of kindness, not to mention the removal of his own burden of carrying the bench all the way home?

He spent the better part of the morning reshaping the wood, removing the old timber, and installing the new piece in its stead. He finished the job with a coat of clear varnish, touching up the other stairs as well so there was at least some sense of similarity between them. He knew at least two more coats of varnish should be applied, but he was content knowing the safety of the backyard had been restored. Satisfied and feeling quite invigorated by his good deed, he marched off toward the tree at full speed, walking briskly, almost skipping as he put time and distance between himself and the now safe house with such an ambiguous identity.

He had lost several hours, and he began to question his stop to repair the step but then quickly discarded any regret. It was the right thing to do, and he felt so good about doing it that he thought of it often afterwards. He was even more encouraged by the impact the accomplishment had on his self-worth, because he had done the deed anonymously. The old adage that "the joy is in the giving" was illuminated clearly for him.

Joseph realized he would not make it all the way to his usual transit lodging that night. He hustled to gather his travel pack and scurried around half aimlessly before finally bidding farewell to the massive tree that had afforded him some shaded rest, dropped a tear of grief onto the well-travelled ground for the poor, mateless mother and her son, blessed with a fatherless destiny, and sped off along the roadway feeling much lighter without the heavy step and much happier with the purpose it had fulfilled.

He walked along briskly for some time until it began to get dark. He was off in the countryside and following a rough path that shortened his trip considerably but left him far from any community. As he strode through the field, he began to wonder exactly where he was going to spend the night. He did have a small blanket, but he was not looking forward to curling up with a hay bale for company and perhaps a rodent or two.

As if his thoughts were being read by some ethereal busybody, he came around a small hill in the field and saw the glow of a low burning campfire with the clear silhouette of a solitary figure leaning beside it, drawing warmth and comfort from the adolescent flames. He approached carefully from the front and made enough noise to draw the attention of the camper. He didn't want to startle the man. First impressions are important, and although it was not so cold that the fire was needed, the waft of fresh coffee was a powerful lure.

The man stood as Joseph approached, and Joseph was careful once again to walk slowly as he spoke, saying his hello in a soft and friendly tone. The young man relaxed visibly after hearing him and offered a hello back, although the tilt of his head and the glint of his eyes revealed a posture of cautious pensiveness.

They stood in an awkward silence for a few moments before the stranger beckoned Joseph to sit and share a cup of coffee. Even though Joseph had no cup, he accepted the offer to sit with more thanks than was required. He reached out to shake hands, offering his name and explaining in one breath that he was travelling and had been delayed unexpectedly, leaving him between where he was and where he was heading. The young stranger understood, expressing that he was also between places, but more between where he was and where he wanted to be. He also offered his name: Tection. It was an unusual name, Joseph thought, not biblical and not local. Perhaps he was from a distant land, though he spoke with the same accent and pronunciations that Joseph did. Well, it wasn't something to worry about tonight. He seemed friendly enough, and Joseph was thankful for the opportunity to have a fire, a companion, a quiet field in which to rest, and a coffee now cooling in Tection's tin bowl.

The two men were of similar age, more than boys for sure but not yet the full bodies they would become. Joseph was larger and a little more mature, but Tection had a palpable difference in his body language and in the way he spoke. He had the same inflections and used the same words, but he had a different way of putting them together, like he was seeing the same painting but from a different angle. They spoke superficially at first, each using many words to say very little about whom they were. They were socially conscious of each other and wanting to be sure there was no offense offered or liberty taken. It took some time for the barriers to soften, but a couple of cups of coffee and some bread with fresh tomatoes proved to be a formidable icebreaker, and soon they found themselves chatting aimlessly but obviously growing comfortably familiar with each other.

Unfortunately, as often happens, the weight of the day's travel squeezed the energy from them, and sleep became the sole topic of discussion. Tection stoked the fire a little, ensuring it enough life to at least get them to sleep, and they settled in for a restful night.

Tection woke first in the morning and, too lazy to seek fresh water, rekindled the fire to reheat the previous night's drink. The unmistakable smell of old coffee roused Joseph. Following their "good mornings," they spoke more about where the path was taking them. Joseph had a defined destination and laid that out, while Tection was quite ambivalent, expressing only that he was heading dangerously close to somewhere he'd already been. This caught Joseph a little off guard, but he didn't feel the time was right to pursue the matter further.

They decided to travel together, at least for the short term, as sharing company and strides provided them both with a less arduous trek. Joseph recounted a short compendium reflecting in broad strokes what had been his life so far, dwelling on the sad circumstances of his father's death and the cycle of bewilderment and reflection that followed. He was in a healing period, and his indecision about the future was revealed, though with little detail and no mention at all of his lack of any amorous adventures. His past was indeed littered with sadness and most deserving of Tection's sympathy, which was offered honestly and without sign of indifference.

They dwelled on Joseph's situation for some time, and it was only as the day was nearing its end that Joseph realized he had been very much the center of discussion and had neglected an invitation for Tection to share his own musings. Joseph flushed with a noticeable embarrassment, feeling certain he had tarnished the harmony of their newfound friendship and indelibly etched an "X" or at least a "?" beside his name in Tection's mind. He decided it would be best to mention such thoughts openly, accompanied by an apology, in hopes of salvaging his character.

Tection laughed, a small laugh of irony. He replied with equal honesty that he appreciated Joseph's carriage of the conversation, as he had shied from telling his own tale, for it was one of broken lives and fraught with recollections of trepidation, turmoil, tyranny, and terror. That hung in the air for a while, Tection wary of opening the door into his recent past and Joseph completely unsure as to his role in the discussion. Had Tection's comments been a stern request to avoid delving into his past, or was it a plea for him to draw out the history through quiz and response?

They walked along quietly for a time, and when they broke into conversation again, it was concerning the best place to stop for the evening and whether they would be travelling together again on the morrow. Joseph, thoroughly enjoying the shared travel, answered both points quickly. He had been along this route before and knew of a pleasant inn just a short way ahead that he had stayed in previously. He had planned to stay there the night before, but his short travel day had swallowed that idea.

The inn was run by a kindly, somewhat elderly lady who hovered endlessly over her guests and ensured their contentment with the stay. She was motherly in all respects and possessed a healthy experience around the stove as well. Joseph decided to, and then decided not to, mention the young chambermaid who also lived there. She was somewhat distant and aloof, but her pulchritude was undeniable. As for travelling together, he decided to risk the moment and told Tection he was still keen to discover more details about the stories of his past that seemed so arcane.

Tection was caught a little off guard and hesitated momentarily before realizing he not only wished to tell his sad tale but was even anxious to do so. It would be a great relief. Just thinking about doing so brought him a fresh calmness, a usually elusive feeling. Still, Tection faced another problem, for he had limited funds and was unable to risk a future shortcoming by paying for a night's stay at the inn. He tried to hide the fact by indicating he preferred to stay out under the canopy of moon and stars, but Joseph assessed the situation quickly. Without embarrassing Tection, he manipulated his request in such a way that refusal was futile. After all, Joseph was going to pay for a room anyway, and having a second person share it would bring Joseph some comfort and camaraderie he surely missed when travelling alone. Tection wasn't sure if Joseph had pleasantly swindled him, but he accepted the invitation, and the matter was settled.

That evening, after a sumptuous meal served by the gorgeous young chambermaid, the two men reclined on the inn veranda and sipped their digestives. Soon, Tection began his account of his earlier life, letting the episodes flow out in scattered groups. Joseph fell into the flow of words, agonizing at times and sympathizing at others. He wanted to reach out and hold Tection as he knew this was a most difficult divulgement, but it would have been intrusive, even if it was comforting. Tection was reliving much of his past and Joseph was not part of it. He was the bystander now, the audience and very much the vessel that would receive and relieve some of the pain Tection was carrying around in his seemingly meager back pack!

Joseph was aghast at the tales and waited until Tection was seemingly done, signaled by a series of deep breaths and a slow recline back into his chair. He wrestled for a while with his search for a comment that might ease Tection, even slightly, but he found none. He had to say something; he had to recognize that this man had just told him tales he had told no others and that he was spent from the discourse.

Joseph stood up and walked behind Tection, slid his hands over the base of his neck, and gave a few stern strokes with his thumbs, providing a point of physical contact that indicated his understanding that this had been a somewhat harrowing revelation. He followed up with a soft pat on his shoulder.

"Let's get some sleep. We have far to travel tomorrow".

The Sign, the Shadow, and the Shape

Tection was elated, or perhaps even euphoric, when he strode from the orphanage for what he thought was the last time. He was dangerously close to oblivious of the world around him at first, walking calmly in body but racing willfully in mind, cherishing each step as a blow to the barrier that kept his soul bound to the institution he was leaving behind. He did not want the last impression he left to be that of an impetuous youth, uncertain and frenzied, loosened on the unsuspecting land of the free born. He was a bird just given wings. His feet did not touch the ground; they slid in a hovered zone just out of reach of the ties of solid earth. Freedom could not have been more unexpected. He was incapable of understanding the impact of being loosed from all that was the orphanage, the hardship and obedience, the servitude and oppression, even the friendships and commitments. His impossible promises to fellow orphans for relief, future attention, and some kind of deliverance were lost right now in the rush of conceptualization. Free. He cared not that he had but a few belongings and so little personal fortune. In his mind, he could have walked down that road for an eternity without being burdened by the time it would take.

Once far from the peering eyes of those left behind, and after hours that seemed like days of trudging along the roadside walkway, Tection departed from the main road and chose to test his stride among the fields of tall grass, sprouting crops, and indifferent livestock. He had never stood on unkempt earth. It was a simple but glorious pleasure for him. A fellow traveler would have thought him unstable for preferring such a difficult path over the unbroken hum and ease of a flattened roadway, but they would have had a perspective too narrow to appreciate his decision. If their understanding was that the purpose of the trip was to get from start to end, they would miss entirely the experience Tection was enjoying by taking the more difficult but also more rewarding path, embracing the journey long before any thoughts of the destination were considered.

Along the way, he encountered a grassy field with several cows gathered together in a single crowded corner, happy with each other's company even though the entire field lay at their command. He approached them and was curious at their aloofness, granting him nothing more than a minor turn of their heads. He had never felt the rough hide of a live cow, tight hair like bristles from a scrub brush and breath pounding in and out of its being like a bellows to fuel life onward. He rested both hands against the beast and allowed his ear to drop onto its dusty flank to experience the sound and ripple of the creature's heartbeat. It was like an entire world within the entire world. The cow was indifferent at first, happy with this spot in the field where fresh greens grew and the sun shone down from behind, until it felt enough time had passed and its tail went to work swatting away at the nuisance of black flies and curious ex-orphans.

Tection had never plucked a fruit and eaten it right on the spot, neither washed nor trimmed, just gulped down in the natural way it was offered. The strawberries and pears, each with their own minor struggle before snapping from their perch and fulfilling their secondary purpose of giving in to the hunger of a footloose wanderer, stayed his lunchtime craving admirably.

He felt the grain stalks with his hands as he strode by, surprised at their rough texture and humbled by their height, strength, and resilience. He had not imagined that when viewing them from afar, from whence they looked like soft noodles swaying like puppets in the breeze.

At one point in the mid-afternoon, he heard a distant voice berating him for trampling through these fields of cash crops, and for a flashing moment he thought it was one of the brothers who, having followed him from the orphanage, had caught him misbehaving and was preparing to return him to his past. He realized immediately that that was not the reality, but it was too late. His legs were already churning, and the dust of summer earth sprang from his heels as he put significant distance between the voice and his ears.

He didn't stop running for a long time even though his fears had subsided and his breathing was ragged. The joy of the boundless space, unbridled except for that which grew from the ground, open to his forward push and without judgement of anything at all, was something he had never experienced. He wanted to run in four different directions simultaneously, and he tried, changing course many times, which he recognized only because the sun was alternatively on his left, his right, and then possibly in front of him.

His speed began to diminish as his body took control once again, and he was about to come to a complete stop when his foot caught the edge of a downed fence wire, and he flew forward like a bag of potatoes thrown onto the kitchen cutting table. He landed hard on his back, flipped over as it were, but unhurt.

He looked skyward at the blueness, clouds speckled indiscriminately on the canvas that was framed by the stalks that surrounded him, and he laughed. It was a long laugh without clear foundation or expectations of distance. His laugh subsided at times before roaring back to life, impervious to reason and direction, unconcerned with the ongoing life around him, and completely exhausting his capacities. Finally, it slid to a silence on the bump of several giggles and wistful whines, leaving Tection tired and dusty but desperately happy. He lay there for some time before reality tugged him from the joy of being alive once again and convinced him with dimming skies that it would be appropriate to find a suitable place to spend the night.

It was dusk, but he was sure there was at least another hour of light, and before long, he found a sheltered pit of a valley with tall stacks of hay on either side. It was protected and relatively well hidden, so he settled in and built a small fire. He had a little coffee remaining, and a nearby stream provided some fresh water for drinking, boiling, and washing. With the coffee brewing and a small inconspicuous fire snapping at the circle of gathered rocks, Tection reclined against a pile of hay he had heaped on the earthen slope.

He was fatigued and half dreaming when he heard the unmistakable crunch of footsteps approaching. He sat upright and peered out into the dying dusk. A sole figure appeared, and Tection stood as the man moved closer.

The stranger offered an overly kind hello and apologized for disturbing him in what seemed like a genuine and honest manner. If life in the orphanage had taught Tection anything, it was a flawless sixth sense from first impressions, and he was eased by the manner in which the stranger had approached him.

His journey to this point had been without human contact except for the odd passer-by or farmer yelling admonitions at him for disturbing the harmony of his field.

He welcomed the stranger, who identified himself as Joseph, a fellow traveler, and Tection served him some coffee in the old tin plate he carried. They chatted and ate tomatoes with bread before settling in for the night, Tection happy for the company and Joseph calm and curious about this young man and his unusual demeanour.

The next day brought an early rise, and the two men easily agreed to travel together, at least for the day. They shared anecdotes of their lives, punctuated by the endless patter of steps and displaced pebbles, tales that were packed with information and revelations unusual for such a newly formed friendship. It may have been that they considered theirs to be a fleeting time together, as their directions were not harmonious, and sharing such personal information was a quick avenue towards a more solid footing.

The conversation also sped up the clock, and the day went by with but a few breaths to slow it down, and soon they were chasing a place to rest for the night once again. Joseph knew of a small bed and breakfast that he had frequented previously, and although Tection had no extra currency to afford such luxury, he was inwardly gracious that Joseph had offered to share the room without embarrassing Tection or his pride. It was clear that a bond was building between them, and Tection had, without realizing it, been anxious to verbalize his haunted past. It was a cleansing he needed desperately and one that he knew Joseph would absorb without judgement, conditions, or artificial pity. It was equally important that Joseph had offered his own story first with a sharp honesty and openness that demonstrated both trust and trustworthiness.

After a delicious dinner, and while sampling the cool evening air and the smooth flow of after dinner drinks, after the whimsical walk by of a beautiful young chambermaid and an appropriate period of silence to whet the appetite of ears and brain, Tection felt the moment was right to share his tale.

He began his story of past life, the one he was fleeing now either to or from, with a seemingly distant recollection, almost as if he was telling someone else's tale. He was so focused and precise, languishing on the smallest details for a while and dropping off huge chunks of time in the next breath, that it was clearly a recounting from memory, a story too detailed to be fantasy and too sad to be false.

He told of a childhood ripped from him by a great fire. Watching his parents and sister burn before his eyes was an impossible horror thrown upon him at a most tender age. But that was the least of his terror. He could deal with the anguish of such an episode, finding a will and a way to carry on in the face of endless sorrow, but what followed was a different kind of sadness. He lost his family in one cold night of flames, but he had his spirit, though so badly scarred with memory it would be an endless battle to heal, and that could sustain him. In fact, it was probably the scar and the steel that encased his soul after the incident with his family that saved him from the horror to come.

At the orphanage, he was herded into what was a different hell, no flames there but an endless pit of abuse, physical, mental, and spiritual—hands on his body, hands on his heart, and hands on his soul. He recounted as much as he could to Joseph, as much as possible while still keeping the tears from flowing and avoiding the deepest recesses of memory that would bring him back to inescapable anguish. His days and months and years at the orphanage, dragging him endlessly through the mud of guilt and condemnation, though his recollections were sprinkled lightly with memories of other young characters, brothers in hell as it were, of their tiny lights and his stoic fondness for them.

Tection finished his narrative without specific accounts of his encounters with Winter, which were still not available for his conscious disposition. Those dark episodes remained entrenched in his internal quagmire. He leaned back, eyes closed, slightly lost in the past, signaling the end of his recollections for the night.

He was a little startled when he felt Joseph apply a short but firm massage to his neck, which was obviously tense from the reliving of a crooked childhood, but swung back into the present under his grip and recognized it as a perfectly appropriate response. Joseph followed up with a soft pat on Tection's shoulder and said, "Let's get some sleep, we have far to travel tomorrow."

They travelled together for a couple more days while their direction was generally aligned. They meandered for perhaps a couple of miles left or right but headed towards the future in a close enough harmony. As they walked, Tection explained to Joseph about the seminary being his preordained destination. Through his recantations of his past life, it was clear that such a path was his destiny, whether fate or fortune or faith had delivered it. Joseph did not try to persuade him otherwise, nor did he encourage him to follow the path chosen by the brothers. As a matter of fact, his longstanding internal battle about his life direction aside from carpentry left him intrigued about the possibility of becoming a professional Christian.

When they parted company, with much babble about reuniting soon and reverberations and accolades towards their friendship, it was with the promised intention to meet at the seminary in about a month's time. Tection would introduce Joseph, and as long as he had his school papers and recommendations from previous professors, he would surely be welcome to attend the school. Although Tection could not provide any information on the cost of such an endeavour—he was under the scholarship of an orphan—he assured Joseph there was always enough room in God's heart for another student!

The Lost Sermon

Not far from the dusty streets and lazy shift of life in the town below the hills that climbed their way to the cottage and her magic, was a small but sturdy and distinct skeleton of a church. It was clearly a church, because several crosses were embedded in its walls and windows. A crooked cross hung solemnly on the back wall of the nave. Another cross hung high above, stretching from the bell-less bell tower and pointing directly to God—or directly at God. Perhaps when the church was active and full of believers and bystanders the cross was pointing *to* God, but now that the building was seemingly abandoned and void of clever morality, it was more likely pointing *at* God, with a sad complaint about the lack of attention it had received recently. After all, it was a long journey from being the focal point of a village to being an eyesore swaddled in undergrowth with no apparent future, a sullen and sedimentary present, and nothing valuable other than the excitement of a distant past.

Some people from town still visited the church to offer prayers or seek forgiveness, to remember loved ones and find comfort in the once sanctified space, but their attendance was dwindling. Since the old priest had died, there had been no one to gather them and keep them assembled. They had allowed their visits to dwindle, and for most the long walk to the unkempt edifice was an unnecessary trek to make on Sunday mornings. Without a priest, they could offer their prayers and make amends at home within the comfort of their kitchens and bedrooms. There were grandparents to pass on the teachings and stories of doom and destruction to children to keep them both fascinated and a little apprehensive, two good tools to manipulate thoughts and quadrate behavior. For important ceremonies like weddings, funerals, new births, and special holidays, the townsfolk would travel en mass to the closest active church, which was about thirty miles away. The priest there was always very nice and receptive, and many friendships were sprouted with the neighbouring community, but they were hard to nurture over such a distance of space and time.

It was here, in this non-functional, weary, and worn building that John P and Julian took refuge. John P thought the little church to be beautiful and was in awe of the cathedral-inspired structure that climbed gracefully towards the heavens with just enough echo and stone to give it reverence and a suitably somber personality. The pews and furnishings were a little worn and in slight disrepair, the beauty of the stained glass windows hidden by dust and dirt, the pulpit slightly crooked, and the back rooms cobwebbed and cluttered, but it was a beautiful church indeed.

John P was unaware of the truth, that a newer, bigger, brighter church was being built close to the center of town, and that a fresh young priest would probably journey from afar to minister to the area. The young priest would no doubt bring many important books with leather bindings and gold inlays from an important source and surely hold the Word of God. But until the priest and God arrived, and unless God objected, John P decided he would stay at the old church.

Julian did not view the structure with nearly as much reverence, but it was dry, and with the fireplace humming and crackling up the bones of dead trees, it was even cozy. They didn't ask permission from anyone, as there was no one accountable. The former priest had been God's solitary representative in the village, and his departure had left the townsfolk unsure of their responsibilities to the building.

Concerned and committed members of the congregation had made the effort to inform the church leaders in the big city about the unfortunate passing of their old priest, and a delegation, more like an entourage, of appropriate size had been dispatched to oversee a proper burial and evaluate the town's needs. The success of local farmers and the appeal of a quieter life for labourers from the city had helped swell the town over the past decade or so. Despite the elderly population, it was clear that the town would continue to grow. The proximity to the sea, the encroachment of the urban centers, and a potential key point in future commerce routes ensured it. The people of the town didn't really follow the delegation's train of thought, but that didn't matter, since the entourage didn't ask for or offer opinions anyway.

An old vegetable market had stood near the center of town once, where ladies would come to shop and chat every day after the farmers delivered their products early in the morning. As the town grew, the farms flourished by supplying the encroaching urban centers with fresh produce that the concrete and commotion of the city could no longer provide for itself. To support this new commerce, an expansive new market was built on the edge of town. This market was at the intersection of the main road leading to the city and was more accessible to the farmers, who had heavy loads to carry every morning. They hired workers to help them, and the workers brought their families and relatives to join them. The town grew, but the spirit and community of the old market in the town center was lost and sorely missed by most of the aging matrons. That had been their contact place with their friends and neighbours. They understood the need for a newer and bigger market. They knew why the change had occurred and could not argue with the process, but they missed their time together just the same.

As a replacement to the lost gathering place at the market, they found some semblance of camaraderie through the church. When the central market closed, the old priest was surprised at how many people attended the Sunday service and the amount of time they spent lingering after his sermons. It made him feel proud and fulfilled that his presence was so keenly appreciated. He felt no need to ponder why the Sunday flow had grown so quickly. He was not concerned if it was the market closing that brought the people to him; it was reward enough that they came.

He prepared coffee and cakes to be served in the nave after the service, and he floated among the ladies and children as they gossiped and confabulated. He knew the social value of these Sunday mornings was a key component of the experience. After all, rejoicing in a celebration of the Supreme Being and swallowing the teachings and parables of their Savior was not sufficient fuel to drive the crowds to him each week. Good coffee was essential as well. Most of the men were less anxious to remain so long at church. They had worked all week, including on Saturday, and were eager to enjoy their Sunday respite, not to mention relief from the lingering hangovers Saturday night had gifted them. Still, it was a great joy for the old priest to see these fruits of his toil before he passed away, and it was with considerable sorrow that the ladies of the village lost their gathering place once again when he died. With no one preaching, the church became vacant and quickly lost presence and form.

As the church and the community of ladies fell into disrepair, life in the town grew a little more somber as well. Work was a little harder, washing a little more tedious, lovemaking less frequent, and baking almost nonexistent.

The special church entourage from the city decided that a new church should be built; one that would serve the growing needs of the town and ensure the Word was spread and that new young families were introduced properly to their responsibilities to the Church and to its God. They met with the town leaders and agreed that the site of the old vegetable market would be deeded to the keepers of the big church in exchange for having a new local church built by them, at their own expense.

In general, the town was excited by the idea, and the initial buzz was everywhere. It was only after they realized it would take at least two years to complete construction that a few disparaging remarks were heard. The old church had already been empty for more than three years as the process of burial, replacement, planning, consultation, dialogue, discussion, deliberation, and decision making had been undertaken. Another two years to build the church would mean five years in total. It was a long time to be without spiritual leadership, but the Church comforted the people by confirming that one of their brightest young seminary students would complete his training shortly and be groomed specially to take over the position of pastor to this important and growing town.

Oblivious to this process, John P and Julian brought the old church into a more appropriate state. They cleaned out the back bedroom for sleeping quarters, straightened the pulpit, and coarsely mended a few pews. They swept and washed, scrubbed and scrapped, and brought the warm, welcoming atmosphere and coloured, stained glass sunlight hues back into the building.

The few people who still came on Sundays noticed the change, and conversations with the polite young men who had moved into their church became warmer and more sincere. John P explained his love for preaching, and his understanding of the written Word and its interpretations was evident to all. Any anger over their intrusion and trespassing on the church washed away easily. John P especially continued his daily work to restore the old building, and although he was a rather poor carpenter, the improvements were evident.

Julian was very much the support staff of the two. As the flock grew each week, he rested comfortably on the circumference of this new inner circle John P was building. He was happy his friend was engrossed and fulfilled by these new developments. But he was not as enthralled by the process as John P was, and he found himself heading to town frequently when time permitted. He enjoyed the odd knowing nod from someone who recognized him from the old church, and he wondered if they thought he was "doing God's work." He smiled inwardly under the weight of that possibility.

One Sunday morning, a rather large group of people arrived at the church. An elderly gentleman, who was greatly respected by many townspeople for his dedication to family, hard work, and his contribution to community projects, wanted to have a service to honor his dead mother. She had died thirty years earlier and was buried in the small graveyard that lounged a short distance from the back of the church. He felt death was closing in on him, too, and he welcomed the anniversary to pay these last living respects to her before he died. It was important to him, and he refused to migrate thirty miles to a distant church to have the service when she was lying right here in the town. Besides, the priest up there was performing the wedding of an important local celebrity with a prestigious party full of influential people afterwards, so he could not travel.

Several of the old man's family members had journeyed to be with him during this time of sorrowful reverence, and the group that showed up at the church was substantial. The daughter of the elderly gentleman brought him over to John P and introduced them.

"Father, this is the preacher, John P, whom you have heard about. He is young but very skilled in the ways of God. I hope he'll be able to share some appropriate words with us."

The elderly man extended his hand to a very surprised and suddenly apprehensive John P. He had no choice but to take it, and he felt the effort made by the man to produce the firmness of his grip. Before John P could protest the overzealous introduction, the man spoke.

"I can't tell you how grateful I am for your assistance today. It is so important that someone with your closeness to God says some words to capture the feeling I shared with my mother. All of us here loved her, and we want this to be a special day."

John P was more that shocked. Who had suggested that he could say words of comfort and condolence to such a large group and about someone he had never met? How could he capture any part of the essence that was this matron when she had died long before he was born? It was a serious request, and it took all his fortitude not to turn and run.

"Well, I hope you will be satisfied with my work. I, uh, I have, I mean, I know a little about some things, but I.... "

The gentleman's daughter could see that John P was fumbling, so she stepped in to ease the situation. "Come along, Father. Let's sit here in the first row so you'll be able to follow closely."

She led him to the pews, and he leaned back carefully before plopping the final few inches into place.

Soon, others took their seats, and a buzz of quiet conversation filled the room. Several people had prepared small readings, and the man's daughter was trying to organize an appropriate order for their delivery. It would be important that she select each person in order of his or her importance in relation to her father, not to the dead woman being honored, for she no longer cared.

After a little consultation and a bit of give and take, she finally got it right. She had each presenter sit in order of their turn and then slipped to the side as they began. Most were old friends who had anecdotes and reminiscences to share with the gathered or narratives on some period of time spent with the long-deceased matriarch.

During these recitations, the daughter moved closer to John P and apologized for putting him on the spot. She realized he had been caught off guard and could not explain why she was under the impression he had been informed about these proceedings. John P assured her he had not. She sympathized and asked if he could come up with something, anything. It was so important to her father that a spiritual person put a final stamp on the proceedings, even if it was only a short prayer or story, not even a real eulogy. John P had no choice but to agree. Although he was very uneasy about these expectations, he had to admit he was also excited at the prospect of preaching to such a large group. It had been his dream for so long.

He excused himself and went to his bedchamber, hoping some of the presenters would take longer so he would have more time to prepare. Julian was parked at the back of the room hoping to remain inconspicuous, but most curious and somewhat excited by this large gathering. He noticed when John P departed and he slid quietly into the back room to join him and ensure all was OK. John P was obviously agitated, or perhaps more accurately, flustered.

He explained the situation to Julian and asked him to retire and allow John P some time to reflect on what he might say. Accordingly, Julian slid quietly out of the back room, expressing confidence in John P's deliberations and commenting how this was his first memorial service aside from that delivered for John P's mother. John P returned to his considerations. How could he write something profound enough for the occasion without any knowledge of the people involved? Should he just make a statement about the importance of God and heaven? Would that be enough, or would the fellowship, being experienced, be disappointed in him? What would Joseph, his mentor, do? What did John P know about dead mothers and their relationships with sons?

Of course! The eulogy that Joseph had presented at his mother's funeral! He still had it word for word. As a matter of fact, he had memorized it word for word. After all, the old man had said his relationship with his mother was loving as well.

John P slid up to the pulpit, sweat on hands and furrow in brow, as was to be expected, and then he delivered the same eulogy, the one Joseph had delivered for his mother. He changed only the names and left out the dates, but he spoke with such passion, emotion, and commitment that the assembled group was stunned. People cried. The old man was so captured emotionally that he had to be held and given water. John P teared up as well. He had not reflected on his mother's passing so intensely for a long time, and his emotions swept over him.

The people gathered had no way of knowing this, and they just assumed he had become so involved with the whole process that he had been caught up in the spirituality and ethereal atmosphere that prevailed. For many, it became the most spiritual event of their lives. The accolades showered on John P were sincere and heartfelt, ranging from a simple "thank you" to a banter of "amazing" and "unbelievable." The people leaving the church that day were like messengers loosed upon the town. Word of John P's powerful preaching spread like fresh ripples from a stone thrown into a stagnant pool.

Most amazed of all was the daughter of the old gentleman, the granddaughter of the woman she had met but didn't really know. She had been a child when her grandmother passed, and no real adult relationship had ever developed. How had this young preacher captured her essence and spiritual importance so gracefully and completely? Not only was she moved by his words, she also expressed that it was the first time she had ever really felt a kinship with the woman whom she had visited only once a year with her father to lay fresh flowers at her graveside. More than that, she realized that John P had prepared those powerful words and images without sufficient notice and in only a short time. He really was amazing.

When the church lay empty again and the last head had bobbed across the road, leaving behind fragments of the praise and wonderment that would soon populate the town palaver, John P sat down gently into the last seat of the last pew. He looked up at the pulpit, still in shock and still unsure of what had just happened. It had all been experienced so quickly. In the span of a couple of hours, he had gone from trespassing church repairman to ecclesiastic pulpitarian. Naturally, he questioned his decision to use his mother's eulogy. He asked himself if it was appropriate; if it was ethical.

Julian slid onto the bench beside his friend and expressed his own wonderment at the amazing delivery John P had presented. He recognized these were the words from his mother's funeral but reflected that, though the words were the same, the use of the sermon to facilitate the desire of remembrance and honour for the visiting congregation also honoured John P's mother. He praised John P for having the generosity to share with others, that which Julian knew was most precious to him; to lend others the power of his mother's sermon to assist in their own consolation. What an unselfish act that actually was.

John P looked back at his friend. This young man who had but a while ago been an angry renegade struggling to break the bonds of an unhappy childhood. Yet this ragamuffin had once again amazed John P with his intuitive remarks. He had found the moment and the comment to bring clarity to John P's thoughts, and did so without plan or purpose other than to support him.

John P himself was buoyed by Julian's observations and could find no wrong in using the sermon to support others. It had delivered great comfort to him at the time of her funeral, and now it had returned to bring more comfort and relief to many others. In that way, he felt it was a great honour to his mother and to her memory. He had had no time or intention to explain where the eulogy came from; for that was too personal and would only diminish the warmth and intimacy it had afforded those who had gathered so affectionately. He had not been looking for credit for the words, he just felt their true source and real inspiration was too personal to share with a group of unknown mourners.

This serendipitous event sprouted the beginning of what would become John P's illustrious reputation. It fired his passion to preach as much as it impacted the local flock. Word of his verbal prowess spread, and though it was unintentional, it was inevitable that rumours exaggerated his qualifications and credited him with that which was not his to claim. No one had asked for any verification of his license to spread the Word, and he had not offered any. He was just a man doing what he enjoyed, finding validation in the attention of his listeners, chasing neither glory nor reputation.

Julian and the Café

The old church was home for Julian for only a short time. He parked his things there and managed to sleep and eat occasionally while he helped John P repair it sufficiently to set up a livable cooking and sleeping area. After that, he left John P to continue the reparations of the church and headed into town every morning to look for some short-term work that could help build up their limited coffer, get them a little thicker for the journey across the sea.

He knocked on the door of every business in town, but the people were a little wary of this young stranger. They weren't sure if he was old enough to work or if he could be trusted with any kind of responsibility. He managed to get the odd physical labour job cleaning walkways and yards of debris and waste, or stacking old items into controllable piles. It paid poorly and was as much a charitable opportunity as it was needful employment.

After those hard days lugging old timber and building material from one dump to another, Julian enjoyed a short stop at the café for a cold glass of water and a small coffee. The café owner was a kindly old gentleman, but business was way down, and the empty chairs on the terrace captured more dust than bottoms.

On days when Julian could not find any local labour, he would stop at the café even earlier in the day, not wanting to make the few kilometers walk back to the church, just to sit there and wait for tomorrow. On those days, there were almost no customers, and Julian spent some time talking with the café owner.

He was a gentleman who had been softened by time and seen his middle grow in proportion to his patience. Nothing really bothered him, but he was rather plump! He was equally casual about his business, lamenting a bit about how the closing of the central market had put a heavy damper on his daily flow of customers, but he was too casual to be concerned. Life had carried him along for many years, and he was happy to have so few regrets and so many memories.

He had built the café in his younger days with his father's help. The town was much busier then, even though it was also much smaller. Everybody gathered in the center of town, heading to the market after church and the café after the market. All those conversations that remained unfinished by the time the ladies had to bring their warming groceries home at the end of a Sunday afternoon were planned for completion at the café during one of the evenings of the following week. Many of the men also slid over to the café after sundown to finish their stories and enjoy a few drinks and a little escape from home. As they walked out the door, their wives would usually bid them off with sarcastic comments about never seeing them, but they were also happy for a little down time by themselves or perhaps an opportunity to renew some banter with a neighbour.

The café owner had grown up in that environment, knowing almost everything about everyone that anyone knew or made up. Both truth and fiction were good for conversation, and conversation was good for business. He went to bed late and woke late. His cycle of life was just a little out of the ordinary, and although he heard and saw more than he probably should have, he never really became part of the town's fabric. His was not the life of a hardworking farmer or tradesman. He was more the paid servant who provided a comfortable spot for relaxation and repose. He didn't mind though. It never occurred to him that he was viewed in such a different light from others. He never questioned why he was invited so seldom to weddings and funerals. Anyway, he had to remain behind to prepare for the crowd that would flow his way afterwards—wine for weddings and whiskey for wakes.

He did not have a wife or a child or a dog or any other pet, although a funny orange cat started to hang around at about the same time as Julian showed up. The café owner wasn't sure why it started to visit or where it came from. It just appeared one day, and he assumed this was its rightful place in the world.

The café owner had seen the business grow and drop over several years, and his life sort of followed along. When the café was busy and lively with both locals and tourists, he had managed to share many nights with various ladies who passed through. He even rented out his upstairs room a few times when the hotel was too full. With his reasonably good looks, his status as owner of the café, and the ladies loosened slightly by his liquor, the opportunity for adventure came by fairly often. Tourists were always more casual and liberal when they were away from home, as if living out their fantasies one week at a time with no baggage or aftermath to deal with. He had spent some time with local girls as well when he and they were young. They went on to become wives and mothers with other men though. They always avoided eye contact with him, but they knew they could trust him. He would never say anything of their pre-marital affairs. That would cost him the ladies, their husbands, and their friends as customers. His lips were sealed for business reasons at least. It was the affairs with married ladies that gave him his few regrets. It wasn't that he couldn't control himself, but he did miss companionship from time to time, and if he was safe for them, they were equally safe for him. He did not regret that he never married and that he had no children. His lifestyle and demeanour were suited for a bachelor, and even though he had periods where he craved some companionship, they usually passed fairly quickly.

It didn't take long for the café owner and Julian to become casual friends. They found something in each other they were missing in their lives. It wasn't really a father and son relationship; more realistically, each provided the other with some insight and understanding of the generation that separated them. This understanding was fresh and revealing for both of them. It was the kind of thing a father and son might afford one another, but it was not the full weight of a child and parent relationship. Julian was far too old to be learning new roots and the café owner too old to teach any.

With the eventual growth of their affinity for one another, Julian began to spend more time at the café, and he just naturally began helping out. He didn't do so in expectation of payment. It was the same kind of assistance he would provide any friend in need. The old man was finding it increasingly difficult to carry the tables, sweep the floors, and handle the cases of drinks and condiments, so he appreciated the young man's help and was aware it would be reasonable to pay him a small amount. If he paid him it would not only reward Julian for his kindly offered assistance, it would also allow the man to make certain demands and enjoy certain expectations. He began to give Julian small amounts whenever he had a good day at the cash or whenever he had a particularly difficult day for moving and storing items, such as the second Wednesday of every month when the deliveries came, or Friday and Saturday mornings. Those were the weekend preparation mornings. Friday meant dusting and washing the chairs and tables, resetting them with the candles and ashtrays, and waiting for the evening crowd. A few tablecloths and a little music brought the tired workers and restless wives out to celebrate the end of another week.

Julian began to realize the old man's ruminations about his lifecycle being contrary to the townspeople was surprisingly accurate. The tablecloths came off on Saturday afternoon when the café became a refuge for the idle, mostly the older folk who no longer worked or held households and the younger who were perhaps too old for school but not yet committed to the fields and to a family. It also harboured those who couldn't, or wouldn't, work, those on vacation, those taking a day off, the gamers, and lately, everyone's favourite, the young Philosopher. He had been published in the local newspaper recently, and his concepts and speculations on a few specific ideas had flourished into a reputation for espousing wisdom on every possible topic. With his stimulation of conversation and penchant for dramatic responses, he was always a welcome addition on Friday or Saturday nights.

From noon until dusk, patrons played chess, backgammon, cards, or dominos. They conquered and then saved the world, and they talked in rhythm, exposing their weaknesses as they boasted of their exploits and convictions. The Philosopher was a bit of an exception. He seemed to have a little better grasp of the world's working parts and seldom missed an opportunity to illustrate the conversation, haranguing the gathering until there was little else to do but return to the chessboard.

As the afternooners melted back into the town, Julian and the café owner took advantage of the lull to re-cloth the tables and reset the bar, ready for the lazier and less passionate Saturday evening crowd. It was also an interesting if not predictable group, a light flow of pre-dinner drinkers exchanging "hello's" and "how-are-you's" to the other passersby.

Then, a little later in the evening, the post-dinner crowd. Many of them were the same as earlier, but the warmth of a good meal at the hotel restaurant, some ripe wine, and common conversation had brought them together again, and small groups formed around different tables to reflect on the past week and the next generation.

Finally, after most of them left, only the drinkers and gamblers remained. These were people whose lives were in a particular state that they felt satisfied with drinking, betting, and generally outlaying their hard earned wages for a boisterous and festive evening. Together, the departing couples whispered about them and their nonsense, but privately, most of the men welcomed those Saturdays when their families were off to see the relatives or otherwise occupied so they, too, could join the Saturday night riffraff.

Julian and the café owner served and humoured them late into the night and made sure every one of them left in a safe and secure condition, either with a clearer-headed friend guiding them or a new sobriety poured into them through several cups of old coffee. Occasionally, one of them would be too far gone to make it home, so Julian would help him into the back room, where a small but comfortable cot was waiting.

Once the café was quiet, the two men cleaned the messiest part and then tried to get a few hours' sleep before rising Sunday morning to polish and prepare for the after-church crowd. Julian would ensure the setup was done before he half ran to the church to hear John P preach.

The after church group were more civil and sensible than the Saturday night bunch, and Julian often pondered the fact that both the wildest and the most governed of guests were patrons with but a few hours between them. Was it so with the world, that opposites were both part of a circle, really right next to each other and could be encountered immediately, or only after a longer journey in the alternate direction, depending on which route one took from one to get to the other? And was it so with all things? With good and evil—or was it good and bad?—with truth and lies, happiness and sadness, or was that one happiness and unhappiness? He came to the conclusion that God must have planned it so that his moment would come immediately after the people had reached their lowest point so that he could excuse their indiscretions immediately after they had been perpetrated.

Then he came to a new dilemma. Did God create Sunday as his time with man, and men, therefore, made Saturday night their time? Or did men make Saturday night their time because of the completed working week and God, therefore, made Sunday his time so He could get them back on track again for Monday morning? Were men following God or was he following them? Julian decided he would have to ask either John P or the Philosopher to clarify this important point.

And so the weeks went by, the routine so predictable that any variation or deviation was a welcome event. Sometimes a bit of a brawl broke out, and everyone had a great time breaking it up and spending an enormous amount of energy getting the combatants to make up. Usually, they ended up being best friends by later in the evening, buying each other drinks and professing their friendship and the insignificance of their dust up. Julian decided this, too, was of the same fabric of thought; from the point of physically harming each other to the point of hugging and sharing, all within a few minutes. He realized that drink had fueled the event, but he also knew there were truths in their actions. Opposites were at such close quarters once again.

He and the café owner were outside the cycle of life the town followed. They were more like guardians or performers than participants. They worked while others played, slept while others worked, and their own pleasure came from doing nothing. They did nothing together quite a bit, and except for the occasional extended visits Julian made to see John P, they spent most of their waking hours together. Julian used the back room cot on an increasingly regular basis, avoiding the long march home in the dark. He learned the various responsibilities involved with running the café, including the small snack menu and drink mixes that kept up with the variety of the clientele. He didn't remember exactly when he became a bona fide employee, but it was sometime between when he asked to work there and when the owner agreed to it.

The owner was very happy with Julian, and he felt blessed that this young man had happened into his life. His trust was well earned, his work ethic boundless, and his attention to detail beyond his years. He even knew a decent amount about the sausages and snacks that were offered for consumption. He wondered how Julian had learned these traits and understandings of food preparation, especially sausage and snacks, but he never received clues through their discussions. The boy never spoke of his past, other than his close friendship with the young preacher out at the old church. It was a curious situation indeed. The people of the town got to know Julian as well, bit by bit, through encounters at the café, the familiarity of his face strolling through the streets, and his frequent presence at the old church for Sunday services. As the seasons rolled by, the café owner and Julian became closer, still without the intimacy of a father and son relationship but more developed than that of mere friends or acquaintances.

It was a day of great honour for Julian when the owner gave him his own set of keys. He had made them during his last trip to the big city, finally finding a shop that could reproduce such an old model. They had a rather playful and somber official key-giving ceremony, broken up by frequent jabs of humor and bites of sarcasm delivered by the Saturday night crowd that remained late enough to witness it. The owner scuffed Julian's hair after handing him the keys, and patrons gave him small pokes of approval. It was all in good fun, but for Julian it was a most significant moment. He had never been trusted with anything in his life. His parents had never demonstrated any confidence or faith in him, and other than John P, no one had ever taken him seriously enough to even have such a thought fall onto the table. This was indeed a special night, and although he smiled sheepishly and turned a little red, the pride he felt was almost overwhelming. That night, after completing an impeccable clean up with nothing left over before the Sunday morning set up, he ran nearly all the way to the old church to see John P and tell him of great news.

The sun was just peeking over the graveyard fence when he arrived, and John P was awake at the table sipping coffee and reading one of his books through the dancing light of a solitary candle. He was startled to see Julian so early, having become well versed with the late night Saturday crowd and Julian's need to sleep over to be ready for the Sunday preparations.

Julian's exuberance was visible immediately, and John P sat there with a huge grin as Julian recounted the happenings of the night before. He held up the keys like a collegian would his diploma, proud of a significant accomplishment and hopelessly happy. As much as the café patrons had not grasped the significance of the moment, so did John P realize it for the important step it was in the transition of Julian from the scared and determined rebel with a bitter, abusive childhood to a young man of integrity and promise, finally enjoying the great reward that this feeling of self-worth was delivering.

After catching his breath, which he had lost just listening to Julian, John P stood and grabbed him, twirling and spinning him in a dance as they hooted echoes off the stone walls of the church and shouted cheers at the tired moonlight above.

Soon afterwards, Julian was back on the road, moving briskly though the morning light, to be back in time for the Sunday setup. John P yelled after him, reminding him to get some sleep, but Julian ignored the words. Sleep could definitely wait until tomorrow.

Julian began opening and closing the café, and soon he was shouldering most of the workload. The old man was definitely slowing in both physical stature and mental capacity. It was a quick and distressing tumble from a jovial veteran of life to a mercenary on the road to purgatory. Fortunately for Julian, the café owner recognized that he was dwindling in capacity and undertook the necessary steps to ensure the café would, after his passing, become Julian's.

As might be anticipated from the last breath, last thought, last emotion of the dying soul, the old man had a brief moment of inspirational clarity and spoke with Julian about taking over, clearing the path for a continuation of his life's purpose, but also reminding Julian never to forego his dreams of sailing the seas of the future for the stability of a single island among its vastness; somehow imparting in a notion of last regret that he himself had made such a mistake many years earlier. It was the first time Julian had ever heard the old man reflect on what might have been. He always seemed endlessly content.

The sadness brought on by the old man's departure was a lasting one, and Julian lay in his bed at night wishing often for a good chuckle with his newly lost "old" friend. He reminisced about various conversations or situations and sometimes even caught himself giggling out loud at a particular recollection. The cat would lift its head with a confused perking of its ears and scan the room for some elusive understanding of why this young man was making such sounds.

John P was awed by the inheritance Julian received and, at times, seemed to be even happier for Julian than Julian was for himself. It wasn't long before Julian realized two important things: First, owning and operating the café was a significantly more complicated and time-consuming responsibility that he had imagined, bringing him sixteen-hour workdays and a completely different kind of stress than his rough youth had offered. Second, while the café offered great independence and financial reward, it also demanded more subordination and commitment than even friendships or future lovers.

The sea always lurked a few miles away, and calm mornings on the terrace allowed for faint echoes of the pounding waves. Their endless call and the last words of the old man lingered in the recesses of Julian's mind, and he went down below the cliffs to the edge of the sea often and looked across the water. He never felt the desire to climb the mountain for a possible view of the distant shores across the water. He couldn't see land on the other side and was not sure he wanted to. That would drive much of the mystery away from the dream. Still, he knew it was there, and each time he arrived at his favourite spot, he half expected to see something, as if the far shore was a growing entity that would expand somehow and become visible. He didn't realize that it was he who would grow and expand his own horizons through happiness and sorrow and finally realize the visibility of a distant shore.

Reflecting On Butterflies

The Philosopher's hunger for knowledge and excitement with texts depicting concepts and ideas from outside sources was not unknown to his parents. They recognized that he needed to be nurtured in this passion, and they realized they were not capable of doing so. He was the most important part of their lives, and seeing his intellectual strength grow with his physical maturity was a rewarding sight. So, at great expense and suffering to their own quality of life—a fact the Philosopher would realize only much later in life—his parents arranged for him to attend a preeminent university in the city. He had demonstrated an aptitude for conceptualization and comprehension that easily allowed him to exceed the expectation of regular school curriculum, and his teachers were both supportive and vociferous in their recommendations to the university that his application be accepted despite his young age. Although the university agreed to admit him, the movement to secure a scholarship fell on deaf ears, inflicting the need for such financial sacrifice on his parents.

He left home bursting with the excitement of adventure and with every expectation that embracing the outside world would bring him the peace of mind and spirit for which he lamented. He never imagined that this last financial burden would be the catalyst for the demise of his parents' relationship as well. Their destiny was sealed long before this commitment, and were it not for this burden, some other would have sufficed.

Meanwhile, the Philosopher excelled at school—new friends, new ideas, alcohol, sex and all the other trappings of university life, even a little enlightenment from time to time between the living of life! The four years flew by in a blur of harmony, philosophy, scholarship, and revelry. Most importantly, he gained the tools he needed to build his ideas into recognizable foundations and become literate in his own beliefs.

The bittersweet return home, complete with a collapsed parental relationship and a house much smaller than he remembered, was balanced by his newfound confidence and worldly demeanour.

His certainty of ideas was a little young, perhaps, but he wrote down his thoughts as they crystallized. Once there was some coherence to them as an essay, with much effort and cajoling, he convinced the editor of the local paper to print them, even though the publisher was hesitant to be too controversial in his content. The advertisers did not like anything that veered away from the happy and contented world that bought the paper. Still, on one Saturday morning, insignificant to most and lost to tired workers and busy shoppers, the Philosopher's first postulations were printed on page eight in the editorial section.

—

The greatest expectation of God's favour is harboured by those least confident or compatible in their own beliefs. They are attracted by the ease and convenience of a "greater power" and slide comfortably onto the constructed road to salvation. Meanwhile, those who have challenged and questioned their purpose and existence are left cold and shivering in their search for answers, seeking calmness for their agitated souls. Insecurity seeks affirmation, and an inability to adhere to the traditional religious images and dogma championed by the religious institutions leaves the seeker perplexed and somewhat anxious. Consequently, without a support system to calm the uncertain soul's temperament or guidance to lead the frustrated individual towards some form of understanding, the entire process of spiritual harmony reverses itself. This solemn individual faces nonconformity with these institutional traditions, whether willingly or spontaneously, and with no footing for an alternative appeasement to the insecurity being experienced, the confused and desperate soul is driven away from the social pack. Subsequently, the search for reasoning to discredit or encumber the traditional image is espoused freely and frequently, offering a self-justification for the discontentment with traditional imagery and rhetoric.

While unsuccessfully indoctrinated with the social and institutional perception, with the preparation and attention towards the greater being, the questioner lacks a reliable and, more importantly, embraceable image to soothe his soul, and indeed, even resents the institutional pressure brought to bear on his psyche. In retaliation, he smudges the image, contradicts the edicts, and questions the reality.

This contradiction is harmful for several reasons. Not only does it inhibit the development of an acceptable and understandable image in the consciousness of the individual, it nurtures a resentment and perhaps even anger towards those who are comfortable with either their own imagery or their underdeveloped faith and consequential capitulation to the institutional image. As there is a strong social requirement to embrace the institutional image, the resentment often manifests itself in the form of ridicule towards the believers themselves, towards the standards of the belief, or even as a physical reaction such as defacing institutional buildings and artifacts, drafting derogatory text and, in a frightening manner smacking of belief-phobia, going so far as to bring direct personal harm to the human targets of their anger.

The decision to pursue such action is not necessarily an anti-social one but one of self-preservation. The struggle to find a form of inner peace compatible with the individual's spiritual needs, no matter how rudimentary, runs head-on into the constant bombardment of external religious and quasi-religious dogma, fueled by those engaged in personal interaction with the poor, underdeveloped soul and the constantly stalking world that awaits it at each day's waking. The buzz and hum of work with its ever-demanding performance evaluation theme, the complication of relationships and their demands on time, integrity, and responsibility, the energy commitment to hunting for, holding, and harbouring a mate, rearing children, and generally forging ahead in our relentlessly active world hinder the inward journey towards clarity of the soul. It is not a shame, indeed it is a blessing, that institutional religions are established firmly with the few who have found some harmony and the strength to dedicate to it, being shepherds to the multitudes who have either never started their own journey or have, at some point, slipped from the path and floundered into the hands of a steadying faith.

And it should not be misunderstood, as this paddling towards the closest safe harbour (i.e., religion) is not a journey of faith but merely of the shortest path. It is not a process of education, information, and evaluation but one of tradition and cultural pressure. Once the individual is committed to the institutional faith, osmosis is inevitable, and the evolution of the soul, no matter how contrary to its instinctual or archetypical footprint, is re-directed. It can be argued that the institution only assists in the development of basic fundamentals of faith that we already manifest in the soul embryo, as genetically viable as life's inherent building blocks and as sure to develop in some form internally as arms and legs are externally through physical activity and minds are through education and experience. This argument might see institutional religions as the equivalent of schools for the soul. As the world of education branches off into specialized philosophies and fields of study, so the schools of faith cleave to their own radically diverse interpretations of the same truths.

Regardless of such reflection, the incomplete soul, perhaps unprepared to journey inward or not yet capable of the journey or, even more frustrating, not fearless enough to begin the journey, remains in dangerous limbo. He resents both the individuals who have found some satisfaction or comfort in their spiritual development, whether real or imagined, as if such a difference truly exists, and the institutions that embrace them, whether classical, tribal, or fundamental in nature. The searching soul goes through a sort of metamorphosis. Once gaining the conscious knowledge that such self-revealing journeys can be taken, with or without the help of external forces, a period of preparation follows before the first strides of the journey are broached, if they ever are. This purgatory can be fleeting or festering. It can both harm and heal depending on the importance and value it is assigned by the potential traveler.

Of course, the easily stated precept of "gaining conscious knowledge that such journeys can be taken" is itself a journey. It is not expected that all, or even most, will come to this conclusion. Indeed, both the blind attachment of the childish or underdeveloped spiritual consciousness to an institutional and socially validated faith and the opposite, yet similarly resulting, void of inspiration towards conscious reflection of the soul result in little progress being made on an individual basis. This does not forego the very real prospect of a handsome, vibrant, and active development of the unconscious spirituality.

Our demeanour, morality, and compassion may reflect a strongly developed unconscious spirituality that reveals itself spontaneously in our daily interactions but remains distant from our conscious understanding of what we seek and why we seek it. The battered ego remains defiant and lashes out at the calmness of quieted souls, not jealous or envious of them just insecure and incomplete, perhaps unnecessarily, feeling a sense of inadequacy. Consequently, the person embraced safely and warmly in the cocoon of institutional and traditional faiths may yet develop a decidedly hostile and unsympathetic unconscious spirituality, whether inherent to their nature or inspired by an unconscious resentment towards the very faith they embrace, as it not only hinders the concept of self-revelation, it blocks the pathways with dogma and indoctrination. The internal drive for self-value is frustrated with the roadblocks and fraught with self-doubt, which manifests due to a lack of perceived alternatives. In such a case, capitulation to the institution devalues the internal soul and dims the sparks that internal development should provide.

Unsurprisingly, the poor soul who has undertaken the beginnings of his journey and seeks guidance and validation from both external and internal resources faces the prospect of ridicule and rhetoric of doubt from those embracing traditional institutional faiths, with their certain, self-indulgent security in numbers, and with God on their side; and from those certain in their unbelief, not yet cognizant of their world beyond the two-dimensional concept of body and mind, either ignorant in their bliss of not knowing that their spiritual self is developing below their conscious surface, or content with the intellectual certainty of mental mathematics and its ability to hibernate the soul. This searching individual clings to the self-constructed dormitory of spiritual ideas, hoping for inspiration from one faith or the other or from one philosophy or the other, unsure of his ability to decipher the many mysteries hidden within his unconscious universe.

Finding pathways through the maze of spiritual unconsciousness, without compass or means of passage from supporting external resources, is ominous and usually an insurmountable task. Yet, like the mapmakers of old, who defied the accepted truths of shorelines, lost rivers, and flat planets to forge ahead and diagram the reality they had witnessed directly, the searching soul must use the tools available and find the courage to sail its own course, and map its own conscious understanding, which it derives from the unconscious sea of spirituality it harbours, having been fed by genetic archetypes, parental influences, self-indulgences, dreams, and lively debate.

As this road develops, and the revelation plot thickens, it may well be that some mainstream faiths reveal themselves as the "most congruent" with the soul's onward journey and be embraced as the weary traveler tires. After all, millions of journeys have been taken before his, and even if the mainstream faith in question does generalize, compartmentalize, and bastardize the sharp images of such individual revelation already embraced, it does offer a soft and leisurely continuity to the path already initiated. It eases the journey, which may have taken a rather trying toll on the searcher, bleeding his energy even further than the demands of life have done already. Having found the enlightenment to realize there was an inner journey to take and having put significant energy into initiating it, the continuous effort required to maintain it may be overwhelming, leaving the explorer content with the knowledge that he has satisfied some unidentified longing from within and is ready to embrace an incomplete but compatible doctrine that has evolved through generations of seekers before him. How unfortunate!

This giving in—or giving up—is usually an end to the truly personal journey. It is an easier path back to the more "important" world of mind and matter and a convenient way to tuck the living soul back into its cocoon with the dreamed of metamorphosis incomplete and unlikely to progress—unless and until the more mature years bring a pinch of mortality and the accompanying inspiration to know and understand more about the "self", combined with a new abundance of time provided by some form of retirement from a fully active work life and less burdened, hopefully, by children now grown and independent.

If the energy and desire remains to regenerate an individual journey, and the indoctrination received during years of perfunctory attention to a faith institution are not too prohibitive, these years may indeed be golden and be received warmly by the soul as a calming and contemporary counterbalance to the anxiety delivered by encroaching mortality. The realization that this journey might have been pursued at an earlier age may not even be recognized, let alone regretted.

What of those who do take a journey to self-realization and spiritual enlightenment? How do they cope in a world of chilled souls and diagrammed belief structures, where their contemporaries and peers are not engaged? They may be willing to endure the ridicule of the masses by trying to explain and reveal their enlightenment despite an inadequate lexicon for doing so and, in the end, may be victims of their own deceit by trying to convert the "unbelievers" into new believers, putting themselves into the same predicament the founding fathers of modern religion did when they shepherded the seeking into their corrals of belief—corrals that ever widened but also diluted to envelope the entire flock.

Alternatively, they may become completely internalized, as reclusive to their own spiritual world as subsistence permits. This is a regrettable journey as well, although it is encouraged in the vocabulary of several faith-based doctrines. It is even considered an obligation to seek and an honour to reach in some more transcendental and spiritually-centered faiths. This greatly limits the value of such successful journeys, and although certain admiration and awe may accompany the successful sojourner, such accolades are egotistical at best and clash directly with the serenity of spiritual realization. Sharing the joy and fulfillment of one's enlightenment without preaching its revelations and without lulling in its temptation to delusions of superiority is no easy task. How can you explain a feeling to someone who's never felt it? More precisely, how can you explain a colour to someone who's never seen it? And when they are unable to capture even your most eloquent and thoughtful interpretations, how can you not feel frustrated and maybe even a little superior? It is just the ego at work.

Where does all of this leave us? We can summon the courage and muster the strength to make our journey, inevitably isolating ourselves from our closest soul mates, unable to share the intricacies and esoteric weavings of our spiritual growth. We cannot embrace or endure this isolation, so we shave the edges and whittle the fabric until we come to the basic common ground again, to the place where we are comfortable together, sharing in common spirituality, back to the common faith, the one that has been captured even by those who have not journeyed.

The fundamental difference is that those who have not journeyed may find a spiritually-diminished contentment therein, but those who have journeyed, even to an immature place of some limited personal enlightenment, may only feel cheated and self-effacing, because they have allowed their spirit to be undressed until it is communally recognizable, bringing forth sadness, a sense of self-betrayal and perhaps even resentment towards the socially developed faith with which it is obliged to swim.

—

So was the Philosopher's own pathway written as well, the pride of being published and the pressure now of being certain in his thought and prepared to respond to both praise and criticism.

The moment he read the printed words, he wished he could change some. Had he been too hasty to admonish so many for their lopsided efforts of self-discovery? Was he risking the social wrath of prickly critics and the weight they might carry among the masses? Did being different mean being wrong, or had he only stated what was obvious to many? Much rambled through his thoughts on that first day of publication. He remained indoors the entire day, both apprehensive about the reception he would receive and the potential for ridicule that haunted every divergent dissertation.

The morning after, he slunk from his abode and drifted cautiously, with head somewhat huddled and downward bent, towards the marketplace. He passed a few souls, giving the standard courteous nod and curl of a lip in that prevalent poor excuse for a smile.

The first person he encountered who had read his words and was well enough acquainted to initiate conversation was an elderly lady who had babysat for his parents occasionally when he was a much younger man. She was nice enough and always let him go to bed without having to take a bath, which was endearing enough to bring him a sigh of relief when he heard she would be supervising his little world on a particular evening. She was certainly more appealing than the alternative, a much younger but tougher woman who probably did not like sitting but could not afford to lose even the slightest income. This elderly former caregiver was a fairly religious individual, at least she went to the old church frequently, insisted on a prayer of thanks before eating, and was surely a little perturbed by his musings. Her comment, therefore, was appropriately surprising.

"I read your column today, (inappropriately named as it was), and must say that I was both pleased and surprised at the depth of thought and understanding you seem to express, especially as you are still quite young. I guess that trip to school did help your imagination, even though I would not have expected this from the little boy I used to have to force to take a bath."

The philosopher could only muster a feeble "thank you" and, with blushing cheeks and vibrant eyes like lamps to light his way, push forward into the day. Inside, he was excited though, his adrenalin pulsing and his spirits floating above the ground. If she was positive, surely he was in for an abundance of praise and adulation! Besides, maybe he did have to take a bath when she was sitting him. Who could remember such insignificant things?

Despite his trepidations, the Philosopher was gratified to see his work in print. He staggered over his ego as he strolled around the town waiting impatiently for others to greet him and share an opinion on his writings. At this young age, he felt he had identified what lay wasted in the social fabric of mankind and surely dug a deserved spot in the annals of philosophical history. Of course, he was a little overzealous, and his shining beacon of a face dimmed slightly as he realized few agreed with him in what he perceived as this backwards town of individuals, seemingly bound by their adherence to the confines of religious doctrine. Soon, he also realized he would have to be careful in how he projected his ideas. He longed for some admiration and future publishing opportunities much more than he wished to convert anyone to his particular dogma.

—

Far away in the big city, the publisher of the second-largest regional paper sat scouring the incoming news and outland papers for something he could use to scoop his rival paper, the larger and more widely read journal belonging to his uncle. Much had been set askew in the family when, following principle-based disagreements with his uncle, he decided to publish his own paper. Despite a resounding feeling to the contrary among his relations, he insisted his decision was not sprinkled by the fact that he had been courting his uncle's daughter, his own cousin, and that his uncle was so vehemently opposed to any contact between the two that he sent his daughter off to boarding school. Therefore, the nephew enjoyed finding anything that was newsworthy and not covered by his uncle. Anything that would drive a reader to his paper first was his small piece of gold, his sliver of revenge. The publisher also continued to pine for his distant cousin, beyond and throughout his own comfortable marriage to a very pleasant and socially appropriate wife.

When he came across the Philosopher's piece in the local town paper, he read it with a little boredom at first; just another wayward young man chasing an old agenda. He even put it down and went on with his scavenger hunt for a scoop. At dinner that evening though, during the main course, between a second gravy pour and the last scoop of potatoes, his wife commented on the text she had found lying on his desk. It was interesting she had mentioned it and that it had challenged her thought process enough to burrow past the routine evaluation of the dinner menu and the direction of the post-meal stroll.

His eyes rose from his plate before his head did, and he glanced at her as if peering over his glasses, which he did not wear. She stared back at him, continuing to impart her opinion on the challenges such ideas brought to her contemplations. His head lifted slowly as she delved deeper into its impact on her. By the time she had finished, instead of engaging her further in the concepts and sharing her revelations, he flashed on the possibility of this being an article in the next day's paper, perhaps inspiring such interest in other wives and mothers around the city, perhaps even readers of his uncle's paper.

He rose quickly, hurried down the length of the table, snatching his napkin from his shirt and dropping it over the half-full plate of green beans, cradled his wife's face in his hands, kissed her firmly on the forehead, and moved on to his office, spinning once as he exited the room to say "thank you."

His wife had no idea what had come over him, but she relished the fact her comments had spurred such action and a sweet kiss to her face. She allowed a smile to crease her lips as she shook her head in wonderment and proceeded to clear the table. No desert tonight, she guessed.

The Philosopher's article was published two days later, as it had been too late to get it done immediately despite a significant push from the publisher and a few heated words with the pressman. Those words had been settled with an apology, and the article came off the press without consequence from the delay. It was indeed a success, and it captured the attention of many local readers in the city, becoming the trendy conversation piece of the moment. The edition sold out and brought with it an introduction of the paper to many who had not explored it previously.

The publisher's uncle read the piece as well and, while not overly impressed with the content, recognized the interest it had generated. So, while his nephew wallowed in his glory, savouring the fleeting fame of the moment and anticipating a significant rush of subscribers, his uncle travelled to the small town and met with the Philosopher. He struck an exclusive deal for a follow-up article, of which the Philosopher already had several, and returned home with a series of additions to the original published work. He paid a very small amount to the Philosopher, who had no idea of the value a hot topic could generate.

The Philosopher, on the other hand, who was immersed in his newfound income and elevated ego, was shuttled to the pathways of the sky when he received the contract from a newspaper that was published in the big city. It was a journal with a significant following, having not just prose but also pictures on occasion, most often in the weekend edition. It contained news and opinion, sports and weather, local and national information. Truly a significant document, it was produced daily, not merely weekly like the local paper that had published his writings.

All in all, it was a fortuitous day for the uncle. Over the next four weekends, he published four additional articles by the Philosopher, and his paper enjoyed a hot circulation bump during that time, on weekdays as well. Still, like most jumps for joy, the interest in the Philosopher's commentary petered out, and the hunt for new bumps of interest resumed.

The nephew publisher tried desperately to get the Philosopher to provide him with some follow-up articles, too, but the uncle had ensured his arrangement was exclusive and impenetrable. The poor nephew, in his haste to garner a single scoop, had missed taking advantage of the full opportunity at a lengthier run. To ensure his lesson was well learned and to cap off his month of disappointment, his cousin also wrote him, informing that she had met someone else in the village near her school and could no longer carry on their illicit communication.

The Lost Lover

Joseph continued to consider the prospect of seminary. He was searching endlessly for purpose and direction in his life, and it seemed that residing in the service of God was a decent and reasonable trade-off. He would provide dedication, belief, and distribution of the Word in exchange for companionship, basic comforts, camaraderie, and perhaps a little adulation from the masses. Joseph was also acutely aware of his shyness in the area of romance, and being a priest would save him any embarrassment at being mateless. All in all, it seemed a good, fair, and equitable arrangement.

He discussed these thoughts, excluding the romantic shyness, with his only other confident, his mother. She knew his expected path was towards that of successor to his father's trade as a carpenter, but she also recognized inherently that he was not enthralled with that destiny.

With her blessing in hand he gathered his school records, which if not awe-inspiring at least covered the necessary prerequisites for admittance to the seminary. Funding his education would not be an issue, as his social life was almost nonexistent and his tastes quite frugal. He had saved money from his work and his mother still held in hand the bulk of their inheritance, which was more than sufficient. She was herself in poor health and had limited need of funds. She would surely be most pleased to buttress the cost of such a prestigious education, agreeing it would be a great fallback to support any decision contrary to a carpentry career.

He made the application at the seminary and referenced his recent encounter with Tection. The brother reviewing his application did not know Tection, but he inquired with his superiors and was told that Tection was indeed a new pupil beginning with the ensuing year. After some scrutiny, a couple of raised eyebrows at some of the weaker marks Joseph had accumulated, a review of his finances, and, most importantly, news that a previously accepted pupil had suddenly and unexpectedly rescinded his intention to attend the seminary, leaving a small dent in their revenue projections, Joseph's application was approved.

Joseph wasn't as elated as he thought he would be, but he was happy to finally have some purpose and prospect in his life. He was anxious to tell Tection and sought him out among the hallowed and holy structures of the school, but Tection was apparently absent, having journeyed back to the orphanage.

Joseph bid his farewells and went home to prepare for the beginning of school. He did not have much time. He had some small jobs he was doing for local customers that had to be finished, and he didn't want to leave any task incomplete. To manage it all, he would have to work many hours each day, hopefully hammering in the last nail just in time to return to the seminary the day before school began.

As Joseph marched home, feeling a little more enthusiastic about his decision, he rested at a small roadside diner about halfway from where he'd been to where he was going. He settled in over his coffee, seemingly motionless but inhaling the aroma rising among the small waves of steam from his mug. He was lost in thought of no particular theme, of no particular time, when he heard a soft and uncertain voice call his name. He wasn't sure at first, but there it was again. The first time woke him from his daydreams, and the second confirmed the reality of the voice. He spun his head before his body and found himself confronted by a young lady he did not recognize at first.

"Hello," she said, drawing the word out in an exaggerated ending. "Mary," she continued, spreading her hands slightly and tilting her head in body language that said "obviously." "High school" she finished.

The realization of who it was got Joseph's adrenalin flowing, and he certainly blushed before responding with a broad smile and weak "Hello."

Mary leaned in and kissed him on the cheek as if it was the most common event possible. Joseph, however, had to shift in his seat to contain his excitement at the touch of her lips. Then it all happened so fast Joseph didn't realize it until much later. He was in a trance, a daze, or a haze, somewhere outside his real body, unsure what to say or do but certain he wanted to be right where he was.

She chattered, and he listened. Time passed, and dusk arrived. She offered lodging, and he accepted. She came to him in the night. Joseph exploded far before he wanted to, and Mary giggled before assuring him she would have to take the time to help him refocus, so to speak. Their night of passion was a delight for both, and the next day found them remaining in bed for most of it.

When the excitement of their trancelike encounter finally ebbed and reality set in, Joseph told her of his admission to seminary and his intention to become a priest. She was shocked, remembering him as a carpenter, and surely saddened by the news. She had thought of him often over the past while and felt their serendipitous meeting was a sign of a potential relationship, *a meeting touched by the hand of God,* she thought. How ironic.

Joseph languished in her arms for another delightful day, finally drawn from her by the realization that he had jobs to finish before seminary and precious little time to accomplish them. They parted with sweet kisses but no promises. Mary was already in love with Joseph but would not say so. Joseph had possibly always been in love with Mary but didn't know it.

—

The adventure of seminary unfolded day by day in a cloud of revelry and transformation. Joseph and Tection laughed knowingly at the fact their chance meeting in a hayfield had led ultimately to the life they were enjoying behind the safe and secure gates of school. Joseph had no regrets about leaving behind his carpentry career or the destiny that had been delivered to him by his father. Neither did he have any regrets about binding himself to Tection in an emotional risk-taking adventure, uncertain of his friendship at first but rewarded for his commitment as they grew and gathered together. His only regret, one that hounded him, one he kept secret from everyone, was the lost lover he left behind.

Mary crawled into his mind on many evenings during his time at seminary, laying softly on his pillow and stroking his face gently in a dance that spread seamlessly from thought to dream. Although he and Tection both took full summer sessions in order to complete their education in the shortest possible time, he did find occasion to venture once again to the roadside diner and small town surrounding it in hopes of another chance encounter with Mary, but it was to no avail. She had moved away, and those living nearby were not sure where.

Her memory dwindled from his conscious reflections but remained ever strengthened in his psyche. His commitment to celibacy reinforced his migration from thoughts of her, but his occasional choice of pathway through her last known town was a quiet reminder that she still dwelled somewhere within him. When Tection used the various holiday breaks to visit the orphanage, Joseph went home to see his ailing mother, always passing slowly though Mary's neighbourhood.

Tection flourished among the students, letting his natural leadership qualities float him effortlessly to the surface of the masses. Joseph was more than comfortable being the constant, reliable, stable influence and sounding board throughout their time together. As Tection rose to valedictorian, travelling occasionally back to his roots at the orphanage and building a reputation of almost celebrity status, Joseph was content to augment his education with readings of other literature, both scientific and romantic in nature.

Many casual friendships were built at school. Joseph was generally liked but unable to really bond with the other boys, all of whom seemed to come from some other world, one laced with wealth and opportunity or political influence. Most of them were attending school to appease parents or fulfill family tradition, destined to continue post-graduation to a university to study engineering or medicine. Tection was from a tragic and impoverished background, which made him much easier to embrace. He did not look down on Joseph or discuss topics that were esoteric to him as some others did, even though they didn't mean to be condescending. Tection had the other boys wishing they could possess the spirit and charisma he had, and they cleaved to him in a sense of belonging and, for most of them, superiority. None was likely to follow him beyond the walls of the seminary.

Graduation brought much emotion. Joy at their success, except for a couple of lads who had to remain for summer courses to pick up on some particular failings, but also a certain sadness at a final departure that would surely see many of them depart from each other's lives forever. Joseph and Tection had a particularly emotional farewell laced with shared sentiment, commitment to future meetings, and some quickly wiped tears. Joseph never told Tection about his adventures with Mary. That remained too personal.

Tection had already been recruited by the central Church and left seminary with an apprenticeship safely tucked in his sash. Joseph would return to his hometown with little fanfare and serve under the priest in their local church to learn the practical responsibilities inherent in operating and maintaining a house of God.

On his final trip home, Joseph passed one last time through the land of Mary with a final hope of bumping into her. Now he wore the frock of his position and received a completely different welcome from acquaintances and strangers, celebrity status indeed.

For the first time, he stopped into the small church the town housed. It was eerily similar to the church in his own town, with a similar layout and position within the community. He met the priest, an elderly man with extremely kind eyes and laborious physical movements; much like the priest with whom he was off to apprentice. The old priest embraced Joseph with genuine affection and welcomed him "home." It was the first time Joseph sensed the tremendous camaraderie and inclusion that being a priest provided, a brotherhood of common men sharing their belief in God, savers of lost souls, and sharing their lives with the masses in a harmony of prayer, penance, and repentance. This was much more interesting than carpentry.

As he bid his final farewell to the priest, promising to look in on him once again, he turned and saw a young mother sitting in the last pew, head bowed and baby held firmly in her arms. He strolled towards the exit, not wishing to disturb her.

As he neared the end of the walkway, she lifted her head, and their eyes met in amazement and some slowly building elation. Mary stood and moved towards him. He reached out and brought her close in a soft embrace, mindful of the child asleep in her arms. The elderly priest was not far behind Joseph and was also surprised that they knew each other. Joseph explained that they had known each other in a younger life back in his hometown. The old priest was satisfied and chuckled at the unexpected encounter as he moved off towards his daily duties. Joseph looked around nervously before whisking Mary out of the church and onto the street. They both blurted out questions without answers and then laughed at the exchange. They walked purposefully yet somehow spontaneously towards Mary's place. They needed to be alone.

When they arrived, she laid the boy down on the couch and sat there with a bit of a grin on her face. They exchanged short tales, Joseph mentioning that he had passed through town occasionally in hopes of seeing her again and then confirming with pride that he was now a priest, effectively dampening the feelings of arousal they were both harbouring.

Mary explained that she had moved back to her mother's house temporarily to have her baby and get through the first couple of years. It had been arduous though as she had to endure the constant nagging of her mother about the child being born out of wedlock, and despite her significant contribution towards the initial upbringing of the young boy, Mary had to return to a life on her own. The fact was, Mary's mother was herself a single parent, and her nagging was more realistically a poor substitute for the empathy she felt from the realization that Mary would endure the same hardship and stigmatizations she had suffered while living through the process of child raising.

By this time, the child was awake and in good spirits, spewing out the few words and half-formed syllables he could muster. Joseph played with him while Mary made coffee. He was not experienced with children, but this lad seemed friendly enough. Joseph wondered where the father was. There were no signs in Mary's place of a man, no indication that anyone but her and her child lived there. He did not want to pry and kept his questions simple.

"What's his name?" Joseph queried.

Mary hesitated before replying, almost as if she was struggling to find the answer. Joseph thought that a little strange.

"John P," she stated finally, looking over at Joseph as though she had just posed a significant question.

Joseph looked away and then back at the boy. "An unusual name. What's the P stand for?" He thought it must be the father's name—Peter or Phillip perhaps.

"Priest," she replied quietly after a moment, her gaze focused squarely on him.

Joseph took a half moment to realize the implication of that and lifted his head slowly, his eyes turning up to Mary's in a locked embrace she could not identify clearly. He looked back at John P. Why hadn't he noticed the similarities before? The face that looked back at him was unmistakable. A picture of John P could have been passed off as a picture of Joseph at the same age.

A very tricky stairway of emotions followed. Bewilderment, euphoria, trepidation, compassion, and certainly fear. He leaned forward, his elbows on his knees and his hands cupping his mouth and nose. His head was bowed, but his eyes looked up at Mary, who was standing several feet away with a face full of anticipation. Joseph wasn't sure why, but he broke into a broad grin, then a slightly confused giggle, and finally a full out laugh. Mary smiled, happy but a little confused. John P was quiet, looking at this strange man and not sure what all this commotion was about.

Joseph stood and moved towards Mary. She reached out, and they embraced in a most tender moment. Mary felt the tears tumble from her cheeks; tears of joy. Joseph could not hold on for long. He broke the embrace and returned to John P, picking him up over his head and jabbering at him. The boy was a little frightened at first but soon broke into his own little grin and giggle, happy with the attention and secure that his mother was close by.

Joseph stayed with her for a couple of days, sleeping on the couch despite the offer to share her bed. (She was not nearly as committed to his celibacy as he was.) By the time he insisted he had to return to his hometown and assume the responsibilities of apprenticeship at his local church, they had come to several conclusions. Joseph could not be the known father of John P; it would put an end to his dreams of a career in the priesthood. Joseph would do what he could to move closer to Mary, as she did not want to move back to their hometown, where her mother still lived. And he would provide financial support, emotional support, and some type of role model for the young boy as he grew up. It was a lousy situation driven by harsh realities, but it was better than no contact at all.

Hope, Chance, and a Liaison

The first day Tection returned to solitary travel following his initial time with Joseph was a sad one. He longed already for Joseph's companionship, and he was acutely aware of the much longer day and still shorter night that followed.

He arrived at the seminary quite ragged and dirty, not realizing the same until one of the brothers there shooed him away from the door with a comment about beggars needing to collect themselves and seek honest work. It took some time and pleading to convince him that this was indeed his destination, but no progress was made until he flashed the finely written and sealed letter from the Patriarch of the orphanage. This was received with much reverence, and Tection was ushered quickly into an anteroom to await a more senior brother.

Tection's only thought, as the huge entrance door squealed and bumped shut, was whether the brothers at the seminary were similar in nature and disposition to those he had escaped from at the orphanage. He did not yet understand that the seminary was a place of learning and reflection attended by those who chose to do so and the staff was handpicked by the bishop and his various committees for their intelligence, integrity, spirit of community, veracity, and, of course, their commitment to God.

After introductions, a general clean up with real soap and a stiff brush, one being most pleasant and the other an assault to his tender flesh, Tection sat down with the seminary vice principal and went through the residency program in great detail—the curriculum, the general rules and regulations, and the expectation towards his commitment to God. Tection was stunned by the respect he received from the staff in general and the vice principal or VPG, as he was known (Vice Principal of God) in particular. They seemed most excited that the orphanage had provided a student worthy of a seminary education and assured him that all expenses, food, and living, would be taken care of. He would even receive an allowance in return for the various chores that were expected of him.

Tection could not have been happier. It was as if God had smiled his way and provided advanced facilities in exchange for the balance of life he was expected to devote in return. Tection even found the opportunity to mention Joseph and the interest that he also had in seminary. The VPG told him that all who were interested would be received, but others were not as fortunate as Tection in that they had to pay the costs of such an eminent opportunity, and it was doubtful that one as young as Joseph, who was fatherless and no doubt impoverished, could carry such a costly load. Tection's initial discouragement was set aside as he imagined that Joseph would indeed be able to cover the costs and that they would spend the next three years in a robust entanglement with the instruction of God's teachers, the folly of young men, and the promise of a bright future.

The commencement of classes was still nearly three weeks away, and Tection had no desire to remain solitary in the first-year dorm. He wanted to wander the area a little and sleep out beneath the stars. He had spent so many years in cubbyhole rooms with thin slit windows that the open expanse of starry night skies was a most exhilarating opportunity. Tection needed some provisions and other comforts, however, and to arrange the same from the seminary, he told the VPG he intended to return to the orphanage and express his great thanks to the Patriarch for affording him this wonderful opportunity, and try to inspire some of the other boys to dedicate themselves to following the same path. The VPG thought it was a noble and unselfish gesture, which he fully supported.

Once Tection was outfitted with quality clothing, supplies, and even a small purse with an allowance advance therein, he bid farewell and thanks to the brethren, the hallways that echoed as they pined for the returning students, and finally to the squealing entrance door. He had formulated a plan to try and locate Joseph based on the tidbits of information he had collected during their conversations and share his newfound knowledge about the seminary.

Alas, as he took his final walk towards the seminary exit the VPG handed him an envelope that was to be hand-delivered to the orphanage Patriarch, properly addressed and sealed, which he commented would require a reply from the senior brother. Tection had no choice now but to actually undertake the sojourn to the orphanage for which he had professed to be preparing, and forego any plans to visit Joseph.

The road back to the orphanage was far less interesting for Tection. The first couple of days he passed some landmarks that he did not recall, and he questioned if he was retracing his steps correctly. As doubts mounted, he always seemed to spot something familiar and felt a renewed reassurance. He surmised that the long walks with Joseph and the discussion on which their attention was closely held, had left him less attentive to his surroundings and, consequently, less familiar with the scenery.

Soon enough, he came to a quiet juncture in the road, and he remembered that the bed and breakfast where Joseph had so kindly shared his room and listened empathetically to his harrowing history, was just beyond the rise to his left. It was the wrong road for him to take if expediency was his consideration, but the thought of a refreshing bath, a tasty stew, and a comfortable night's sleep between clean linen sheets was most enticing. This time though he had the funds from his allowance advance and could cover the room costs himself.

When he arrived, the matriarch of the small inn was glad to see him again and fussed considerably more than was necessary over his comforts. The young chambermaid, still there from the last visit, her beauty present constantly in the room, served him dinner under the supervision of the matriarch. He learned that she was the daughter of a distant cousin of the innkeeper and had had been left in her care when her mother was convicted of something more than a misdemeanour, and subsequently sentenced to time in prison.

Tection enjoyed his fine meal, for which he extended more than sufficient thanks, and retired to the same veranda previously shared with Joseph. He rocked quietly in his chair, remembering the evening and feeling happy, which for him was a rare emotion indeed. After a while, he rose to his feet, stretched a "good evening" to the stars and vacant clouds above, and climbed the stairs to his room.

The tenants of the inn shared the bathroom on the second floor, but Tection understood he was the only visitor that night. He stripped down to his undergarments, picked up a clean towel, and walked across the hall, anticipating a nice, long, and soothing shower. He opened the bathroom door and froze. The chambermaid was in front of him naked, meaning without clothes!

She was toweling herself off, having just stepped from the shower, and she also froze for a moment. Tection had never seen a naked woman before, and quite possibly, this woman had never been seen naked before. He quickly regained his senses and backed out of the room, saying nothing, just closing the door in front of him.

She remained for a moment not moving, just staring at the now closed door, a little bewildered by what had just happened. Then she lunged across the tiny room to turn the handle lock into place and lifted the towel up high to cover her body completely, even if it was too late for such action. She became angry as she thought, for just a moment, that Tection had no right to spy on her, but she quickly discarded that notion, realizing he was a very considerate young man, and it was she who had left the door unlocked and precipitated the opportunity for such an encounter. Of course he was going to use the bathroom before bed.

Tection slammed his bedroom door shut and bolted it. He was very ashamed he had not knocked first. Of course she might be using the bathroom. She wasn't a guest, but she lived in the house. He lay on the bed and buried his face in the towel he still held in his hands. How was he going to face her later? What should he say? All he could think about was her naked body. She was slender and well proportioned. Her legs were long and muscled from the work she carried out constantly, and her hips framed her femininity in perfect harmony, stretching the skin from her torso taught against their edges before flowing down to her legs. The towel she held had covered her most sensitive areas, but her breasts were not covered at all. They were not large, but they were firm and rose with nipples pointed slightly upwards from their enviable perch.

So beautiful, he thought, and he could feel the desire building uncontrollably within him. He wasn't sure how long he lay there, frozen in memory of her body and fear of the future confrontation, but he bolted upright when a knock came to his door. Who could it be? Was it the matriarch, angered by the invasion of her young ward's privacy, here to demand his immediate departure from her house? Or was it the chambermaid, angry and determined to chastise him properly for his indiscretion? He knew he had to answer; they knew he was in there.

He crept quietly to the door and took hold of the bolt, holding it for several seconds. A second knock came, and he stumbled into opening the door.

The chambermaid stood there, now dressed in her housecoat, and looked him straight in the eyes. He turned away slightly, casting his glance to the floor.

"I'm so sorry," she said, "I never should have left the door unlocked like that."

Tection looked up at her. It definitely was not what he was expecting to hear. Before he could utter a word, she went on, offering apologies for embarrassing him and begging him not to mention it to the matriarch, as she would surely punish her.

"No, of course not" he managed to blurt out, completely surprised by the turn of events. Now it was her turn to glance downward, but before her vision could reach the floor, it reached Tection's underclothes, which were being tugged out of shape by his clearly revealed excitement. Her eyes widened, and it took Tection a few moments to realize why. Here he was standing in front of a beautiful young lady, whom he had just seen naked, with his member pointing straight at her, shamelessly dancing and dipping!

His hands dropped immediately to cover himself with his towel. She smiled and then giggled. Tection undoubtedly turned red. They stood like that, awkward and trapped, neither wishing for the moment to end or the encounter to pass.

"Last time you were here, I heard some of the things you and your friend were talking about," she said finally.

Once again, Tection was completely unprepared for her words. He was not sure if it was merely some banter she had eavesdropped on or part of the life story Tection had detailed. His response was another stumbling and juvenile one, but the conversation had begun. They chatted in the doorway for a bit about what was irrelevant, and soon she told him she was not allowed to be out of her room at night, especially not "bothering" the customers. Tection could feel his sorrow choking upwards, as he did not want her to leave. Then she surprised him for a third time. She looked at him and smiled a crooked little smile that defined her face whenever it appeared, shaking up the balance of her beautiful features.

"Can I come inside your room for a little while? We can close the door and continue to chat, but we must be quiet."

In the morning, Tection was robust and invigorated. He parted from the inn with a slight skip in his gate, a wave to the matriarch, and a wink to the young lady. They had said their long and lamented goodbyes under his cool sheets the night before, and this parting was only ceremonial.

As Tection continued his journey back to the orphanage, his thoughts wandered eerily in the direction of the horrific memory of Winter, the sadistic and brutal purveyor of nightmares who had scarred his life so deeply. As cleansing as it had been to verbalize most of his sad story to Joseph, and as strong as his character had become with the buoyancy of success and accolades from both the orphanage Patriarch and the VPG,

Tection had never recounted to anyone the abuse he had suffered at the hands of Winter. His name and deeds had not been included with the Joseph diary, and it was doubtful that even the Patriarch had a full understanding of what had transpired in the bowels of the orphanage. The Ogre was the only one who had actually witnessed any of the atrocities, but he had been far too perplexed himself, trapped in a convolution of confusion as he despised the abuse but was also the dispenser of "just" punishment to young boys, to track down such vermin as Winter. It was true that he would have wrung his neck on the spot if he could have, but the Patriarch, in an inexplicable display of ignorance, had freed Winter out into the general population of the world, in a classical "out of sight, out of mind" scenario. He had to have known that Winter would continue his predatory ways as he moved off into the cities and skylines of the outside world, littered with unsuspecting and vulnerable targets.

It had been four years since the dreadful encounters with Winter, and Tection had grown significantly into a young adult with a physical presence, gaining stature and maturing alongside his mental and social capacities. He longed for an opportunity to confront Winter, but at the same time he was entirely afraid of allowing those harsh memories to resurface, afraid of the reaction he might display. For him, the hatred and anger he felt towards the man was deeply entrenched in his psyche and would remain a burden to his development as a truly happy individual for years to come. These thoughts soured the last leg of his journey and sucked the joy of his night at the inn like black oil covering his heart.

When Tection reached the orphanage, he was received with great fanfare and revelry. It was true that his departure had been hasty and indifferent to what ceremony might have been enjoyed, but his return came at a time when his lore was legend and his name was invoked on a daily basis by the boys and even some of the brothers. He was proud to confirm to the Patriarch that he had met successfully with the VPG and decided to attend the seminary that fall. He was even prouder to present the wax-sealed envelope from the VPG, adding a somber request for a response to its unknown contents.

The Patriarch promised one would be forthcoming. He arranged private quarters for Tection, with what was basically run-of-the-house for the next two days. He asked only that Tection read a small prepared speech at dinner that evening as a favour to the Patriarch and for the good of the orphans. It was a fairly harmless speech, dwelling on the need for obedience and conformity to the institutional rules and offering Tection as an example of what could be achieved with perseverance, dedication, and the support of God.

Tection read the speech, providing the Patriarch with a smug sense of victory in claiming Tection's loyalty despite his renegade status among the boys, but Tection added a few unscripted comments at the end, encouraging the lads to stay loyal to each other, report any inappropriate action they witnessed, and, most of all, to be ready for the outside world. He reminded them there were many options besides joining the army, which was the usual institutional path for almost all of them. He informed them that once they reached age eighteen, they were free citizens and able to move from the orphanage and travel where they wished and work where they could. Many of the boys were unaware of this, being under the impression that life brought them from the orphanage to the army in a straight line of tradition.

The Patriarch did not appreciate the ad lib comments, as they stirred non-conforming thoughts among the boys, but he did not admonish Tection for them; he just moved gracefully to the pulpit from which Tection spoke and gently pushed him aside with loud barks of "thank you" and "welcome home" as if he were a father receiving his wayward son.

Tection returned to the seminary shortly thereafter, stopping purposely at the inn with the hopes of another encounter with his young lover, but she was away in the city with one of the hands purchasing new linens, soaps, and other comforts for the guests. Tection stayed the night, and before departing he asked the matriarch to remember him to her when she returned. She replied that she would, but the matriarch did not do so.

Over the next few weeks, the school began to fill with students. Some were senior young men, returning for their final year and anxious from the day of arrival for the day of graduation. Others were happy to be back with friends missed over the summer months and pleased to be away from doting mothers and demanding fathers who were replete with rhetorical comments about the high cost of school and the fact that God had enough shepherds and that fathers could use a few as well. Then there were the aunts and uncles or grandparents who wondered constantly at the great accomplishments of the lads doing God's work and bringing pride to the family name. There were also the new boys, some following older brothers, some scared and introverted during this first trip from the shelter of home, some fulfilling a long-dreamed calling, and finally, one orphan with nowhere else to go. Most of the boys came from well-to-do families and were unfamiliar with any life but that of artificial harmony and occasional skullduggery. This was vacation and a way to avoid responsibilities to the military. They had spent their summer gallivanting among the crop of young ladies on their way to their own futures.

Tection managed to make some acquaintances and managed to avoid some prickly personalities. He was resigned to facing a year of ups and downs when, on the last day of summer break, the day before classes were to start, a final young man walked through the door to his dormitory. Joseph!

The Philosopher and the Café

The Philosopher's theories were fairly well received in town despite his slightly questionable approach to God. He hadn't specifically criticized God, so there was no reason to disregard the text completely. Besides, there was no priest in the church right now, only a young preacher, so there was no mention of blasphemy or sacrilege. The locals were proud in some ways that one of their flock had the ability to philosophize and write down his thoughts in a manner worthy of publication.

Before long, locals mentioned the Philosopher regularly during afternoon walks or during idle chatter in the midst of dinner preparation. They claimed to have known him when he was a wee child or to have been close with his parents. The Philosopher gained a fairly immediate reputation for being a thinker and even a wise spirit, even though he was still quite young. People noticed him now as he walked along the streets and invited him to the café to discuss various issues. It was always nice to find a new, fresh face to shed creative opinions on issues that were rehashed over and over every Saturday and Sunday on the café terrace.

Having finished his schooling, and armed with his published resume of work, he landed a job at the newspaper writing copy for the various stories that held enough interest to be published locally. Most of the big stories and news events were bought from the larger newspapers that could afford to have professional writers and reporters processing events from a firsthand point of view.

The Philosopher was quite content with his work. It allowed him to earn some keep with a job that he found extremely easy to perform and, most importantly, afforded him the time to read, postulate, and write about his ideas before discussing them with the locals. He spent every afternoon and all day on weekends at the café, unless it was raining, which was a rare occurrence. If it was wet, he would move over to the hotel restaurant and languish there with both the locals who followed him and, occasionally, a guest who was involved in an idle itinerary.

The locals who frequented the café and hotel enjoyed his theories, and he fed them his concepts as they developed, piece by piece. By spending so much time on philosophizing while others around him were working or fulfilling family responsibilities, he became an interesting diversion. Eventually, he became more of a lecturer than a conversationalist, but that suited the audience fine, as they were usually tired and wanting only to relax rather than debate.

Julian, now the café proprietor, also liked the Philosopher, because he brought more people onto his terrace and kept them there longer. He had a special reduced price for the Philosopher's drinks and often, when he thought he might be getting ready to head home for the day, provided him with an extra cup of coffee at no charge, ostensibly to help him regain some sobriety but in reality just to prolong his patronage.

The Philosopher became more popular as time went by, and the demands on him for additional theories and opinions on just about everything, from politics to home medicinal remedies, became frequent. He did not like to disappoint his audience and often made up his thoughts on the fly, bluffing though issues and events he knew little about and offering advice on situations he had never faced.

On days when he felt less talkative, or perhaps to avoid some particular individual who was expecting something profound on their topic from the day before, the Philosopher would go for long walks. The problem was that he would invariably meet someone who would be going to the café later. The person would say, "See you over there later. I can't wait to hear you tell that old know-it-all Michael how wrong he is about the best way to hunt wolves." And if he didn't show up at the café, the person would tell everyone, "Sure I saw him. I thought he'd be here by now." Then the Philosopher would have to create some excuse to explain why he hadn't shown up. Therefore, it was better to take his walks far from the busyness of the town.

He began by climbing the hills that separated the town from the sea. They were steep and thickly forested. It was not that nobody ever went to them—several paths led though the lower elevations. They were traveled mostly by adventurous children stealing their first cigarettes or young lovers looking for some privacy from the prying eyes of neighbours, parents, and friends. Or maybe an elderly person, left lonely by the loss of his or her lifelong companion, strolled there in solitude while pretending the lost mate was still there, conversing silently in the elderly person's mind and sometimes no so silently, head bobbing and shaking in a whispered conversation with an invisible sweetheart.

One Saturday, while feeling particularly apprehensive about interacting with the usual folk, the Philosopher decided to climb the hill to its summit. He had never done so and had hardly heard of anyone who had, just some old myths and fables about that which lurked among the darkened corridors.

He set out early in the morning, draped with a jacket he knew would be removed soon and a light lunch to keep hunger off his back. He spent most of the morning and early afternoon climbing skyward, and he felt the labour in his legs. He began using his hands to push off his thighs as the terrain became steeper and more convoluted. He was not too concerned about finding his way back, as the direction was clear—down.

Just as he began to feel that he was at the limit of his desire to go on, he noticed a swath cut through a rather thickly flowered bush that was too big of a passage and too cleanly cut to have been made by an animal. Following it as it curved around a giant tree, he found the path meandered through a small clearing and ended abruptly at the entrance to a small rudimentary structure, incomplete in most every way but obviously quite aged. He pushed his way through the door and found himself in a small single-room cottage.

Although unsophisticated in appearance, it was quite comfortable and functional. The ashes in the small fireplace and the water, stagnant but wet, still sitting in the small kettle hanging over it, assured him that it had been visited recently. He wondered if someone lived there but discarded that idea, as there were no clothes, dishes, or toiletries to be found. The only light came through two windows at the front of the cottage, and it was obvious he had entered through the back door. He pulled open the front door and stepped out onto the porch. He was engrossed immediately by the most spectacular and prodigious panorama that yawned back at him.

He gazed in slow motion at the spectacle, and after a minute or so, realized he was not breathing. As he gulped down a fresh supply of oxygen, he realized that he understood now what the expression "takes your breath away" really meant. He had heard it before but never experienced it. The horizon was lost, muddled somewhere between sea and sky, seemingly higher in one spot and lower in another. So entwined was its fabric that there was no distinguishing characteristic, no tangible definition to its presence. How interesting for such clear concepts to be so undistinguishable from afar! Like different religions or different philosophies, seemingly in conflict when examined under the microscope but indistinguishable from a casual distance other than their condemnation of each other. No doubt fodder for some deeper reflection.

The sea sparkled from the late day sun with beams of light that were too distant to impair his vision. The shoreline spread left and right like arms reaching out to catch a running child, and he was in the eye of the earthly being, seeing nature enjoy some constant reunion between shore and sea, lover and loved. The sun lay softly in the distant sky, crackling to sleep on a dwindling string.

He leaned back against the doorframe and laughed. He wasn't sure if he laughed out loud or just inside his chest. What a spectacular moment! Actually, the word "spectacular" was a poor substitute for his reflection. He was learned and possessed a well-developed lexicon but was unable to source from it a single word that could truly encompass the emotion of the moment.

He stood motionless for some time before his hands gripped the two door handles, spreading them open like a pair of wings. It was almost hypnotic as the vista lured him outward and skyward; not corporeally but metaphysically magnetized to a blueness unsurpassed. He felt the pull inhale his being, attempting to drag it from the tiny prison of a body that held it firm. Such exhilaration and at the same time such fear.

The Philosopher pushed the doors back together and gathered himself. He was crying. He caught his breath suddenly and swallowed deep gulps of newly refreshed air from inside the cottage, realizing he had not been breathing while engulfed by the spectacle moments earlier. He gathered his senses and blinked, rubbing his eyes with sweaty knuckles. His mind raced with thoughts of vision, epiphany, miracle, mirage, hallucination, he didn't know what. No, it was none of those; it was something beyond earthly life, something from an alternative existence perhaps. He didn't realize it then, but it would become a short but lifelong contemplation and evaluation for him, an unattainable destination from this world, as elusive as capturing smoke in the clasping of hands.

When calmer, he opened one of the doors cautiously and peered out through a smaller opening, feeling back in control. Then he opened the door wide enough to slip through it out onto the porch.

After some time, he allowed his compass to reset, and he noticed the thick forest peeking around the corners of the cottage. Realizing he was dangerously close to the edge of the cliff he felt sideways along the wall with his hand, feeling some security in the rough texture and solid structure.

He looked down to his right and saw the bench so carefully constructed, as far as possible from the edge but unhindered in sightlines. Feeling the wall behind him as he shuffled to his right and found the closest seat, which was needlessly guarding the cottage entrance, he sat down on the smooth surface, still captured by the sights before him but now in control and measuring his wonderment.

He sat there for some time, lost in what would be unremembered thought. Eventually, he relaxed a bit, leaning backwards, feeling a little stiff from the rigid position in which he had been holding himself, or perhaps from the climb itself.

The bench upon which he sat was smooth and glossy, renewed some years ago perhaps but certainly newer than the cottage. It was dark and mysterious in its natural colour and littered with a soft, continuous grain running across its width. The appearance reminded him of a tiger's stripes running dark against its amber skin. As he examined the bench, he felt a renewed rush of adrenalin, a quick rise in his pounding heart rate. He tilted his head in a curious contemplation, much as a young puppy does when first trying to understand his master's call for him to "sit."

In that moment, he realized it was identical to the repaired stair from his backyard so many years earlier! The broken stair that he felt had brought rise to the calamity of his parent's marriage before delivering harmony once again when finally repaired. The same color, the same pattern of wood grain, and the same finish. Not similar in a casual way that one might feel something was a lot like another thing. This was without a doubt identical, hewn from the same raw timber and cut with the same craftsman's hand.

He stood up and spun to examine it closer. In doing so, he brought himself dangerously close to the precipice at the edge of the porch. He realized this in time and pulled back towards the cottage, bending to one knee with his head bent sideways like that puppy, listening for the repeat of some distant noise, caressing the bench in a slow, pensive manner.

At that moment, another reverberating thought struck him: His father had repaired the step. But how could that be? Had he also trekked to this cottage in the sky to renew old benches? He contemplated this for some time but finally agreed with himself that his father must have purchased the wood from a craftsman somewhere; one who had either repaired the cottage benches or also sold the wood for such repairs to another carpenter. What a small world it was. Definitely the same wood, of that there was no doubt.

He lifted himself carefully and sat back on the bench, expelling another long-held breath and beginning a rhythmic breathing, almost panting, in its stead. His eyes were open, but he was not focusing on the surroundings, only upon the epic blueness that ringed his sight line, from peripheral shadow to distant horizon. Here was a moment, a long moment, of complete clarity. All the ripples of life, perhaps even existence, returning to their source, a reversal of the outward learning experience he had followed his entire adult life. The opposite of the stone's ripples spreading through the water; his was a gathering together of related and unrelated information, unchecked emotion, sinewy thoughts, and great crashing chunks of his lifeline. The shadowy world of physical life spun around unceremoniously and was revealed for the theater it really was. He was the leading man, finally able to throw off his disguise of impersonation, drop his intellectual character ruse, and return to his real self, the universal self. Free to choose life or death, for they mattered not. Free to express from within, from his wholeness in its entirety.

It was a most fulfilling experience for the Philosopher. It was a moment that lasted for the balance of the afternoon and early evening. At the time of his awakening from this revelation, he was astounded by the length of time that had passed. He felt more complete within, and although he could not recollect every detail of this daytime dream experience, he knew it was life-altering. He couldn't understand exactly what it was, but he definitely understood that those moments had changed him. He knew that this place and emotion, this understanding and completeness, was what he wanted to write about, what he wanted to capture in prose and share with an unsuspecting world. This is what he wanted to share with the masses. For the first time in his life, he felt a true enlightenment and a sense of spiritual superiority over the life being led by those back down the side of the mountain. His need to record some of these feeling was most powerful, and he could do little but lament loudly and profanely over his lack of writing equipment.

Neither pen nor paper lay about this darkening structure. He decided, or more realistically realized, the need to spend the night in the cottage, even though he was quite hungry and very thirsty. He had no desire to be caught in the dark forest halfway home and spend the night either searching for the poorly defined pathways or providing a remarkable evening feast for the black flies and mosquitoes who owned the whispering woods at dusk. He would begin in the morning, a morning that could not come soon enough.

The Province of Salvation

What a fabulous three years they had! Tection rounded out into a most skilled pupil and leader of fellow students, gaining notoriety through his accomplishments despite his unfortunate beginnings and earning the respect of staff and congregation through his leadership and compassion. By his final year, he was valedictorian and a true light shining on the transformation process that all assumed God had made possible. The perception of his past was that he had been a delinquent and troubled child—even though his only crime was watching his family burn—who had been transformed through the glory of a proper Christian education into a valuable and worthwhile member of society. What a huge burden for the young man to carry!

Joseph, on the other hand, was a quiet and introspective student, always punctual and prepared in his studies, amicable though not overly popular but appreciated especially for his carpentry skills when repairs or maintenance were required. Tection and Joseph became fast friends and built many stories to enrich their memories as life moved on. They shared their deepest thoughts, troubles, ambitions, fears, and fancies. But Tection never told Joseph about his misadventures with Winter. That remained too personal.

Tection carried the burden of hidden demons as most do, but his were of a nature not common to most. He embraced the idea of returning to the orphanage as some sort of avenger or saviour, swift from the halls of the seminary to the hearts of the orphans, snatching them from the callous clasp of hungry hands and the twisted dreams of their oppressors.

He made several return trips to his old home, becoming more than an acquaintance to the staff that still ruled the confines of the residence. He saw several boys turn that magic age of eighteen and head off to their military commitments. He also met many new boys, fresh from their own tragic circumstances that turned the wheels that brought them to the gates of that place. He guarded his feelings of concern as he encouraged them, fearing for them and their future with less apprehension than he thought, as the landscape of the orphanage had changed since he left.

The new oversight from the Church, some change in personnel, and the fully buried episode of Winter's mistreatments were all catalyst for a revamping of the orphanage platform. There was still much corporal punishment and expectations of obedience beyond what a young boy could contribute, but there was also some compassion and a concerted effort to teach and transform these youths into working adults.

Tection did not realize it, but his own survival and success were more inspiring to the collective mindset of the staff and residents than he could have imagined. His solitary tale was a tangible confirmation that sadness, military servitude, or lives of crime were not the only avenues available to the boys. The staff was inspired to view the young population more personally and with more value, while the boys were buoyed by the tales of Tection's transition. It was a rewarding day when Tection realized his value as an avenger was fulfilled by his example of living and the contribution he had made to the orphanage was not to stampede in on a white horse, leaving a trail of false promises and casual reflection, but instead as an example of character, dedication, and understanding that he had delivered even before he realized it.

Sometimes life is good, he thought, but Winter always lingered in his mind.

His animosity towards Winter, the evil troll of a human that had scarred his life much more than the tragedy of his family's death, was buried during his school years but festered continually as the callous memories chased him from below. The horrific death of his family had been a personal tragedy but was tucked safely into Tection's psyche as an unfortunate burden for the living to endure. Winter, however, represented the evil that arises in some, the black heart and devious character of a psychopath, and a psychopath that chased the soft lives of children. As Tection's days went by, as his schooling neared completion, he dwelled significantly on Winter, wondering where he was and who he was abusing now.

With each return trip to the orphanage Tection managed to spend the night at the inn where his first and only lover had been employed. During his first few visits, the matriarch expressed apologies for the chambermaid's absence, blaming travel and employment responsibilities, and she whiled away at the misfortune of their uncoordinated schedules. She knew the young lady was the catalyst for Tection's visits and feared telling him the truth about her pregnancy and banishment to a distant relative, her new baby boy delivered to a different orphanage on the other side of the city. She had no idea that the child was the fruit of

Tection's night of passion with the young lady, and Tection had no idea that their revelry had brought forth a small life.

By the fourth visit, the matriarch informed Tection that the young lady had relocated permanently to a place with which she was not really familiar, something about a distant relative and their expressions of promised guardianship. It proved sufficient to appease the flutters of anticipation Tection brandished with each nearing visit to the inn. In time, the memories of his lover melted into a rich but undefined syrup, pouring over the few good moments of history Tection had lived.

The young child that their passion had produced, as yet unknown to Tection, ended up similarly orphaned, and by the time Tection graduated, he was a waddling three-year-old, the favourite of the young ladies working at his orphanage and the one everybody poked in the tummy and to whom they made incoherent gurgling sounds. The young child was to enjoy a fabulous life for the next few years, complete with numerous mothers and endless gifts of both substance and spirit. It was not until he moved from the infant ward to the youth school section of the orphanage that his life would hit barriers similar to those his father had endured!

Following the revelry of graduation, there was much sad fanfare to fellow students, both those who had yet to complete their training and those moving on to life's next episode. There were many carefully constructed friendships, and none more so that that with Joseph. They had served each other well during this schooling period, providing support or encouragement when needed and comfortably approaching one another with issues or predicaments beyond solitary resolution.

Joseph was more than content to return to the proximity of his roots and find shelter in his own church, seeking not the fame and fanfare of being an official messenger of God. Tection, however, was fully free from the cocoon of his childhood misadventures and spread out to capture the world, as he knew it. His personality and work ethic were both infectious, and he was recognized as a special student, much the same as he had been identified as a special orphan. He was called to the big church in the big city and offered a position that was referred to as an apprenticeship, which really meant working hard in exchange for little reward. He knew no better and was both proud and happy to receive such a calling.

His journey to the big city was littered with awe and inspiration. He saw that which he had never seen and recognized much that he had never perceived. It was a great awakening for him, not only as a physical structure and mass of humanity beyond count but also as an awakened understanding that there was indeed much in this world that he had neither seen nor imagined. It was a brand new canvas on which he could dabble, and the excitement he felt was palpable.

Among the first tasks he undertook with the church was to join a visiting committee that was investigating several smaller towns in the region to determine their needs for a separate church structure and determine the cost of erecting the same. The expense would have to be supported by a strong contingent of new believers, rejuvenated believers, and a community familiar with the principles of tithing and the strength of disposable income that could foster such activities. In time, these forays into small towns and villages became rather routine. The visits blurred into a single process, and the people they met and interviewed warbled a singular refrain of persuasion and commitment, all of which was politely heeded and then discarded. The church had a master map and a predetermined disposition, their great scholars having determined long before exactly where and when the newly constructed edifices would be. The process of the investigation committee was to impart a sense of fairness to the masses and assure them that every consideration was being reviewed.

Early in his career as a committee member, perhaps two or three years along, Tection was most fortunate to become aware of a small town nearby that had seen the recent passing of their local priest. It had been rather sudden, and the committee was scrambling to find a suitable successor. They preferred someone young and not too ambitious, for the long life of a local priest was seldom a catalyst for growth in the church hierarchy. One needed to be on a committee for that. Tection rather shyly put forward the name of Joseph, entirely unsure as to whether this was something he was seeking. From their numerous discussions though, he knew that Joseph envisioned himself as a local priest rather than a travelling one, and he also knew that he desired an opportunity to settle down in a single community. He did not know then that this would be the greatest kindness he could bestow on his friend!

Joseph was embraced quickly as the perfect candidate, and Tection was praised for his foresight. Joseph was summoned to meet with the committee, and the details were put into place without interruption. Joseph had his church. Not just *a* church but the one he coveted more than anyone knew.

Another town stood out from the mass of communities that Tection visited, one with a small café nestled comfortably at the crossroads, an old church far out on the north edge of town, and a sickly and elderly priest hobbling along with but hope and determination to propel a body that could no longer perform the tasks requested of it. It was a town that clearly needed a new church.

The old building had been central to the farming community, serving as both a social and spiritual gathering point for the hardworking people. It was the growth of commerce fueled by the new road passing on the south side of the town that had led to a shift in the local workforce from farming to trading. Several farms consolidated, and sons found opportunities in delivering produce rather than growing it, as their fathers did. The old church had grown isolated and distant from the community, and the vigour of the vicar was seeping earthward along with his physical being. Tection felt some kinship to this town. Even though it was far from his birthplace, it held many similarities, including the soft hum of life, the folly of children with happy voices, and the preoccupation with destination rather than journey, all so familiar.

This was the first place Tection stepped forward to promote during the ensuing committee review meetings and the first time he was told politely but firmly to keep his opinions congruent with the senior members of the committee. This town was already earmarked for a new church in approximately fifteen years, when the roads were completed, the population developed, and the prosperity of the region more established. The purpose of the visiting committee was to encourage and reassure the locals of their importance to the church, not to give them hope of a new building so soon. Of course, this was not their vocabulary during the visit, which brimmed with hope and anticipation, but it was their determination long beforehand.

For several years, Tection toiled on these committees. He was a skilled conversationalist and easily slipped on the cloak of "church representative." He became a lead spokesperson for the church, and soon he sat on the main development committee. Fiscal analysts, theologians, engineers, resource managers, and public representatives also sat on these committees, but Tection was at the top. He was well liked by both internal and external societies and was often flattered with comments about the great future he had within the Church. He had the credentials, the piety, the benevolence, and the humility to function at the highest levels.

Soon after his rise to such an eminent position, Tection was travelling with fellow priests to seek an administrator for a new church being built further to the south. Among the candidates for this important job was an administrator currently employed at an orphanage run by the church in a nearby town. Tection's familiarity with orphanages and their efficiencies would be of great assistance in determining if this was the right candidate.

The committee of three priests was formed, and they travelled to the orphanage, where meetings were held and formalities executed in precise order. After further discussions and a general agreement that this could indeed be the right person, Tection asked if he could stroll the grounds of the orphanage. He was granted permission immediately and offered a guide. He declined the guide and began his walkabout with the two other priests from the committee, including the head priest who, although not the committee chairman, was a senior Bother and closely trusted by the Bishop, and thereby had the ultimate decision-making power.

As they strolled, they chatted, and Tection reflected on some of the memories that flooded back to him. Without direct purpose in mind, he left the main corridors and found a small staircase lingering at the rear of a kitchen vestibule. His companions were reticent to descend, but he encouraged them to continue their exploration away from the bright lights of the main corridors.

As they descended, they heard faint sounds that seemed almost like a scream. They glanced at one another to verify that they were all hearing the same thing. After their eyes confirmed that they had, they hurried through the door and down a dark corridor towards the increasingly loud screams.

Near the end of the passage was another door. Tection threw it open with such vigour that it crashed off the wall and bounced back towards him. He reached out to hold it and permit all of them to see inside.

In the center of the room was a small table. A young boy was strapped to it, naked, and an elderly priest stood behind him, also unclothed, holding a short birch switch. The priest was startled frozen by the sudden intrusion. The accompanying priests were equally aghast by the sight before them.

Tection recognized Winter immediately. He needed only to see one of his eyes, nothing more.

Winter, a.k.a. Brother James, took a half second longer to recognize Tection, but his face revealed that recognition just as Tection pounced. Winter held up his arm in defense, but it was too late. Tection's right hand came down on his eye socket with a blow that broke both men's bones. Winter teetered for a moment and then crashed backwards into the wall behind him, striking his head violently against the edge of the artificial mantle that rested there. He was dead before he hit the ground.

Tection lunged forward, ready to deliver another blow, impervious to the mounting pain that barreled up his forearm from the broken knuckles in his fist, but held up when he saw Winter's cold eyes, lifeless and vacant in the shallows of his face. Blood coursed from the back of Winter's head, pooling like a halo around him, a red halo from hell.

Tection untied the boy, who grabbed him around the leg and held on as if his life depended on it. Tection covered him with the robe hanging from the back of the chair next to Winter's body, soothing his shaking with kind strokes through his sweat-matted hair and a gentle pressure against his left shoulder.

The committee agreed that Mr. James had fallen and struck his head, causing severe trauma resulting in death. The administrator of the orphanage, who signed off on the incident report, would become the new administrator of the new church. The young boy would be delivered to the seminary to complete his education far from the memory of what had happened. Tection, whose display of violence revealed a character flaw previously unseen by the Church, would be removed from the committee and provided a job within the confines of the central church archives. He never did reveal that Winter had also tormented him as a young boy.

The killing of Winter brought a great relief to Tection's soul, but only for a short period. It was true enough that Winter deserved to die, that murdering him had provided unknown revenge for many who had suffered and no doubt saved countless others from similar torment. But in killing Winter, Tection had killed part of himself as well. He battled inwardly over the issue. He had not meant to kill him—or had he? If Winter had not hit his head on the way down, Tection was coiled to deliver another blow and probably a continuation of them until the life was beaten out of the bastard. Tection came to some fearful conclusions about his inner anger and what he thought was his controlled rage. He realized what he'd always known, that this black internal demon could surface whenever called through some rage or reaction, and that much of his life undertakings were merely layers of packing stuffed onto his soul to keep it from fermenting. Winter represented much more than a tormentor. He was a receptacle for Tection's anger regarding a number of things. Toward his parents for leaving him alone to suffer at the hands of the orphanage, the other boys at the orphanage for being as desperate as him, the brothers for their demigod demeanour and condescending rhetoric, the seminary Patriarch for his demands of excellence, and even the beautiful chambermaid at the inn, who managed to be away whenever he returned. Only Joseph avoided his resentment.

Tection's banishment to the bowels of institutional life was unbearable. He was a social butterfly of uncommon resolve, and his joy was in the encounter with new people and unrehearsed events. He tried desperately to conform to the new parameters of his responsibility to the Church and to God, but he wavered daily, rolling ever closer to a different path. He was desperately unhappy, and he feared the future. But he feared himself most of all, feared the person he could be if a situation demanded it of him, and he questioned his value as a student of God much more vociferously that anyone should.

It was on a day cooler than summer, either spring or autumn, that Tection departed the Church for the last time. He had ample funds saved from years of moderate allowance and frugal activity, so that was not an issue. He was also skilled in conversation and ways of the word, so finding work would not be a problem either.

His last communication, before sailing across the wide isthmus separating his world from another across the sea was to look in one last time on the young boy who had been Winter's last victim. Tection was most pleased to see him grown up into a very young man, seemingly unaffected by his past abuse and joining seminary with grades and accolades almost as vaunted as Tection's own. Still, he knew that deep down, the young man had to hold dark recesses where his demons, born of the horrors he'd lived, languished patiently for an opportunity to spring forth. Tection knew this, because he held the same demons, which had already surfaced once and were hungry for further life.

Tection was destined to be a stranger, an exceptionally skilled stranger with verbose oration about himself that provided no information on who he was or where he was from. His esoteric reflections and generalizations about life, land, and legacy were poor substitutes for the passionate past he actually owned. A stranger to those he met and to himself as well, unable to reconcile or expel the beasts within, he wandered from land to land, running away from the demons while carrying them deep in his bosom at the same time, a losing battle.

The Lost Father

It was difficult in the beginning for Mary and Joseph, being so far apart and having only occasional contact. During their time of separation, especially when their love was new and all consuming, Joseph composed a beautiful sermon dedicated to Mary. He spoke of her beauty, commitment, fortitude, elegance, ethics, spirituality, and other attributes he felt she embodied. He also spoke of the loss he felt and the courage she displayed. He was in love, and although he did not carry a reputation for poetic prose, his inspiration for this text was unmistakable. He gave it to Mary, and she cherished it as a testament, a bridge to keep them close even when they were far apart.

Mary went frequently to visit her mother, who lived a short distance from Joseph and the town church he had returned to apprentice in. Mary's mother was surprised by her daughter's renewed interest in visiting the local church, and although pleased to see it, she was also curious about the motivation behind her change in direction. It had not been her habit as a young woman, but now it seemed Mary was there once or twice a day whenever she was in town.

On the other side, Joseph would make the journey to Mary's town under the guise of assisting the elderly priest with some particular task requiring physical strength or carpentry skills. There was no shortage of that in the old building, and the priest always provided a small cot on which Joseph could sleep. Occasionally, Joseph bid farewell to the priest early enough to claim he was embarking on a return trip and managed instead to stay the night at Mary's place, always on the couch, before heading back home. With ground rules laid and visits frequent, if not often, they settled into a routine full of anticipation and covert engagements. Joseph's sermon often found its way into her hands for a re-read when she was feeling particularly lonesome.

It was with genuine sadness that all learned of the unexpected passing of the old priest at the church near Mary. God had loaned him to the world for long enough and was bringing him home a little early. He must have had some task for him on high.

It wasn't long after the priest's passing that Joseph received an unexpected communication from his good friend Tection. It seemed he was on a committee that involved itself in decisions on new church construction and the search for suitable replacement priests when an opening presented itself. Although Joseph had not finished his apprenticeship, Tection had recommended him as a replacement for the recently departed priest. He wanted to know from Joseph directly whether he felt, as the Church did, that he was capable of assuming such responsibility, especially as the priest from whom he was gaining experience currently would be close enough to support any complicated situations that might arise.

Joseph answered, "yes" before the entire question was asked. He was most definitely interested in becoming the replacement priest. He had always wanted his own church, it was close enough to his roots, and, of course, Mary lived nearby. He did not communicate that last part back to Tection though.

Life gathered much excitement after that. Mary volunteered at the Sunday school, which became quite popular with the townsfolk. They bubbled at the renewed vigour of the church and the close community ties Joseph was developing. John P was a regular as well, flourishing with the other young children and enjoying his mother's full attention.

Joseph spent as much time as he could with the boy, assisting with his early education and trying to be fatherly in any way that was needed. Joseph and Mary maintained the façade, and although there may have been some backroom gossip, nothing ever surfaced that jeopardized their secret.

Mary worked for the city as an administrator and was compensated well enough to provide a decent lifestyle for her and John P. Joseph assisted in many ways. John P went to the church after school, where the priest would care for him until his mother finished work. Joseph introduced him to many things, including, books, maps, and elementary carpentry. He tried not to direct John P towards religious readings but rather those of adventure.

Joseph felt he had been truly blessed by God. He had his own congregation, a community of respect and honor, close proximity to the woman he loved, and, most importantly, John P. Life was good. Flowers smelled sweeter, and the sun always shone a little warmer these days. Joseph had never felt closer to his chosen path, and he leveraged his inspiration into numerous well-received sermons. He had a knack for delving right to his particular point without much fanfare or circumvention, avoiding the misdirection and sarcasm that littered the fabric of other writings he knew so well. He had had enough of those characteristics in his real life!

Mary grew happy as well, although she longed to rekindle the physical companionship she had shared with Joseph. She was careful not to compromise him, always respectful of his commitment to the Church, but she also embraced any opportunity to linger close to him, to brush against him or spread her kisses gently on his face. He knew her desires but always refrained when the opportunity presented itself.

Mary was promoted several times in her job with the city, eventually becoming a favourite of the mayor and receiving the title of town clerk, although she whispered that she would gladly accept more money and less title. Nevertheless, she had both a position and reputation of respect. She could not really pinpoint why that was important to her, but perhaps it was a reaction to the opposite scenario her mother had faced when raising her. Life was good. Flowers smelled sweeter and the sun always shone a little warmer these days. Mary never felt so complete as a person or loved as a mother. She had John P, her personal light; she had Joseph nearby, a good man with the best of intentions; and she had a career that provided a comfortable living and the promise of independence in the future.

John P grew quickly, too quickly, it seemed. He read veraciously and possessed a keen but calm intelligence. With his mother working and only Joseph as a quasi-father, he became independent quicker that most boys his age. He was not antisocial, but he enjoyed his personal time with his books and ponderings. He did not have any specific friend with whom he shared things until Julian arrived on the scene.

Julian was about two years younger than John P and a bit of a lost soul. Mary had asked John P to talk to Julian away from the formalities of inquisition, as she was concerned about his welfare at home. She wasn't sure what it was that attracted John P to Julian, but she sensed that the two boys bonded quickly and closely. Mary knew of Julian's family through her dealings at work and was not too surprised when John P confided about some of the rough and tumultuous episodes Julian had endured at the hands of his parents. He came from a seemingly loveless environment, and yet he was a quiet and soulful individual.

John P definitely felt some guilt at living such a joyous life and initially introduced Julian into it through some misguided form of pity. But that was momentary. In a short period, he realized Julian was a passionate and driven individual who brought some sense of reality into John P's quiet and sheltered world. They were a great fit, playing off each other's strengths and comforting each other's weaknesses. John P was the older, more reserved friend, and Julian was the renegade, full of adventure and restlessness.

As their friendship developed, Mary discussed the situation with Joseph; always just a little worried that Julian might bring some form of hardship into John P's life. Joseph began inviting both boys to the church after school in hopes of appeasing Mary's concerns and keeping a close eye on them himself.

The boys were getting older—and bolder, of that there was no doubt. Julian enjoyed his time with John P at the church, especially in the basement library, where they read of foreign lands and where Julian's sense of adventure was stoked with the exploits of others. But he had adult responsibilities at home, more than a child should suffer, and his visits were less frequent than anyone except his parents would have preferred.

Life was good for John P though. Flowers smelled sweeter, and the sun always shone a little warmer these days. John P had never felt happier or more secure in his short life. He had a close and reliable friend, a good and respected man in Joseph to guide him in areas of uncertainty, and a loving mother who meant everything to him.

But life would change, as it does. Joseph first received word of Mary's illness while visiting her in hospital for what most believed was a bad bout of influenza. She was there a couple of days, and many were concerned but reassured it was an illness that would pass. She told Joseph the truth though. This illness would not pass. As a matter of fact, it was consuming her at an alarming rate, and she had but a few months to live.

Joseph was devastated. He cried for hours. He threatened every belief he had and offered every part of himself in exchange for some miraculous turn of events. But none came. Mary elicited a promise from Joseph to keep this news from John P. There was no point in having him suffer through months of distress, and she did not want him to turn away from the life he enjoyed to fill hers with pity and servitude.

Joseph remembered how difficult it had been on him and his mother when his father lay sick for long periods, sucking the life from those closest to him. He agreed to the promise and kept it. It was a most difficult task. John P was bubbling to life as a young adult, and Joseph knew the hammer would fall hard when his mother's news reached his heart.

And it did, a cold and cloudy day indeed. Mary lying quietly in bed as she had been for a couple of weeks, always full of promises to get better soon and return to the business of her life. John P worried for her but never realized her condition was terminal. Her last words to Joseph included her lamentations at their unfulfilled physical relationship, words of love and appreciation for all they had shared, and a whispered request to look after John P. She handed him the sermon he had written for her, the private words of hope, love, and lamentation, and she smiled, so beautiful. Then she was gone.

John P was inconsolable, isolating himself for a long period. Even when he maneuvered through the day, he was robotic and detached. Joseph was lost and helpless to reach him. It was Julian who finally jolted him from melancholy and brought some purpose back to his life. But John P was a changed person. Gone was the young, curious boy, replaced by a serious and determined young man. Although he forgave Joseph eventually for keeping his mother's secret from him, there was a sense of lost trust between them that, over time, split into a greater chasm. Joseph tried to bridge the gap, but John P was already gone. Not physically but certainly spiritually.

At Mary's funeral, Joseph read aloud for the first and only time the sermon he had written for her long ago when they were first reconnected but separated, when they were first in love but separated. He modified and augmented it slightly to capture the sadness of the current situation, but it still had the foundation it was originally meant to share. It was his finest work, and those attending the service were captivated by his words and cognizant of the importance Mary had played in his life.

John P was also impressed. The reading brought tears to his eyes once again and seemed to depict his mother the way he wanted to remember her, including her beauty, commitment, fortitude, elegance, ethics, spirituality, and other attributes that he felt she embraced.

Following the service, John P approached Joseph and thanked him for the definitive words, expressing a genuine appreciation for the final testament to his mother and recognition that Joseph had been so close to her. Joseph handed him the pages with the admission that he could never read it again. John P clutched it and promised he would do so, many times.

John P was sixteen and homeless. Joseph convinced him to move into the church, as there was a small spare room. He could have that area to sleep and the basement to wander as his own space. He would still attend school and have chores to perform, but otherwise he would be at his liberty.

It was a generous offer, and John P jumped on it with much thanks and graciousness. He bought a token of appreciation for Joseph, a small wooden cross with a gold tip on the top of the vertical post. It had no inscription, but John P claimed it was a representation of the kindness Joseph had provided to him and his mother. Joseph culled his tears enough to express his thanks, embracing John P more vividly than either expected.

Over the next two years, Joseph and John P spent much time together. Joseph taught him the basics of carpentry and guided him effortlessly towards books on subjects in which John P expressed an interest. They were happy days filled with much camaraderie. Joseph, ever cognizant that John P was his son, delved into their relationship as if a true legacy was being built, but he never told the young boy the truth. John P, however, albeit appreciative of the support and guidance from Joseph, never considered him more than a close confidante and lacked the true sense of love and belonging that Joseph did. His distance and independence was not unnoticed, but Joseph assumed it to be part of the growing up process.

John P and Julian still frequented the church basement together, but they were almost always engaged in personal matters that didn't include Joseph. Joseph understood that. The boys were older, and both had some tragedy and resentment in their lives. Better to let them sort it out together.

It caught Joseph off guard though when, a few days before Julian's sixteenth birthday, John P informed him that the two lads would be leaving their cozy town and striking out on their own adventure. Joseph tried valiantly to dissuade them, expounding the benefits of a full education and the value of a safe environment to continue their development. But he knew it was a lost argument even before he made it. John P had finished his primary schooling, and Julian was driven by issues far more important to him than an education. Joseph tried to at least get a commitment on communication, calendar, and destination, but promises of such were vague and unreliable.

And then they were gone. John P had funds from his inheritance, so Joseph did not worry about that. Julian left a cold and loveless situation, so he did not worry about that either. Joseph was completely alone now. Mary, dead two years earlier, and John P, gone for unknown lands.

He worried about that a lot.

Hard Road to the Altar

Nicholas remembered little from his early years. Vague whispers of memory, jutting out occasionally from jagged edges of thought. Always without complete form and hung hopelessly in the sad magic of the moment. He remembered a beautiful face. He was certain it was his mother. She had a crooked smile, the left side of her mouth acting alone against the rest of her face, jumping mischievously out of context. She held him gently enough that he wondered sometimes if her hands were actually touching him, her instinctive cooing soothing his quiet discomforts.

He couldn't remember the last time he saw her, but he remembered that there was a last time. Passed along from her arms to stronger, less sensitive hands, watching as she disappeared down the tunnel of confusion into which he was falling. He was moved helplessly into a world shared with others, punctuated with strange odors and unrecognized whines and wails. He remembered the transfer, from comfort to control, from delight to duty, from deep blue eyes to wandering glances. The whole landscape of his early childhood was a transparent tablet held up against the staccato memories of those gentle arms, now just helpless tracings across that shifting smile.

By the time he was moved to the regular orphanage for some proper discipline and instruction, the tablet had been wiped nearly clean. While transition to a community, even such a disciplined and rigid one, left much to be learned and understood in terms of interaction and conformity, Nicholas found the demands of scholarly review an easy process. He was more than capable of absorbing all that was expected of him and often felt unchallenged by the curriculum. He accelerated through his level of study and was moved up the proficiency ladder to sit with boys one or even two years older.

He was not a settled individual though. He was reactionary to being torn from his mother's arms and slightly angered by the misfortune of his life, even though he was not aware yet of any semblance of an alternative. He was also overt, even verbose at times—the perfect candidate for seminary!

This fact was recognized early on, and the brothers in the orphanage rarely missed an opportunity to indoctrinate him with the dogma and tenets they expounded. Nicholas had a keen mind, sharp wit, pliable understanding, and acute memory skills. They filled him with enough religious script and episodes to galvanize his indoctrination at an early age.

At six years old, his easy adaptation to an older crowd was clear enough on an academic level, but Nicholas was still a very young boy. He had not benefited from the experiences of growing up with nurturing and mentorship but rather been cast into the quagmire of rhetoric and repartee that should have been reserved for older lads. The brothers remained ignorant to that, all of them except Brother James.

Brother James saw Nicholas as the perfect candidate for his own personal type of education, the kind that steals the soul and batters the heart. Brother James, known as Winter in his earlier life, saw Nicholas as an island in a sea of older boys the first day he arrived at the orphanage, a little bit helpless and unsure in certain situations. Brother James developed his plans to comfort Nicholas in his own special way.

Over the ensuing years, the other brothers began to notice a change in Nicholas, for the worse. He became withdrawn and more than a little difficult in matters of discipline. His change was so dramatic that it was brought to the attention of the head of the orphanage (HOTHOP, as he was known affectionately by the boys).

HOTHOP had a meeting with all the brethren who shared in Nicholas's education and queried them about these changes. Little of value came from the discussions, though some brothers were extremely suspicious of the private tutorial sessions Brother James was having with the boy. They were reticent to be too forward or hint at accusations in their comments though, as Brother James was a senior brother and one with a travelled past, although the reasons for his travel were never disseminated within the religious community. Nevertheless, it was not appropriate to question anyone of his stature without some significant hard evidence. Still, they suggested, under guise that a change in study habits might unlock the old Nicholas, that perhaps all his tutoring should be done in a group environment, commenting that he was possibly feeling a little alienated by the individual attention.

HOTHOP said he would consider the matter and adjourned the meeting promptly. He was under consideration for an important job as a director of a new regional church being constructed a short distance from the orphanage, and he did not want any negative issues to be part of the visiting discussions. He was anxious to leave the orphanage behind and saw this opportunity as a bold career move and a significant ladder-climbing event. His ambition to reach an opportunity in the great cathedral was a guarded one, and he was well practiced in the art of appearing aloof while coveting upward mobility.

The three priests who were due a little later in the day were dignitaries of sorts, and he had to prepare for their reception. He retired to his chambers while his minions scurried about ensuring cleanliness, aeration, and suitable nourishment was all in context. HOTHOP pondered his reflection in the mirror, content with the image, struggling quietly to mould an appearance of contemplative importance.

While HOTHOP ran through his litany of facial expressions and shoulder shrugs with the visiting delegation, Brother James brought Nicholas downstairs for a private session, fully aware that it may be their last. He was quite forward and confident in their privacy, as most of the orphanage was busy with preparations and consternation surrounding the visiting dignitaries, who were now interviewing the orphanage director.

Nicholas cowered behind the desk as Brother James went through his ritual lecture explaining the importance of commitment, secrecy, and submission to him as a senior brother, emphasizing that by doing so, Nicholas was paving his path to a higher calling and usurping the jagged road upwards through his acceptance of Brother James' guidance. As the rhetoric danced, especially that it was important for Nicholas to put his full trust in Brother James and maintain the secrecy of their encounters lest others become envious, his language turned eventually to the sins of the flesh. Brother James reiterated, as he always did, that it was important to cast off those desires by confronting them and experiencing them for the vile acts that they were. Brother James was a specialist at demonstrating their disgrace and shame.

Nicholas cringed as Brother James disrobed him and laid him under bondage on the table. Nicholas closed his eyes into a significant prayer. If only God would save him from this man. If only he would send someone—anyone—to free him from the pain and torment Brother James inflicted, Nicholas promised God he would devote every living breath to his service. His confusion was appropriate for such a young boy, and his illusions about the purpose and protection of God's hand were scattered in perpetual directions.

As Brother James moved towards him, his flesh-punishing switch in hand to climax the tutorial, Nicholas fell trancelike into the strength of his internal pleadings to God for some intervention. He would, he promised again; commit his entire life to the glory of the Lord if only God could bring an end to this horror.

When he awoke from his trance, with Brother James above him and Nicholas falling towards resignation to the insignificance of his measly little prayer, surely missed by the hugely important agenda of God; when he collapsed his will and released his scream of submission, and felt his soul fall to fatigue, the door to the subterranean chamber burst open, and a strange man filled the doorway. The light from the hall shadowed him and shone like a halo around his head.

Nicholas felt the rumble in the floor as the stranger moved forward and delivered a blow of significant force to Brother James. His tormentor fell backwards, out of sight from the table that held Nicholas captive, but the thud of head against mantle and then floor was unmistakable.

Nicholas shuddered, and as soon as this avenger released him from his bonds, he clutched to his leg, as though it was a lifeline flung down from heaven by God himself. He looked up at the man who held him gently behind the head, patting his shoulder with reassurance. Nicholas felt the tremors pulsing through the veins of the large hand. The stranger draped a robe over Nicholas, and although the boy tried desperately to hang onto this angel, he was whisked away by the other two brothers. He would keep the vision of this stranger, this angel, vivid and fixed in his mind for many years. It was the symbol of God's intervention in his life and the marker of his commitment to repay God through devotion and commitment to his cause, promised through a rewarded prayer under the cold hands of hell.

Soon after the incident in the basement, Nicholas was moved from the orphanage to a new institution, the seminary primary school. This school was usually for the offspring of wealthy or influential families and certainly not accustomed to housing orphans. As a matter of fact, Nicholas was the first orphan to enjoy the opportunity for a seminary education in several years. He was quite young to be there and recognized immediately that he was with older companions once again. This did not concern him; it was an expectation to which he was accustomed.

Nicholas flourished in the months and years that followed with his great burden lifted and his belief unquestionable. He was an exceptional individual. His raw talents, keen determination of purpose, and his experience with unwavering belief, even with the mediocre superintendence the seminary could deliver, forged a highly intelligent, adaptive, and resilient young man. He climbed easily to the head of his class, gaining praise and reputation at an accelerated rate. He was a seminary celebrity of sorts, earmarked for his own church before he was twenty years old and groomed accordingly under the watchful eye of the cathedral guardians and his old mentor, HOTHOP.

HOTHOP was in blissful purgatory, under neither the daily supervision of the cathedral nor the predatory eyes of cardinal hopefuls. He had a position of supervision over several regional churches and a secluded office that matched that exalted position.

He also took as much credit as possible for the growth and blossoming of young Nicholas, mentioning their close relationship and reminding all of his tutorship whenever possible, even though he barely knew the boy's name before the "incident" with Brother James. How fortunate he was that everything had been covered up. Tection, the avenging priest who struck the blow, had been banished to the crypts of the cathedral administration, and HOTHOP had secured his enviable position as much in appeasement and payment for his silence as on merit.

Following his graduation, with appropriate bells and whistles, promises of his own church, and a whirlwind tour of the cathedral for inspection by the hive, Nicholas approached HOTHOP with inquiries about his mother and father. The aging man was reticent at first to provide any leads, but Nicholas manipulated him easily through cunning innuendo and garnished the name and location of his mother and, with his access to the records office, the search was easy to complete.

Nicholas observed his mother, Sarah, from afar for some time, careful to follow her comings and goings without conspicuousness or intrusion. His approaches became bolder, and, as was inevitable, there came a point where she looked directly at him with her surrendered eyes. He stepped forward, seeing the sadness she carried and knowing the goodness she embodied. She registered her confusion with a tilt of her head before recognizing clearly the young man she had last seen through the distortion her tears provided as he was carried from her embrace when still a baby.

The tears on her cheeks rolled from joy now, and her disbelief was a catchall for the words that never escaped her throat. Nicholas stepped forward and held her close as if it was the most natural thing he had ever done. Their bond was instantaneous and urethral. That her memories rushed back to her was enough of an event to warrant her explosion of happiness, but that his memories also welled up to the surface of his mind was testament to the loving and nurturing relationship they had developed in that short period before he had been sacrificed into the orphanage by smugly moralistic strangers, distressed by her lack of wedlock.

Over the next while, Nicholas revealed his short and choppy history to his mother. He dwelled significantly on the episode with Brother James and the heroic stranger who had saved him. Talking about the episode was an immense cleansing process for his soul and even though he barely knew his mother she was, well, his mother. He had tried to find out the name of the stranger, but the orphanage and seminary both stuck to the same rhetoric: Brother James had died in a tragic fall; there was no executioner. Those dead ends had hindered his search, but the stranger's face remained embedded in Nicholas' mind.

Sarah watched with pride as Nicholas bolted through his short apprenticeship at the cathedral and prepared for his first opportunity to have his own congregation. He waited patiently for the new church to be completed and prepared for transition from sheltered apprentice to giver of light. The new church was conveniently close to Sarah, and they both shared their appreciation of this fact with God himself. However, they had to keep their relationship a secret, at least for the time being, as Nicholas needed the appearance of complete innocence and honesty and Sarah the perceived position of spinster.

The town where the new church was located had been without an active priest for several years. Ceremonies and celebrations that a house of God was required to fulfill were scheduled at the closest active church, many miles away over dusty and occasionally dangerous terrain. The congregation was probably in a state of disarray in terms of their religious commitments and spiritual awareness, Nicholas surmised, and he organized a short visit to the town to mingle with some locals and get a clearer understanding of just how far off center the lack of a proper church had caused them to drift.

He was both surprised and delighted to hear that a lay preacher named John P, a common but spiritual individual, had been providing some moral, social, and inspirational rhetoric to those who cared to listen. He used the old church outside of town as a pulpit and had collected a fair following of souls who had been left void by the lack of an official Sunday service. Nicholas realized he would have to meet this man and secure his assistance in fashioning a seamless transition of the services from the old church to the new one, from the preacher to the priest. He understood this preacher was also living in the old building, which still belonged to the Church, a building that was to be levelled at some point to accommodate some sort of housing development. The graveyard next to the church remained an issue of some concern, however, impeding these development plans, but such was not within Nicholas' sphere of influence.

The Cat and the Almighty

On the second Wednesday of every month, the supply vehicle passed through town. It stopped at the restaurant, the snack shop, the small hotel, and the café, bringing the provisions and utensils they all needed to continue their ventures. It was important for them to anticipate their needs carefully based on the season and the flow of clientele. Buying too much not only risked the possibility of waste and spoilage, it also used up the cash flow of small currency available to make these purchases. On the other hand, too little inventory, and the menus and customer favourites might be jeopardized, and customers were very fickle.

Even though his was the only real café in town, Julian always feared that the hotel, with its little side terrace, where clients could sun themselves and relax after their various journeys, might decide to open a small door onto the street one day and allow passersby to stop in for refreshment. Those customers would be drawn from his café. If not the hotel, even the restaurant might cut into his client flow one day if it began selling after-dinner drinks without accompanying food and provided a few tables in an environment separate from the dining area. Those who usually visited the café after dinner to sip digestives, snack on some long-anticipated dessert, or ramble their conversations into the night fueled with drink might decide not to have that short intermission in their evening conversation and just stay at the restaurant instead.

Julian liked the after-dinner crowd. Not only were they already in a spending mood, if they decided to continue their evening after dinner, it meant the time was being enjoyed by all, and the spirit and revelry was infectious. It often drew casual strollers from the streets who decided a nice, lively atmosphere was just what they needed to end their promenade, or lured a tired worker or two from their evening newspapers, not yet ready to give up on the day that was. Yes, the importance of managing the supplies and the money was significant to a successful enterprise, far beyond the obvious.

On one such Wednesday in early fall, the delivery vehicle didn't show up. All those involved in purchasing from the supply house began communicating with one another to see if anyone had seen the wayward transport. No sign. Finally, after much persistence and more than a single comment on the irresponsibility of the supplier and the need to search for an alternative if this continued, the very young but very serious weekday manager at the hotel reached the supply company. They informed him that the poor driver had broken down. Assistance had been dispatched to bring him and his vehicle back to the garage, but they could not determine how long it might take to return to his delivery route. To make matters worse, if the vehicle was not repaired quickly, their delivery could only be completed the following Saturday, as they were already committed to a Thursday and Friday schedule. The hotel clerk passed the unfortunate info along to the various enterprises concerned.

Julian was very upset by this. He was almost completely out of his most popular liqueur. He had several brands that did not sell well, but this one was a swift mover and most important to certain clients. He had not noticed how low the stock was the month before and felt fortunate that his dwindling supply had lasted through the current period. Now on the last half bottle, he was sure to run out before Saturday, and Friday night was a popular evening for drinking liqueurs, as the work week was over and his patrons felt comfortable to relax a bit. He was not looking forward to telling his regulars that he did not have their drink. Why else did they come to the café?

This dilemma was occupying his mind Friday morning as he held the last bottle up against the Friday afternoon sky to measure its contents more accurately. He strolled back onto the terrace smelling the contents in an effort to determine which substitute might be the most suitable.

Suddenly, he heard a screech and whine that turned quickly into a growl. Looking down as he stumbled, he realized in a flash that he had stepped on the orange carpet of a cat that always sunned around his tables and along his stairs. He didn't mind the cat. It was like a companion that required no effort to care for and always agreed with him or else just went away. Even then he felt no guilt at having a conflicting opinion to the feline's and never received a rebuff that prowlers of his own species might deliver.

As he crashed to the ground, he felt that last bottle of liqueur fly out of his hands and land with a thud on the street below his terrace. He listened. No breaking of glass, no sign of damage. Though he was a little disoriented and not yet cognizant of what had just happened, he felt a wave of relief that the bottle didn't break.

He hoisted his bruised body up to his feet, seeing the cat staring back at him with slit green eyes that reminded him of a demon. He jumped down the two steps and picked up the bottle. It wasn't broken, but the top was still off because he had been smelling the liquid before the cat tripped him, and the precious contents had all but drained out. There were no more than a couple of drinks left in the hollow of the bottle's side.

Julian stormed up the stairs and caught sight of the cat still hunched on the floor, wary of the ongoing action and a little confused as to why this previously kind young human had stepped on him. With a display of anger unusual to his character but planted deep inside him by the pains of his upbringing, he kicked out and caught the cat in the side just as it realized the danger and tried to leap away.

The cat had never experienced a moment of anger in its life, having lived in and around the café and restaurant enjoying scraps, tasty morsels dispensed secretly by young children with one eye on unsuspecting parents, and the odd snack from older folks. He languished beneath the casual scratching of patrons and pedestrians alike, feeling a simple pleasant life that befitted an animal that slept most of the time and never made a mess where he lived.

Under the impact of the kick, the cat flew through the air, smashed into the square post that supported the upstairs balcony off Julian's bedroom, and flopped to the ground, definitely not landing on his feet.

Julian watched the flight unfold in slow motion, finding the time between the initial impact and the decent of the now motionless animal to run through the whole range of feelings about what had just happened. At the speed only a brain can muster, by the time the cat actually hit the ground, he felt his anger, realized his action, despised that it had happened, felt pity for the poor cat, leaped unsuccessfully to try and catch it, felt a great sense of sorrow and disappointment in himself, and decided he must do everything in his power to save the animal.

He recognized the ability to hurt a helpless and unsuspecting creature was indeed within him, and that scared him more than he realized at first. It revealed the existence of an evil within himself that he never knew was there. Even in his dreams, whenever he lashed out at his loveless parents, he always felt guilt and remorse at the idea of even thinking about it, never mind doing it. He considered himself a kind and caring person completely incapable of performing or even imagining anything as horrible as bringing suffering into a life that didn't deserve it.

He lifted the cat up, found it still breathing a faint whine of anguish, and brought him inside to the back storage room. The remorse he felt for having caused this pain drove him to make every effort to repair the damage. He knew nothing about cats, medicine, or the servitude guilt could command, but he cleared out an old box and laid a soft tablecloth at the bottom to cushion the cat.

One of the cat's legs was obviously broken, so Julian bent it straight. He was fortunate the cat was unconscious, although it did squirm a bit at what must have been a very painful procedure. Julian also applied a splint made from two wooden spoons broken off below the ladle and held in place with a swaddling bandage, solidified by tape around the exterior. Julian was grateful it was a more flexible and less important front leg that had broken and that the bone had not pierced the skin, so there was no blood or changeable bandage to worry about. He stayed near the cat all day, neglecting all but the most essential of services to his customers.

When evening came and the usual Friday night crowd began to grow, he sold the last few drinks of the guilty liqueur, stretching two large drinks into three small ones. When the next patron, a rather elderly man named Oliver, asked him for a drink of the liqueur, Julian had no choice but to tell him the truth.

"I'm sorry, Oliver, but it seems everyone is so fond of it we've run out, and the delivery truck was late, so there was no resupply. I'm so sorry, but ... "

His words tailed off with a bow of his head, waiting for Oliver to dispatch him with a scowl and some comment about his lack of service. But Oliver was enjoying his evening, and the particular liqueur he was sipping was far less important than the company he was keeping, a lesson Julian would continue to learn along the way.

"That's okay, Julian, forget it," Oliver said without much attention. "Just bring me something new then, anything you have."

Julian snapped out of the shrug he had put on unconsciously to brace for the umbrage he felt was due from Oliver and hurried over to the bar. What should he serve instead of the preferred spirit? He did have a full bottle of a new liqueur the supply house had given to him as a sample. It was a new product that they were introducing to the region, and no one really knew what it was like. Julian had hesitated to recommend it, feeling there was no need to change anything that didn't need changing, and his clients were well established in their brands and habits. Perhaps he would provide it one day to an unsuspecting tourist who was only passing through or at least be prepared when the promotion of the product reached his small community. He decided this was the time. Oliver had said to give him something new.

Julian poured a glass, ensuring it was very full, as some form of ersatz apology for the lack of the requested brand, and served him.

"Here, try this special new liqueur."

Oliver sipped it, not missing the fact that Julian had provided an extra-large quantity, and swirled the sweet liquid around in his mouth. He looked up and smiled.

"Very good!"

Then he turned his attention back to the table, not realizing the immense relief his reaction had brought to Julian.

As Julian turned to leave the table, another man ordered the infamous cat-depleted liqueur.

Here we go again, Julian thought, but before he could extend his apologies for being out of stock and letting his good customers down, Oliver spoke up.

"Malcolm, you should try this new one Julian has brought for us, it really is rather tasty."

Malcolm thought for a second, shrugged, and shot Julian an "all right" with his eyes and a little "okay" with his lips. Soon, the whole table was drinking the new liqueur and finding the courage and desire to try some other ones as well.

Julian caught on to the rhythm of the evening quickly and, one by one, brought out all the old liqueurs that had not been very good sellers. It was a perfect opportunity to move the contents of his old bottles. Julian was even tempted to tell them the new liqueur was a little more expensive than the regular ones but decided that would not be appropriate under the circumstances. What a blessing that delayed delivery and lazy old cat had been! All his old stock sold, and his regulars were happy and content.

That night, Julian remained with the cat throughout, so he was there when the poor, pained, and frightened creature awoke. Its eyes were scared from both the strange implement attached to his painful leg and to the new experience of an emotion called anger that had inflicted the pain. It didn't understand that the pain it felt now was one of healing. Still, unable to walk and unsure of these changes to its existence, the cat took some comfort in this man who was stroking him gently and feeding him warm milk. Soon, the pain and experience took their toll again, and the cat slid into a deep sleep, its body shutting down so the healing process could be maximized.

Julian watched the cat as it slept and noticed a definite swelling along the right rib cage, obviously caused by his boot, and he prayed there was no permanent damage. He prayed specifically to the powers John P told him were contained in his religion. He prayed to all the names he could recall and in all the ways he could remember. He didn't pray very often, so each time was a special effort. He even convinced himself that with all the people who prayed to these powers every day, he alone would receive some special attention, exactly because he didn't pray too often. If each person who prayed was on equal footing and terms, as the Bible from which John P quoted with such regularity promised, surely those who did not take advantage of those amazing powers of prayer to right wrongs, those who didn't need to take advantage of the powers because they did no wrong, surely they would have a separate path to the front of the line and receive immediate attention.

Julian spent the periods when the cat slept to consider those powers. He liked the idea that something existed that had such strength, control, and sweeping authority over the multitude. But he worried that, if by chance, the Great Being happened to step on an unsuspecting assembly of people and stumble, could he possibly rise up in anger and kick the whole gathering into unconsciousness? Was that what sudden mass deaths from disasters and tragic events were? Were they the Almighty lashing out because something had angered him? Was the pain, not just physical but emotional, the way restitution was exacted? And if that was true, how did this Almighty get inside every person to inflict that kind of pain? Did we have to let him in, as they professed at the church meetings? "Let him into your hearts," they chanted. Did letting him into your heart allow him to deliver emotional pain when he stumbled unexpectedly? Did the cat think of Julian as the almighty?

Julian smiled and laughed inwardly at his musings, wondering if these were questions he might put to John P when they met next. The levity of his thoughts helped relieve his guilt, and his attention to the cat became gentler and more attentive. He had to ensure the animal recovered as fully as possible. Even if it had a slight limp, it could still survive and flourish, just as a culture, sometimes kicked by the omnipotent unknown, found ways to heal, never exactly the same but always prepared to push on.

Julian didn't realize it then, but the process of praying had, in itself, alleviated much of his guilt and provided a commitment to extend compassion, easily quelling the cold dark side of his nature that had shown its ugly face earlier. Who or what he prayed to seemed far less important to him than the actual act of unselfishness it really was, undertaking the responsibility to ask himself to help someone less fortunate. He didn't pray for forgiveness for his action, only for help in repairing the damage done. Fortunately, he had not learned that sometimes the religion of John P's Bible let believers find forgiveness for their evil deeds without consequence; just a few soft prayers as penance, even though this often made the evil easier to accept and tolerate. But forgiveness was not a weapon against evil; it was only a mask. Julian didn't realize right then that the power of good was not only the sole weapon that could defeat evil, it was also its sibling, sharing space in every soul.

Over the next few weeks, the cat healed, and the pain diminished. An unusual but real bond developed between the animal and Julian. The cat walked a little funny, as the bone had not been set in the right manner, but it was not painful, and it allowed the cat to garnish more sympathy and, consequently, more treats from the café guests. The cat stopped going to the restaurant altogether, finding all the comfort and subsistence he desired to live out his lazy and supine existence in and around the café. He had a green light to travel anywhere at any time and became quite bold. Everyone enjoyed seeing him around again, and the sympathy his noticeable limp brought only added to his acceptance.

Julian never corrected the patrons when they speculated on exactly what had happened to the poor cat. Perhaps a distracted tourist had hit it, or some delinquent children from the next town had teased it too hard, or maybe a stray dog had chased it towards an accident. The cat was his personal reminder that darkness existed in his soul, but with the love and kindness he had the capacity to dispense, he could bury that ugly part of himself below the levels of consciousness. Was it this evil that the Almighty saw in each person after being let into their hearts that caused him to lash out?

The Preacher, the Priest, Broccoli and Faith

John P struggled at times to speak fluidly in front of a large audience. He knew such was a hindrance to his value as a preacher and that the word from the pulpit was his greatest tool. He would lose his edge of concentration often when gazing at his congregation, a slight hiccup in his flowing speech, as it were. If he concentrated on one individual for a few moments, he would be able to regain his full concentration and deliver some dramatic finality to his thought or a clever twist to his tale. He was careful not to look at the same person more than once per sermon to ensure he did not become reliant on that individual to trigger his reconnection with the tale being weaved.

When there was no one present and he was rehearsing his future offerings, he would use the carved cross that lingered slightly off center on the back wall of the room. He would tilt his head slightly to get the cross in direct focus and use it to re-center his thoughts. He often laid plans to straighten the cross, but its value as a re-centering tool, despite its crooked stance, made him reticent to change it in any way.

John P completed his delivery to the captivated audience. As always, he spoke of life and betrayal, the oft-repeated process from his biblical reading. He also spoke of right and wrong, of fact and fancy, of love and lamentation. The words were not special in themselves. It was the context in which he placed them that kept the gathering enthralled.

The congregation was always impressed that he would, at appropriate moments during his oration, make eye contact with one of those in the first few pews and talk directly to the person, creating some uneasiness within the individual but also pulling the parishioner more personally into the tale being weaved. The recipient of his attention felt compelled to answer John P as he posed his questions or situations. But they were always rhetorical remarks, and John P had an uncanny ability to break the stalemate of words just as the target of his attention was sure he was waiting for him or her to respond. John P would continue, lifting the pause from the air like a tablecloth snatched from beneath a fully set table and leaving a slight smile of amazement on the lips of the selected visitor.

At other times, he cocked his head slightly and peered into the distance, as if connecting with some unknown force, pausing again with a dramatic silence before refocusing and dropping a punchline to his tale. Sometimes the congregation would sneak a backwards glance to try and share whatever vision he was embracing, but all they could see was an old crooked cross on the back wall. They wondered why John P didn't straighten it.

This skilled oration was a slowly and almost imperceptibly acquired skill. The many Sunday sermons John P had delivered over the past few years lent a small moment to the development of a whole pulpit personality. The meagre but comfortable living that the congregation provided him through their donations and collections, after the rental and assessment monies for the church, allowed John P to spend countless valuable and cherished hours with his scriptures and other writings, devouring the text and realizing the intentions, helping to form the lines of thought and direction of influence he would deliver to his flock.

His disseminations were well received, because they were comprehensible and worthy of contemplation to those listening. As John P was basically self-taught in the revelations of his faith, he put those ideas in a common language. He shared the wonderment and curiosities of his fellow townspeople, and even though there was but one speaker, his sermons were much more like conversations than lectures. He did not explain what the scriptures meant, as was the case with most preachers when they spoke down to the congregation from the pulpit. John P was at one with his congregation, unspoiled by the learned dogma and rich philosophies of the Church, unfettered by rules of disclosure they may imply and unfazed by any threat of condemnation if he revealed too much or too little, or if he strayed from the classical scriptures into the dangerous underworld of analysis and questioning of the established rhetoric, or invited alternative thoughts and discourse to those of mainstream teachings, for he had never learned nor even heard of any such potential condemnation. That the Church wanted a single, uniform, and controlled expression of faith among followers was never really a consideration for John P, as he had never experienced it. He had never been subject to the influences of its powerful regulations, rules, and laws nor cowed by the confessions and retributions the forgiveness of sins mandated. Did a person really sin if he or she did not know it was a sin? Was it the task of the Church to let people know what the various sins were so they would know they had sinned and then attend church to have them absolved? Not the great and known sins of the commandments but the daily, life-inspired sins of the living, like the fundamental questioning of existence and purpose, or the unavoidable strength of emotions or the feelings of anger and revenge that inevitably accompanied death, before the sorrow and forgiveness consumed the mourners. And if this was so, did the Church update continuously and create new sins to keep pace with the evolution of society, to ensure sins were common enough and important enough, regardless of their seemingly insignificant nature, to prevent anyone from actually avoiding sins altogether, thereby negating a key element to the pursuit of faith and dependence on the Church for absolution? If the Church was gracious enough to allow its followers to interact with God through its cathedrals of faith and powerful enough to forgive individual sins in God's name, surely the faithful could at least oblige it by sinning occasionally, and then confessing.

This must have been a great justification for the priests who carried the good word, for they had sacrificed much in order to build that special relationship with God that enabled them to communicate in his name. They had sacrificed their natural inclination towards physical love, forced either to live in a constant state of frustration or to seek relief through anonymous liaisons, incognito and nameless. To deny all sexual relationships was a cruel obligation to extract, and perhaps, John P wondered, it affected their mental disposition to question, evaluate, and postulate for themselves.

He wondered what adventure life held for those who knew from their very first stages of adulthood the mysteries of the known universe had already been deciphered and laid out for them to follow. John P was young and not yet ready to develop his own philosophies and opinions on the fate, facility, and faculties of mankind. He knew there would be times when he might want to question the ebbs and flows life delivered without being obliged to accept the postulations and predictions extracted from the literature of faith by the self-proclaimed and officially appointed interpreters. He was disassociated from his own simple understandings of the message contained in these books so often that he questioned whether he was even speaking the same language as these explicators. He did not feel the constrictions that priests did, because he was not bound to the physical or intellectual confinements they were, and he was happy about that.

This particular day's sermon had to do with the youth of Jesus and the relationship and influences of his parents. Was his father, Joseph, more influential and engaging than his mother, or was she the force behind his early growth into preaching? It did not escape John P in the slightest that Jesus was neither an ordained orator nor a recognized rabbi. On the contrary, he was ridiculed and scoffed at throughout his short life, finding his internal strength in his beliefs and confidence in his destiny. Not only did he remain true to himself despite the doubts thrown continuously into his path, he carried a multitude of people along with him, countering their shortcomings with his words of comfort and support, propping up their wavering faith and insecure moments with a quiet power of conscience and commitment that could only be carried by someone who believed without hesitation that he held the truth and the "way."

John P admired Jesus greatly for his strength of character and self-confidence and fancifully considered himself a very distant cousin in nature. After all, John P was not recognized or supported by the Church, but, like Jesus, he had a distinct and faithful following. He felt kindred to the passionate relationship Jesus had with humility and forgiveness, and he carried a great sense of responsibility towards those who attended his services—not to mention that his mother was also named Mary!

John P recognized that his respect among those who heard him came from his ability, and indeed history, of being equal to them, being of the same cloth, as it were. His reward was knowing that he inspired some thought and understanding among them in terms of their faith and commitment to God. He valued the fact that he could help them understand what and why their faith was, without limiting them in how they expressed or demonstrated it. This was not something he did through any kind of irreverence towards the Church, for he had not learned the rules and regulation, the limits and boundaries, or the official interpretations. He had studied intently, listened when he found the opportunity, and developed a sense of faith's intentions through his love of the principles and passions of the stories about and surrounding Jesus. He recognized that every person would have to find that on his or her own; it could not be implanted. He realized faith was like broccoli, a delicacy to some and an awful thing to others in its basic form, but when dressed with salt or cream or oil, when steamed or boiled or breaded, it became so much more consumable and enjoyable. John P wanted everyone he knew to have the opportunity to try broccoli in the most varied ways possible so that they could be informed enough to choose their most desirable and tasty form. He came to see himself as a chef offering up different variations of the same dish.

In his talk on this particular day, he offered the two very different scenarios the gospels revealed about Jesus' youth and upbringing. He pondered and postulated about the influence Jesus' young mother might have had as opposed to his busy father. Surely Joseph taught him the gift of his trade, the working of wood and the methods for measuring, squaring, and calculating. But his mother must have shown him the path to gentle humility, patient understanding, and compassion, nurturing his unwavering desire to forgive and even embrace his enemies. John

P was not well read in the published analyses of Jesus' youth, as abundant as they were, but his understanding grew from his own youth, where he had grown up with just such a woman, and he recognized, within his society that the tenderness and devotion a child might receive would come from his mother. After all, hadn't Mary been there to hold Jesus, despite her misgivings about his calling, when he was cast from the cross? Who but a mother could hold her son in death as she had in birth? And what importance would it draw from the fact that the first and last person to comfort Jesus in his natural life was Mary? John P felt there was much more to her significance in the life of Jesus than the Church allowed to be published. Why were the stories of the disciples, some glorious and some condemnable, recounted with such vigour and elaboration while Mary languished in near obscurity, save for the few moments when it was convenient to have her appear? How could this Son of Man, larger than life, hurler of parable and analogy, purveyor of kindness, absolution, and miracles, saviour of faithful and forgiver of the unbelieving, how could this man have reached out for his destiny without the kind of fundamental good that Mary must have brought into his young life? How important it must have been to have the most significant person in any infant's life, his mother, carry a sense of humility, understanding, and passion for the goodness of life and to plant this seed in him and share in the growth and understanding of the strength and value it would produce and provide. Why was the obviousness of this so apparent to John P yet seemingly so trivialized by the dogma and determinations of the scholars? Any good son, and Jesus was certainly all that was good, would always carry a special place in his being for the memories and moments he shared with his mother.

John P was certain the significance of Mary being there to receive him from his execution was more important than the

Bible revealed, and he became curious as to why the Church was so hesitant to expand on her role in the chronicles of their history. The lack of developed female characters in the Bible was a flaw to which John P was particularly sensitive. He wanted to discuss this with someone who could provide a female perspective on these points and who knew or could explain the birth and growth of the Good Book, but all such scholars he knew of were men. As far as John P was concerned, Mary carried a special role in the development of the Christian world and was not properly recognized for her contribution. While it may have been the disciples, especially Peter and Paul, who carried the teachings and galvanized the movement that would become the institution, it was Mary, virgin or not, who birthed and guided young Jesus into the ways of life that would provide the foundation for it. If she was indeed "chosen" by God to literally deliver the Messiah, why did he choose her? What was so special, or perhaps so common, about her that appealed to God? She was young, poor, unsettled, and inexperienced. She was exactly what was needed to produce the kind of person who would lead a new world. Jesus could not have been born into a wealthy or educated life. Otherwise he would have had to unlearn all that his family taught. It had to be Mary, unspoiled, uneducated, and unblemished by life, not yet settled in her ways yet courageous and committed. Imagine defying the centurions and remaining steadfast to comfort her son's sufferings when all others had deserted him. It was Mary after which the Messiah would be modeled. If God was the sculptor of his Son, Mary was the rock from which Jesus was hewn.

By sermon's end, John P had planted certain seeds in the minds of his flock—not seeds of doubt or insecurity but seeds of attraction and intrigue. He had built an interest in the minds of his audience and a curiosity to learn more about the parents of this Saviour.

Several people came to him after the sermon and asked questions or shared thoughts and opinions. John P enjoyed this part of his Sunday most of all. Not only was their interest his reward, he found his own curiosities stimulated by the dialogue. He did not take pride or gain self-importance from these discussions; they were a genuine discourse between people who were interested in the stories and principles of their faith. His satisfaction was filled by the realization that he could, and did, stimulate interest and provide some small understanding of the Good Book and its teachings. That was his reward.

The last person to speak with John P that day was a young man who was unfamiliar to him. John P had noticed him at the back of the room listening intently throughout the morning and guessed him to be a year or two younger than himself. He had assumed he was a visiting nephew or family friend of one of his regulars. He had not seen him around town before, and with the pleasant spring weather, it was common for families to visit and gather for a short while to share news and shake off the distance of winter months.

John P spoke first. "Hello, my friend: I don't think I've seen you here before."

"I'm sorry," the young man replied, "I probably should have introduced myself when I arrived, but you were just beginning, and I didn't want to interrupt. I hope I didn't disturb you with my late arrival. I'm new here and took a wrong turn on my way. I asked directions from an elderly man, and I think it might have been a while since he came this way. He referred to several landmarks that no longer exist." He punctuated his last remark with a slight roll of his eyes.

"Please don't give it a second thought," John P replied, "I'm happy to have any and every face, new or old, early or late"!

He chuckled lightly with his last remark, and the young man smiled back, nodding his thanks for the easy absolution.

"Are you visiting a relative?" John P continued.

"No, no, not at all. I've just moved here and wanted the opportunity to meet with you and discuss the situation."

John P cocked his head like a rooster surveying the barnyard in anticipation of the fox. "Situation?"

"I'm the new priest. Didn't you know I was coming?"

John P was stunned. He did know he was coming. He'd known for several years he was coming. He just didn't know he was coming that day! He tried to keep the shock he felt away from his face and his body language and extended his hand to the young man.

"Well, well, of course I knew you were coming; we just didn't know exactly when, and we didn't know exactly who."

The priest coughed a small chuckle, either a little nervous with John P's response or confused by the delivery. He sensed some deliberate sarcasm in John P's words, although John P had not intended that.

"Father Nicholas," the new priest said, extending his hand.

John P wasn't sure if it was a greeting, a peace offering, a threat, or a poison dart! He shook the priest's hand with caution, looking directly into his eyes. He seemed sincere enough. Perhaps this young man didn't realize he was walking in someone else's garden, stepping on someone else's dream.

"I have moved into the new church and was planning to introduce a first mass today but realized I needed to visit you first and discuss the transition beforehand."

The young man looked quite pleased with himself, not because he was the official priest and religious figure for the town now but because he felt he was being extremely gracious by coming to visit John P and offering to include him in the arrangements for the transition from the old rickety church to the new, larger, and more appropriate one that was close to town, easy for the people to visit, had tall towers stretching purposefully towards the heavens, and a real bell to ring for the events that warranted it.

The truth of the matter was, however, that he could not arrange his first mass, because all the churchgoing citizens were at John P's sermon. Nicholas didn't say that, and he may not have even realized it consciously, but that was the reality of the situation. It could be imagined that if hundreds of interested people were waiting for a mass in the new church, Nicholas would have had no reason to even think of John P today, let alone visit him.

Nicholas went on to explain his ideas about the transition. John P was much appreciated by the Church and its delegation and was to be commended for his ability to rejuvenate and maintain an interest in the Church amongst the townspeople. He was to be mentioned specifically in the first mass and given accolades and other rose petals from the pulpit. Nicholas even thanked him in advance for the help he could surely count on in directing John P's "wayward" congregation back to the confines of a true temple. There might even be some husbandry work that John P could undertake, hopefully with some compensation if the collection plate was sufficient.

What an honour indeed! The new priest would bring many important books with leather bindings and gold inlays that would only be from a very important source and surely hold the Word of God.

The impact of his remarks and the collision with reality that John P felt caused him a considerable adrenalin rush and played havoc with his equilibrium. Of course the Church would have to attract the very same churchgoers John P did. What else could they do? But John P had never considered the possibility that the new church and the new priest would be sheepherding his flock from his pastures to their own. Confusion turned to anger and then to resentment and then to confusion again. Yes, they would have to discuss this in great detail!

Broccoli cooked the same way each time could become a dreaded dish.

The Philosopher and Transition

Following his discovery of the cottage and the overpowering emotional and spiritual impact it delivered to him, the Philosopher attacked the pen and paper he now kept ever ready in this small abode. He was flush with thought and inspiration, ready to hammer out the disseminations he would detail to his readers, never wondering for a moment if the newspapers would actually publish them.

Despite his racing mindset and eager pen, he found it most difficult to begin. He wasn't sure how far back in the epic of man he should travel or how much initial insight he should afford his readers. He pondered the questions for some time until they had gone full circle in his brain.

Just start writing, he told himself. *The flow will come, and the words can always be rearranged!*

He jotted down his thoughts, a little jagged though they were, and patched together a loose facsimile of what he actually felt. Upon completion of the first draft, he realized it was wholly inadequate at expressing the strength of his visions, and during editing he found it rather choppy and lacking in clarity. He fought with the written pages for several days; realizing eventually that he would not be able to express his revelation in worldly words, for there was no vocabulary capable of doing so. It was such an individual and personal experience that even if he could recreate it in text, no one would understand it.

During a return trip to the cottage, he was undeniably surprised to discover someone else had been there. Some repairs and maintenance had been performed. He wondered if he was indeed trespassing on someone's private domain but scuttled those thoughts with a reaffirmation that no one person could own the view the cottage provided or withhold the panorama from others. It opened a door into the self that could only be experienced individually, that had to be experienced in solitary reflection, a personal journey voided by any other presence.

The theme gained momentum, and the Philosopher detailed such thoughts in his best form. His lifelong struggle with the value and authenticity of the religious institutions that regulated his parents remained in questionable status, and this clarity of thought brought some relief, if not explanation, to his dilemma. He wrote for some time, borrowing thoughts and observations from other essays previously unpublished and combining them with a renewed flow of words to create a suitable reflection on his current revelations.

With his dissertation complete and fully edited, he waited only for the morning to begin the descent back to the real world far below. He slept soundly with various visions and dreams dancing in his unconscious mind, dangling their snippets of memory onto his unsuspecting consciousness.

He slept beyond when he wanted and awoke with a sense of urgency. The sun was rising towards mid sky, and he had hoped to be back in town before supper neared.

As he packed his final items and tucked his writings away, he heard an unmistakable crunch of footsteps nearing the cottage. Instinctually, he held his belongings tight and watched the door with anticipation.

When it opened, there was only the shadow of a man cast against the bright light outside. He wasn't sure who was more surprised, because he could not see the man's face, but he was certain that neither of them had anticipated the other. That thought gave them common ground.

Their meeting was brief and friendly. Both men had been there before, and both had seen telltale signs of the other. Neither felt a sense of possession over the cottage, and they shared comments on the beauty and indescribability of the venue. The Philosopher mentioned his writings, and his new companion, Joseph, indicated he would enjoy hearing them. After some light encouragement, the Philosopher agreed to read them, and both men settled in for the occasion.

—

On this great journey to understanding, in our effort to recognize who we are, we make vast assumptions and draw monumental conclusions. We begin with a sense of complete knowledge and even a perception that we are fully capable of recognizing the raw soul we carry and diagnose the various ailments that afflict it. We toss about witty comments on the paths to salvation, we whisper our remedies for others who may be spiritually troubled, and even shake off unfavourable self-evaluations as momentary quirks in our otherwise fluid existence.

As is often noted, but not always agreed upon, we enter this world an empty vessel, unfettered by sin or confused with dogma. We have our inherent capacities to initiate us, reflexes to set our bodies in motion, instincts to guide our first behaviors, and archetypes to capture our essence and help build it steadfast. We would not spend a lifetime lying prone on a pedestal while the world functioned around us, leaving us disconnected physically as an invalid, deriving strength of body as a witness only. Nor would we spend that lifetime cocooned in an isolated chamber, void of study and learning, merely existing without any intellectual capacity or growth.

Yet, this is what fate befalls our psyche, our spirit, our soul when we fail to introduce initial building blocks and cornerstones as a foundation, and we allow it instead to be shepherded into the hallways and chapels of religious dogma, where we are purportedly cast into the living world after surviving the competitive, violent, and serendipitous process of creation in a state of soulful bewilderment. Yet, we hold some expectation of inherited enlightenment, as though the mere fact of being born would provide us the tools necessary to hammer out a magnificent statue from the roughly hewn boulder that our soul actually is.

We build ourselves over time, seeking education to fill our mental void, reading and writing to communicate and enhance our lexicon, and knowledge to boost our value to either an employer or a social community. We sharpen our physical attributes so they conform to our preferred standard and enable us to travel life with some physical ability and perform in sport activities with rules and regulations shared by the other participants. Yet, in many cases, we shelter our soul and spirituality from our own psyche, choosing unconsciously to allow ourselves to be led and swayed by characters who prey on the fragile ego we are trying to support.

The discussion between the mind and the soul is a personal and demanding one. Unlike the physical world into which we emerge, the internal world has no boundaries, no rules, no councilors, and no roadmap. We evolve in a scattered stream of ideas and inquisitions, tumbling about in an eternity of possibilities, probabilities, and uncertainties. From there we begin, but why we begin with a conscious belief that we are in control of this spiritual universe is itself another mystery. That all souls reside in this vast darkness to begin with is a great accommodator. It provides common ground when we look into another's eyes or share another's sorrow and joy. We are often troubled by the lack of order and undefined boundaries of this internal universe in which our souls swim. We make a commitment, large or small, to understand it better, to manipulate it somehow and perhaps even organize it. And when we lose such ambition or fall exhausted and void of such effort, we can slide into a depression and a feeling of distress, a certain melancholy that wears away our spiritual strength, unseen by our fellow travelers but often more powerful than any physical illness we must fend off from time to time. It can plunder our hopes and dreams, ransack our sense of worth, and perhaps even steal our will to live.

So this journey to self-understanding and self-awareness is an important one. It requires much energy and commitment but holds much reward when the barriers are cleared away, even slightly. Here sits an individual, forever wondering of existence yet unprepared to unravel any part of the mystery. An individual unarmed with any standard tool or weapon and alone with his or her internal thoughts, doubts, and questions, lashing about in the darkness without a clear objective, just firm in the realization that continuing the battle is essential for his or her well-being.

Most individuals stabilize this spiritual uneasiness and coexist with it comfortably for significant portions of their lives, a sort of spiritual truce, the mind recognizing that a wandering spirit can be devastating to existence and the soul recognizing its host is unable to suffer beyond what it can bear. Occasionally, this fragile armistice is breached, and episodes of re-evaluation or panicked misunderstanding surface and wrench serenity from the soul, situations usually precipitated by emotional attachments to another, some sort of physical calamity, or some other sudden change in the structure of life. All in all, it is an easy target for missionaries, spiritual scavengers, pontificating clerics, and other wolves of the soul.

Into this world of uncertainty and confusion steps the institution of religion, all religions, with a gasconading vocabulary describing rich and sturdy structures of support for the lost soul, winged journeys to sunlit meadows with good fairies fluttering about, a legion of warriors bent on delivering certain salvation, and the ultimate prize: an everlasting kingdom of milk and honey. Who can resist? So, our lack of understanding, driven by an impotent attempt to embrace the battle for our spiritual development, leads us humbly to the feet of the knight in shining armour on the steed of religious sanctuary.

Apprehensive of this long inward journey we are challenged to take and buoyed by the accessible alternative presented, how easy it is to be embraced by those theological loving arms of forgiveness and sheltered from the turbulent storm that swirls within. Those manning the Church bastions are skilled seducers and shepherds tending the baffled flock, well aware that the strength required to make such inner enlightenment possible is elusive, requiring much soul-searching and contemplation. Antithetically, we are coaxed with superior efficiency to avoid such journeys and embrace an alternative road within the Church, where we can rely upon wiser ecumenical masters. They provide us physical objects to touch and feel, letting our conscious mind find peace and comfort in their solid and tangible form. Crosses, altars, pews, cups, curtains, and other otherwise common objects suddenly gain a higher value and buff our souls into shiny caldrons for our spirit. In this way, the Church fuels our inner cowardice, all the while keeping us paradoxically attached to its righteousness, preaching the value of the inner journey while providing superficial belief in external objects. It is the very reverence with which the objects are held that necessarily depreciates their value. The Golden Calf exposed!

Hoodwinked as it were, by the powerful imagery and substance of the religious institution, peer pressure and damnation in tow, we lose sight of the internal objective. The strengthened ego is fed by the objects and becomes superficially immune to any spiritual enlightenment, content in the accumulation of material wealth and social status. The poor soul is sacrificed to the institution and left to swim among other searching souls, waving the banners of their particular church proudly and ready to die for what they think is "their" belief, especially if death is at the expense of some different, distant, and obviously ignorant banner.

God and his namesakes are externalized as great leaders, so distant and aloof that they must provide sons or facsimiles to act in their stead as saviours of the lost souls riding on the factional crusade. He remains unattainable at all times and even unapproachable except through the Church and her emissaries. The idea of finding our God, both personal and collective, within our own infinite internal universe is heresy and punished swiftly by a social death sentence. And this is not to exclude the so-called Eastern religions, wrapped in a different cloak but similarly attached to the collection of the soul. In simplified terms, substituting the object with the dream is no more different that exchanging cash for jewels.

The paradox continues further as these saviours agree to swallow the sins of lost souls, by definition making the sins objects and not responsibilities, providing absolution without consequence, itself a great contrary. With sin, responsibility for it, and absolution all residing outside the inner universe, what purpose does this vast internal space serve? Some transcendental contemplations of the self notwithstanding, this leaves us hollow shells spiritually, and completely dependent upon an external belief system to get us through the drudgery of our lives.

Instead of being born with a clean slate, an open road of adventure and discovery waiting for us to explore in harmony and tranquility in a world of shared space with our fellow beings, we are anointed as sinners at the moment we slip from the womb, straight into a seething purgatory of sin and corruption, already strapped onto the road to perdition with only the good Church to break our fall. Bumbling along in a beehive of daily struggles and under the external ceremony of religion, the soul loses all ambition to develop and rests in the shadows from whence it should have burst.

How can we deal with the concept that God is omnipresent yet somehow unable to reside in our spiritual world, and only approachable through an institution built across the backs of non-believers? It is fundamentally absurd. Since this inward journey of spiritual soul searching is so personal and esoteric, God must be connected to all. This would foster the idea that the spiritual universe itself, infinite and esoteric, is actually a single infinity that all can access through that exclusive key: being alive physically. Even though we cannot relate to this vast malaise of randomness, chaos, and mystery at first, we can establish some building blocks of understanding on which to deconstruct the significant confusion we encounter. Were it not for the preconceived imagery and standardized dogma of our religious institutions, spouting doctrine in tight conformity to capricious texts, melting historical interpretations with significant poetic license, we might actually, instead of figuratively, become enlightened by this wondrous spiritual journey.

God, in his infinite forms, images, and conceptualizations, holding court in the center of the spiritual and collective universe for all to perceive in their own way, under their own light, can accommodate every whimsical approach regardless of the worldly nature, learned speculation, or naiveté of it; whether they be kings of lands or peons of the soil. Without this inner connection, we remain void and solitary, unable to embrace the very principles described in the elusive texts of dogma. We cannot employ the traits espoused so frequently by the great preachers of the faith, for we are incomplete in our spiritual growth and ill-prepared to grasp the concepts of shared happiness and brotherly love. Born with a black cross on our foreheads, sacrificed by indoctrinated parents into the clutches of an unknown evil empire that is bent on wrenching us from our individuality and fitting us into schools of unoriginal thought, we remain cattle at the trough.

When we do not journey and our soul is offered to an institutional dogma instead, there is no development, no adventure, no struggle for understanding, and no ensuing enlightenment, because the strength of our spirit lies dormant and unfulfilled. Our acceptance of a preordained covenant and attachment to external objects to represent our souls, offered as a pathway to salvation, is a lie perpetuated by institutions or, perhaps more accurately, embraced by us, because we lack the initial influences, guidance, courage, and perhaps even the desire to battle inwardly and construct our faith in an individually honest and hopefully rewarding manner. Like lying on a pedestal or languishing secluded and sheltered in a chamber, we allow our souls to become slaves to the object of religion and void of any real growth or individual advancement.

The danger herein lies in the lost value we have for ourselves, for we lack any true individual enlightenment, and perhaps worse, we see our souls blacken and contorted, leaving them incapable of embracing happiness and joy but troublesome in their potential for evil and malicious deeds. It is as though we are sitting in bleachers watching the Church wage war as our surrogate soul, both manifesting the enemies with which to clash and then claiming the victories on our behalf. If we are vigorous but polite spectators, we are rewarded with a promise of heaven and eternal life. All the while everything happens outside our lives with destinations created like candy to lure us into the clutches of the institution. The internal soul remains stunted with only chaotic black matter swirling around, lost and homeless, uncontrolled, and with the potential to surface at a whim; yes, the beast within!

This scenario provides the Church great power over the "lost" flock. Facing the inner darkness requires superhuman strength, while surrendering to the institutional object is hopelessly easy. Beware! The relief enjoyed is hollow and truly unfulfilling. If we were, on the other hand, from the first moments of cognitive life encouraged and guided to seek our inner selves and build our own internal pathways and bridges to joy and contentment, to seek and perhaps find our collective God, the one inherent to our existence, the same deity the Church chases for us, then we might find enlightenment and understanding individually as well as collectively. Would it not be a wonderful Church that facilitates that process and gathers us unto one another to share and support each other's journey instead of admonishing us for unknown sins and bullying us into conformity of thought and expression with whips of guilt and threats of a fiery death?

We are born with "god" somewhere deep within our being, primordial and obscure, an eternal spark that flows from generations before and after simultaneously. It is a rugged landscape indeed that we inherit from our ancestors and through which we are challenged to navigate. It is the process of seeking our god that builds us into creatures of value, compassion, hope, and understanding. That some will travel further than others and some will find the light more illuminating than others is expected and in complete harmony with the diversity of existence. Some will also wander from the path, misdirected into dark valleys or subterranean canals, turning them bitter and dangerous, void of the very qualities we seek.

For such poor misfortunate souls there is an inherent and collective responsibility to enforce control and ensure they do not bring harm to other unsuspecting commuters along the path, assisting them with rehabilitation and reconnection with their journey. Still others will become completely lost and struggle to build even the most fundamental spirituality, remaining emotionally comatose as their lives unravel. Our god, our deity, our light hovers deep within each of us, and it is the same one for all of us. It can be viewed, embraced, chased, and otherwise engaged from an infinite number of angles and directions—closer or further, brighter or dimmer, higher or lower—but it is collective and shared between us. It has been propagated that it is not the light itself that needs to be demonstrated but the mere existence of the light and our pursuit of it that must be understood. People must know there is a light, that there is an individual of value within, so they begin to unravel it. It is a gift from evolution and creation and is no more separable from us than our reflexes or instincts.

Finding our path to this light is an internal journey that builds our spirituality as we travel. For most it is a pleasant and steady journey, though not without some hardship and disappointment. What of value is ever an easy capture? For a few, the path leads close to the light and shines vibrantly down on the traveler. It is here that final tests are faced, the commitment to enlightenment confirmed. It should not be assumed that enlightenment is a desired end to one's journey, for the journey itself is full of reward and happiness. Just as the absence of all light makes us blind, immersion in complete light has the same effect!

It may be at this wondrous stage that a final confrontation between the ego and the soul ensues. If the soul wins and true enlightenment is achieved, the individual may enjoy great understanding and awareness, an insight to be shared with others or not, solely at his or her discretion. When enlightenment is so close and the ego takes control, the traveler may fall prey to feelings of superiority and power. Now he or she can look "down" on those below, striding along on their own journey, and wonder at their ineptitude and ignorance. Such an ego so close to our collective God might gain visions of grandeur, glory, and even immortality. He might even start a religion.

—

The Philosopher completed his words with that sarcastic final remark and then looked up at Joseph. He was fast asleep!

The Stranger, Dust and Doubt

Moving slowly into town, the stranger glanced left and right, taking in the situation without ever moving his head. Julian saw this. He had his own way of catching the traits of others. The eyes were the best way to learn of someone's intentions. A stranger arriving without fanfare or fatigue and no clear destination or any gaze of wonderment, obviously wanting to appear inconspicuous but contradicting that by being different. How easy it was to spot people who were different in appearance or action, but how difficult to spot those who were different in intention or diversion.

Julian was a regular in the area. You might even say he was part of the local landscape. People could walk by and say hello without realizing it. They might even forget they had seen him. It was the casual hello people tossed at the familiar, not the sincere one they offered to a friend or the passionate one they heaped on lost companions and close relations. Julian didn't like to say those casual hellos. He wanted to be more sincere, but it was impossible to engage every person he saw, especially as he was so well known. The stranger didn't know him though. He hadn't said hello either.

Carrying his head slightly bowed so he wasn't obvious, Julian concentrated on the stranger's eyes. The stranger was shifting his line of sight too quickly to catch this, and he wasn't looking for eye contact either; he was looking for something or someone else.

After the stranger passed, Julian lifted his head and stared more directly. As he did, the stranger lifted himself slightly and turned his body halfway around and his head all the way around, staring directly into Julian's eyes. Although a little startled, Julian was far too familiar with first impression consequences, and he broke into a kind smile and returned the stranger's stare. Diverting his eyes and pretending he wasn't looking would have been the wrong impression. Holding his gaze and smiling was both non-threatening and welcoming. The stranger read that right away, too. He was obviously a veteran stranger! The stranger moved off into the immediate future, rounded the corner, and departed from sight. Julian was curious about him. He had no expectation of seeing him again.

A couple of days later though, they met face to face. Julian was leaving the café en route to visit his friend, the Philosopher, when he turned a corner and nearly bumped into the stranger. The man was leaning against the edge of a dusty wall, one hand in his pocket and the other sliding through his hair like a giant comb. He was a little out of breath and seemed agitated by something. More importantly for Julian, he tried to conceal his distress with a poorly conceived look of nonchalance. It was clear that something of some significance had just transpired in the stranger's life, but it was equally clear that his efforts to conceal it could only be questioned at the cost of any future conversation.

Julian noticed a tiny fire smoldered through a small gathering of garbage by the edge of the street, and he wondered if that had anything to do with the stranger's comportment. Julian decided it was preferable to let any information of the situation flow from the stranger unsolicited, so he just excused himself for the near collision.

"No need," the stranger replied, keenly aware that Julian recognized there was something asunder and had been courteous enough not to pursue the issue.

They stood for a moment, a sort of awkward moment. Julian reached for some small talk, but the stranger spoke first.

"There's a long distance between where I've been and where I'm going."

Julian looked at him, waiting for more information that would contextualize that statement, but nothing came. He wanted to reply but found no suitable retort. After another uncomfortable moment the stranger spoke again.

"My problem is ensuring that I am not actually returning to where I've already been."

Another chance to reply. Another lack of offering one. Instead, the stranger walked past Julian, turned the corner, sauntered up the sidewalk, and slipped sideways into the café.

Julian was a little uneven in his thinking about these comments. Were they literal, figurative, casual, or spiritual? He always thought things were spiritual. Was it a riddle? Was he supposed to follow him? This was a strange stranger indeed.

Julian started to shuffle on with his day, but after a few steps, he realized he could not. He turned and followed the stranger's path into the café. He spotted him sitting halfway along the wall with his back to the door. The stranger knew Julian was going to come in, and Julian knew he knew it.

One of the staff approached Julian to query if all was okay, but Julian held his hand up to elicit silence and moved toward the stranger's table. He did not want the stranger to know it was his café, for that always modified the behaviour of Julian's conversation partners.

Using the table as a support, Julian swung into the seat opposite the stranger. He could see the whole café in front of him. The stranger could see only Julian.

"Are you thinking about the last time you took a trip?" the stranger asked.

"Not really," Julian replied.

"Are you thinking about what trip I'm taking?"

Julian shook his head. "Not necessarily."

"Then what's on your mind?"

"Well, actually, I've been trying to figure out why the dust always settles on my porch in such a great quantity compared to other surfaces long the street."

The stranger raised his eyes and looked into Julian's. He gave the slightest of nods; either confirming that he understood Julian to be the café owner or that he appreciated the complexity of the dust accumulation. It was the former, and after a few moments of quizzical pensiveness, he offered his retort.

"That's almost easy. Your porch attracts a lot of customers, and their movement around the café, walking and sliding in and out of chairs, keeps the chairs dusted, displacing the content and pushing it towards the porch, making the rest of the area look dustier. You also obviously clean quite frequently, which has the same effect as much of the dust is merely displaced by the dry dusters being used. On top of that, the larger traffic itself stirs up more dust, much of which comes off the clothing of weary travelers or carefree frolickers who frequent your establishment, along with their dancing partners, who kick up even more dust. Beyond all that, you are particularly sensitive to the dusty conditions and notice it more when it is attached to your private space, when it appears to tarnish that which you hold dear. And finally, your terrace is located across from the apex of two intersections, so the natural funneling of breezes blows street dust directly towards you."

After a short pause, during which Julian scanned the whole of the café to better understand the stranger's explanation, he realized that his analysis, as quickly drawn as it was, could not have been more correct. A sudden clarity fell upon him, and he understood completely that his small café was destined to be a dusty one.

"I suppose my style and location will inevitably attract dust then," Julian said with a sigh.

The stranger looked at him with a little surprise and then held his hand up as if to say, "stop" and pursed his lips before continuing.

"Your comment is true, but you have lost the real purpose of the dust. You feel it is there to hinder your life and darken your strength, but the reality is far from that. It is actually a catalyst for your success and enjoyment during the short and confusing time you have on Earth."

Julian looked at him with more than a little confusion but without remark.

"Don't forget that the dust rides in on the breeze. It is this same wind that keeps a nice breeze blowing across your guests' heated brows and makes your terrace desirable for relaxation and conversation. The dust also keeps them thirsty and prone to greater consumption of your various brews."

The stranger's reply was more data, detailed and accurate, than Julian had expected, although he knew better than to underestimate the unknown. He considered a witty response but concluded none would be welcome.

"Can I offer you some lunch?"

"Sure," said the stranger, who was now significantly altered in his physiological state, having regained normal breathing and parked away from whatever it was that had been making him distraught.

After a short pause to gulp down their nourishment and find a more comfortable spot on the veranda to sip their iced tea, the stranger broke the silence.

"I answered your question with as much honesty as I could muster. It may not have been what you expected, but it was genuine."

"No doubt," Julian replied, "and it was indeed a little bit off the edge."

"Is it reasonable then for me to ask a simple question of you as well?" the stranger asked.

Julian looked at him and spread his hands slightly while raising his brow and curling his lip, as certain a sign of "sure" as his body could muster.

The stranger's question came out with a little pop, "Can you tell me if I'm heading into new territory or just recycling my previous experiences?"

Julian thought about it for a moment, not too long but long enough to show he had thought about it. After he thought enough time had passed that the stranger would think he had thought about it, Julian replied.

"Let's order more tea, and then I'll share my thoughts on that question."

They sipped their iced tea and watched the town go by, pedestrians safe and secure in what would happen next and who would wander by, untouched by the insecurity of the moment and impervious to the inner workings of the conversation between the two men in the café. From afar, Julian and the stranger might appear to be discussing the upcoming weekend or perhaps the weather and its lack of variety or even the alternate life paths that could have been charted were it not for a little serendipity.

After consuming the iced tea, down to the last rattle of ice in the bottom of the glass, Julian began his approach to the stranger's dilemma.

"I would like to respond to your question with vigour and consequence," he began, "but it is not a simple question you have posed, so first I would like to request some elaboration, or rather information, on your irregular past. I have three simple questions that will no doubt help strengthen the sincerity and value of my response."

"All right," the stranger replied, "if they will assist you to assist me, I will answer them with candor and limited speculation."

"Firstly, I would like to know from where you came," Julian said.

The stranger delivered his response quickly as though he fully expected this question, or perhaps he had just answered it several times in the recent past. "I come from somewhere distant and dark. A place where hunger is a weapon and the spirit is captive to the whims of unworthy guardians."

This response was a little more esoteric than Julian had expected, but he recognized the stranger was no ordinary stranger, even if he was a veteran stranger, and his few words were not meant for trivial discussion. This would not be a simple "I come from the east, and I'm heading to the west" response. Not likely. Still, questioning the response to his question was out of the question. He continued as if the stranger's answer was perfectly clear and concise.

"Question two concerns your path to this point and what major turns it has taken in the past few years," Julian said.

"That's easy," the stranger replied, again without hesitation. "I have travelled from that place of darkness to a new world, one of hope and expression. Once I cancelled the greatest of demons, I climbed from the black hole I was in and turned my heart from anger to calm and my feelings from spite to pity. I was hoping to afford the guardians forgiveness rather than pity, but I could not find it anywhere within. It is a search I continue to undertake."

"No doubt," Julian said, "forgiveness is a lofty ambition encumbered by much of our basic instinctual behaviour."

"What is the third question?" the stranger queried.

"I would like to know what regrets you have carried and the weight they have built into."

The stranger was not quite as prepared for the third question as he was for the first two, especially since it was actually two questions with two very different answers. He began to answer a couple of times, holding back before any actual words came out. Eventually, he took a deep breath and sighed slightly as he responded in what Julian perceived to be an almost apologetic tone.

"Not long ago, I had many regrets." He slowed his words slightly with more than a little pensiveness. "But reality is that now I have only one, and it weighs heavily on my life."

Julian leaned forward slightly in his seat anticipating the stranger's declaration. It did not materialize. He waited a few moments wondering if the stranger was just pausing to collect his thoughts for expressing his regret. Finally, he lost patience and held his arm out, palms up.

"And it is?"

"Oh," said the stranger, "I thought that would be obvious. My only real regret is leaving behind those I shared the blackness with and failing to protect my fellow foundlings who suffered, and may still be suffering, in that wretched dark hole out of which I was reborn. I should have found the will and the way to free them from the burdens I escaped, but I ran too fast and too far to act upon this regret in time. I pursued a personal reprisal and retribution agenda at the expense of a more compassionate and collective one."

"Is there no opportunity to return to this 'black hole' and remedy that burden?" Julian asked.

"Well, that brings me back to my question, doesn't it? Whether I am heading towards new territory or just recycling my past experiences."

Julian sighed so the stranger would know he was considering the remark. "I see your point, but I'm not sure I would view it as such. Your answers have provided much for thought and pondering."

After a few more shuffles and more lip pursing, Julian continued. "I would appreciate the opportunity to respond to your question after having a while to consider what's been revealed. Shall we dine again in the morning? This will give me some time to measure my comments."

"Sure," the stranger replied without surprise.

Julian wondered at his easy agreement to a delayed reply. Perhaps he was appreciative of the time Julian was prepared to give in weighing his situation, or perhaps he wasn't that interested in Julian's response at all.

Julian also offered the stranger lodging for the night, which he accepted readily. It was clear he was weary, maybe even very weary, but from what was not easily determined. Was it from the travel and tired miles of road or was it the weight of burdens he was lugging around the countryside?

With that mystery foremost in Julian's thought, the clatter and clang of the evening service at the café was almost a blur. Regulars came and went. One server was ill and had to leave early, but her counterpart stepped up and carried the load. As often happened, a small argument broke out between two farmers dueling over exactly where their fields met and who had the right to harvest the last line of produce. It all finished with harmony and last call. Then Julian retired to his room, and the stranger, who had observed the evening's folly, to the spare bedroom upstairs behind the office.

The spare bedroom was nothing spectacular, but it was certainly comfortable and close to a bathroom and shower. The stranger utilized both, washing away the dust of the day, or perhaps even a piece of the decay that comprised his quandary, and soothed his stress with the hot stream of water.

The stranger woke early and dressed before descending to the café. It was not yet open, but the kitchen was not complicated, and he moved over to start a pot of fresh coffee. His experience in large institutional kitchens was significant, and he had little difficulty in getting things humming.

He glanced around at the surroundings, simple and efficient as they were, and then strolled out into the sitting area to watch the town rolling to life along with the rising sun. He poured a large cup of the freshly brewed coffee before dropping into a chair next to the window. A few early risers spotted him and wondered what he was doing in the café before opening, but he was relaxed enough to appear as though he belonged there, and they took no action.

The stranger barely noticed them, engulfed instead by the underappreciated beauty of a simple dawn and the world of possibilities it was bringing to all as the day grew from it. He was careful not to judge the day or those waking into it. It would be mundane for most, exciting for some, and life-altering for a few. He thought about those still with the guardians and shook his head slightly knowing that they seldom looked forward to a new day.

Julian crawled from his slumber with the aroma of coffee tickling his senses. He was enjoying it with a slight curl of a smile when he realized there should not be such an aroma in the air before he made it so. He threw back the covers and hustled downstairs.

As soon as he spotted the stranger over by the window, he felt his body relax as he realized he was the one who had ground and brewed the beans. Julian sauntered over to where the stranger was lounging and sat down while quietly refusing his offer of a cup of coffee. He never let his eyes stray from the stranger's brow, hoping for some small revelation as to his early morning demeanour before sharing his thoughts on the yet unanswered question.

The stranger waited patiently, but when Julian suggested breakfast first, he made it clear that the answer was expected before then.

"I will be leaving before breakfast. As a matter of fact, I would have left some while ago were I not waiting for my last piece of luggage."

"What luggage?" Julian asked.

"Your answer to my question, of course. I am hoping it will lighten my load."

"Why do you feel I am even capable, never mind worthy, of answering this important question?"

"Because you were concerned about dust, which tells me you pay attention to that which others may take for granted. It tells me you are concerned about the appearance of your café and, therefore, have a fairly high level of self-esteem. Although you have referenced God, indicating a belief in his existence, I note also that you have no overt religious artefacts within your café, telling me you do not conform to either the whims of patrons or threats of clergy. That might indicate I can expect an unbiased response and, at the very least, an honest consideration."

Julian appreciated the words of confident evaluation, accurate as they were, and realized the time had come to reply. He had pondered the night before and developed some opinions, though they could not really be considered conclusions.

"Your path is obviously an emerging one and far from a worldly landscape. Therein lies the dilemma. If it were merely a road to be travelled, it would be easy to return to that which weighs on your soul. I surmise then that your route is challenged by both the dangers of wind, storm, and highwaymen as well as the burdens of soul, faith, and charity. Two distinct yet tangled roads indeed."

The stranger nodded slightly, feeling even more certain that Julian would be able to provide some beacon in the restless night through which he wandered.

Spurred on by the nod, Julian continued. "It is difficult for anyone to depart from what is comfortable, even if that which is comfortable is also brutal. I come from a stinging past, littered with hardship, and what I felt very much was injustice. It was only upon the realization, spurred by the guidance and consultation of close friends, that I recognized I was ultimately responsible for myself and only valuable as a guide or mentor to others when I was powerful internally as an individual. I could not walk their miles in my own shoes, so to speak. But there is more than that even, as my good friend the Philosopher often details. We must each find an internal resolution, a personal light if you like, that can bring us some sense of purpose and genuine value. We need this internal progress in order to be of value to others, especially those who have not yet pondered such inner assessments."

Julian paused for a moment, just to be sure the stranger was not repelled by his offerings and to ensure the comments were not being delivered in a monotone type lecture. Realizing neither was the case he continued.

"Once you have come to terms with yourself, your internal nature, and not necessarily with others you hope to provide assistance to, for they would also need to be active participants in any such revelation. The journey to self-realization is empowering and affords the opportunity to bring the most value into the world in general and, more specifically, into the lives of those preferred. Become who you can be and who you want to be first, and then you can help, literally, to save the world. If you try in vain to consume the burdens and hardships of others, like some sort of self-sanctifying atonement, without first building your own character and self-worth, you will be doomed to drown in an inevitable flood of anguish".

"In direct response to your first query, I suggest it is not what you are doing but rather what you will do. Your confusion about your journey is piled on your doubt about being able to be effective in your self-appointed task of salvation. But the real question is whether you are capable, without first making a strengthening and illuminating journey of self-realization, to find a path towards purifying your past through the liberation and emancipation of those struggling under the same sad destiny that you were once burdened with."

Julian had much more to say, both he and the stranger knew that, but time was ticking, and the day was fully dawned. The café had to be opened, and the road had to be walked.

The stranger smiled in appreciation of Julian's offerings. He flipped a small medallion with his thumb, leaving it spinning in the air before landing in his palm.

Julian spotted the outline of a crescent moon and five pointed star. As the stranger's hand closed over the medallion, Julian reflected that it was unusual.

The stranger smiled again and slid it into his vest pocket. He raised his cup for a final swig of cold coffee and then rose up through the strength of his hands pushing against the chair arms. He nodded, and possibly winked, at Julian, and then strode toward the door.

Before he went out, he turned back and stared directly in Julian's eyes. "What is your name, café owner?"

Julian told him, but he didn't ask for the stranger's name in return, as he seemed very private and mysterious, perhaps preferring to be nameless, but the stranger offered it just the same.

"Mine is Tection. Hope to see you soon." He closed the door and turned left or right, away from Julian's view. It was a strange name, but he was obviously not a stranger anymore.

As the dust continued to swirl and float, dive and settle around the café, Julian reclined emotionally and was far from bothered by it. It was a part of his life, good and bad, that was going to be there until he moved away from it physically.

A short time later, in an otherwise uneventful day, John P came by the café for a visit. It was a rare occasion, and Julian was pleased to see him, lunging forward to hug his friend and clamouring on sarcastically about what a pleasure it was to be graced by his presence. It was usually the other way around, with Julian venturing out to the old church in order to share a little time with him. John P explained that he had been in town to visit a sick member of his congregation. Julian expressed his concern, but John P assured him it was not that serious. Julian offered his best wishes just the same, and the two men sat comfortably for a late morning espresso.

Julian felt easy in the preacher's company. Theirs was a close relationship born from shared experiences and lived adventure, though the gaps between their times together had drifted wider recently as they both went about living their lives. This morning was casual and quiet for both of them though, a chance to relax and chat, to share company like they use to do so often before. Julian knew his friend had a seemingly unwavering faith in his beliefs, or at least a thick veil over any insecurity that might have dwelled within, so he was a little surprised when John P reflected casually on some spiritual misgivings.

"I am perplexed to understand why I continue to have doubt even when those around me seem able to accept faith and religious values daily without questioning it. Why are my doubts more frequent and more troubling?"

Julian thought long and hard on this perceived dilemma and was cautious not to answer too swiftly, thereby trivializing his friend's concerns. He was also conscious that some reply was necessary, as the young preacher would otherwise feel somewhat abandoned and perhaps reticent to approach Julian in the future. Although the comment had been offered in a rather impromptu manner, Julian recognized it as significant, because John P was all about faith and the embracing of it.

As he contemplated an appropriate response, Julian reflected back on his conversation with Tection and the duality of his dust problem. He leaned forward into the conversation and offered his thoughts with no objective other than to enlighten himself as much as his friend.

"That's almost easy," he began. "Your life is so full of faithful people that their certainties and comfort with their faith highlights your own doubts. You struggle to reaffirm your faith so frequently that every doubt gains more prominence than it deserves."

Julian looked closely at John P, wondering if he was out of line to make such assumptions about someone who was much more learned about matters of faith. John P stared back at him with a little surprise at the nature of his remarks but without any sign of discomfort. Buoyed by this reaction, Julian continued.

"In addition, you spend time regularly with people who do not hold the same beliefs, and though they do not try to change or criticize your faith, their influence cannot be easily disregarded.

Sometimes you yourself are overly sensitive to your doubts, because you want faith to be an easy adventure, but you don't want to give in to a belief without questioning it."

John P shifted in his chair, trying to capture the full value of his companion's words.

"You hold close two separate groups of associates," Julian continued, holding his hands outward like scales of evidence, "those with near blind faith and those with a distinct void of such classical faith. As you gather friendships and gleam some wisdom from each group, you struggle to come to an internal consensus."

John P nodded, half in some current understanding and half in the knowledge that he would have to reflect further on these comments before gaining a full understanding.

"Don't forget though," Julian went on with even further clarity of thought, "that these conflicts of ideas are also the drivers of your intellectual and spiritual growth. I think you should be pleased to have these doubts and accept them as affirmation that you are a growing, expanding, and uniquely diversified individual. There is no obligation to find and attach yourself to a single belief structure or philosophical genre at any age, let alone while so young. In actuality, we should all share a small bit of envy for the diverse and challenging position in which you find yourself."

Julian sat square and direct to John P. It was the first time he had ever assumed the role of scholar in their relationship, and he felt a little awkward but also quite confident in his expressions. The young man looked at John P, who had not said a word, and cocked his head slightly.

"Let's have another drink"

The preacher looked back at Julian, still a little dumbfounded at the intuitive and perspicacious content of his remarks, and cocked his head.

"Where did that come from, my friend?"

Julian shrugged. "I don't know. I guess your faith is a little bit similar to my dust, that's all."

John P could not capture the analogy, but his coffee cup was empty, and Julian's offer of a fresh espresso seemed like a good idea.

Later, Julian recounted his conversation with the stranger, and John P nodded with a slight smile on pursed lips, shedding a bit of the curiosity Julian's analysis had spawned. When Julian mentioned the stranger's name, Tection, John P sat up, noticeably surprised. He explained that Joseph, the priest from their hometown, the one who was like a father to John P, the one to whom he had been saddest about saying goodbye, the one who let them sift through the basement library unhindered, had spoken often of his great friend Tection. He wondered if they were one and the same. But of course they were. With a name like that, there was no doubt.

Julian's Dream

On one of those endlessly sunny, bright, sea breeze mornings that whisked Julian's life to a plateau of comfort and contentment, on the porch of his café, freshly tabled and chaired, fate delivered a middle-aged couple and one of life's ironic twists.

As Julian moved from the interior dining room to greet the visitors, menu in hand, he recognized them—his parents! The exact emotional disease from which he had run away: selfish, unloving, dried-out souls, lunging through life with nothing but greed and regret to steer their course.

His adrenalin rushed, and his body trembled. He had placed them so far back in his recollections of life that he was sure they would never surface again. In that moment though, they were yanked straight up through his being, bumping and grinding his fragile spirit as their memory elbowed its way to the surface once more. They had no idea their son was about to walk out the door and serve them the coffee they had been craving since their early morning journey commenced.

Julian reached out for the back of a chair, still inside the café and concealed from his parents' view by the reflection of daylight across the picture window. His parents sat idly, their backs to the café, chatting with unrecognized words while gazing harmlessly out at the street flowing by. Julian sat down, feeling weakened and unstable from the high blood pressure his heart was delivering.

He looked around, seeking someone else to serve, hoping he could excuse himself from waiting on his parents, letting them drink their coffee and fade away once again to the distant past. But no one else was there. It was still between breakfast and lunch, so the kitchen clerk was running errands, and the lunch waitress would not be in for an hour. His visual search for an alternative was as useless as a broken egg on the ceramic floor. He had no choice but to confront the situation.

As he came to this realization, he also became emboldened. These two had brought him enough pain in his life. There was no way he was going to let them back into his psyche to wreak havoc on his unsuspecting soul.

He marched purposefully out onto the porch and delivered the menus in the most deliberate and nonchalant manner he could muster.

At first, his parents didn't realize it was him. After all, why would they look at the hired help when they sought only a confirmation from the menu that their coffee of choice was available at this dusty little café? As they looked up to order though, a shocked expression spread across their faces. Words were not immediate. Julian peered back, holding the artificial demeanour of waiter to customer.

His mother reacted first, beginning to rise in what might have been an attempt to hug him, but Julian held his hand out, palm open, and froze her in place. She relaxed back into her chair, still unable to procure any words.

"Where have you been?" his father blurted finally. "Do you realize the concern we've had; the time we have spent looking for—"

Julian held up his hand once again, blocking the words before they could reach him. He asked them politely, as a good waiter would, if they would like something to start. They looked at each other and then back at him, as if sharing the same neck, and ordered some coffee.

Julian fled back to the sanctuary of the café and released a huge sigh. What a battle that had been. What a struggle to confront, between the evil his parents represented to him and the good of the café. He realized immediately that he had fought and won that battle internally in just those few moments on the porch. It would be all right, he told himself, just before he raced ahead in thought, realizing they knew where he was now. Would they return again, unannounced and unwelcome? Would this end his desire to remain at the café? Why had this happened? How could they have walked into this small out of the way spot, but a speck in the dusty trail of life?

He stood behind the counter and prepped the coffees instinctively, his mind otherwise occupied as he let his hands do the work without direction or distraction from his brain.

As he brought the coffee out to their table, he saw the cat saunter over to his father's leg and rub against it, as cats do. The cat knew this usually brought him some attention, and this big round leg looked like another opportunity for a good neck scratching. Julian's father was a wholly uncompassionate man, however, and he pushed the cat away quite roughly with a sideways swing of his leg, mumbling something about the uselessness of the species.

Julian lunged forward, balancing the tray in one hand, and grabbed his father's shirt below his chin. His anger was more than evident, and his parents received his action with utter disbelief.

After a moment, he loosened his grip as he regained a sense on control over himself and the situation. He slid the tray of coffee onto the edge of the table and crouched down, bending his knees but not kneeling, bringing his eye level below that of his father, who remained glued to his chair.

"I am more attached to that cat than I am to you," Julian said. "Be very careful not to disrespect him again."

His father had no reply. What could he say? He looked over at his wife and threw his head in a sideways nod, indicating they should leave. They stood, and he almost pulled her away as she looked back at her son, standing resolute and somewhat defiant on the top step.

"Don't worry," Julian said, "the coffee is on me."

He never saw them again. More importantly, he never thought of them again. He gathered the cat onto his lap as he sat down and took a sip of his father's coffee.

A little bitter, he thought as he added a healthy spoon of sugar.

He told no one of this encounter, preferring to let his parents' memory slide quietly out of his body and into the damp earth the unexpected late afternoon shower was steeping.

His last contemplated recollection of them was later that night as he lay in bed with the orange fur ball nestled against his left foot, feeling happy that the event had transpired, as it provided some final relief for him from a burden he had not realized was still superfluous baggage in his ever-growing closet of memories.

Later that week, following a busy Saturday night that eventually delivered a most welcome bed and blanket, Julian shuffled restlessly between the cotton sheets enveloping him and the vivid visions that surrounded his sleep. The quiet of the town square howled silently across the patio of his café and scattered amongst the tables and chairs stacked neatly and ceremoniously against the exterior wall.

The cat curled into a single form on a small pile of dirty linen not yet captured from the night's revelry, with only a single perked ear confirming that more than mere fur lurked within. It had been a difficult week. He had dealt with the memory of his parents, but other visions rose in his head, some unknown and others unwanted. Though he tossed and turned, at least he slept. That in itself had been difficult to do for the past several nights.

As he slipped deeper into the mysteries of his unconscious, unusual events and unexpected situations claimed him. These new visitors to his dream did not frighten him, but he was most curious about their origins and their intentions. His attachments to the conscious world seemed further away than ever. He wasn't sure how he knew that. Surely it was not a conscious understanding that his consciousness was drifting. He knew he was sliding deep into unknown space, and he was a little surprised to realize he actually wanted to be there. It was not so much the appearance, or even the possibility of help within the experience, but the promise of some possible revelation that might remain with him when he journeyed back to the corporeal world. Many times he had pondered the question of which reality was more valuable, the boundaries of the days among the living or the vastness of the potential beyond that, even if that world, too, was shared by many. His conscious world now put to bed, he drifted forward into an unconscious dreamscape.

—

Julian lay on the surface of the water. It was shallow but he could not feel the bottom even though he thought he should be able to. He hovered, not flying or swimming just floating. But not on the water, more like in it, like he was part of it. He rolled from back to front, from head to foot, like a gyro without axis or gravity. It was a pleasant though unusual feeling.

As he adjusted to the sense of his mobility, he glanced down at his feet but saw nothing. He could feel they were down there attached to his legs, but he could not see them. Nor, he realized, could he see his legs or arms or body, even though there was brightness surrounding him. His entire body was there but unseen, invisible but not hidden.

A moment of panic followed, an acceleration of the heart, a tingle of limbs, and a mist of sweat. But that passed. He relaxed back into his circumstances. There was no discomfort or tangible conflict. What a wondrous feeling actually, freedom of movement without responsibility towards, or consequence of, gravity. Only in this vast world of dreams was such fantasy possible.

Julian lost himself in the magic of the moment, twisting and turning upside down and inside out. The horizons around him were painted with blended colours and woven lines of no particular purpose.

As he bathed in his blissful pool of nothingness, he did not notice the mountains forming around him. Just shallow mounds at first, they crunched and crashed together pushing upwards silently into great towering peaks, pillaging the very crush of formation that had built this world. By the time Julian recognized what was happening, the mountains had surrounded him. Tall walls of stone herded his ethereal sea of nothingness into a liquid canyon.

Julian felt trapped suddenly. The almost mystical feeling of unobstructed freedom crashed around him and evaporated as he tumbled around the canyon without purpose. The mountain walls had grown insurmountable and continued to contract into his space. Fear dove into his heart, and he searched frantically for escape from the collapsing stone.

As the canyon's complete disintegration seemed inescapable Julian pounded on the stone walls. It seemed futile, but little else was possible. He screamed with a foreign voice and banged with unseen fists. Moments before certain and complete destruction, his hands punched through the mountainside and broke free into a cave that lurked there, just waiting for a poor panicked soul to provide a chance for it to invade the valley. As if some great force within the mountain had heard his cries and finally broken through the stone barriers, the nothingness spilled from the canyon into the cave like water flowing its course.

Julian rode the currents into the mouth of the cave and was consumed by the darkness within. He bobbed and banged along the corridors on a raging stream of energy without pain of collision or concept of destination.

Somewhere down an offshoot channel, he heard his voice echoing a warning to return to the café. It was a frightened call. It was his own voice but from many years before, from the sad and painful times of his childhood. Or perhaps it was his voice from some distant time, a future yet unrevealed.

He tried to redirect his flow into the tributary that held his voice, but he could not navigate. There was no substance to influence his flow. His voice was lost behind him.

Then another side channel approached. He could not see it. He could only sense it, feel it. As he drew closer, he heard his voice again, calling, pleading for him to come towards the sound, to avoid the path he was on. This was a different voice. Although still his, it hailed from a different time, from a different point of emotion. Again, he did not have the ability to redirect his course. Despite his pleading, the energy on which he sailed carried him obdurately forward, oblivious to his efforts or pleadings.

This event repeated itself several times, and each time Julian tried to maneuver his flow towards his voice, he failed. Once he realized the effort was futile, the voice and the side channels stopped approaching.

He continued to travel this black and unyielding space at an accelerated speed. He was falling but not as a victim of gravity. He was a passenger on the flow of energy, driving forward, or backward, without horizons. The speed and the silence reached a crescendo. His heartbeat crashed like a landslide into his lungs.

Just when the flow reached what seemed like a point of no return, a point of explosion, the flow began to thicken, to solidify, slowing him down and letting his energy dissipate into it, like being in the pit of an elastic band as it draws taught. When the momentum of the energy flow reached the moment of equilibrium with the elastic flex, and all movement hovered for that slightest instant, waiting for action or reaction, he felt an amazing moment of calmness and serenity. Then the moment exploded, and he was thrust through the elastic membrane that was once a cave wall and tumbled out into a glorious midday sky under a blue and cloudless canopy to lush green fields and rolling hills far below. But he did not fall towards

Mother Earth. He floated down gently like a feather dancing on a warm breeze.

And there were others, hundreds, even thousands, bursting from the energy membrane into the sunshine and fluttering downward. Many already lay, smiling warm and soft on the carpet of grass and fern that bathed the valley below. What a beautiful place to be. What joy and happiness radiated from these surroundings! It seeped into the pores of existence, fueling harmony and beauty within it. He had transcended the terror of the cave to the purity of the valley. Julian wondered why his voice, his many voices, had tried to call him away from this direction.

As he floated down to his final resting place, he noticed an expanding brown patch on the ground. It seemed to grow outwards as water does on dry cloth. Others floating down with him noticed it as well, trying helplessly, or more precisely, wishing that their flight might not bring them within the sphere of this patch. But Julian realized his path could not be manipulated, and this patch of brown was his destination. Others so destined looked at each other with expressions of bewilderment, while those fortunate enough to be headed for the huge green pastures looked on with surprise, which turned to pity.

The closer Julian got to the ground, the clearer his landing spot became. Small spikes of steel or bone sprang from the ground, which bubbled as if molten rock or boiling earth sat there. Despite his renewed and invigorated efforts to avoid the cavity, Julian touched down.

The spikes pierced him, the earth boiled over him, and the flow of energy collapsed over his being as he sank into the ground. He was horrified. Shots of flame licked at his presence. The others who had descended into the pit with him turned ugly, their faces contorted and twisted. Some blackened and shriveled before him. Others wailed helplessly at their predicament. Julian wept to himself, although he thought he heard his own voice wailing in tragic harmony with the others.

He sank further into the ground. Hope drifted away, and desperation engulfed him. As he spun aimlessly, capturing the vision of those around him, he realized he must appear the same to them. Why had these few missed the beautiful green valley? What was their offense?

Julian sank further. As his desperation gathered strength over his essence, he saw a soft, glowing hand pierce the fury of the raging pit. Many others reached for it but tumbled by helplessly, resigned to some unknown horror further down the depths of the abyss.

Julian reached out as well; with all the strength and extension he could muster. His fingers touched the hand, and it glowed a little brighter. The arm extended, and gentle fingers slid around his forearm, holding him firmly but surprisingly without any pressure. His descent into the hole slowed to a stop. The arm was warm and soft, warmer than the heat of the pit. It pulled Julian sideways towards it and then up and out through some unseen hole in the burning walls of the pit.

Julian's heart raced, and his spirit cried out silently as he slid through the wall up onto the green mat that was the valley floor. He paused for a moment, tears on his cheeks and gratefulness in his heart. He turned and looked upwards to see his saviour, unable to believe his eyes as he peered into the radiant and relieved face of John P.

After a moment, John P turned away and gazed back towards the pit. Tears rolled down his cheeks, and sadness ruled his posture. Julian wanted to shake him, to tell him everything was okay, that he had been saved. But as he saw

John P return his arm into the pit in search of another victim, he realized his tears were for those not yet saved, or more precisely, for those who would never be saved.

Julian lay back down on the grass, totally exhausted and bewildered by the course of events. A large orange flower bent towards him, urged on by the breeze that drifted across the valley. The pedals of the flower stroked his face. He lay there forever, his eyes closed, the breeze drying him off, and the pedals brushing the dirt from his face.

Suddenly, the valley began to crack, as if it were made of glass—or was it ice? The scene fractured around him. John P toppled over, shattering into thousands of splinters. Julian didn't see it; he just felt it. He wanted to call out, to save John P, but the reflection from John P's splintered being produced specks of light that grew in unison into an enormous and aggressive light stream, firing directly towards Julian.

—

Julian raised his arms to protect his eyes from the brilliant onslaught of morning sun gleaming through his window. It took him a moment to regain consciousness and focus. He opened his eyes and looked up into the face of the orange cat stretched peacefully on the pillow beside him, licking the sweat from his forehead and the salt from his tears. He reached up and stroked the purring animal behind its ear, a small smile curling his lips. Then a curious frown crossed his brow. The dream remained vivid in his mind for only a moment, but the crux of its message lingered. The vision of John P as his saviour was easy enough to digest, but the shattering of his image was an omen he was not prepared to examine, a forewarning of the separation they were destined to experience.

John P and the Light

As might be expected, John P continued to search for the truth, not only deep in the light but also in the shadows that grew from the light. He reflected that bright light could be blinding as it captured our attention but left little revelation or discovery from within the brightness. As we adjusted, the shadows fell softly around its glow. Many sharp and simple shadows lay dark and dimpled around the light's point of impact, but more distant and dramatic ones began to be recognized as the eyes followed the flow of light. It could be the light that created the shadows, but the shadows were what gave the light its character. They defined its purpose and gathered effortlessly around its emanations. What would the light be without the shadows? Nothing more than an empty promise of clarity, a curiosity for memory.

Was the relationship between light and enlightenment a metaphor for that between God and Church, or perhaps between truth and gnosis? John P was unfamiliar with the light examination process. As a matter of fact, he could not recall any previous experience with it. He was certain there were moments in his younger life, somewhere in his past experience, when he had encountered the light, but he was unable to draw upon any memories that revealed when and where. His previous curiosity for the memory had been so underdeveloped that the foundation of those memories was well entrenched in the hidden drawers of his past. Now he had a greater interest in the light. He wondered with a renewed curiosity for a while before a more urgent and intense desire to explore and understand took hold of him. This, in turn, grew into a significant interest, almost an obsession with a journey to understand and digest the significance of this experience. In a younger man, as John P was, little significance was given to the shadows that surrounded the light. The light itself was enough of an anomaly to enthrall his curiosity and sufficed to consume the attention that might have drifted into the shadows.

Now, with a more learned part of his mind being stimulated, John P had a tremendous revelation centered on the importance of the shadows. The shadows actually revealed the light, although the light created the shadows. It was such a symbiotic relationship that he was surprised he had not recognized it earlier. Light in itself was a useless and brutal tool if it had nothing to illuminate and no one to observe its illumination.

As he realized that his previous astonishment with seeing the light was actually a rather juvenile emotion, he felt a wave of understanding caress him like a soft pool of water encompassing a hot and thirsty traveler. It even bothered him that he had spent so much of his life without embracing an understanding of this perspective or even a realization of its existence. A whole different landscape was unraveled in his mind, and concepts of reality were crushed by this sudden understanding that the greys of his black and white world were lurking in and around those shadows. Visually, these shadows were merely occasions where an object intruded into the light's journey toward its destination.

Metaphorically, the shadows became thoughts, emotions, and concepts that battled perception and understanding and challenged belief and betrayal. They were the third dimension to a flat spiritual existence.

John P reclined at his small desk and held his head away from the light. His eyes softened, and he relaxed into a semi-sleep-like state, not completely unconscious but certainly relaxed enough to enable his thought process to unbind from the rigours of consciousness.

Did the truth exist without knowledge of it? Did God exist without followers to worship him? Could the world and its masses believe in a truth based on the knowledge they were provided or acquired? Similarly, could God be defined by the projections man made of him? Were the anger and hatred generated by subtle differences in the various religious projections of God a service to God or a disservice to the projection altogether? It certainly seemed to John P that the indoctrination of selected knowledge, sliced from the truth with a star, cross, or crescent, diminished God's value, limiting him to but a handful of the many possibilities he embraced. Like the love of a child, there was always enough for one more. The emotion was not diminished or diluted by additional embracement. The truth could not be diminished by a more complete knowledge of it. God would not be devalued by an encompassing tolerance of faith. Sharing the knowledge and embracing the growth of faith would deliver it more power and more understanding. Every person safe within yet shared without, sliding gleefully among the shadows of truth below the glow of light that shone within and the shared knowledge that flowed without. If spiritual existence and faith were natural phenomena of humanity, then religious confinements were created, and that which is created is not natural. A conflict was emerging from the battlefield of his known dogma.

In the full circle of love and hate that John P had witnessed in his life, in the battle and building that had developed, the understanding of what mattered to him and what was real for him was clouded by spiritual authorities that floated arrogantly in and out of his thoughts. Images and ideas that had been developing for millennia were hardly prepared to be questioned by such an adolescent soul. Yet, from within this vast spiritual landscape and conceptual allegory, John P was able to call upon some obscure understanding from an unknown origin and see the faint light of hope riding on his visions of angel wings, and his path was illuminated by the light, as yet un-sourceable, that grew into more and more light yet was covered in the confusion he felt towards his purpose and place within this landscape.

His mind swirled among the pictures that his religious studies had painted for him. The battling angel perched upon the rocky outcrop unaware of the horned demon crouched and breathing fire below him, lurking close at hand while his thoughts and dreams perused the distant landscape seeking opportunities to fulfill his destiny. His trusted sage, somehow aware of the danger but unable, or maybe unwilling, to warn the great avenger of the imminent threat. The story was destined to end in a crash of calamity and a struggle of forces that, in the great scheme, had almost no significance. What was this battle for?

While this scenario played out, other reflections on his learning breached his thoughts. The wise and wonderful earth mother wobbled forward on her crumbling cane, hard pressed to place one foot before the next, embracing every living thing. She harboured no ill will or judgement based on the beliefs or commitments of humanity. She had an obligation to all that was living, but she was being eroded by the will of institutions and the humiliation of all forms of discrimination and intolerance.

So much was occupying the living in their lives, the gathering of belongings and properties and gold. This was not a new revelation for John P. Every philosopher, preacher, and politician throughout history had reflected on the values of wealth versus knowledge, of possessions versus passions, specifics versus spontaneity. And each and every one of them was unmistakably right and wrong. Such was the grey nature of black and white. Yet these cravings for wealth, status, and power lay ever swirling in the corridors of each person's castle. John P saw his clinging to the walls of his worn out chapel and illuminating his visions of a new and wonderful structure to house the followers of his sermons. He was distracted by the prospect of a new and grandiose church building, one that would require much contribution from the congregation, especially in cooler months when the heating costs would be significant. But they would, he reminded himself, have official pews, an official altar (probably even blessed in an even more important church before being brought to town), official crosses and effigies, and alas, even an official priest. A very dark shadow did that illuminate!

It was clear to him at that moment that he was less useful to these souls than was a warm loaf of bread. He was a place they could go to cleanse their remotely managed spirituality while they waited patiently for instructions, promotions, and policy. He was a convenient connection to the rhetoric they had been fed, and whether truth lay in its doctrine or not, it was better to err on the side of caution. John P was a more accessible and less demanding pulpit than were the rigours of the institutions of forgiveness. Besides, as he knew they perceived, he told tales of their lives with reference to their realities, sparing them the burden of great tragedies and shoulder-bending responsibilities towards the heavens. With John P, there was a less judgmental and more understanding community, and he knew this was appreciated. He was counting on it to gather his flock into a less cynical and more contemplative place. His original vision, of being a deliverer of the value message for the journey to seek individual truths, was corrupted by the realization that he was more accurately providing the soft landing that allowed those he chased to actually lay down their quests and ride on the river of his ramblings. Did the light of God have any value without the shadows cast by the institutions serving him and the multitudes of worshipers born into the shadow of their ancestor's sins, never able to step out of the shadows? Even when leaving their own shadow behind, they were imprisoned by that of the institution. How he longed to shepherd them out of the shadows!

Meanwhile, under the hammers and mortar of builders, the new church grew strong and proud within the town. It neared completion and was adorned with symbols and sculptures of history. It had representations in marble and story-laced glass to demonstrate to the people that they were about to become a more important group. The visitors buzzed about the strength the new edifice would hold, not only physically and as a temple to the testament of faith but also as a demonstration of the will and interest the town was receiving from the Church and, by transference, from the glory of heaven itself. The young priest would place his hands on the controls of this glory machine and drive the forces of evil back to their rightful place—into the hearts of non-believers. John P knew this perception itself to be a far greater sin than any other sin these individual followers were remotely capable of producing.

The Church seemed content to have her followers chase the gold of wealth and privilege, exclaiming gleefully that such persons of wealth should, could, and would make greater contributions to their cause, to secure their own glory and salvation. John P felt that it might be more important to find some balance in their lives before they tried to save the world. After all, if the new church was not quite so magnificent, it would not have cost the town quite so much. This building was really the dream of some expansion-minded visionary at great distance from them. It was a plan and execution without consultation and invaded the pocketbooks of every person in town without providing an opportunity for them to discuss its merits and costs. And there was no escape for them; repentance and salvation were not to be undervalued.

Once John P realized the threat he posed to the Church, he began to understand why there had been such lack of dialogue with him towards a transition from his abandoned little church to the new cathedral in town. He understood a little better now that he could not coexist with the new priest. He would be a contradiction to the forces that drove the Church and a nuisance to the full implementation of the new religious direction. It became clearer to him that the new priest was dwelling in the shadows now, fearful of alienating John P because of his popularity among the townspeople but holding no intention of sharing the spiritual wealth the town possessed. John P would have to go, but could the Church get him to redirect his flock their way, or would they have to crush him and steal them back? John P could hardly take a breath as he realized the distasteful shape into which reality was morphing. Could he hide in the shadows that toppled off the beam of light heading his way, or would he be caught in the open with only his forearm to shield his eyes from the powerful stream?

John P sat quietly and contemplatively for some time after gaining this insight. Yes, the light was shining on him, but the shadows were lurking all about. He reflected on all that he had hoped to accomplish as a preacher, the good he hoped to bring into the lives of so many. He had never anticipated he might be perceived as a counterproductive force in the social and spiritual community of the town. He wanted only to be a positive light in their lives. Would he be forced to criticize the Church in order to gain understanding from his followers, or would he be pressured to turn them around and into the arms of that which he felt was an ill-advised path? Would he have to sacrifice his dreams to avoid the self-destructive challenge of being at odds with the Church? Weren't they chasing the same result? How had it come to such adversarial conditions? How was it that the brighter the light shone, the more shadows it revealed?

John P rose up from his chair and paced slowly through the old building, his hand rubbing his chin and the back of his head alternatively, as if trying to massage a clear understanding into his thoughts. Lost in his contemplations, he paid too little attention to his path, and he stubbed his toe quit firmly on the corner of the altar steps, tumbling earthward with his hands forward to break his fall.

He rolled onto his side to lessen the impact and lay still for a moment, smiling sheepishly at this circumstance. As he pressed down to lift himself up, he glanced towards the far wall where the sinking sun sent beams of light through the stained glass and across the altar to capture his shadow. It was an eerie, twisted projection that he saw, just for a moment, his hands planted on the floor giving the shadow an appearance of hoofed front legs and the candles from the altar framing his head like horns, his shoulder providing the accompanying snout. Surely a demon with nothing but evil intentions. His spine tingled at the false reflection of his position, and he lost his grip, collapsing back onto the floor once again, breath sucking from his lungs. His legs cramped tightly together as shivers vibrated through his being. What a terrible vision.

He lay motionless for some time, all kinds of crazy half-formed thoughts racing through his brain. Was it an omen? Was that how he actually saw himself, as a horned beast? Was that how he was perceived by the Church? His flock? Was such a shadow cast honestly by the fading sun, or was it manipulated somehow by unknown forces or, worse, by his intuitive imagination?

He slammed his eyes shut for a few moments, his cheeks scrunched into his brow, framing the pathway of light in an effort to banish these thoughts from his mind. He wasn't sure how long he remained in such a tense and void position, but his facial muscles began to ache, driving him back to full consciousness.

He reopened his eyes with a sense of cleansing light filtering inward. After a few moments of recovery, he pushed himself upwards again, almost afraid to glance back at the shadow on the wall, but he could not prevent his gaze from returning there. This time, he saw something completely different. The sun had wandered lower in the dusk sky and shed an entirely different hue of amber light across the room, almost fire-like in colour and visual texture.

He reached up to hold either side of the altar table for support and glanced back over his shoulder to the far wall. His shadow had been transformed. His legs, now together, bore a resemblance to the stock of a post; his arms seemingly stretched against a cross, framed by the edges of the altar, and the candles, merely thorns in the halo that encircled his head. There lay his shadow, crucified by the soft light of a setting sun and silent in the pain of realization, a vision he saw more deeply for himself.

Julian and Sunday Morning

Julian wasn't sure about his future. Doubt and curiosity etched a cold border across his thoughts. He had already journeyed beyond what he had known as a child but had not scratched the surface of where his studies and readings had taken him. He knew that love had evaded him. He enjoyed the occasional liaison, much like his predecessor, which was provided by being the owner of the café, but they were merely luscious nights without substance. Love was one journey he dreamed frequently of taking. His young passions dancing, untainted by life and unfulfilled by encounters, hovered constantly on the edge of his mind. At the oddest of moments and during the least expected tasks, he found his thoughts drifting to a future filled with love and family. These diversions were like sweet strings of honey stretching across his dusty days.

In all the stories he had followed, love was the most common reoccurring theme. It ravaged and enthralled souls and shaped destinies of men, women, societies, and cultures. It possessed the beckoning paradox of being both reason to live and reason to die.

He tried to identify those things that carried such weighted value, life and death, or even happiness and sorrow. Even at his young age he had identified the combat of opposites that fueled life. It was not difficult for him to understand that any one thing was hopelessly attached to its opposite. Even the ultimate attachment of life and death was obvious, though he felt that life held so many more emotions and experiences while death was, well, death. Life could be shared casually, intermittently, collectively, devotedly, and even lived solitarily. It was unclear to him why so much of life was dedicated and directed by the penance for living it and the preparation for leaving it.

He was not oblivious to the fact that life always ended in death or to that fact that the fear of dying must have inspired the very concept of life *after* death. Why did those who wanted so profoundly to control and regulate life use death to do so? Regulated by the fear of retribution at death and controlled by the promises of life after death. It seemed to smother the joy that was life itself. Instead of experiencing and experimenting with the wonders that our senses and intelligence could muster, many spent their lives trying to follow the ordained path to death. Existing to serve collective memory instead of individual imagination, they failed to reach for the apogee their lives might attain and instead herded themselves towards the end, proud to be within the prescribed borders and fulfilled to see their children surrendered to the concocted dream of post-death paradise. It was difficult to follow the concept that life should be lived most attentively in a manner that would be recognized only after death, that life after death was the destination of life before death. Who on Earth had actually figured this out? He thought himself naïve to an extent for not being able to understand or appreciate this concept. He hoped no one would notice!

Even though he neither understood nor adhered to the principles of living in a manner that would help facilitate his life after death, he realized that many of his customers were dedicated to that idea. They almost seemed to be living to die as it were, as opposed to dying to live. He knew by the scowls he dodged frequently from mothers tugging young children towards the church on Sunday mornings while their husbands sat sipping coffee and cognac in his café, that a problem was developing.

The first time he asked a previous regular why he hadn't been around lately and got a reply referencing his wife's association of the café with the devil because it served alcohol on Sunday mornings and lured the otherwise committed away from the righteous path, he knew he had to make peace with the situation. Possessing only a small café, a few words of greeting, and a bottle of fermented juice, how could he possibly stand against a power that could deliver life after death? Hence, no alcohol before noon on Sunday became the rule. This was fairly well received among the general population, but it did not have the desired effect of returning his café to the good graces of those who did not visit it.

One particular Sunday, as he rose early to serve those dwindling customers who skipped church to sip coffee, now without cognac, on his terrace, the thump of the boisterous Saturday night still palpitating with his heartbeat through his swollen head, he had a moment of clarity. From that Sunday on, the café would be closed on Sunday mornings. This announcement was received much more favourably. He began to open the café only after midday on Sundays, ostensibly as recognition that God deserved at least half a day. He seldom had many customers seeking Sunday morning coffee anyway, as most of the townsfolk were listening to the wonders of life after death in the big new church. Those few he did annoy with his new policy would find other distractions during his "closed for church" period and return after morning gave way to afternoon.

On the other hand, those more ardent about the importance of Sunday morning dedication were thrilled with his policy and commented often on how the old café owner should have implemented such respect for the times of church service long ago. Some of them even felt that the café was now a suitable venue for an afternoon coffee and perhaps even a glass of port after church. Not only had he appeased the ladies who tugged children towards that transcendent steeple and earned a meter of respect from the townspeople in general, many of whom did not go to church on Sunday morning but nevertheless honoured it from afar, he had also provided himself a few extra hours of sleep to ring out the hangover that had haunted his Sunday mornings previously. It also occurred to him that if there really was life after death, he might be building up a small cache of credit towards its quality.

Later during the week, when reflecting back on what a simple yet significant and valuable decision the Sunday morning closing had been, he wondered for some time about other small and simple changes that might benefit his life. That there were opportunities to improve and increase life's livability with such simple decisions captured his attention for some time. It even pushed his daydreams of love and family aside, but only for a short while.

Indeed, Julian noticed a definite upturn in Sunday afternoon business. He even heard from some of his customers that the very knowledgeable, though rather young, priest, Nicholas, had mentioned his new policy during his general remarks at the service. This was almost an endorsement and enhanced his status greatly with the more devout portion of the community.

During one particularly inauspicious afternoon, Julian even received a "thank you" and "bless you" from one of the local ladies whose husband used to sit in the café sipping coffee and cognac on Sunday morning while she attended church. Now, as the café was closed during the church period, not only did he got to church with her, they both stopped by for a few libations afterward, usually leaving around midafternoon with much more than the washing of clothes on their minds.

As a matter of fact, on Friday evenings, after beer and brandy had broadened his vocabulary, the husband regaled his table with tales of his newfound love life. He was amazed how this short time of going to church with his wife had rekindled their affections and turned Sunday afternoon into playtime instead of work time. He lamented the idea that such activity brought chores to Saturday morning instead but was firm in his belief that it was well worth it. His colleagues remarked as well how spirited his wife had become and how carefully she seemed to be dressed regardless of the day.

Julian understood the fact that the church, and the couple's attendance there, received credit for turning their love life sweet, but he realized full well that the appreciation they shared thanks to the glory of the divine was definitely enhanced by three of four drinks from his bar. What a forceful team he and the church could be, influencing lives and spreading happiness. He wondered what other symmetries he might find between his café and the church. He was wise enough to know that asking the church "mothers," as they were known by the locals, those few ladies who not only attended every service and occasion but were also responsible for the social calendar supported by the church, for advice and guidance on how he might support their efforts further could be most endearing and cement the bridge that now spanned the schism of exalted worship and libertine debate. He could always beg off their suggestions with excuses of excessive costs or previous commitments, but if he could implement any of their ideas, even one solitary recommendation, he would definitely find a warmer spot in their collective heart. If unable to make them an ally, at least he would not foster an enemy within their perceptions.

And so were born the spring and autumn church bazaars. At the mothers' suggestion, and with the church's blessing, he sponsored and promoted what would become a semi-annual trade market. With unbridled credit to the ladies, and with the appearance of great sacrifice on his part, the event was born. What an opportunity for the church to travel out among the flock, the young priest to build relationships and friendships beyond what he could garnish through services, weddings, and funerals.

The bazaar became an overnight success. The townspeople were able to bring items that no longer held purpose for them and trade or sell them to neighbours who could use them, or at least wanted to have them to enjoy the thrill of barter and the promise of something new or different. Children's clothing was a favourite, passing down from one family of teenagers to another family of toddlers. Farm tools and utensils from retiring farmers were also passed on to the newlywed son-in-law of a friend. It also provided a venue for the freshly baked pies from that lady by the brown house with potted white flowers around the windows, who was able to make them taste better that anyone else, and for books or magazines that had long since been read by their original owners. Many people made sweets and toys for the children. Games were spawned spontaneously, and laughter painted the landscape of the city square.

The café did a burgeoning business with both tired hagglers and new negotiators all wanting a relaxed corner to consummate their deals or with the multitude that just enjoyed sitting and watching the event unfold before their eyes, not participating, just being part of the moment. Julian was allowed to have a small temporary booth at the bazaar; his lack of license for such a venue carefully overlooked by the local authorities as they sipped the reward for their blind eye. It was his most fruitful day of the year. What a great idea this had been. And it was so simple, as simple as closing the café on Sunday morning. And to think that all those times the old café owner had seen the church as a topic to avoid, if not an enemy altogether. Julian saw it as his trusted ally now and a conduit to new business and a new harmony. He even began to have semi-regular discussions with Nicholas, as he accepted, on occasion, Julian's frequent invitations to enjoy a coffee and croissant, gratis, of course, as it would be inappropriate to charge a purveyor of God's word undertaking a social task of merriment, for such a humble offering. Besides, it never hurt to have the priest sitting and savouring at his café. It was an obvious blessing and validation of the café as an acceptable meeting point; though it was also recognized that the priest should not linger too long lest the patrons of regular attendance or excessive consumption harbour concerns that they were being watched or evaluated.

Although they never discussed it directly, it was pretty clear to both Julian and Nicholas that Sunday had become a mutual time. The church had seen renewed vigour in the attendance, not only with those souls who could no longer sit patiently in the café while their lives were directed to salvation despite their absence, but a whole new group of people who came in the morning now because of the additional promise of social time in the afternoon. Those who had been indecisive about the ceremony involved with rising, dressing up, and participating in the service, an event that often made them feel guilty but also gave them some sense of absolution, could follow that up with a few hours of interaction with their neighbours after the service, enjoying some time at the café to gather for gossip and camaraderie. This made the whole process more worthwhile and, consequently, more alluring.

Julian recognized that this new social partnership made his café a valuable asset, certainly monetarily enriched but also socially empowered. It occurred to him that this would be the ideal time to sell it. He could surely support a transition in ownership and provide the acquirer with someone, perhaps even a veteran stranger, who possessed the necessary information and skills to maintain the current success. Julian's attachment to his dream of travelling was never more beckoning. But who had the funds he would demand for the café? Who had the interest and the assets to buy him out and free him from a future filled with obligation and commitment, though also some fortune? He wanted to travel and explore life beyond baked goods and bar supplies, beyond life in this now organized and predictable town. The only possible buyer he could think of was the church. They had exorbitant amounts of money and now a vested interest in the café as a Sunday partner. He decided to approach Nicholas right after the rather bizarre bazaar.

The Theory of Hungry Hearts

Following the departure of John P and his young sidekick Julian, Joseph rambled into a soft depression of sorts. Over the ensuing years, he lost interest in preparing his sermons and let his church fall into disarray. Without young curious hands to flip their pages or old priests to extract their messages, the books in his basement library gathered dust. He ate sparingly and drank shamelessly. The foundation of his life was cracked and weathered, crumbling into small chunks around the broken soul they sheltered. He was lonely despite his congregation, which was dwindling and decaying with his lack of energy.

By the time Joseph began to notice the same symptoms of the illness that had claimed his father's life, he was already contemplating the end of his own. He longed to see John P, to reveal the truth about their relationship, to look him in the eye as father to son and confess all the moments of pride and love that had been left dangling around the corners of the room for fear of discovery. He had much to offer the boy that he had not yet shared. Although he had had the opportunity to be fatherly on many occasions, especially after John P's mother died, he was never able to connect with John P in such a way that theirs became a lasting tie, a binding cord whose grip was known only by fathers and sons.

Joseph had come to terms with the fact that he was dying. He was destined to suffer the same fate as his father, melting away day by day in a bed somewhere, unable to care for himself and, consequently, being a burden on those who would have to do so. And who would those people, those caregivers, be? Strangers trudging through their workday, cursing the aged patients under their auspices who needed their assistance for even the most basic and mundane tasks, wishing they would pass away sooner rather than later or at least sleep most of the day. He had seen the unhappy faces circling around his father during the last months of his life, and even though the occasional bright and cheerful young nurse popped around the sick asylum, the general population had a collective sense of foreboding and, driven by endless dealings with sickness and death, was hopelessly void of empathy, humanity, or compassion. At least his father had his mother and him to visit and bring small snippets of joy into his imploding life. But who would Joseph have to tickle his life light? There was nobody left whom he cared about or who cared about him. Surely some of his practitioners would visit him and shed sympathies on his dying situation, but they could not be expected to share responsibility for any type of routine support during a prolonged palliative period.

Joseph worried about this, not wanting to complete his life journey as a burden on others still wandering on their own. If only his son knew him as the father he was. Then he might enjoy some last months of purpose and companionship. Joseph grew painfully cognizant of death's certainty as the hereditary sickness he housed continued its march through his body.

Joseph spent most of his time at the cottage or travelling to and from it. He tinkered with the structure, keeping the framework and contents in passable, if not good working order. It was his escape and private domain.

On one occasion, he arrived at the cottage and found a younger man standing at the kitchen table clutching his notebook like a child in the face of imminent danger. They were equally shocked to encounter one another, and after a brief and uncomfortable introduction, they recognized that each of them had found his serenity, if not destiny, out on the front porch.

Joseph was tired but polite and agreed to listen to the young man's dissertation on the need for internal spiritual commitment. The topic seemed interesting enough, and Joseph relaxed on the bed and leaned against the back wall as the young man began his oration. It was interesting to hear some original thought, but Joseph, weary from the long climb and previous week of labour, fell fast asleep. When he awoke, the young man was gone, no doubt chasing a more interested and vivacious audience.

Joseph came across the young man again sometime later and shared a nice conversation with him in the middle of the woods. Joseph was descending with a few planks and tools, the young philosopher climbing back towards the otherworldly vista. The young man was the only other person Joseph knew who shared his wonderment with the cottage. They chatted again briefly, the young man greatly interested in the benches Joseph had built and the accompanying stair he formed for an unsuspecting widow and her young son. Even though they could not articulate the powerful experience of visiting the cottage, they recognized that each understood the other's experience, perhaps in different ways but not without similar significance. Joseph always felt some intangible security of sanctuary in the knowledge that another soul on this vast planet was witness to the majesty of the cottage.

Joseph still managed to mount the pulpit on Sunday mornings, usually rehashing old sermons or reworking previous deliveries, but the kind of social and communal support normally inherent to a local church was almost extinct.

Monday mornings, indeed sometimes Sunday evenings, saw him back on the road to the cottage. There, he felt close to some greater existence. He was able to push the thoughts of physical mortality and failure from his mind to experience the beauty and serenity of the landscape afforded by the cottage view, languishing on the sturdy benches he had installed so long ago and comfortable in the belief that his next journey was pending, one that would bring him far away from his lonely life.

Joseph battled internally for some time with the demons of his sins. He had abandoned the carpentry profession for which his father had worked so diligently to prepare him, thereby ending a family tradition. He recognized that he had actually become a priest for two reasons. First, to spend a few years hanging out with Tection at seminary without care or responsibility other than some studying and reading, which were his passions anyway. Second, because he was hopelessly shy around women and felt being a priest would deflect his shame at never having a companion beside him, and perhaps even bring him honor for the great sacrifice he was making. How ironic it was for him that he had finally enjoyed the intimate company of a woman just as he was about to confirm his commitment to celibacy!

As a priest, he was expected to be celibate, and although he had conceived John P before his actual ordination, he had never revealed the fact that he had a son. He had lived the lie of his celibacy while dwelling but a few blocks from the mother of his child. As his self-pity mounted, he had allowed his church to fall into some disarray, and he suffered a growing failure to provide even the basic comforts and services his profession demanded.

The spiral towards depression spun ever more quickly, and soon Joseph lay lost in its vortex. He considered himself a failure as a son, a priest, a lover, and a father, yet he did not fear the journey to his next destiny. For all the sermonizing he had done, waving the threats of heaven and hell around the room like whips and salve, he realized he didn't actually believe his own rhetoric. His own passive descent into such melancholy had provided new insights and recognitions for him.

While preaching, he gazed across the hopeful faces of his congregation—the spirited elderly ladies so truly joyous to be sitting before him, the tired young workers happy to be through another week, children yet in wonder of this foreboding building to which they were brought each Sunday to be scared into thinking they were partially responsible for the collective actions of mankind and, therefore, fortunate to be able to choose a forgiving and reflective path through this esoteric great-grandfather called God.

What folly, he thought, as he spewed out the words and warnings he had learned so well from the Bible and accompanying texts.

Yet, his attachment to belief did not necessarily crumble his faith. He knew the importance of his church to the social fabric of the neighbourhood. It was where folks gathered on a regular basis, where they built friendships and embraced each other collectively in the spirit of community. And the children loved Sunday school. Parents were no doubt blessed, and the children were certainly fortunate to have a special young lady running the program, herself void of an ability to bear children but hopelessly enamoured by them. She would bring to life the stories of the Bible and perpetuate the true principles of joy, love, and friendship that young lives deserved.

Joseph's dwindling belief in the structured universe presented by the religion he embraced outwardly fueled his sense of failure and revealed a cold hypocrisy at the core of his life. He was comforted somewhat by the fact he was convinced he would not dwell in the flames and agony of damnation, and as his certainty of death became stronger, his desire to reach out for its result grew. Each trip to the cottage brought him closer to the edge, literally and figuratively, but the final catalyst was delivered by an unexpected source: Tection.

Joseph informed the elders of his congregation that he would be taking a short sabbatical of sorts, a break from responsibility to gather his thoughts and sharpen his dedication to the Church. These elders had witnessed his slow descent from vigour and his slide away from the exuberance and work ethic he had always embraced.

During the final, fateful journey to the cottage, one that began as so many others had, with some bark at the drudgery of life and some anticipation of the relief the cottage provided, Joseph walked along the steepening trail with his head bowed, seeing only the ground that lay a few feet in front of him, disinterested in the flowering life and endless hum of the wild forest around him. He certainly was not expecting anyone else to be walking along that day. He knew others also visited the cottage including the young Philosopher, as small signs revealed that, but it seemed that anyone who did go there respected the place and was careful to keep it clean and comfortable. There was also the occasional hiker, usually too distant to recognize or be recognized by, but other than that, it was a solitary trek.

On this particular journey, as Joseph left the trodden path and began his vertical climb, he was startled by the clear call of his name.

"Joseph!" cried a figure from the main path below.

At first, he thought it must be one of his parishioners wandering far from home, but as he peered up to focus on the source of the greeting, he stopped dead in his tracks and allowed his eyes to widen with the surprise and bewilderment that accompanied it. Tection!

Joseph was stunned momentarily, but then a great sense of excitement overcame him. He raised his hands like a young child would to greet his onrushing parents and called out Tection's name as he raced down the hill towards him.

The thick branches of the forest were helpless against the rush of bodies, and the two men embraced in a short spin that reflected their joy and helped decelerate their forward push. What a surprise! What a moment!

Joseph responded to the inevitable questions of how, why, and where he was going by explaining to Tection about the cottage and the surreal charm it held. Tection on the other hand found much embarrassment and consternation as he stumbled through an explanation excusing his lack of contact with Joseph, claiming it was fueled by his desire to erase a woeful past experience. Joseph was too happy to see him to dwell on such matters. With those words hanging in the air and lungs too consumed by the climb to be busy with chatter, they moved upwards through the forest on a path undistinguishable by sight but unmistakably embedded on Joseph's soul.

It took some time, but they finally reached the summit. Joseph tingled with the excitement of knowing Tection would experience the amazing vista for the first time. As he skipped through the cottage to open the front door, he noticed the Philosopher's notebook lying open on the kitchen table with a large number "8" drawn in a repetitive series of interlocking lines; a doodled figure eight. *What an odd drawing* he thought, *and what an unlikely item to be left behind by the young sage.*

He was momentarily consumed with his own memories of their first encounter and the step repair. They fluttered through his thoughts, and at some point he found they were actually words he was offering Tection. He wasn't sure when the thoughts and memories turned into verbal recantations, but they flowed with the easy comfort that defined the warm friendship the two men shared.

Joseph talked for some time. Tection, seemingly speechless as he drank in the view and its implications, listened with a hungry heart as Joseph gradually transformed his storytelling from casual joy at the panorama of the cottage to the brutal pain of lost love and imminent death. It was a seamless transition, and Tection was caught off guard by the casual shift of Joseph's dialogue. It became clear that Joseph was revealing his innermost feelings in a spontaneous manner but with deliberate intent. It was his confession, Tection realized, but he did not ascertain it was his final one!

Joseph laughed and cried as he emptied out the long list of memories and regrets, revealing for the first time to anyone that he had a son, John P, and that he had an incurable disease and a broken heart. Talking about all these issues, verbalizing them, was a dichotomy of sorts, providing some relief and softening in their telling of sadness on the one hand, but also delivering a strong and soulful reminder of the harshness he had endured.

Tection was captivated by Joseph's outpouring and even a little bewildered. He thought of his own life, filled with misfortune, and recognized that sorrow, like love, was merciless and infinite, corralled only by the strength of the individual and the randomness of emotional competition, greater sorrow hibernating lesser sorrow.

Joseph was always the better listener of the two, and he was comforted by Tection's patience as he unraveled his tale. It did indeed turn into a confession of sorts, and Tection was uncertain what his role was now. Was he a friend or a priest? But Joseph was not separating these issues internally. The disclosure of his darkest and deepest past reaffirmed the trust and friendship he felt for Tection. They both realized this was more than a mere conversation.

Joseph sensed that Tection also had more than chatter on his mind, so he took his turn to listen intently to the crazy past that Tection had not revealed previously. Joseph had always felt some sympathy for the harrowing history that Tection had already recounted long ago during that evening on the veranda of the inn. That there could be even more significant experiences yet untold was unexpected.

The feeling of comfort and ease they shared led Tection to find the courage and motivation to express his hidden history. If not a confession, it was at least a revelation for Joseph. The entire Winter saga, from an orphan's abuse at the hands of this devil to a priest's sacrilege and self-doubt fostered by his murder, was recounted in the usual varying degrees of detail.

Joseph listened in silent agony; shaking his head slightly from side to side in disbelief on occasion and closing his half-open mouth to swallow. What was clear was that the impact Tection's history with Winter had had on his life was more than meaningful; it was a catalyst for the very paths of existence he strode.

The two men sat in silence again, neither sure what words would be appropriate next. Finally, Joseph broke the silence by recounting a chance encounter he had had with the beautiful young chambermaid from the inn.

The tale of her exile to deliver the young boy she had been gifted from an unknown traveler and guest at the inn was barely fresh from his mouth when Tection leaped up and held his hands forward, as if to embrace Joseph's face but holding them firmly to the sides and shaking. He questioned Joseph about the timing. How long ago? How old was the child? Did she say anything about who the father was? Joseph responded with his best understanding of the situation, and Tection relayed the story of his wonderful night together with her at the inn. They pieced it together rather quickly after that.

A strange yelp escaped Tection's mouth as his head swung backwards and his hands slid towards the ceiling, or perhaps heaven. He turned in a circle, as if dancing, and finally came over to hug Joseph. The revelation and conclusion was hopelessly improbable but surely true. Her son was Tection's! Joseph went on to reveal that the boy had been placed in a local orphanage, and following the somewhat suspicious death of a priest named Brother James, had been moved over to the seminary, the same one that he and Tection had attended.

If Joseph was a little shocked at Tection's initial reaction to this news, he was subsequently astonished with the even more dramatic impact the reference to Brother James had elicited. He judiciously sat back, looking on with some lost wonderment. After Tection regained some calm, he explained that the man he called Winter was the same man who had been known as Brother James. It all came into sudden clarity for both men. They spent the rest of the evening bantering in quick and easy fashion reconstructing what was becoming an obvious chain of events. Tection had to find the mother, married or not, and connect with his son!

They headed to their beds, physically exhausted but emotionally vibrant, Joseph greatly relieved to have finally told his hidden story, and Tection spinning with the news of his son. Sleep was a difficult companion to find for both.

The following morning, they awoke only partially rested. After some trivial but cordial early morning dialogue, Tection commented on the unusual name of Joseph's son, John P. Joseph explained that the boy was to be the child of a single parent, and the "P" was a representation of the word "priest" in reference to

Joseph. He remembered how John P had asked often about the significance of the letter, but Mary had dismissed the subject with a comment about it being just a distinguishing component to his otherwise common name.

Joseph recounted again the great love he had shared with John P's mother and the drama life had delivered with her illness. As he retold these tales, he also began to reveal a deeper conflict that tore at him from within, his betrayal of his vows of celibacy. The child had been conceived and raised while Joseph was professing his priesthood and the commitments that accompanied it. To live with a daily reminder that he had not adhered completely to those commitments perpetuated a gradual erosion of his self-worth. He reflected that he had not really articulated it before, but once he began his ruminations, the words flowed out in another river of negative self-evaluation.

Tection tried valiantly to reassure Joseph that small deviations from the path were not only common but also even expected. After all, who was perfect? But Joseph was not appeased easily. He considered his broken vows and endless secret of fatherhood to be significant and brought much guilt on himself by reaching conclusions that God had punished his insolence by taking his lover and son from him. His analysis subtly but ultimately left him convinced that he had doomed his lover through his disobedience to God, and he had been called upon to "sacrifice" his firstborn to make further amends. Tection rallied another round of reassurance, but the battle was lost long ago. His words only fanned wisps of smoke from the dead embers of life's fire.

After a full morning of mutual support and several cups of harsh coffee, Tection departed from the cottage, anxious to begin his search for his wayward son and promising to return to continue their discussions and revelations. He extracted a promise from Joseph to wait for his return and not do anything foolish in the meantime. Tection was certain he could help Joseph overcome his distress. Joseph was content for the moment with his friend's sudden joy and shared vicariously in the emotion.

Following Tection's departure, Joseph's thoughts trickled back to his son and the realization that the very joy Tection was about to embrace was lost to him forever. Joseph clutched the small wooden cross with its golden tip that John P had given him when he moved into the church following Mary's death. He carried it around his neck at all times.

He tried to stay busy with some puttering and reading of the Philosopher's journal, which sat curiously on the kitchen table. It was unlikely that one so passionate about his perceptions of life's struggle would be careless with his notes. The presence and content of the book confused him further, but in all instances he slipped back into his assumption of guilt, betrayal, and loss.

At one point, he lapsed into a trancelike state for several hours, waking only as he realized the sun was setting. He did manage to stroll out onto the front porch in time to see the last rays dwindle across the horizon in a final wink for the end of the day, a day that was gone forever as well.

The following day, Joseph was even less energetic. He didn't eat, sipping only a small amount of water to wet his lips and tongue. His appetite was lost, and his will to continue dancing with his sorrow and guilt slid from his psyche. He found his last joy in a final sunset, embracing every moment and turn of colour that convinced him that his purpose and contribution to life were exhausted.

For the first time in recent memory, he slept peacefully, letting his thoughts and then dreams wash over the great memories of joy and love that had permeated his life—a time of pride in his father's eyes, of love in his woman's, and wonderment in his son's. He plucked moments of time from his history and corralled them into one glorious dream. He longed for such moments to be his again but realized they were hopelessly elusive.

In the morning, he felt serene and complete. Regrets had been buried and debts paid. His friend Tection was safe and happy; soon to be happier, no doubt.

Joseph lamented at the eroded relationship he had developed with God. He was certain, with his sins towards his responsibilities as a priest, he was receiving some sort of punishment. How had he travelled from a time of wondrous joy when he had received his church, one close to Mary and John P, with nothing but bright skies and hopefulness ahead, to his current situation, with all lost or dead and hope but a sunset in the sky?

Joseph stepped out onto the porch, slipping closer and closer to the edge until his toes passed the pressure of earth. The midday sun climbed eternally into the center of the earthly universe, and Joseph closed his eyes, leaned forward and washed in the eruption of adrenalin that exploded through his body. He couldn't breathe as the welcoming hands of death gripped his throat. The pain of lost loved ones flew from his hungry heart like bats from a cave in his own personal hell. He was washed with a relief that was as inexplicable as it was unexpected.

Past that moment of commitment, as he donated his body to gravity, Joseph heard a distant voice call "Father!"

Just an echo in the wind, he thought. Then he heard it again, more clearly, more desperate.

He tried to look back, twisting his body as it plunged to the soft rocks and sand below, and he glimpsed a solitary figure peering over the cottage porch, now far distant and swallowed in a telescopic tunnel of sight. He lifted his hand skyward.

"John P ... " he said in an inaudible voice through a vision of confusion.

As always, he was too late.

The Philosopher and the Cottage

Following his enlightening experience at the cottage so deep and steep in the forest, the Philosopher changed in both demeanour and direction. Gone was his desire to enthrall those at the café with his "universal" knowledge. Left behind were his musings about the thunderous relationships between man and spirit, God and ceremony. He became focused on the otherworldly. In the café, he would no longer chat idly about human passions, spiritual challenges, or wolf hunting. His entire conversation emanated from and traveled along the pathways of his new curiosity—existence beyond the physical.

At first, the townsfolk, especially those who shared the café terrace, were enamoured with his latest ruminations. They humoured him, not really understanding what he was jabbering about, all this talk of an alternative existence, of clarity of mind and spirit without the body, of sanctuary from life's torment through a higher calling, and the blinding impact of understanding and enlightenment. Most of them would be more that content with a better knowledge of what the weather was going to be in the coming days!

And so the schism between the Philosopher and the townsfolk, especially the café patrons, grew. Julian no longer felt it worthwhile to provide special prices or the occasional complimentary beverage to him, as he often chased customers off with his dominating clatter about the other dimensions, rather than hold them captive with his perceived understanding of man's journey to spiritual achievement. Still, Julian continued to deliver a coffee here and there just for old time's sake.

Over time, the Philosopher stopped coming to the café altogether. At first, his absence was barely noticeable, but soon enough, there was a distinct void in the atmosphere surrounding the wobbly tables and languishing cat. And it was appropriate. The café patrons had not changed at all, but the Philosopher had. He would be remembered for a few months in tales of "remember this" and "remember that," but his name and teachings would fall off the table of conversation to join the dust that swirled on the wooden floor. Within a short period, he had shifted from a patron whose arrival was anticipated to an avoided companion to undesired company and finally just an indifferent anecdote.

The Philosopher became more reclusive with each day. He no longer enjoyed chatting at the café with meaningless narrations of the mundane existence life provided. He was no longer empowered by the feelings of importance and superiority that his elevated status had delivered. He even quit his job at the local paper, citing a desire to write on a full-time basis but really just feeling the retelling of stories that had happened to other people, far and wide and away, was a waste of precious time and a casual disrespect of his own being.

He tried repeatedly to capture in words the tremendous feelings he had experienced during his visit to the cottage, but he was unable to do so in any way that fulfilled him. He wrote pages and pages of prose, grasping at the essence of what he wished to relay to the reader, but it was never enough; it was always insufficient and incomplete.

He made several journeys to the cottage. Each one was a pilgrimage of sorts aimed at furthering his understanding of this ethereal contemplation, and each one left him further enthralled with the vision but less able to recount it in any worthwhile reflection. He became frustrated and fixated, incapable of gaining clarity on any other matter than the cottage and its gateway to some intangible light. What a burden his body had become!

During one of his forays into the woods, while high on the pathway and close to the cottage, the Philosopher heard a distinct rustling sound in the thick brush ahead. At first, he stopped and contemplated seeking cover from what might be a large animal, or worse, a curious individual, but he maintained his ascent nonetheless.

Shortly thereafter, a middle-aged gentleman emerged from the thick underbrush, slightly sweaty, slightly stooped, and slightly unaware of the Philosopher's presence. He carried some small pieces of wood, a hammer, and other tools reminiscent of a carpenter. The forest was so dense that they were nearly on top of each other by the time they were mutually visible.

The Philosopher whispered an "Ahoy," and the preoccupied man stopped hard in his steps and straightened up with more than a little surprise to encounter another person at this elevated spot on the mountain. The man gathered himself and laid down the tools and tote he carried and whispered a "Good day" that included extending a large calloused hand to the Philosopher.

They stood awkwardly among the circling vines and branches before they recognized each other. Joseph was the visitor who had fallen asleep during the Philosopher's reading. Joseph, meanwhile, recognized the Philosopher as the young, witty lad who had read him to sleep with his spiritual confabulation. They agreed to move over to a small clearing and make use of the dead tree sofa that dwelled there.

They quizzed each other on the journey they were taking, and it became more than apparent that they were both regular patrons of the cottage and were mutually aware that it was owned by no one and available only to those worthy of understanding that. They once again tried feebly to share some expression of the majesty of the cottage but soon realized their folly and succumbed to more tangible conversation.

In the short moments they spent together, an intangible bond developed; the kind of mutual respect or admiration that comes with having shared an experience that few others had shared. It was an understanding of the power the cottage held, but also delivered, that united them, though they never spoke of it directly in such terms. Somehow they were both empowered by their awareness of the cottage and understood its importance in terms of life and the understanding of it.

Their half-hour conversation was the only other time these two would meet; yet it was a lasting and significant memory of kinship that they both held onto. Even though they never shared a moment in each other's company again, they remembered this meeting as significant. The Philosopher was greatly relieved that someone else in this vast world had experienced the un-documentable joy of the vision, and the carpenter was equally pleased with the realization that his labours and attention to the cottage were so appreciated and welcome.

As they rose to part company, the Philosopher queried as to whether the carpenter was responsible for the beautiful benches that adorned the cottage porch. Indeed, he was, the carpenter replied, recalling the rickety ones that were there when he first found the place. The Philosopher expressed how impressive that was and asked if the carpenter had sold any of the wood he used to someone in the town below the mountain.

The carpenter explained that the benches consumed all the wood he had prepared in such a skilled manner, except for a small piece, which instead of carrying all the way back to his town, he used to repair the broken step on some unknown back stoop in the town below. He recalled how he'd seen a young mother distraught over the inconvenience of her broken step and watched a young boy having to jump dangerously over it. When the boy was marched away by his mother Joseph had jumped into the yard and changed out the broken wood.

The carpenter eventually departed without either of them making a commitment to a future encounter, and the Philosopher remained seated as the revelation of the broken step repair gained momentum in his brain. His recollection of the great healing process the step repair had brought to his parents' torment was as vivid as if having transpired the day before. He remembered the great pride he had felt in his father when he had shattered the stalemate in his parent's relationship that the broken step had delivered. To this day, he felt it was a turning point in his understanding of the values a man should possess; certainly those of temperance, sympathy, and tolerance. The fact the step had been repaired serendipitously by a stranger passing by, looking only to lighten his own load, was devastating. That meant that not only had his father not repaired the step but also that he had taken credit for doing so! He was not only incapable of the very compassion the Philosopher admired in him but beyond that, he was also a liar and thief of another's work! Even though his parents' marriage did not last, the Philosopher had carried for many years the warm recollection of his father doing his best to keep the family together. In his eyes, the step repair represented all that was good and admirable in his father, a representation that was shattered with the stroke of a single sentence. The balance of his ascent was a blur, timeless and wholly unmemorable.

The Philosopher's outlook on life and the love of it shifted that afternoon following his encounter with the carpenter. The broken step had only been a small crack in his existence, but it was a crack that grew ever wider and deeper as time went by. His realization that enlightenment could only be experienced and not taught was pivotal. He knew his self-imposed ambition of enlightening others was an impassable trail that left him hollow and without purpose. His lost faith in his father and his entire family unit was as deep as a blow to his psyche.

He began to spend more and more time at the cottage. It was the only place he gained respite from the torments of a soul now void of purpose and faith. He longed for the relief he envisioned beyond the cliff walls, beyond the edge that was an invisible wall of steel bars, holding his spirit prisoner while laying out the fruits of utopia before him, tempting him to take a bite!

Some time passed, and his visits to the cottage folded one on top of the other. They were indistinguishable except for one particular visit when he found a hammer with a ribbon tied tightly around it on the kitchen table. He collected the hammer and hung it on a small nail that was probably meant to house a washcloth or hand towel. The hammer remained so hung throughout his subsequent visits. He was certain it belonged to the carpenter, and he wondered often if the carpenter had, for some unimaginable reason, decided not to return to the cottage.

As his depression spiraled downward, his joy of living followed close behind. Gone were the sunny days of revelry on the café terrace. Departed were the bittersweet memories of a childhood steered happily by a father's unselfish commitment. Dead was the purpose of prose to enrich the lives of others. All were replaced by a longing to experience what could not be experienced.

More and more time passed unnoticed as the Philosopher reclined on the porch bench staring into the void of an unseen dimension. He began spending most of his time at the cottage, pen and paper left idle on the kitchen table, save for the continuous scribbling of the symbolic image for 'infinity', similar to a number eight, laying sideways across the page. Food and water became a solitary afterthought. He began to wither away, his body seldom replenished with nourishment and his mind unstimulated by thought or process.

And so it was, on a particularly sunny afternoon, with the heated rays of sunlight probing the slits in his eyelids, that a moment of clarity rushed up his spine and captured his brain. It was a lightning bolt from within, powerful and hungry, striking recklessly through his neck into all points of his head. The thunder of thoughts that followed was decisive.

He stood tall and straight for the first time in a long time. His eyes widened, and a smile crept over his lips.

Of course! Why couldn't he move onward to the next dimension, to the enlightenment that he knew was but a short leap of faith away? What were these invisible bars but an illusion of limitations reinforced by the false confines of the body? He could travel inward on the infinite trails that were surrounded by memory, fantasy, and dreams, and all contained in this finite vessel of flesh and bone. Infinity confined within his body—what a paradox!

He stepped forward and took in the wonderment of the scene. The world lay before him, but a temporary plot to stage the soul while it sought greater vision and purpose, a temporary house for the wayward spirit, willing to consume all those who did not venture into the unknown realm of existence beyond primal understanding. Beauty and enlightenment lay waiting, far away from the chase of possessions and sex and status and legacy. It was more than clear. He had waited his entire life for this moment. Everything that had transpired before had been a beacon on the pathway to this moment—his ragged childhood, his published introspections, his shallow friendships, and especially, the broken step, all steering him towards enlightenment.

He leaned forward ever so slightly, feeling the balance of weight shift towards the edge of the cottage porch. His legs were together, and his arms spread slowly upwards as if dragging wings behind them. All he had to do was continue his tilt a few more inches, and he would teeter over the edge, his worldly musings and endless barrage of explanations and contemplations left behind for those who pursued his wisdom. How they would ponder the senselessness of his decision. How they would judge him and share opinions on what drove his final actions.

"He was always a little confused."

"Those blasphemous words were bound to bring trouble."

"Don't you know? He was very much in love but she left happily in the arms of another."

"No, no, I heard he was embarrassed by some action or rejection and couldn't bear it."

"No, that's not so, it runs in his family. I think his uncle also killed himself."

Fools, he thought. *You and your limitations* are *my catalyst. How can I share the vision that you are unable to see? How can I chase your wonderment into open space from the lonely corrals into which it settles nightly? Sheep and chickens, wandering the earth under the weight of manmade chains, happy in captivity only because even the existence of freedom has never even been conceived, yet alone seen or embraced.*

His head bent back, and he looked up at the universe, brandishing a growing smile that opened to inhale the ocean breeze that never ceased to gust along the cliff wall. The rocky beach lay half a mile below, the tug of eternity but a breath ahead of him. He continued his lean until it was far enough, gravity taking over and pulling his body effortlessly down towards Mother Earth.

As he felt the exhilaration of descent, his spirit leapt forward, sliding from its cocoon like a butterfly in its summer ritual, driving out into the light with an unexpected acceleration. His hands were in front of him now, leading the way to another dimension, steering him through the inexplicable wash of light and energy, twisting and spinning his evaporating thought and emotion into dust behind him as he embraced an entirely new existence. What joy! No regrets, no blame, no loss, and how immediate was there indeed, no recollection of earthly life. He was free from his physical confines and thrust into a new chaos of unknown excitement and tangled mystery. An entirely new eternity, caught in the blink of his eye, a snap of his finger, in the last wisp of breath that fueled his launch into the misunderstood realm of the unknown.

His body, now a vessel empty of spirit and soul and a burden to Earth's gravity, hit the beach with enough power to loosen dirt and small stones from the surrounding cliff wall, which tumbled down after it. The crooked twist of what had, moments earlier, been the confines of his enlightenment lay crumpled and distorted on the twinkling sands of dusk. Within a few seconds, everything returned to exactly how it was before the sudden impact. What a feast was served for the crabs and scavengers and birds of prey.

Fathers, Sons, and Serendipity

Tection was growing fond of the town. His encounter with Julian was a positive catalyst for some long-sought revelation about just how much he missed being himself. Winter had stolen much from him, ironically, more in his dying than in his living. The warm breeze brought dust to his throat, and the far distant hum of endless waves brought a tangible serenity to his tired life. He began to frequent the café, and although he shared several interesting conversations with Julian, he never really became a regular, preferring to avoid the obvious questions that accompanied post-introduction encounters. He was cordial, the patrons thought, but a little too contemplative. He had that "don't bother me" look when he sat relaxed and distant in his favourite chair near the back of the terrace, one arm draped over the railing and one foot perched on the bottom step of the neighbouring chair, making a claim on it and indicating it was not available to any inquisitive onlooker.

His serious though often esoteric demeanour and his slight aloofness to the customers made Tection a reliable escape for Julian when he wanted to be sheltered from his patrons' musings. Julian was fascinated by Tection's recent journeys to the land across the sea, the land in which he was a stranger, and whenever the time seemed appropriate, he slid into the chair reserved by Tection's foot and carried the slightest curl of a smile on his lip.

Tection knew the look, and as often as not would roll his eyes as the young man sat down, but always with his own slight smile and a little shake of his head. He knew it was story time, and inevitably the conversation, after a few innocuous remarks about the day's traffic or the previous evening's landscape, turned to, "Okay, where were we?" and the tales of the foreign land would renew.

Tection was a gifted storyteller, having always possessed a strong faculty for oration, and whenever he saw Julian's eyebrow raise a twitch as some situation or topic was introduced, he would let his story languish there, with all the actuality he could remember, and often some poetic license driving his embellishments.

Julian cared not if fancy was mixed with fact. He chased the dream of travel every evening as he slid into his bed and transformed from café owner to distant adventurer.

As time brought familiarity to their relationship, Julian realized he could count on Tection to handle the café when he had other, more pressing, matters to which he needed to attend. The customers respected Tection, if only because of his distant nature, and the staff followed his direction, because they remained unsure as to exactly who he was and the precise nature of his relationship to Julian. It all worked out uneventfully.

When not busy reading in his room above the kitchen, which he had finally agreed to rent from Julian, or languishing at either work or play in the café, Tection toured the boundaries of the town, finding an undisturbed calmness in the quiet streets and slowly changing scenery that helped quell the calamity of his life. Tection was cautious not to tread on any avenues leading to his past life, at least for the time being. Eventually though, he ventured further out, breaking away from the town boundaries and walking along more rural and rustic pathways. He had an occasional run-in with others on the paths, but they were few and dispatched quickly with a courteous nod "hello" and possibly a grunt of "good day" in passing.

On one particularly normal day, neither warm nor cold, a few clouds speckling the sky and the actual day of the week undetermined, Tection saw a slightly distant figure leaving the main path and climbing up into the woods. They were moving towards each other, but the other man was also moving upward. As they neared each other and the distance between them was insufficient to hinder recognition, Tection stopped dead in his tracks.

"Joseph!" he called out, half with a statement of excitement and half with a question of bewilderment.

Joseph, who had been completely oblivious to anyone else as he trudged upwards, cocked his head for a moment to be sure he had heard the voice, and then he spun around towards Tection, hands flying outward and his mouth gaping for words.

"Tection!" he blurted out finally.

The men moved quickly towards each other, ignoring the lack of a pathway, and fell into a comfortable laugh, enclosed by their happy embrace. What a fortuitous moment! How impossible was it that their paths had crossed at the same moment in the same place after so long. Tection's last contact with Joseph had been shortly after he recommended him for the priest position in the church of a small, rather distant town around twenty years earlier. Joseph had embraced the opportunity, and Tection's occasional visits during that first year had always found Joseph happy and content.

Following the killing of Winter, Tection's contact with his previous life all but disappeared. Joseph had wondered for a long time as to the whereabouts of Tection. He had sent numerous letters and even travelled to the city church to find out where he had gone. The answer was always the same: "Tection is no longer with our church; he has left this area."

There was much to catch up on. Joseph explained that he was enroute to a cottage high up on the mountainside and deep in the blanket of forest. They agreed to travel there together and spend some time putting words to the blank pages that were their recent histories.

Tection noticed dimness to the glint that had always shone in Joseph's eye, a small clue to the sadness that he had endured. Joseph also recognized a change in Tection's presence. He had always been so jovial and gregarious; punctuating his conversations with whoops and whistles, slaps and tickles.

They had much to discuss, but they journeyed up to the cottage with only trivial conversation. The task was too demanding on the lungs to afford any verbose interplay, and the climb was an opportunity for both of them to absorb the impact of their meeting and ponder the questions they might ask each other. Joseph knew the path well and led Tection through some rather thick areas before they reached the small clearing that introduced the cottage.

Tection expressed his wonderment that Joseph was familiar with this place and then, after experiencing the view from the front porch, revealed bewilderment with the entire situation. The view was as if flying among the clouds, enjoying the panorama for the first time, being a bird.

Joseph rattled off the stories of his discovery of the cottage, its refurbishment and building the benches, the serenity he felt when there, and the irresistible attraction the edge of the cliff had built into him. This fascination with the edge did not impact Tection when first disclosed, but when taken in context with the stories that were retold, it became a great concern.

Tection, in turn, delivered his own excited prose, elaborating on the journeys he had made to the other side of the sea with details of strange people and sights that could not be imagined. He made long stories of small details and skipped over huge chunks of time, something that made Joseph reminisce about the first time he and Tection had spoken of sincere matters back at the roadside inn where the two young travelers had stopped for the evening. The bigger question hung in the air like a ghost unrevealed. Why had Tection left behind the seemingly joyous and fulfilling life he had carved from his birthstone of misfortune and grief? As usual, Joseph was not overly inquisitive and allowed Tection to reveal his story at his own pace.

Meanwhile, Joseph painted his own story of sadness, leaving out no detail. He spoke for the first time to anyone about the son he knew was his, John P, about the woman he loved so dearly but was unable to be with because of his vows to the Church and the glory of God. He shed unexpected tears when recalling her illness and long anticipated death. Then he perked up with the remembered joy of having his son come to stay with him even though he had never revealed to the boy that he was his father. That joy soured as well, chased away by the memories of his son's departure to "see the world" and the years that had passed without communication, a boy who had asked about his "missing" father, and Joseph, head turned away with deep breaths to control his tears, explaining that such was destiny. Joseph lamented his past and concluded that all that was good and loved by him had been taken from him—his father, Tection, his one true love and the mother of his child, his son, and with all of them, his lust for life. And now he was encumbered further with the initial signs of the hereditary disease that had taken his father from him at a relatively young age. More fuel on the fires of destiny.

Tection sensed the deep sorrow Joseph was projecting and feared that his friend was unsure about life and living. Once Joseph slipped into a quiet and contemplative posture, signaling he was talked out for the time being, Tection felt that he might shed light on the entire history of his erratic life. He decided to reveal his own secrets, for the first time to anyone, believing his own sorrows might diminish Joseph's. Perhaps shared sorrow would build some pastel alleviation to the pain Joseph suffered and, by including him in this other sorrow, reduce his own.

He reminded Joseph of that night long ago on the veranda of the inn when Tection had recounted the stories of hardship and misfortune from his childhood. Joseph recalled every word like it was yesterday. What an honour it had been to be the sounding board for tales of a lifetime left behind. Not all had been revealed, Tection explained, and he began the disclosure of the Winter stories. They were harrowing to tell and horrifying to hear. Tection went on to recount the visit with the church committee and the circumstance that had led him to kill Winter and, ultimately, drove him from the new, sweet life he had discovered.

Joseph was shocked. He had no idea of Tection's past hardships, on which he had shed such sympathy, were actually even more abominable. He reached out and held Tection, each man finding comfort in the embrace. Comfort from the moment, from the disclosure, from the discovery and the battle of life itself.

Joseph broke the silence with a sudden revelation, asking Tection if he remembered the beautiful chambermaid from the inn. Then he went on to tell of an encounter with her in his hometown, where she had been sent to reside because she had become pregnant and delivered a son into the hands of the local orphanage. It seems a visitor to the inn, one who came by on occasion, had enjoyed her company one night and left behind more than expected. The poor chambermaid never saw the father again and cried openly at her situation. She had begged the innkeeper to let the father know the situation so they could decide on their future path, which the old woman promised to do, but later she told her that the father had never returned to the inn.

Joseph saw the sudden change in the hue of Tection's skin, turning a very pale blanche, accompanied by some mild shaking. The story of Tection's liaison with the young lady was soon recounted. Once they put the ages and the timing together it was clear. Tection was the "stranger" who had been the chambermaid's lover one fateful night. He had a son. But where was he?

Joseph was the first to put the puzzle together. Brother James being Winter and Tection saving his own son! It was all more than could be consumed at the moment. After running through the range of emotion generated by this revelation—astonishment, deep sorrow, lamentation of what could have been, shock and awe at the realization of fatherhood, anger and disappointment at the innkeeper for harbouring the news of a child, and finally to joy and bliss at learning he was not without a legacy, something that had tormented him endlessly—his uncertainty about the direction of his life gained sudden clarity and purpose, even though it was through a foggy and undetermined lens.

They slept a little restlessly that night, Tection the "guest" on the bed mat and Joseph displaced but comfortable with bedding along the wall. Tection swirled in and out of slumber as he dragged every sliver of memory back to the surface, visions of his son dancing in and out of the shadows. He remembered his evening with the boy's mother, but why did he have difficulty remembering her face? It had always been so clear before. He also recalled more vividly the dramatic moments involving Winter's death and the young boy who clung to him in a "thank you" embrace. Finally, he settled into a somewhat peaceful sleep when he realized the pathway to finding his son was not a difficult one. The seminary was close enough, and the notoriety of the boy meant he could be traced easily. Those thoughts comforted him, but what he didn't realize was the huge importance of this news to his psyche as it injected a direction and purpose back into his life as a stranger.

In the morning, Tection was anxious to begin the journey to find his son, but he tempered that with a desire to delve deeper into his friend's troubled expression. He was not pleased with Joseph's apparent depression and sense of loss. He was concerned with the aloofness towards life and regretful prose that permeated their discussion.

Joseph explained his self-doubt and elaborated on the conflict he felt with God, lamenting his own perceived betrayal and suggesting his hardships were possibly retribution from God. Tection thought this rather absurd but was careful not to trivialize or question the relevance of Joseph's concerns. He elicited promises from Joseph to remain calm and take no harsh action. He extracted a commitment to allow them to continue their reconnection and promised a most supportive friendship going forward. Joseph smiled at Tection's energy and persuasiveness. He agreed easily, and Tection took his acquiescence at face value. His own mind was racing ahead of his body, however, and he left the cottage convincing himself that Joseph was all right and only needed a little time to allow some healing to take place. It was an incorrect assessment.

—

Tection reached the town late in the afternoon, the sun tumbling from the sky and evening's shadow growing and claiming its place as ruler of the night. Despite his anxiousness, he would not be able to begin his hunt until morning.

He wandered over to the café and sat in his usual chair, releasing a long sigh and realizing he was exhausted from both the news of his son and the significant journey up and down the mountain.

What a beautiful spot the cottage was, he thought, and he made a mental commitment to revisit it sooner rather than later.

Later that evening, Julian joined him and was overpowered by the flow of words Tection delivered. He recounted meeting Joseph and shared the drama his friend was living, with the onset of illness, the loss of his loved ones, and an estranged son. He paused to express his concern at Joseph's demeanour and seemingly frivolous attitude towards the future. His tale trailed off momentarily at that point but then revamped itself when revealing the discovery that he also had a son. His voice tried to portray his thoughts and emotions on the subject, but his mind was too sporadic and scattered for his mouth to capture. He tried in vain to capture the vision in words of the enigmatic, enormous, and ultimately esoteric panorama of the cottage, seemingly in a single breath.

Julian was used to seeing Tection in a reflective and contemplative mood, usually choosing his words with care and significance. This explosion, almost childlike, was so sudden and out of character that it brought a broad smile to Julian's face.

"What are you smiling about?" Tection asked.

"You, my friend. You sound like a little kid who just discovered the sound of music."

They both laughed, and Tection shuffled his feet quickly to regain his usual composure, though only on the outside. His internal engine was still racing with plans and hopes concerning his son. He forgot temporarily about the concern he had for Joseph's depressed state!

As their laughter faded, carried away on the evening breeze, Tection tried to express his urgent need to locate his newfound son while, at the same time, reflecting on his sadness for Joseph's inability to do the same. For the first time, he named John P as the wayward son.

Julian jumped from his chair almost before the name left Tection's lips. John P! Surely there was only one John P. He came to the realization that the "Joseph" of which Tection spoke was the same one with whom John P had lived and whom Julian himself knew, the same priest who sheltered John P and let them carouse through his library like tadpoles in the muddy pool of a post-rainstorm morning. But Tection had just said that John P was Joseph's son! Was it possible? Julian knew that John P lamented the fact that he knew little of his father, but this news—or, more precisely this realization—was staggering.

John P had just passed by the night before following his short trip back to his hometown to see Joseph. Joseph had not been there, now an obvious fact. What an unusual coincidence. Julian and John P had shared an extended evening of drink and discussion. It was, unfortunately, too late to travel out to see John P at the old church with the news, but Julian told Tection it was a must trip for early in the morning.

Tection was also flabbergasted by the series of coincidences unravelling before him. He confirmed that Joseph was up at the cottage and gave Julian the basic directions for how to get there, upwards and then towards the sea. Julian knew that John P would be elated to hear the news and chase after his newfound father. Tection also knew that Joseph would be uncontrollably elated to see the boy again, and with the news of their relationship being discovered, the moment would be outstanding.

Tection sank into the fact that both he and Joseph were on the cusp of a new relationship with their sons, he with a son he had just discovered and Joseph with a son long lost; but not too late to learn about.

Too Late to Learn

John P slipped his legs over the side of his bed and pushed himself up into a sitting position. His hands moved to his face, and he leaned forward so his elbows rested on his knees. Not quite the position of prayer but excellent for hangover relief. He wasn't much of a drinker, but he had certainly overindulged the night before. He was still feeling the results. He didn't visit Julian at the café often, but the previous night had been a welcome respite from the sorrow and torment he had been feeling about his visit with Nicholas, the new priest, and the consequences his arrival invoked, acerbated further by the wasted voyage back to his hometown to see Joseph.

Julian had been most sympathetic, as was expected, and offered various scenarios in which John P could maintain his purpose and position with the townsfolk while being inclusive of Nicholas and the new church. Unfortunately, John P knew them all to be fantasy. There was room for only one "sheriff" in town, and John P was about to be excommunicated. His options were limited. He could seek to compete with Nicholas for the attention and commitment of the people, but that was unlikely in that Nicholas had God as an ally now. John P could seek new, greener pastures elsewhere, but without the official credentials of a priest; he would be unlikely to achieve such a lofty ambition. Most realistically, he could return to his hometown and reconnect with Joseph at their local church. Although he would not have his own church, he would at least receive and deliver respect and emotion with the shared space.

John P had recognized this as his most realistic option earlier and wondered if Joseph was still there after these few years. He was struck suddenly with a pang of guilt at not communicating with Joseph. After all, he had been a significant friend to his mother and helped John P enormously when she passed away.

He could also seek a new faith, a new religion of sorts, something that would not require an official church in order to be qualified. He knew such streams of thought were elsewhere in the world. As this idea gained momentum in his mind, he went on further to think that perhaps he could start his own church—his own religion, as it were—but remain committed to God and his ways. That idea died quickly as he realized such a church would in itself be contrary to God's requirement of service and commitment through the official structures to his omnipotence.

The first time his congregation moved to the new church devastated John P. He had not attended, and Nicholas had assumed he was ill or otherwise indisposed. The locals who had become accustomed to John P's sermons and spirited pulpit deliveries queried about his absence, but as many excuses were offered as there were questions asked.

A few recognized that John P must be feeling distressed, so they organized a small band to visit him following the official service in the new church. They arrived under the guise of being concerned about his health but were clearly sensitive to the unavoidable transition of religious venues. John P covered his feelings well, professing chills and fever as the reasons for his absence. The visitors cooed apologies and well wishes for a speedy recovery, but they knew such was not the real factor behind his truancy. In and around various suggestions for a cure for fever, were salutations of good wishes and hopes for a visit from him the following Sunday. John P felt grateful when they arrived and even more grateful when they left. It was the last time he held court in any manner with these folks.

Once armed with the clear realization that his days as a lay preacher for the little town were history, John P made some firm decisions about his future, or at least about his immediate direction. Nicholas, and by default, the Church, had offered him continued use of the small old church, which John P had restored and rejuvenated, so his immediate accommodation needs were covered. Although he had taken little from the service offerings, his life was extremely frugal, and he had accumulated a fairly handsome purse. He also had remains of the inheritance from his mother, so there was no pressing concern for funds. No, John P's problems were not matters of residence and income; they were issues of his spirit and purpose.

John P reflected on his departure from his hometown, how he had articulated the value that Joseph, as the town priest, provided the community and how honourable his profession was. He felt a definite carving of those thoughts now. He recalled having felt that he would never return to his little town and now he felt some distant sense of failure in his journey so far, including a lost value to all the good and joy he had showered on what he now perceived as his defunct flock. He wanted desperately not to dislike or blame Nicholas for the situation, but he did. He felt it could have been handled much differently and that his own value as a community leader should have been recognized and nurtured by the new church. Bitterness was only beginning to fester.

John P decided he would venture back to his hometown and reconnect with Joseph. He would seek solace and advice on his situation, perhaps even a small amount of sympathy, which was always a soothing balm. He informed Julian of his plans, but his friend was distraught over his decision. They had set out together to challenge the world and were now at a crossroads of uneven familiarity. Julian's eye remained fixed on adventure, even though he had settled quickly into the café and accompanying lifestyle, while John P's reticence at too boisterous an adventure had made a small circle back to home base. Not really the exploits of explorers, they reflected. John P assured Julian that it was only a temporary visit. To demonstrate that, he asked Julian to look in on the old church occasionally and ensure everything was in order. He also asked him to mention to the townsfolk only that he was on a short trip away and would return soon. All was agreed, though not all was necessarily believed, by either of them.

The journey home was hopelessly uneventful and seemed much, much shorter than the outbound one had been. In realizing how relatively short the journey home was, John P readmonished himself for having never taken it. He could think of many exaggerations he might offer to Joseph to support his lack of communication but knew in reality that straight, honest talk was the most valuable kind. He would simply explain the flow of life and how his consumption with the present had kept his eyes away from the past.

John P arrived on a cool, drizzly morning, the town activity hidden well behind doors closed to the elements. His steps grew heavy as he neared the church, and his mind raced with an overflow of thoughts and emotions. In his worst moments, he feared Joseph might be irrevocably distant, but in reality, he knew that was highly unlikely. His nature, kind and understanding, could not entertain such negativity. He had played out several scenarios that all ended positively with him living back at the hometown church and supporting Joseph in his responsibilities towards the community.

He hesitated before opening the church doors, just long enough for quiet drops of water to find his brow, and breathed deeply. Then he swung the large wooden doors inward and stepped inside out of the rain.

He was greeted by an elderly man, the church keeper of sorts, handy with mop, hammer, flame, and muscle, when required. He recognized John P immediately and left his mop standing in its bucket, opening his arms in a warm hello that John P returned with enthusiasm. It was a kind and honest way to be received and left John P much more relaxed and welcome than he had felt a moment earlier.

After acceptable greetings and small talk, the church keeper explained that Joseph had not been around for nearly a week, or perhaps longer. It seemed he had taken some time off to reflect on matters of life and would not return for a while. This was most disappointing to John P, a dead end of sorts.

He stayed at the church overnight and then set out in the morning to undertake the journey back to the life he was looking to leave behind; a rather quick turnaround for such a trip of adventurous undertaking. He left word for Joseph with the church keeper and promised to return in a couple of weeks.

Once again, the journey back felt much shorter than he remembered, and John P wondered if each subsequent retracing of the route would seem equally less arduous.

He stopped by the cafe to let Julian know his journey was shortened due to Joseph's absence. Then he arrived back at the old church, deciding to take a few days off to reflect on life's happenings.

His first night back was restless at best. He dreamed of unusual spirals and strange visions turning in on themselves in a constant evolution.

The next day, John P was in a bit of a fog. He had some uneasiness in his step and walked about the church unsure of what to do next. No sermon to write, no visits to make, and no reflections of value. He decided to visit Julian, as that always brought some levity, if not laughter, to his soul. They drank far too much, and John P managed to stumble home. He suffered the following day and slept early that night. He slept even less comfortably than when he was intoxicated and was awoken rather early by the calamity of Julian crashing through the outer gate and barging into the church in a clumsy, excited manner, not unusual for him.

Julian rambled on about Joseph and the cottage and Tection and the relationships and anything else that could be mustered. It was a blur for John P, and he finally got Julian to relax and repeat the entire tale.

John P sat and listened with casual interest at first but then slipped into a concentrated attention to every word Julian offered. The story of Joseph being at this cottage was coincidental enough, but the comment about John P being his son was a confusing one indeed. John P figured it might be a metaphorical expression, but Julian was certain it was not. John P flashed back to several moments and markings in time that lent credence to the idea of Joseph being his father. The depth of his gaze, the tenderness of his patience, the almost sad reflections, and the poorly disguised sadness at John P's departure all make sense if he were his father.

What about his mother then? That hit him harder. Numerous times, he thought there had been close contact between her and Joseph, but he, as a young and innocent child, had always assumed it was an embrace of comfort or appeasement from the priest to his follower. It made much more sense now. Of course Joseph was his father and those tender embraces with his mother were a continued expression of their shared life. How crazy. How could he miss that? How could he not know that?

John P leaned back further in his chair and lost himself in deep reflection on the situation. So much became clearer as pockets of revelation emptied into his thoughts in rapid succession. Within a few minutes, he travelled from lamenting the difficulty such a secret life must have brought upon both Joseph and Mary to a realization that he actually had a living father, and one for whom he felt great respect and endearment. That last thought snapped him back to sharp reality, and he shook his head slightly to clear it while Julian rambled on.

As John P's eyes focused, Julian realized John P had been only half attentive to what he was saying. Julian repeated that Joseph was at the cottage right now, that he was a little ill and definitely disheartened by his lack of contact with John P. Tection had mentioned the hereditary illness that plagued Joseph and how it would probably afflict John P one day as well. The tale unraveled into one describing the distress and discomfort Joseph was enduring. It was obvious that John P had to go to the cottage immediately!

He jumped up and began to head out before stopping and asking Julian exactly where it was. How funny, he thought, so anxious to leave he had no idea where he was going. Julian explained what Tection had told him and drew a small map with some known reference points on it. He cautioned John P that it was a fair distance, and he should expect to spend the night there. John P prepared a blanket wrap, some food and water, reviewed the location with Julian once more, and then they set out for the mountain.

They walked together for some time, as they were heading in the same general direction, before splitting up with offerings of sincere good luck from Julian and a nervous thank you from John P.

John P climbed the mountain with swiftness and purpose. He barely noticed the underbrush thickening around him or the sweat soaking his shirt as the day grew hotter. The buzzing gnats and flies were pushed aside as he powered his way upward using his hands and his feet. It took a few minutes to regain his bearings as he ran out of a clear path, but he made out some broken branches and lightly trampled brush that indicated others had come the same way. He knew he had to head towards the sea, which was to his left, and climb until there was nowhere left to go.

As frustration crept into his anxiousness, and the midday sun reached its pinnacle, he saw the clearing Julian had described in his relay from Tection. Across the clearing he saw the soft outline of a structure, certainly the cottage he sought.

He fumbled through the last bits of forest and found the door. He pushed it open carefully, expecting to see Joseph sitting there and anticipating a heartfelt reunion with the man whom he now believed to be his true father, but no one was there. He perused the room, actually two rooms that formed one larger space. Nothing. From the corner of his eye, he saw a shadow break the stream of light darting through the cracks of the window shutter.

"Father!" he blurted out and swung the porch doors open just as the shadowy figure plunged out of sight over the edge of the sheer cliff wall.

John P lunged forward, falling to his knees in order to crawl to the cliff edge. He saw the body tumbling away from him at an alarming speed, and the horror of the moment struck him in an avalanche of adrenalin and electrical impulse.

"Father!" he cried again with a loud, cracking voice, but it was too late. The falling body seemed to twist slightly in one last purposeful action before it hit the rocky beach far below. There was no sound at all. It was too far away, and the ocean's symphony swallowed up every stray noise.

John P remained motionless for some time. The body, now a lifetime away, blurred in the tears that appeared in his eyes, although he didn't know exactly when they did so. His mind raced in an extravaganza of questions and postulations, each one struck down by the brick of reality.

Finally, he rolled onto his back, gazing up at the midday sun, hurling anger towards the heavens and anyone who dwelled there. Too much had bitten his life in the recent past, and this was but a final exclamation point on the downfall of his faith and purpose. He had always believed that living a good life would bring goodness in return, that sharing would bring abundance and kindness would return grace. He was both confused and annoyed at his beliefs, feeling used and somewhat the fool. His commitment to God, heaven, and salvation had returned naught but disappointment, banishment, disease, and death. Faith and belief should exalt us, not condemn us!

He contemplated rolling backwards over the same cliff, joining Joseph in the escape death might provide, but he found reasons not to, reasons drawn from memories of his mother, reflections on the history he had with Joseph and some good friendships he had, and even the flock he no longer led.

A short time later, he stumbled back into the cottage and sat in one of the two chairs. He squeezed the small kitchen table so hard that his thumb tendon bruised. If only he had been there even five minutes earlier. What was going on with life? Did it all revolve around a few trigger moments? Did it all fall into the destiny of a few shifts of time or collision of events? He was sad, frustrated, and exhausted. He passed out leaning on the table, tears drying on his cheeks and his brain too confused to remain awake.

He awoke either late at night or very early in the morning, before light shone, and sprang up to descend the mountain as soon as possible. But a quick step outside convinced him he could not possibly do so in the darkness. He couldn't even find the clearing behind the cottage. He was a prisoner there until the sun freed him, with nothing to do but build his remorse at arriving late and still trying to grasp the reality that Joseph was—had been—his father. He was sure of it.

The first cracks in the night sky broadened, and light shone for another day. John P hurried back down the mountain, but then he slowed. He was still full of confusion, and he barely recognized the path with any conscious understanding. He shivered in the forest heat with an emotional collapse that grew heavier with each broken branch he trampled. He exited the forest in a continuing state of shock and wandered towards the café, where Julian was just sweeping up from the morning service, sharing a coffee with Nicholas, the new priest.

When John P delivered the news to Julian and the priest, they were unmistakably shocked and truly concerned for John P's fragile state. Nicholas recognized his presence in the town was a huge hurdle for John P, but this was a time for comfort and consolation, both of which were his specialty. Tection was away from town, chasing down his own family.

The three of them enlisted the assistance of some townsfolk and ventured out along the rocky shore to find Joseph's body. As they neared his lifeless form, the odor was overwhelming, and John P rushed forward to ward of the birds that hovered and cackled nearby. But they were bird's intent on another body, one decomposed and badly gnawed at by the scavengers of the land and sea. It was unrecognizable, but it was painfully obvious that this other body had also fallen prey to the long journey from the cottage porch to the rocky beach, either by accident or by choice. They removed Joseph's body and left the other there, deciding to notify the proper authorities once back so it could be reclaimed properly.

The journey back was an arduous task, burdened, as they were, both physically and emotionally. Joseph's lifeless, broken body was the journey's goal, but certainly not the prize.

The Exceptional Journey

Tection woke early, transiting from full sleep to adrenalin-fueled morning in but a few breaths. He was more anxious to begin his journey than the sun was to light his road. A few sips of coffee and a quick bite of a day-old croissant had him fully energized.

Julian appeared briefly before he departed, himself anxious to reach John P with the news of his father, bidding Tection a fruitful hunt for his son. They were both oblivious to the fact his son was actually sleeping but a few hundred feet away.

As Tection powered along the side of the main road on his way to the seminary, he drifted into flashes of memory. The moments of contact he had shared with his son, even though he had not known it was his son, the potential future together, and then the reminiscence of his mother, Tection's lover, where she was and what she was doing all washed over his mind in a swirl of chaotic reminiscence. Was she with another man? Had she married? Did she have other children? A second wave of questions and very little in the way of answers.

After spinning with these thoughts for a while, Tection found his memories falling further back into his life. He recalled his early days and the labours of the orphanage, realizing his son had also lived that life. He felt an uncharacteristic sense of pride in his own accomplishments in escaping the dark destiny thrown at him, a pride that he realized was driven by the same pride he had in his son for not only surviving the harsh past but hopefully becoming someone valuable in spite of it.

As he continued his trek, physically purposeful and mentally whimsical, he passed a young boy playing just off the side of the road. He was slashing his way through tall stalks of wheat and grass whooping like a wild turkey and laughing at the wind that teased him. At first, Tection thought him a little strange, hustling a little joy from such a huge field of agriculture, but in a moment of electric impact, he recalled his own journey through tall fields of wheat, running aimlessly from the orphanage when he was first released, relishing the sharp slap of the stalks against his young hands and the relentless earth happy to receive his pounding feet. He remembered too, the few times he passed those travelling on the road and how they had looked at him with a curiosity hewn by their lack of experience in running through wild fields.

He stopped, looked at the boy, and began to laugh. The boy looked back, and he laughed as well. Then he danced away, his laughter trailing on the morning air until the short horizon swallowed them both audibly and physically.

Tection stood motionless, allowing his laughter to quiet down with a few last chuckles. He stared at the field for some time, held to it by the memory of it and the entire part of his life that memory represented. A tear slid down his cheek. He had not cried in many years.

He laid his travel bag down by the side of the road and walked towards the field. He climbed the animal fence with ease and walked deeper into the crop. He began to jog and then run and then sprint—hands out, palms up, slapping the stalks. His eyes went skyward. The sun and clouds danced in harmony with his bobbing head. As he tired, he stumbled, falling into a small clearing, dirty and dusty but desperately happy.

—

The doors to the seminary were much smaller than Tection remembered. As a matter of fact, the entire school was but an outline of the memories he held. The VPG was still there, much older but still recognizable, and he was ecstatic to share words and drink with Tection once again. He had always favoured the boy and took great pride in the accomplishments he had achieved. The VPG knew from where Tection came and recognized the weight of his journey to achievement. He was also aware of the episode with the death of Mr. James, or Winter, as he was also known, and the huge toll it had extracted from Tection. But that was neither discussed nor mentioned.

After suitable small talk, it was clear that Tection was anxious to channel the discussion towards the young boy who had survived Mr. James' last attack, the catalyst for Tection's tarnished legacy within the Church. Normally, the VPG was hesitant to divulge information concerning past students, but this situation was truly unique. He was actually surprised that Tection was not already aware of the great success the boy had enjoyed over the last few years, completing seminary and, last he had heard, excelling as an apprentice in the Church. The VPG mentioned that the boy had often sought reunion with Tection, the man who saved him, but was told by the Church that he was on a long sabbatical. Tection had not wanted to see the boy again at that time anyway. The impact of the killing of Mr. James was crushing Tection, and he had wanted only to get away. If he had known the boy was his son, he would have carried a much different demeanour.

Tection and the VPG had a long and happy goodbye punctuated with hugs and promises of reuniting in a much shorter time thereafter, but Tection never mentioned the boy was his son!

After the rest and reminiscence at the seminary, Tection headed towards the church, towards his last point of contact with the priesthood and the last place he expected to be revisiting. He had not left on bad terms, but his self-imposed shame and exile following the reassignment to clerical work had rendered his welcome depleted. He had been gone for many years and was uncertain as to how he might be received, but his desire to reunite with his son was much stronger than his old nervousness.

It turned out he had no need for concern. He was gathered into the flock like the prodigal son, embraced by his brothers and celebrated by smiles of sincerity from all. What a lucky man he was, wayward and distant in action but loved and embraced in reality. It was a rewarding homecoming. Tection was equally surprised to find that, in order to maintain his name on the register of priests and avoid his excommunication, the church had kept him on staff and under salary. Of course, this had nothing to do with the possibility that an excommunication might inspire Tection to regale the public with his tales of misfortune! His back pay had been deposited to his account on a monthly basis and had grown to be a rather significant sum. His attempts to donate it back to the church were met with shouts of refusal; implying that the reason his donation was being refused was the same reason he had been kept active. He was an outstanding, generous individual who deserved more in life than he had received. Tection was overwhelmed at the outpouring of accolades and a little uncomfortable with the praise, but he accepted the funds and broke bread with laughter and harmony.

In a quiet moment, reclusive with a former committee member, after throat clearing and curious contemplation, Tection asked about the young boy he had plucked from the clutches of Mr. James. He tempered his inquiry with a ruse of mere curiosity, preferring not to reveal that the boy was his son until he had the chance to meet and confront him personally in case there was any residual that might be compromised. He did not know if the boy's status as an orphan provided him any privileges or if there had been any adoptive figures in his life. It would be better, Tection decided, for him and his son to keep their relationship private until they could decide otherwise.

His friend's response displayed little drama. The boy had been a superior student and seemingly carried no ill effects from the episode in question. Other than lamenting often that he wanted to see Tection again, he had not suffered outwardly. Of course, the inner workings of his soul were not as easily determined, and both men agreed there was undoubtedly some significant anger repressed within his universe. He had graduated with flying colors though and ploughed through his apprenticeship without deviation. He was sought after by several dioceses but had decided to work as a priest in the new church alongside the ex-administrator of the orphanage where Tection had saved him. Nicholas, right smack in the middle of Tection's current place of residence, a full circle indeed!

Tection could only smile ironically at the journey he had taken these last few days, running from place to place chasing a memory that had been lingering right in front of him the entire time. It was another opportunity to reflect on the importance of not just looking but actually seeing that which surrounded our daily lives. He couldn't help but comment to his friend that he was concerned about the boy's reaction when confronted and the memories it might jar.

"Not to worry," his friend replied. "He has been seeing his mother regularly and seems to adapt well to such recognitions."

Tection was floored. The boy's mother, the chambermaid, still in the picture and now entrenched in their son's life? What was her name? He realized he could not remember it.

"Sarah," his friend informed him.

Sarah. Tection swallowed and closed his eyes to regain focus. After composing himself, he was able to get his friend to reveal Sarah's whereabouts. Before his departure, his friend even provided a small note introducing Tection as her son's benefactor.

How ironic, Tection thought. *She will recognize me as much more that a benefactor when she sees my face!*

Armed with this information and charged by a sense of final encounter, Tection bid farewell his friend.

Tection was torn between paths now. Should he reunited with his son first and then confront his mother together or should he bring his tale to Sarah first and have them meet their son together? He decided on Sarah first, if only because she might be with a new man, and Tection's presence might skew their harmony. It was better that she had the opportunity to embrace the change away from her son's eyes. Tection realized with sobering impact that Sarah and Nicholas might have a different man in their lives already, a surrogate father. His mind reached for the possibility that he might not be welcome back into their lives, but his heart pushed the thought back into the abyss from whence it came.

Tection followed the simple but detailed instructions and located her easily. She worked in a large house, a mansion, for a wealthy and influential family.

Still living a life of servitude, he thought, *just like chambermaids, butlers, orphans, and priests.*

Sarah recognized him immediately, eliminating all concerns about how he would explain who he was. She not only recognized his face from their brief liaison, but Tection was also the somewhat-aged mirror image of her son. There was no doubt in her mind he was the boy's father.

She captured her breath in due course, but her heart pounded for significantly longer. Words were difficult to find and curiously disjointed when she did speak them. The weight of discussion and explanation was lifted finally by the strength of an awaited embrace. Soft at first, like a wild animal unsure of the outstretched hand, but growing firmer with mutual reassurance and finally into a strong and passionate one with the accompanying caresses and tears expressing infinitely more that any prose or dialogue could hope to offer.

They stumbled together through the short history of their affair, alleviating long-held doubts about each other's intentions and lamentations towards the circumstances that kept them apart, the lies they had been fed to ensure the absence of any further communication once the baby was known and the secrets kept about the boy after his birth. Sarah laid out the simple facts of her life, the loneliness during her pregnancy and the sorrow upon relinquishing Nicholas to the orphanage, the several years of serving the current household, strict conditions but fair enough in disposition, and the great joy and elation that the reunion with her son had poured into her life.

Nicholas! Of course that was his name, Tection thought, *surely after Saint Nicholas, a giver of great gifts. Nicholas!* He interrupted Sarah to toss her in his arms and sneak a small tickle to her side, which brought a simple laugh and toss of her head. She was still beautiful. She smiled with her eyes as much as her mouth. He brought her close to him.

"Nicholas," he repeated, letting her peer through his eyes and see the happiness in his soul, "Thank you."

She told him Nicholas had reached out to find her after graduating from seminary. Armed with the confidence of his position, the strength of his limited knowledge of the system, his access to records of the orphanage, and, most importantly, his relationship with the former administrator, he was able to find her with very little effort. Their reunion had been a bright wonderment. The initial shock of meeting each other was followed by embraces and tender touches, lamentations and apologies, apologies and forgiveness, forgiveness and commitments, and in the end, the simple truth of a mother's love.

Tection contributed his own tale, his fruitless search for her following their time together and the tales told him of her changed residence, his complete unawareness that he even had a son, and his frequent recollections of their time together. He did not share his entire history with her during that first encounter, his own experiences with Winter, or the residue of spiritual suicide killing him had left, but he did reveal the story of Mr. James and the rescue of a young orphan. He was surprised to learn that she was aware of the story. Their son had revealed his memories of it soon after their reunion. Although it differed from Tection's version—the boy's being much more dramatic and punctuated with awe of the larger than life saviour who crushed the evil priest—the basic revelation was aligned.

They laughed at the irony of the situation, the years lost because of miscommunication and misrepresentation. Then they cried for the same reasons. Tection wondered what a difference it might have made in his life if he had known he had a child. Would it have prevented him from joining the priesthood? Would it have led him on an entirely different path, one with this wonderful woman and their offspring? An endless conversation for sure!

Their relationship was re-cemented with significant passion under the soft sheets of Tection's hotel room between noon and eight on her day off. It was not nearly enough time.

Despite the great joy that surrounded those first couple of days back in the arms of his lover, Tection was restless and anxious to greet the young boy he had saved from Winter, but this time with the knowledge that it was his son. He discussed it relentlessly with Sarah, and despite the fact her commitment to her job was very demanding, they agreed to travel together for a true family reunion.

Her employer was not pleased with her decision to take several days off, but she explained that her son was taking on a great responsibility with the church, and his installation was an event she could not miss. It was a soft white lie, as his instalment was already completed. God, she told him, would be disappointed if she were not there. Of course, her employer could not resist her request once she claimed to have God as her travelling companion! She did not mention the fact that the boy's father had suddenly appeared, for they were not married, and such news would have raised her employer's ire.

With her employer's approval in hand, she left the mansion, met Tection where agreed, and headed straight for the church. They were bubbling like young preschooler's heading to the candy store. As they journeyed, they smiled continuously at the situation, guessing alternatively at how their son would react to such an over wash of news. It occurred to them almost simultaneously that Nicholas could actually marry them! That would be an unusual but exciting possibility.

They arrived at the church and entered at a brisk walk with every intention to blurt out the happenings to Nicholas, but they were surprised to find the room filled and the mood somber. Their son, the priest, was at the altar reciting in Latin from his richly detailed and gold-bound Bible as a precursor to a sermon he was unable to deliver.

Tection looked at Nicholas from afar, easily recognizing the hard lines to his face that were his inheritance. Tection's heart pounded with anticipation, and he took some time before he realized Nicholas was conducting a funeral service. He couldn't help but notice his friend Julian from the café up on the stage as well sitting beside another fairly young man with a sad and forlorn look on his face. It was John P.

Nicholas did not notice his mother walk in as she and Tection sat in the back, quietly discarding the various looks from townsfolk who gave slight frowns of admonishment for their perceived tardiness. The reunion would have to wait. Tection looked up at Julian, and as their eyes met, Julian shook his head ever so slightly. Tection understood his gesture, realizing this was not a happy time, although he wasn't sure why.

The Delirious Journey

Tection wondered how he had transformed from a time of tragic sorrow, where he had suffered through the life at the orphanage, lost his young lover, killed Winter, and travelled the Earth with nothing but stormy skies and hopelessness ahead, to his current situation, with all found and vibrant and hope now a sunrise in the rose-blue sky.

News of Joseph's death was indescribable. Tection howled when he realized what had happened. Julian came down from the apse when Tection arrived with Sarah and whispered the sad news of Joseph's suicide into Tection's disbelieving ear. He lost his balance momentarily, and Julian clutched him and lowered him back onto the pew.

"No, I told him to wait ... " trailed from Tection's lips. In his heart, Tection knew that Joseph had been void of the will to continue living. He had seen it in his eyes and heard it in his words. He shouldn't have left him alone.

The gathered few, Nicholas and John P, all looked over at Tection following his vocal outburst and, following a few whispers and disapproving glances, returned to their task of eulogizing the deceased.

Tection's initial shock turned to guilt and then to anger—anger at himself, at the world, and at God for "allowing" this to happen. He feared Joseph's soul was lost now in murky isolation, kind and giving as it had been, excluded from the promise of rapture in the afterlife due to this self-inflicted demise. He speculated often whether God would bar him from the soft luxury of heaven because of Winter's murder. Ultimately, it was clear that suicide was a burden for the living to carry. It was their loss, their pain, guilt, and regret that brought them suffering. The victim was removed from the emotional conversation now, battling only the consequences of eternity.

Nicholas could not speak as God's representative, because Joseph's death had been a suicide. John P delivered the eulogy and brought tears to all eyes present as he delivered a heartfelt reminiscence of the man. His usual style of oration never shone brighter, and he managed to maintain his voice despite several moments of quivering and after the occasional deep breath or steadying hand from Nicholas. John P did not mention the word "suicide" and was careful to attribute the demise of Joseph to that of an unbearable inherited illness.

At the conclusion of the service, Joseph's body was led in procession to the rear of the church and returned to the anteroom. John P had already made the arrangements to return Joseph's body to their hometown for a final burial at the old church, which had been Joseph's home.

Following the service, many of the attendees went to the café to reflect on the happenings and to glean some insight into the sad story. John P was not very talkative on the matter, save for a few special anecdotes from his early life. Julian also shared some measure of admiration for Joseph, recounting the long hours spent in his basement library and the kindness he had always received from the gentle priest.

The tragic event more than dampened the anticipated reunion between Tection and Nicholas. Nicholas recognized Tection immediately as the man who had rescued him from Mr. James, and after allowing him to find some momentary composure, embraced Tection in an unusual hug, one seemingly gentle but carrying a huge weight into its fold. Tection looked at him, a strange look Nicholas thought, full of more emotion that might have been expected.

As Sarah passed Nicholas just inside the doorway, Nicholas on his way to the washroom and Sarah on her way back, they embraced in a mother and son way before she asked him to sit down in a quiet area of the café. Nicholas found it a little strange but did as she asked.

He was still babbling about seeing Tection and reminding her that he was indeed the man who had saved him when Sarah held her fingers to his lips, bidding him to be silent.

Tection watched them from outside, tilting his head to see past the reflection of the busy terrace the window held. He saw Nicholas look up at him first in some form of disbelief and then rise and walk slowly outside, never taking his eyes off Tection.

John P and Julian both saw that something was happening and interrupted their conversation to witness the reunion. They both recognized that this was the moment of reunification between father and son. For John P, it was ironically bittersweet.

As Nicholas neared Tection's chair, the older man stood up, and they faced each other momentarily before Nicholas threw his arms around Tection. Tection returned the embrace in a more reserved manner but just as sincerely. They stood for some time, just living in the moment of sheer joy, both of them shedding tears in silence. Tection's hand moved up to cup the back of

Nicholas's head and rubbed gently back and forth, confirming the sanctity of the moment. It was, Nicholas recognized, the same hand that held and rubbed his head many years earlier in the bowels of the now distant orphanage.

As the crowd thinned and the evening melted away, Julian, John P, Tection, Nicholas, and Sarah remained on the terrace. It was an amazing time, the sorrow of Joseph's departure balanced somehow by the delight of Tection and Nicholas's reunion. This was as close as Julian and John P had ever been to having any extended family, and they both enjoyed hearing the crazy tales of misinformation, silent glances, and critical coincidences that littered the history of Tection and his family. Not everything was revealed that night, not Winter and not Mr. James, but enough was shared to understand the sadness of a missed life together and the significance of the newfound harmony.

Before the evening ended, everyone at the table knew that Joseph was John P's father, and there was much discussion on the tragedy of that, not only Joseph's death but also the hidden and now lost relationship. Tection brought the irony of the situation to light without minimizing the value of John P's emotions. He also had a strong and witty style of conversation and used it carefully to include John P in the wonderment of the father and son reunion despite his recent loss. The world of opposites gathered strength once gain among the living, sorrow and joy, love and loss, tears and laughter all sharing the table with the bottles, glasses, idle hands, and, a contented orange cat languishing on Julian's lap.

John P and Nicholas were still not fluidly comfortable with each other. Nicholas didn't realize as quickly or as fully as he should have that he had brought some ruin to John P's quiet existence. Tection was firm in pointing that out, however, and once Nicholas gained at least the beginning of an understanding, he was sincerely remorseful about the situation. Whether that remorse was fueled in part by the events of the past few days was inconsequential. John P knew he had to repatriate Joseph's body to their hometown, and he was wholly unsure about where and how his own future would unfold. It didn't seem to be here in this dusty town with bitter memories. Although he didn't vocalize the feeling, the air was thick with a sense of departure, not just his own but Julian's as well.

As Tection, Sarah, and Nicholas were coming together as a family unit, John P and Julian were about to put asunder their own close relationship. Even though they did not see each other nearly as often as they would have liked, there was a certain familiarity with them living in the same community and being only a couple of miles apart. If they departed now in opposite directions with vastly different agendas, there was little doubt they would fall even further from each other's lives.

As the evening progressed, Sarah spent some time reflecting on her own life, especially committed to the period after Tection's departure from the inn and her struggles to birth and care for Nicholas during his first few months. She bore lingering guilt about placing him in the orphanage, but each person present knew it was an option she was unable to avoid. Tection was clearly disappointed in the fact he was unaware of the young boy's existence, and he felt much could have been different if he had been.

Eventually, after a period of negativity and some regret, John P was the one who stepped up and summarized the situation, demonstrating to all that fate, and nothing else, was driving the past, and the future was a more favourable target. A head turned to the past saw only history made, while one turned to the future saw destiny waiting. Pragmatism and persuasiveness were traits he demonstrated at all times, and at this point, they were much appreciated.

As the darkness dwindled and the pre-sunrise skies brightened, John P prepared to bid everyone goodnight. He had a fair distance to walk and was unexpectedly overcome with an exhaustion that flamed both his physical and emotional weariness.

Nicholas recognized the situation and insisted that John P sleep in the spare room in the church, the one usually reserved for visiting clergy or travelers of significance. John P hesitated, but it took little convincing for him to accept with much thanks.

Sarah retired to Tection's room above the café. As John P left with Nicholas, he saw Tection and Julian engrossed in whispered conversation that he knew was centered on some type of formation of their futures. Nicholas had informed Julian of his conversation with the priest from the church acquisition committee and the negative reply he had received concerning a purchase of the café. Partnering with a café was fine for a bazaar but completely indecent for a church. Julian shared that information with Tection, as he was quite entrenched in the café operations. Tection did not reply but rolled an old medallion across the back of his knuckles as he pondered Julian's comments. Julian thought he recognized a crescent moon on it.

Full Circle

Death always brought pain to the living. *It was a crooked and unreasonable twist to life*, Tection thought. We fear dying for so long that we forget the grief it delivers to the living. And why this great pity for the dead and dying? Was there not a rich and beautiful afterlife? If we really believed such an afterlife existed, then we would be happy and joyous for those ending the hardship of earthly existence, while racing to encourage them towards an end of life that would bring endless and everlasting peace. A rather interesting paradox; blindly faithful that a well-cared for life would deliver an everlasting oasis of happiness, but fearing death so much that it drove people to despicable and critical acts of self-preservation and selfishness. Living convinced with the unabashed certainty that heaven waits while feeling the head-on clash with the unparalleled fear of actually dying. Maybe people didn't really, deep down, believe that such an afterlife hobbled along in the fields of eternity, bountiful and patient for new arrivals. Perhaps the postulating and fostering of such an ideal playground was only a relief for the living, an appeasement of their grief, a filter of emotions enabling the survivors to feel that the departed were still okay, off to a better place, and that their own impending death was more palatable. Whatever the afterlife delivered, it wasn't enough to prevent the sullen grief of the survivors, especially John P.

Tection felt a heavy burden for many reasons. He felt he had not supported Joseph through those many years apart and believed he might have been a deterrent to Joseph's journey towards sorrow if he had been a more regular part of his life. He also felt a deep guilt about leaving the cottage, spurred by the joy of realizing he had a child, while Joseph was in such a delicate state. Of course he hadn't realized the severity of Joseph's emotional collapse or he would have certainly remained with him, but Tection questioned whether he had missed those signs of depression because he was in a selfish whirlwind. He also felt guilty, perhaps unnecessarily; that he had enjoyed such a wonderful reunion with his son while John P suffered with the realization that such joy could never be his. His feelings of remorse drove him to seek out John P and provide whatever comfort he could.

John P lamented incredibly following the death of Joseph. He had journeyed with Julian and some townsfolk to recover the body. There had been another body nearby, longer departed and unrecognizable but obviously originating from the same precipice from which Joseph had leaped. They were not able to bring both bodies back, but the authorities were notified and organized to collect the second corpse the following day.

The journey back was harrowing enough, and the Church's stand on suicide exacerbated the grief surrounding the situation. Nicholas agreed to allow John P the opportunity to eulogize Joseph, although he had no idea at that point what the true relationship between Joseph and John P was. The fact that Joseph was a priest provided some favour from the Church, and there was at least a kind and loving expression of grief for the departed.

Under other circumstances there would have been a significant outpouring of both people and lamentation over the death of a fellow priest, but the suicide component of the tragedy put pressure on such expressions.

John P was grateful for the opportunity to deliver a final homily inside the great new church, and though the congregation was rather diminished, he was pleased to see many of the faces from his previous congregation gathered to support him in his time of sorrow, especially the young lady who had inadvertently extracted a re-reading of his mother's eulogy some time before. None were aware that Joseph was John P's father. The presented tale was that of pseudo-father, mentor, and male role model for the young preacher during his formative years. John P and Julian had agreed without equivocation that disclosure of the relationship would provide nothing but further negativity for the sullen occasion; and perhaps worse, to Joseph's legacy, which was battered already by the form of death he chose.

Unfortunately, the joyful reunion of Tection and his family was road-blocked when they arrived during the funeral and were hammered by the news of Joseph's death. Tection took it especially hard and was fortunate to have Julian there to provide some support. Later, as they gathered at the café, John P met Tection and learned that he had been a close friend of Joseph's and that he was the father of Nicholas—at the same time Nicholas did! It was not without irony that John P witnessed the joyous reunion of Nicholas and Tection while he endured the emotional pounding delivered by the loss of his own father. His very nature was a loving one though, and he held no animosity or animadversion towards Tection for his untimely departure from the cottage. Nor did he bear jealousy towards them, but perhaps a small wave of envy did creep through his pursed lips and reddened eyes.

He managed to snatch a few moments of personal time with Tection to share some anecdotes, and John P was especially attentive to alleviate any guilt Tection carried. Joseph's journey to self-demise could not have been prevented by anything Tection might have provided, and it was a long and undoubtedly lonely odyssey far from any normal concepts of reality.

Tection was impressed with this attitude from John P. He had every reason to lash out at both Tection and Nicholas, but he was obviously an exceptional character. How unfortunate that he was not engaged officially with the Church. He was far more worthy than many of the ordained with whom Tection had been acquainted. In the end, John P elicited the same commitment to secrecy about the relationship between him and Joseph from Tection, Sarah, and Nicholas when they sat together on the cafe terrace following the funeral.

When the dust settled and John P took stock of his situation, he realized that little remained for him in this small town. He wondered why it seemed so much smaller than before. Nicholas was entrenched in the new church, and Tection was busy in some kind of arrangements with Julian. It was clear that Julian was anxious to undertake new adventures, as he probably had been for some time, perhaps even from their first days in this dusty and predictable town. John P also began to recognize the first tinges of discomfort that were symptoms of the illness from which his father and grandfather had suffered. Tection had explained Joseph's revelation about the disease and whispered a forewarning to John P of this negative legacy that would undoubtedly accompany his future.

No, not much positive remained here for the young preacher, save the few lasting relationships he had developed among the townsfolk. Those would be suitable for the occasional reunion with warm embraces, back patting, and smiles and nods. Armed with these realizations and the task of transporting Joseph's body back for a local burial, John P decided to return to his hometown for a while. He wasn't sure what would be done about the vacant church, with Joseph now departed, but he knew many people there and had been well received during his short return earlier.

As he reflected on his desire but a short while earlier to remain with the big new church and work with Nicholas, he recognized the folly of it. Nicholas was a strong and ambitious individual, reticent to give an inch of ground on his climb through the hierarchy of the religious landscape. The mere fact he was given this new and slightly ominous church, with his youthful and inexperienced career just blossoming, was enough of a proclamation to confirm his rising stardom.

While John P prepared his departure, complete with lengthy goodbyes and sad farewells, he was unaware that Tection was appeasing his own guilty conscience though a strong lobby of the main Church administration, extolling John P's character, demeanour, and dedication and suggesting without reservation that he be employed as a caretaker and lay preacher at the now vacant church in his hometown, not just until the new priest arrived but on an ongoing basis. He expressed further that John P had provided a significant interim galvanization of the church community before the new church was built, and his service should be rewarded accordingly.

Tection's history with the Church and the hushed recantations of his exploits with Winter made him both a favoured character and one to be cautious around, for he could easily shine a spotlight on the Church's negligence in dealing with matters like Winter and his deviations. Although Tection never intimated that he might shine such a light, it continued to hang in the shadows.

He mentioned nothing to John P about this until he received a confirmation from the highest authority that his recommendations would be entrenched. John P would be compensated decently for his past service to the Church through a bonus payment. He would also be given full-time employment at the church in his hometown as caretaker, with the elderly gentleman there already aiming at retirement any day, and lay preacher. It was not a significant salary, but when accompanied with the bonus, the lodging provided in the church, and his inheritance, it would allow him a very comfortable and rewarding financial future. Beyond that, the fact that he was officially the lay preacher there meant that when a new priest was assigned to the church, John P would still be an integral part of the environment.

John P was ecstatic about this turn of events and found it difficult to express his appreciation properly. Tection waved off John P's gratitude with a quiet "No need" and an unpretentious move on to other topics. Tection was not unaware that the arrival of Nicholas had collapsed John P's *raison d'être,* as it were, and the solution achieved was both satisfying to correct that void as well as to help appease his lingering guilt over his premature departure from the cottage, and perhaps even some form of unusual farewell gift to his departed friend.

Tection had proven to be a resourceful veteran stranger indeed!

With the disclosure of these new responsibilities in his hometown, John P prepared more thoroughly for the trip. This was to be a move to a new life and not just a potentially prolonged visit to familiar territory. The long goodbye with Julian was fueled by numerous drinks, inevitable laughter, and stifled tears during a last warm embrace, both men assuring each other that they would be in touch regularly.

Later, Tection encountered the two young men and was told of their firm commitment to stay in contact. After gathering in those last comments, he shook his head knowingly, remembering his own friendship with Joseph that had been poorly nurtured due to just such a separation. The two young men had started out together in what seemed like a mere wink of life's eye gone by, visions of conquering the world held precariously in their fingertips. The reality of survival had helped those visions vanish, and the harshness of reality itself had brought changes beyond expectation. Julian's plans were a bit fuzzy, but John P had no doubt he would find his adventure. Armed with a broader understanding of the shifting world, unburdened by commitment or relationships, fueled by funds from the eventual sale of the café, and inspired by Tection's tales of strange lands and peoples, he was ready to go get it!

During the trip home, John P thought back to those moments on the cottage porch, Joseph lifeless on the beach below, when he doubted both his faith and purpose. How sharply things changed. How dramatic the shadows shaped the world, delivering their truth one small piece at a time. If this engagement at the church in his hometown was his reward for contributions to the good and glory of society, why did he have to suffer so greatly to receive it? It seemed coldly ironic that great joy might only be achieved after significant sorrow, love only after indifference, trust after betrayal. Why not have a world where joy, love, and trust were inherent and the carpet of grass covering the Earth was smooth and silky? He chuckled at the reflection. He knew every person had that rage within, the sorrow, betrayal, and indifference that lurked ominously below the surface, closer in some and more distant in others. He shivered. Life's prospect, at the moment so full of potential and opportunity, so well determined for him, could only get worse at some point. For all the positives he was experiencing here, negative opposites lurked somewhere out there. And if these positives were just the opposites of the negative impact that Joseph, the disease, the Church, and the lost congregation had already delivered, then he was merely catching up on the antithetical realm. The counterbalance of life's very existence was behind any corner, every corner. He decided to live in the "now" of it all, enjoying the good and fortuitous side of life he was experiencing at the moment, realizing that the dark side of such experience, the empowered opposite, hovered in a curious flight barely an arm's length from reality, around the shadow's corner, waiting to slide into unsuspecting lives.

His arrival in his hometown was met with a friendly and even gracious reception. The core of the local congregation had been fully informed of his past exploits and commitment and even schooled on the forward intention the Church had for him. The locals were quite curious about Joseph's demise. Comments on his lack of recent interest, his distance from their daily lives, and the seemingly sorrowful expression he wore frequently, all fed their questions.

John P had already organized his story internally and his clarifications surrounding Joseph's sickness and his desire not to impact the congregation with the burden of sympathy. He detailed how Joseph had suffered at the thought of not revealing his illness to them and his regret at not having the opportunity to express an emotional departure to all the churchgoers. They were aware of the nature of Joseph's death, so that could not be hidden, but John P made it clear that it was for the relief of the tremendous pain accompanying Joseph's disease that he dove towards destiny. That seemed to satisfy their curiosity and enabled Joseph's name to retain some dignity. The fact that Joseph was John P's father was never revealed to anyone. It would go to the grave with the five people who knew.

Prior to John P's arrival they had prepared his quarters and organized a welcoming dinner. In all, it was more than John P had expected. His questions about how he would be received and the most effective way to reintegrate were all answered.

During that first dinner, he found his mind wandering off in reflection on what direction his first sermon would take. Words of praise and context for Joseph no doubt.

The positive life flow continued for him and would, deservedly, continue so for a long time.

Julian and the Obvious Shore

Julian had never felt the pain of another the way he did for John P as they marched along the cliffs to collect Joseph's body. The excitement and exuberance John P had when he left to visit the cottage were palpable, and his crash down into the pit of sadness in which he swam now was an ominous one. Julian was unable to comfort him in any way and felt like a useless appendage that took up space but provided no value to the situation. John P was most grateful for his friendship and accompaniment, but he was dealing with the devastation of Joseph's suicide internally, deep within the inherent sanctum contained in the physical body. Julian would have to wait for the internal forgings to be refined before he could greet and support John P from without.

When Tection walked in on the funeral with an unknown lady at his side, Julian knew he would have to let him know what had transpired. He didn't want Tection to learn of Joseph's death from an ordinary stranger.

He went to him immediately and shared the sullen news while supporting him physically and emotionally. It had been a tiring few days for all, the reunion of Sarah, Nicholas, and Tection notwithstanding. Tection was certainly levelled by the news of Joseph's death, but he was also engrossed with a sense of responsibility towards John P. He had left Joseph at the cottage and missed the severity of the signs of his depression. He had discovered his son was Nicholas, who had basically taken over the religious component to the town's life and usurped John P's position, and he shone with the joy of fatherhood now that could do nothing but remind John P of what a loss Joseph had been. All in all, it was a large load for one stranger to carry.

He set about remedying the situation as quickly as possible through his connections and relationships in the Church. He concentrated on getting John P entrenched with the Church for the future and used the success of his efforts to appease at least part of the emotional burden he was harbouring. He shared the news of the Church's acquiescence to his suggestions with John P who was shocked initially but then ecstatic with the news. He hugged Tection and offered his unfettered gratitude, but Tection was not seeking that. He did not tell John P how he felt about his early departure from the cottage or how he viewed his son's effect on John P's life. It was easy enough for anyone to ascertain. He was content to know he had helped John P going forward and enabled himself to begin the process of forgiving himself.

John P's departure was a bittersweet occasion. He was happy to be heading to a new beginning yet sad to be leaving behind Julian and their friendship. Julian sat with John P for a while, just the two of them out behind the café on an outcrop of sorts. Julian carried a bottle of suitable spirits, and they shared sips as they ingested their intended separation. Julian reminisced about their early years and vocalized how much he respected John P and how grateful he was to have him as a friend. He had no idea what would have become of himself without John P's support and guidance. John P replied with his usual graciousness, commenting how it was Julian who put the fire in the relationship that enabled them to strike out on their own. John P repeated the comment that he also wondered where he might be without Julian. They chuckled. It was a symbiotic relationship for sure. They embraced in a long and sturdy hug, surely recognizing that their futures were on different paths. Julian had already decided he would travel. It was only a question of when and how. John P had his own destiny waiting patiently back in their hometown. They were cautious not to say goodbye, only a casual farewell.

Tection's family reunion was tempered acutely by the ongoing events, and it wasn't until John P prepared to depart that Tection revealed his thoughts to Julian. During their afternoons together, Tection had often shared stories of his travels and escapades across the sea, always with a little poetic license and an occasional narrator's exaggeration. Julian always responded with an expression of desire to create his own adventures so he might also share his exploits with another someday. They laughed often at the possibility that Julian might encounter some of the characters Tection had.

Once John P left, their discussion gained some seriousness. Tection wanted to remain in town, close to his son, but he had no intention of returning to an occupation involving the Church. Julian had been most disappointed at Nicholas's abrupt refusal to consider a church-funded purchase of the café, and he saw his opportunity to engage his dream of adventures slipping away. Tection had considered the situation most carefully, and the decision was actually quite easy. He proposed buying the café. He had a rather handsome sum from the wages set aside by the Church for the past years, and he and Sarah could maintain the good name and quality establishment that Julian was running. Julian was shocked and delighted, although he found Tection's offer far too generous. But Tection insisted. Julian would need funds to support his travels, and Tection had no need for a stuffed mattress. This meant the reality of an adventure was imminent for Julian. He took some time to digest that reality, but it was inevitable that he would accept Tection's generous offer.

Tection couldn't be more pleased with the turn of events. Finding Sarah and Nicholas was more than outstanding, providing significant help to John P was most rewarding, and securing the café from Julian provided him a future occupation where he could embrace the joys of family while also providing Julian with a means to realize his dream of travel.

It wasn't long before Julian had secured passage on a fishing boat heading back across the endlessly undulating sea and packed his life's belongings into a travel bag of acceptable weight.

His last request of Tection was that the orange cat be well cared for and protected. Tection assured him it would be. After all, the cat had surely been mistreated at some point and was deserving of a comfortable retirement of sorts. Julian never told Tection that he was the one who had mistreated the cat, never wanting to reveal or even recognize that dark space that languished somewhere deep in his being.

As he bid his final farewell, he looked for the cat to give it one last stroke, but it was nowhere to be found.

No on never owns a cat, he thought, *not even God.* He also hoped to see the Philosopher one more time before he departed, but he had been incognito for some time now. He elicited a promise from Tection to pass on his regards once the esoteric scholar reappeared; all of them unaware that he was last seen as an anonymous and lifeless form keeping Joseph's body company on the jagged beach.

As they shook hands, Tection gave Julian a small medallion he had carried since his days at the orphanage, the crescent moon beside a five-pointed star. He explained that the medallion had gained him much acceptance among distant peoples, and Julian could show it to those he encountered as validation that the two of them were friends, and that he travelled in friendship with all humanity. Later, Julian drilled a small hole in the top of the medallion and strung a chain through it.

As he stood on the boat and drifted slowly from the shore, he bid farewell to the gathered few. Soon, they were out of sight, and with them the remnants of his life to that point. He was blessed with the exhilaration of excitement and the adrenalin of trepidation.

He held the medallion by its chain and spun it with a flick of his fingers, trying to consider the possibility of diverse religious beliefs. Surely they were beyond his current scope of understanding. He was familiar only with his local rendition of spiritual salvation. He knew the precepts were basically an expectation of peace and happiness in exchange for devotion and obedience, but he had difficulty reconciling that. He knew people were inherently good. They toiled at labour and embraced recreation. They sacrificed for one another and shared joy and sorrow with equal abandon. Yet there was something inconsistent with the procession of life. He couldn't disseminate it in a coherent evaluation, but he grasped the concept that reality did not always match expectations. He reflected on John P's own struggle with faith, even though he was now in a position of contentment, and on Tection's encounters with institutional expectations and his subsequent disengagement, on Nicholas's blind commitment and unintentional disregard for his impact on John P, and finally on Joseph and what must have been a catastrophic emotional whirlpool for him. He could not imagine the possibility of ending the preciousness of life on purpose. He could not imagine the experience that would drive anyone to such a destination.

Julian lost himself in a reflection on individual religions as a defined entity as opposed to individual spirituality as a pathway through life, on the one hand being provided a path to follow and on the other seeking the path to follow, only being preached to about the qualities that evolve and empower happiness—love, faith, kindness, charity, and honesty—as opposed to actually embracing them spiritually. There was specific religious dogma from every church, a requirement for almost blind obedience that effectively devalued all alternatives and established a perimeter of barriers to hold off the heathen. Or perhaps it was to keep in the committed. Individual spirituality, on the other hand, could seek compromise and common ground, embracing diversity and flaming acceptance, understanding, and perhaps even assimilation.

Designed religion, he thought, *leaves the soul void and floundering, seemingly worthless to the individual who must gather all value from outside himself. The spiritual or soul-searching adventure however, nourishes the soul, building value and treasured experience through the process.* Julian was definitely on a soul-searching adventure!

He slipped the chain over his head and let the medallion fall inside his shirt next to his heart.

Julian leaned forward on the stern of the boat, resting his arms on the railing and his chin on his hands. This would be his last look at his homeland, at least for a long time.

As they left the safety of the harbour, the water became rougher, and he stepped back a bit. He looked up at the disappearing cliffs and saw a glint of sunlight reflected high up near the cliff's summit. As the angle changed, he could just make out the form of a small cottage standing guard over the expanse of the world, carefree and emotionless, sturdy and dignified. He pondered the direction life was taking. For him it was forward towards unknown adventure and not upwards towards the heavens and that recondite cottage, whose own adventure seemed to be separation from the corporeal. Julian had heard the stories of the glorification, magnetism, and spellbinding beauty the cottage held. He wondered if it was a first step on the pathway to true enlightenment or a last and lost gateway to sudden endlessness.

Better not to look, he thought as he turned and walked towards the front of the boat, steadying himself while gripping the cool steel railing and preparing internally to become a stranger in a distant land.

Soon, the cottage disappeared into the misty horizon, perched with confidence on the precipice and waiting patiently, endlessly, for another visitor seeking clarification, or perhaps confusion.

END

About the Author

David Cocklin is a consultant and occasional lecturer who is now retired from mainstream corporate life. He has only indulged his passion for novel writing over the past five years, due in part to an increasing realization of eventual mortality and the corresponding desire to leave a legacy for his children. Apart from writing, these days David is focused primarily on the pursuit of happiness, embracing new experiences to share and promote growth, while building on the wisdom gained from past adventures. He splits his time between Montreal, Quebec and Fort Lauderdale, Florida. *The Cottage: Recondite* is his first book.

Printed in Canada